ONLY ONE

THING MISSING

ONLY ONE

THING MISSING

Luis Manuel Ruiz

Translated from the Spanish
by Alfred Mac Adam

Grove Press
New York

Published simultaneously in Canada
Printed in the United States of America

FIRST EDITION

Library of Congress Cataloging-in-Publication Data

Ruiz, Luis Manuel, 1973–
[Solo una cosa no hay. English]
Only one thing missing / Luis Manuel Ruiz ; translated from
the Spanish by Alfred Mac Adam.
p. cm.
ISBN 0-8021-1730-9
I. Mac Adam, Alfred J., 1941– II. Title.
PQ6668.U3238 S6513 2003
863'.64—dc21   2002029723

Grove Press
841 Broadway
New York, NY 10003

03 04 05 06 07   10 9 8 7 6 5 4 3 2 1

"Only one thing missing. Forgetting."
—Jorge Luis Borges, "Everness"

ONLY ONE
THING MISSING

T o know a city, she thought, you must first empty it. If you don't, the city fuses in your retina with its own metabolism, dissolves in the routine traffic of cars and faces, of winking window shades, of buses with full stomachs, of all those things we mistakenly identify it with, things of which it is nothing more than the submissive depositary. To understand a city, she concluded, like probing the depths of a friendship, you need silence: Sometimes we regret that we don't really understand someone until they're gone.

For that reason, the city she had before her, the city that wrapped around her like a shell, the concave panorama of eighteenth-century-style buildings orbiting her, proliferating in balustrades, plazas, facades, tiled roofs, was much more perfect and transparent than all the blurred cities she'd explored until then, cities darkened by their traffic, whose truth is revealed by their inhabitants and shops, cities buried under tourism and maps. This city, the blue and gray skeleton clogging her eyes, was empty, and that rendered its sincerity incontrovertible: It had the violent frankness of an insult. She could almost feel that the avenues and alleys were extensions of her own arms and legs, that the sidewalks of the outlying neighborhoods belonged to her like her own supply of teeth and nails.

She suspected that the uninhabited city was a symbol, a suggestion, an emblem obliquely alluding to some kind of truth that she'd lost or left behind in some obscure byway of a memory that wouldn't come back. She loved the city for its mystery, the empty mystery sighed by mirrors, by words in other languages and nights that precede certain events; she feared it because our fascination with mysterious things always, inevitably, leads to fear: Monsters horrify us because they are magnetic.

All that alchemy of confused sensations was churning her stomach, pushing her blood wave by wave toward the exhausted drum of her heart: It seemed that after each beat, once the blood was again flushed out of the bag of muscles, another hot, silent tide flowed through the city with the slow treachery of the night's own light. She had no doubt that the empty city was one of her own attributes, like her green eyes or her ineptitude at ironing shirts, and that in this precise instant a subterranean kind of energy she couldn't name and which was born in her shoulder blades was irrigating her and connecting her to the city, as if through a minute and ubiquitous network of shapeless roots. Then she began to move forward, and it was the same as brushing aside the successive veils blocking a memory, and they reached, in an inexorable, almost axiomatic order, a boulevard, a yellow clock, a plaza with the statue of an angel.

One

Visits with Mamá Luisa were always games of blind-man's bluff dotted with feints and ambushes, a game without rules she sadistically inflicted on her visitors to test their courage. No one could predict where Mamá Luisa's questions or comments would lead, and she seemed to take an absolutely cold-blooded delight in smashing conversations by launching, at just the right moment, an inopportune question, an out-of-place reference, or naming the thing everyone was thinking but decorously chose not to mention in order to pass at least one tranquil afternoon. Those underhanded maneuvers appalled Alicia to the point that right after the death of Pablo and the girl she opened a parenthesis in her relationship with Mamá Luisa and let two or three months go by before visiting the dark little flat on Francos Street where the old woman was slowly withering away, eaten up by diabetes and colds.

From time to time, in the fleeting bubbles of peace or sanity despondency left to her, Alicia would give in when Esteban begged over the telephone: It wasn't right that after losing a son and a granddaughter in the mangled chassis of a Ford Orion she, her daughter-in-law, should leave her to rot with her age and her grief, without even trying, even if it were out of pure compassion, to toss her a life preserver by sitting down at her side with her smile painted on and the muscles of her cheeks stiffened. She would have to accept coffee and put up with the swarms of words that flew like wasps out of the old lady's mouth, those wary, cruel words that spoke about Pablo's boyhood, the gray eyes he had inherited from his father, and his predilection for nougat, which he shared with poor Rosita, may she rest in peace.

Mamá Luisa's conversational labyrinths were as complicated as they were difficult to map out. And just when Alicia, seated in the colorless, flower-print armchair, facing the firing squad of photographs, the rows of surviving sons, daughters-in-law, and grandchildren, had resigned herself to burning eyelids and that spiral of ash in her stomach—the inevitable result of focusing her memory in certain directions—Mamá Luisa would pick through their names, hygienically isolate the parcels of her past contaminated by the existence of the dead, and the whole afternoon would go by with great tranquillity amid false plans for the summer and recipes for strawberry pie.

Esteban, hiding behind the smoke of his cigarette, witnessed Alicia's samaritan patience, her way of squeezing her hands together until the nails dug into her palms at the moment when Mamá Luisa, perhaps abusing the privileges granted her by senility, would punish Alicia with the usual apostrophes which he would rapidly try to soften by changing the course of the conversation. True, he sometimes felt remorse for coercing Alicia into those encounters that, instead of granting her a necessary dose of oblivion, served to scrape away scabs, including his own, and he suspected that Alicia, who lately was on the very edge of the precipice of depression, needed silence more than she needed his mother, whose age had confined her in a happily impenetrable deafness to disasters. Knowing Alicia, he had no trouble speculating about what condition the simultaneous deaths of Pablo and the girl had left her in, just as it wasn't hard to identify the ominous ghost of her nights, visited by the alternating presence of despair and insomnia.

Esteban had always loved her: her thin, elastic silhouette with well-defined breasts, her straight hair, always falling down over her eyes (two green wells), her fingernails, indecisively sprouting from the tips of her fingers, her hand holding the watering can over the *conibras* in the living room (prettier with each summer), her way of caressing Rosita's hair, of talking to her about Humpty Dumpty or the Queen of Hearts—oh yes, her face hovering over the edition of Lewis Carroll loaded with illustrations that Pablo had given her on her birthday. That entire combination of happy coincidences which transformed her into the ideal lover Esteban found in his readings of the Argentine writer Julio Cortázar, readings which included the absolutely necessary—when reading Cortázar—Charlie Parker records properly scattered on the shelves next to the bottles, really made him envy his brother's luck in having met that timid student of library science during a demonstration one foggy morning. From that moment on, a secret link, a kind of surreptitious current, bound him to his sister-in-law, the woman with young knees he'd run to embrace the November day in the cemetery when, shot to pieces by torrential rain and expressions of sympathy, she'd collapsed in a messy pile of sobs.

It would have been miserable for Esteban to admit that the death of his brother left the way to Alicia open to him. But even if he didn't formulate that thought in explicit clauses, he felt that an obstacle between them had been cleared away, that her voice was closer or her touch more distinct, and perhaps for that reason (no matter how much he'd wanted to abort filthy hopes) he would call her three times a week. On Thursdays or Fridays, they would browse in bookstores and record shops, ending up with coffee or a drink. He was always there when she visited his mother. And it was always Alicia's waves of chestnut hair falling over her forehead, her eyes distracted for a few minutes from her memory full of traps and badly aired nooks and crannies, her body which, closing his eyes, Esteban imagined flexible and hot, breathing regularly with her head on a pillow where one head was missing, where no one would ever rest his head.

"I didn't think she was too badly off," Alicia said to him as they got into the elevator. Mamá Luisa had fallen asleep watching a soap opera.

"No, you're right," Esteban poked the letter *B.* "Lately she's been calmer. I don't know, maybe she's forgetting. She has to forget."

"Your mother's mind is too sharp for her to forget anything that quickly." Alicia was speaking with certainty. "I think it's a maneuver, one of her many maneuvers. I don't know, your mother upsets me."

The sky was flat and neutral; it was going to rain. They walked to a shop that sold religious articles. A bust of Christ was bleeding in the window.

"Can I drop you somewhere?" asked Alicia. "My car's right over there."

"No, I'm going to the watch repair shop." Esteban pulled up the collar on his parka. "It's that damned watch of Dad's. It hasn't worked two days in a row since he died."

"The pocket watch?" Alicia laughed.

...

Rosita never liked elevators. She was horrified by that coffin with buttons and mirrors in which she must have seen a vague anticipation of the little white mahogany box where she was ultimately locked up. Alicia mechanically opened the door, entered, and pushed the button with its faded 4. While the flow of white tiles was running up and down the wall opposite the mirror, she again saw Rosita's softened face in the apartment entryway, her wool cap muzzling her hair. She'd said good-bye and had stood on tiptoe to give her that kiss on the cheek, that prickly kiss indistinguishable from all the others, from any of the others Rosita had given her over the course of eight short years before going to school, before going to Cintia's house, before going to Grandma's, before going to the movies: It was the same kiss, the same moist squirrel at her cheek accompanied by the scent of cologne and Rosita's freshly washed leotards.

How could Alicia guess that the kiss would never be repeated, that it would remain there suspended like Rosita's never-to-mature face in the entryway with the wool cap, horribly fusing with that other face which was also Rosita's but which wasn't Rosita, that white, made-up thing with its features corrected, that awkward doll in horizontal position presiding over the assembly of family members, surrounded by the suffocating stench of lilies and chrysanthemums? That other Rosita, that wasted, broken mask, that voiceless double frozen in an unbreakable dream was the one who visited Alicia's nightmares, until horror or suffocation returned her to her bedroom, to her glass of water, to her weeping alarm clock, and two, three cigarettes. Rosa and Pablo came back to her every night, sailing on their coffins now dispossessed of their owners: Rosa and Pablo reduced to two wax dummies eternally condemned to play the part of sentinels in the merciless dream of the wife and mother, of the survivor who chased absences ever since that day through the empty rooms of the apartment on Reyes Católicos Street.

She left the elevator, curtly greeted an old man who was closing a door, stopped opposite the plaque engraved with letters appropriate for a Roman monument: CARMEN BARROSO. PSYCHOLOGIST. Sitting in the waiting room, she amused herself by leafing through two or three magazines. She finished a cigarette. She usually liked Mamen's office because of the colors of the walls, those foamy pastel tones that diffusely brought her back to a summer in Florence, where there were frescoes that color. Pablo, after having told her he intended to many times, had decided to try them at home before what happened truncated all such decisions.

Even now she wondered if she'd really been in love with Pablo. She wondered if the feeling that linked her to him during those nine years was legitimate, nine years in which a fiction of intimacy had made them share loving words, two apartments, vacations, that intelligent, tender thing that was Rosita. Perhaps she'd expected something more from the person with whom she was supposed to build a future, perhaps something more than proximity or security, and not that rather unclean sensation she felt at times of being an epitome or suburb of the other's life, of being relegated to the epilogue of the readings, movies, political discussions, Rosita, and work, always work. Pablo had done his job as copy editor for the Almadraba Publishing Company and its affiliates all over Europe with religious fervor, without caring that his professionalism distracted him from other matters.

Pablo's death was not inside her the way Rosita's was. It wasn't that refusal with compact walls to accept something impossible, it wasn't the sacrilege and the flagrant breaking of the rules of the game that rendered further play pointless. Actually it was wounded security, the roof falling in, being exposed. Saved from the shipwreck, Alicia had been left a naked, deaf animal that doesn't remember the way home. And sometimes, even if she blotted out that possibility each time it insinuated itself by closing her eyes or playing a record, the other side remained as magnetic and beautiful as an empty beach. Called from time to time by a dream with velvet edges, she thought about turning on the gas or reaching for the tranquilizers on the night table which almost eclipsed her husband's face: It would have been so simple to dissolve the nightmares that tormented her every day at dawn in the bottom of that mercury swimming pool, in that final pit which was only turning out the lights. But some sort of undefined impulse kept her from taking the leap, a force like the right to protest continued making her heart beat and feeding her lungs, to say nothing of friends, Esteban (poor Esteban, so unabashedly attentive), Joaquín and Marisa, the Acevedos, Mamen naturally, and, of course, her beautiful, very needy *conibras,* which absolutely had to be watered three times a day.

When Alicia entered the office, Mamen was finishing a telephone conversation, and again she was twirling her pen between her fingers as she did whenever she listened to her patients. "Patient": Instead of alarming her, the word now seemed curious to Alicia. Never, when she'd visited that office facing toward Torneo Street and the ruins of the Universal Exposition, that soft interregnum occupied by reproductions of Kandinsky and Matisse, could she have imagined herself being admitted into Mamen's space as anything but a friend.

She was confident in Mamen's ability to untangle the skein that had her hands tied and kept her from developing, and not only for the sake of her brand-new title, made even more valuable by master's degrees from Milan and Boston, but exactly because Mamen since long before had been an ear, had shared beers in the cute apartment with modern ashtrays where she could leave Rosita on nights when Pablo suggested a movie or a Chinese restaurant. Aside from the almost ten-year difference in their ages, Mamen was always the person who best understood her madness, that unresolved balance between loving Pablo and not loving him, the opportunity that she'd supposed she'd found in Rosita, a channel to redirect her repressed marital anxieties. With her thirty-nine long years, Mamen was a complete woman with resolved aspirations, gifted with an acid clairvoyance that had ordered her to sacrifice a short-lived marriage and a few silly protocols in order to bring to fruition a career that had made her one of the most sought after psychologists in Seville. Alicia noticed that the lazy light coming through the window drew reddish reflections from Mamen's hair.

"You've dyed your hair again."

"Yes I did." Mamen shook her hair; the charm bracelet on her wrist jingled. "It's henna, chemicals make my hair disgusting. Mind you, you've got to spend four hours with the paste on your head."

Rather than dealing with the problems straight away, they preferred to let their conversation lead them slowly in the direction the words were pointing, leaving spaces to talk about decor or last night's movie, sliding along carefully so as not to hurt themselves. Finally, they would open into the thing that was there, like it or not, no matter how much Alicia might pretend to be deaf or turn her back: No matter, it was Rosita dead and Pablo dead and Rosita made-up inside a box made of white mahogany on which she had no tears left to go on weeping.

"How are you?"

"What do you think?" Alicia's voice had no light. "I still can't believe it, Mamen."

"It only just happened," there was a musical delicacy in Mamen's tone. "But how are you getting along?"

"I don't know. During the day, I go from one thing to the next, work, Esteban, the neighbors, I don't remember much about it. I don't cry too much anymore, really, Mamen. At night, it's worse."

"Nightmares?"

"Yes." A wheel of needles ran down Alicia's spine. "They're not getting better. They're still there, the two of them, in their coffins. And they rot. They're rotting."

"Okay." Mamen wanted, as it were, to undo those images. "You haven't noticed any improvement?"

"Are you asking because of the hypnosis sessions?" Alicia waved her hand in the same way she would to dispel a bad odor. "No, everything's the same. I told you I didn't have much faith in that stuff."

"What you're saying makes me feel silly, because after all I'm the psychologist around here. Anyway, I recognize that hypnosis isn't a panacea, but it could have helped clear you up a bit."

"Well, as you can see, it didn't. Five intensive sessions and nothing."

"Still taking the tranquilizers?"

"Yes."

"What about them?"

"Bah." Alicia stuck out her tongue. "I don't think they're doing much good. I do sleep a little more, that's true."

Mamen's hand wrote down sentences in a notebook.

"I'll increase the dosage," she said. "Take another half pill. I know it may sound silly, but you have to realize you've got your whole life ahead of you."

"You don't say so."

"Imagine you've just come to a new city, and you don't know anyone. You've got to make friends. Above all, take it all calmly. What about Esteban?"

"Esteban's fine," Alicia answered from a half smile.

The problem did not involve accepting the fact that they were dead, that is, that they'd carried out that canonical and unavoidable form of absence. To see that, all you had to do was walk through the apartment and see the dressers intact, the piles of paper perfectly lined up on both sides of the desk; the torturous thing, the unbearable thing was that they were dead and that they would go on being there, inside, waiting, kicking, disturbing her memory as if to punish her for being so ill-mannered as to go on being alive. Why, Pablo, why, Rosita, why, it was hard enough having to go on breathing and raising soup spoons to one's mouth. Why,

Rosita, that improbable mask without expression and not the cap and the waves of hair in the vestibule and the repetition of the same kiss like a bee and that distant smell of cologne, distant but not distant.

...

Those hands were two mummified animals. Esteban stared at the hands holding up the watch, stared at the deliberate way the middle fingers caressed the crystal, the thumb slipped over the tin case darkened by time.

"This watch has been here before," the man observed.

"Yes," said Esteban. "My brother brought it in."

"What's your name?"

When the man stood up from the counter, Esteban noted that his body magnified, until the tininess of the shop transformed him into a black, squalid giant. The shop, a narrow cave aspiring to be a junkyard, was carved into the Plaza del Pan, at the rear of the Salvador church. To negotiate the place you had to step carefully to avoid tripping over divans or umbrellas. In the back, behind Mr. Berruel, who was now rummaging through a file box, there was a display cabinet mistreated by dust and scratches inside of which were rows of watches and ancient, vague toys alternating with tiny tools that looked like shrunken versions of pincers, levers, and screwdrivers. Pablo had always had a blind faith in that watchmaker, no doubt because he fixed the diamond-studded Rolex he was given as a wedding present, a watch declared beyond help by all the other watch repair shops in Seville. Berruel made a show of his expertise and speed, which probably had suggested supernatural interventions to Pablo.

"Here we are," said the giant looking at a card. "Pablo Labastida you said, right?"

"That's it, Pablo Labastida."

There was an obscure ritual of succession in the gesture of bringing Dad's watch to be fixed, like an indirect ceremony through which Esteban took possession of the family inheritance, transmitted from his father to his brother and now from his brother to him, as if all the blood of the Labastidas and the tangled circuit of their lives were gathered up in that round, filthy thing that went all the way back to some obscure great-grandfather. He'd never wanted Pablo to die—really—not even because he was in love with Alicia and desired, to the point of despair, to sleep against her naked back. Yes, to be sure, from time to time the fantasy of a sudden, irreversible absence had come into his head—Pablo dispatched to Canada, Pablo reading Joseph Conrad and deciding to retrace Nostromo's steps—but never, never that immolation, never blood and Alicia in a state of collapse, dodging nightmares and swallowing tranquilizers. No, that wasn't worth Dad's watch.

"It's a Lancashire watch." Mr. Berruel spoke in appraising terms, dividing his only eye between the watch and the card. "From 1910, tin case, platinum lid, balance wheel set between the plates, wound at the stem. These watches turned out to be very bad."

"It's a family heirloom."

"Fine." Mr. Berruel held the watch as if checking its weight. "But it isn't very accurate, it's badly designed, and expensive to fix, aside from the fact that the original price was excessive. According to my card, it's already had problems with the escapement."

"Yes, I really don't know."

On the other side of the plaza, next to the display window filled with brides, there was an antiques shop Esteban liked to look through. He would wander among the *bargueños* and console tables, he would evaluate the ubiquitous still lifes with the cadavers of pheasants, vases, some piece of furniture covered in damask. That afternoon, after leaving Mr. Berruel's shop, Esteban lit a cigarette in front of a darkened Saint Lucy locked in a frame with grotesque tracery. Of course he wasn't in the slightest responsible for Pablo's death, even if passion or jealousy might have obliquely begged for that conclusion: From time to time, alone in his room, distracted from his music or a book, he discovered he was completely fed up with the role of second son, with being the good Esteban, as docile as he was useless, who would look after Mom so attentively when she became a widow, while Pablo, glorified by his career and his incursions into foreign countries, would start a family with Alicia and create grandchildren to amuse Mom on Sundays.

Esteban's life was supposed to fall diligently into the mold prepared for it; the glove was supposed to correspond exactly to the hand that was supposed to fill it. Pablo's death obliterated that road, and for that reason Esteban was secretly happy about Mom's disillusion, by the surprise of all concerned, by the mild madness of poor Alicia, who was going to have to see in him something other than the sweet Esteban domesticated by family imperatives, something other than the precarious pup Esteban tortured by a hidden love for which his words never managed to find an exit. Because he wanted to infiltrate her nights, corrupt her life, contaminate with kisses that angular body Pablo's hand would never touch again, would never caress again with his fingers because they would never be able to free themselves from the moss and mushrooms, from all that poisoned vegetation imprisoning them down there, in that empty night down there.

...

She'd just returned home and had barely finished hanging up her duffle coat, when Nuria walked in with a six-pack of Cruzcampos and two cans of smoked clams. After reeling off her ghosts under Mamen's sharp scrutiny, Alicia was not especially in the mood for excess conversation, but for Nuria this was not the case. She'd just returned from work, after being cooped up the whole damn day with two other people in an asphyxiating Gothic chapel one hundred square meters in size, sick and tired of scrambling up the scaffolding like some monkey to fix retables or to remove, with the care the Ministry of Culture demands, all those moth-eaten saints from their niches.

After a long day of wood, solvents, and salami sandwiches, Nuria needed a beer as much as she needed a good shower. However, she really couldn't complain. This was the first really important job she'd had since she'd opened the restoration studio along with two university friends. They were in line for a ton of good assignments plastering and sealing all those yellowed martyrs. The chapel of Our Lady of Blood, which occupied a narrow plot of land on one corner of the Puerta de Jerez, between a branch bank and a pharmacy with a neon sign, had been suffering a threatening deterioration for forty years, the result of disagreements between church authorities and the municipal government. Over the past decades, each side had insisted the other was responsible for taking on the restoration of the church and, especially, the back wall, which contained various pieces of religious statuary of the Sevillian and Cordovan schools, almost all of them from the seventeenth century: San Fernando, San Bartolomé, Santa Lucía, and a kind of bearded African with a shepherd's crook and sandals whose iconography Nuria hadn't yet managed to decipher.

Although the condition of the saints and the windows, ⁀red by holes and cavities, called for urgent care, the poor ⁀g of the Virgin of Blood, the virgin for whom the en- ⁀apel was named, needed emergency work. The block ⁀ gazed mournfully at the faithful from the rear of the ⁀nantle reduced to a rosary of patches and splinters, ⁀d, at the knuckles, transformed into a fan of trun- ⁀s. They'd had to defer attempting to reverse those ⁀ powerful Madrid bank put a check decorated ⁀le number of zeros at the disposition of the ⁀servation of the national patrimony.

⁀ood deal all around, and they're going to pay us well, ⁀ admitted as she surveyed the records. "But I work like a dog, Alicia, and I'm so fed up with saints. . . . How beautiful your *conibras* are, Alicia."

"They are, but you should see how hard it is to get them that way."

"How feathery, they look like plush chicks. Lou Reed, now you're talking."

Before Pablo and the child had moved elsewhere, Alicia's relationship with Nuria was limited to the elevator, the supermarket downstairs, and dietary conversations that could end up in a couple of beers or a coffee in the modest little flat on the fourth floor whose walls were impartially divided between René Magritte and Jimi Hendrix. Before, held back by marriage, Alicia hadn't dared venture into that life full of noises and colors, which was a bit like her own life without Pablo and without routine, the life of an irresponsible and content Alicia liberated from the heavy dictates of her family. Now events had pushed her strangely in Nuria's direction, had removed the burden of all those obligations that had blocked the adolescent exercise of her freedom.

But that freedom was a dirty freedom, contaminated by a past that disfigured and reduced it to a clumsy parody of itself. The slowed-down voice of Lou Reed was rebuking a vicious transvestite while Alicia extracted a cigarette from the pack of Ducados and inserted it in her lips: That was Nuria's style— to turn her back to Alicia, squat down on the rug, read record jackets with a burned-down cigarette between her fingers, leaving her bottle on the table and reciting her morning misfortunes. Nuria's energy was too brilliant and versatile to waste lamenting disasters, her own or those of others, and she preferred to skip over it all, affirming the animal need to go on breathing, to go on perpetuating herself in the clams and beer.

"What's that noise?"

"It's the assholes upstairs. They bang a broomstick on the floor, I think."

The noise was repeated every five seconds, drowning out Lou Reed's little voice which, pushed by the drums, was tenaciously repeating the same refrain: *Babe, you're so vicious.* It was a hollow artillery blast that shook the fringe on the Chinese lamp with every broadside.

"What bastards." Nuria was showing her teeth. "You can't tell me this music's loud."

"It isn't. They do it for the sheer joy of being a pain in the ass, especially because I can hear their voices at four in the morning as if I had them in the living room. Lower the volume a bit anyway."

Nuria interpreted the neighbors' crude threats as an intolerable abridgment of her free will and proposed, playing with the last bottle, going down to her house to listen to something else. Alicia turned her down without saying a word, with a movement of her hands through which she seemed mysteriously to rid herself of some object, some presence, some smell that had been left clinging to the hollows of her fingers, and began to pick up the plates and bottles with the slow-motion diligence of someone who considers the visit over. But Nuria was not a soft opponent in this game. After the fourth invitation, Alicia, in despair, smoked a cigarette and nodded assent in bovine fashion.

"Come on, then." Nuria's long hair was beginning to turn into a pony tail. "Besides, you'll see the statue I told you about. Very pretty, but the shape it's in will bring tears to your eyes."

The studio she shared with her two partners—a cramped apartment in the Santa Cruz neighborhood—enabled her to make use of a more or less acceptable number of rooms at the same time, but even so, every so often, the space limitations obliged her to bring work home. Nuria had knocked down two walls and stolen the space from a couple of rooms in order to make her living room into an anarchic studio that looked as if it were somewhere between a carpenter shop and a laboratory.

The first thing Alicia noticed when she walked through the vestibule was the lacerating smell of ammonia masked by another strange, sweet fragrance that made her mouth water.

Then she saw the cabinetmaker's table in the rear, next to the balcony, where there was a mountain of wooden wedges and shavings; the blackened oven that bit into the wall and from which sprouted a laborious intestine of rubble that led to the terrace; planes, brushes, chisels merrily scattered on the floor, along with the odd empty beer can and substances half-covered with aluminum foil.

When Nuria crossed the room to turn on the music, after choosing *Morrison Hotel,* she pointed out a silhouette that was timidly hiding in a corner, on top of some newspapers, right next to a complicated device with a motor and sprayer that was something between a fumigation machine and a flame-thrower. It was a broken virgin; time had torn her tunic until it had pulled off the colors, had left her one-handed and one-eyed, tattooing into her face a moving expression of supplication that transformed her into a kind of maimed orphan. Nuria showed her a blueprint covered with angles and lines on which a Day-Glo marker had amused itself by marking crosses, many crosses. Accepting the glass handed to her—cheap wine was all that remained in the refrigerator—Alicia looked at the paper. It was the plan of a church.

"Our Lady of Blood," said Nuria. "You've probably walked past it a million times."

"I have, but I never went in."

"Neither you nor anybody else for years and years. It's closed to the public. Practically in ruins. The crosses on the plan are the sculptures that have to be repaired."

"This one's pretty," said Alicia, crouching down to contemplate the orphan's face: A brutal, black bite broke her forehead just above her left eye.

"She is, but just look at the shape she's in," Nuria sighed.

"I've got the X rays somewhere. In the two previous restorations, they put in four nails so her head wouldn't fall off, and I'm thinking of putting a strap hinge in her hand. Yes, this one will require my close attention. I've already given her a bath in stabilizers to see how much the wood can take, and now I'm treating her with gases. Termites, woodworms, annoying tenants that have to be evicted. That's why it stinks in here. Some more wine?"

Fatigue had finally gotten the better of Alicia's will, so she now allowed herself to be dragged along by the decisions of others. This was the thing most like forgetting she was likely to attain: a no-man's-land where words didn't climb up to her ears, where innocent acts would not be forbidden or executed by an electric charge that rose up from some deep, sordid cellar inside her she couldn't seal off. But the very instant when her fingers accepted Nuria's glass, she felt that in some way she was tying a blindfold over her eyelids, neglecting the unbearable command to purge her memory, playing a trick so she could, like a coward, sidestep what she had to endure, what she was condemned to endure. She put on the best smile she could manage, left the glass next to the fumigation device, and gave Nuria two kisses.

"You're leaving?"

"I am."

In the center of the silent hiatus, Jim Morrison was waiting for the sun: "I'm waiting for the sun."

"How are you?"

Alicia smiled.

"Okay, silly."

Nuria's hand was trying to extricate itself from some red goo that had trapped her fingers with its little tentacles.

"Really? Don't you be silly now, because whatever you need, you know . . ."

A docile Alicia nodded her head in agreement. It was so easy to agree, all you had to do was nod your head, say you agreed: not remember, dam up that avalanche of mangled memories whose fault it was she was not attending to the unavoidable obligation to live. Saying yes was the easiest thing in the world, saying any old thing is always so easy; the tongue is the most elastic part of the human body.

"Whatever you need . . ." Alicia allowed herself to be hastily kissed. "See you tomorrow."

She went up the stairs to her floor two at a time, while her left hand rifled through the pocket in her sweater and scratched itself on her keys and lighter. Before opening the door, she took a deep breath and put a cigarette between her lips. She was exasperated by this self-imposed imperative to martyrdom as if she had to force herself to suffer to be at the same level as the love the dead had dedicated to her. But at the same time, a perfect deafness, which she longed for and for which she'd failed in many aspirations, seemed to her the most miserable sort of betrayal, like not performing the role assigned in the choreography of the tragedy now that the other two had finished their parts and left the stage. She was inhaling the first mouthful of smoke when she saw how her neighbor's door was opening in a surreptitious way and how two eyes materialized in the narrow crack. Then the door opened wide, and a shrunken, wrinkled creature smiled joyfully at her from the rectangle of the doorway.

"Hello there, Lourdes."

"Hello, my child. Don't run off now, wait just a moment."

In a brief moment, the creature disappeared and reappeared on the landing with a pot wrapped in aluminum foil. The smile was still deforming that face made of dried clay.

"Take it, child. Go ahead, take it."

"But Lourdes, I owe you so much already."

"Don't be silly, child." The two blue eyes were the only vestige of energy remaining in that face creased with trenches. "You have to eat, you're turning into skin and bones, and I know you don't have time to be in the kitchen. It's just a little vegetable soup. You'll see how much good it will do you."

"Thank you, Lourdes."

Thank you, of course thank you, always thank you, accepting that others do the work of living for her, accepting that they relieve her of those small, prosaic obligations to which the fact of existing was almost, with irony, reduced. Mrs. Acevedo's lips scaled Alicia's cheek and released the kiss in that central area between the temple and the jaw, where all kisses sounded like bubbles. For that retired couple, slowly resigned to tedium and Sundays, taking care of Alicia had become a service they would never abandon, one to which they were obligated both by compassion and by the curious resemblance between Alicia and a daughter they'd lost a few years earlier after a bitter struggle with leukemia.

Lourdes often took unfair advantage of the key Alicia had given her so she could water the ficus tree on the terrace and mop the bathroom or empty the dishwasher, to say nothing of the ashtrays that every afternoon she found empty and shining. Don Blas also attentively offered to fix the drain from the tub or check the plug on the water heater, all for the modest price of one of the detective novels Pablo had lined up in the library, between the Larousse dictionary and his collection of Spanish classics: Agatha Christie he liked, but Simenon was too disorderly for his tastes. Detective novels should consist of a murder, a closed circle of suspects, and an imperturbable inspector—neither more nor less.

"It's because Simenon's French," he declared. "The French go off on tangents all the time."

There was nothing on television: a movie with explosions, the back of a head confessing to rape. Alicia watered the *conibras* and placed them next to the balcony so that the dawn would gild them with the proper amount of light. Really, they were extremely beautiful, with all their white and yellow plumage, looking like bear cubs playfully licking cubes of sugar. If only there were an empty space, she said while putting on her pajamas and filling her glass of water, if I had an escape hatch or if there were a garbage dump where I could toss those thick presences, those dizzying ghosts, the invisible conspirators who were now waiting for her at the foot of the bed, waiting for her to swallow the tranquilizers and place her head on the pillow, for her to stretch out her hand to push the button on the light switch, when a darkness with blue edges would erase the bedroom. Then, after a brief interlude of amputated voices and figures, the hunt, the escape, and the hunt would begin again, along with the suffocation and gasping and again the light switch, the glass of water, cigarettes.

Two

Paralyzed, not daring to move her feet, Alicia observed that the wind swirled around darkly through the alleys until it poured into the great horizontal space. She was waiting next to a vaguely art nouveau–style streetlight and holding either a flower or a teaspoon in her hand. Before her eyes, the boulevard extended infinitely, a long tongue of asphalt flanked by the flat shoulders of the buildings. It was night, but the constellations were not like the ones she used to contemplate on summer vacations. In the distance, at the horizon, the howl of a dog mixed with the whistles of the gale. When she did start to walk, she discovered she could cover the length of the avenue in a few strides, because in that city her steps were much longer. She looked left and right: The buildings were actually enormous stage sets with painted supports. Rows of gray windows were repeated everywhere, the same quadrilateral divided by crosspieces multiplied on the wooden surfaces that closed off the streets.

Alicia felt she was suffocating. She thought as she squeezed the teaspoon that the world contained nothing else but that unlimited extension of faceless windows. But in the center of the avenue, capping a frozen pediment, a clock stood guard, a vast, yellow clock like the eye of a lizard, its hands frozen in an obtuse angle. It was four o'clock.

It was only then that Alicia noticed there were more people on the avenue of that city, which looked like something left over after a holocaust, the useless relic of a humanity effaced by catastrophe. There were human backs in vague spots on the boulevard, next to the art nouveau lampposts, facing the wall, fleeing toward the corner where more avenues were beginning to grow. Sometimes the backs spoke in low voices, dissolving their words in a shapeless crackling. Alicia wanted to stop them, show them her flower, ask the way back to her house, but the flocks of backs scattered, and they all chose different paths to make their disappearance.

Saddened, Alicia sat down on the sidewalk, picked the leaves off the teaspoon, and blew her nose into the little blue velvet dress Mom had made for her. Then a faint music called her from above and, stamping her feet with joy, she discovered a lighted window and, against the background of the yellow gridwork, two shadows dancing. The masculine silhouette clasped the feminine silhouette around the waist and led her with exquisite violence from one side to the other of the quadrilateral; he bent her back until it seemed she grazed the floor; he pressed his face with its finely etched profile against his partner's neck so she would break down in sighs and giggles. Those silhouettes, Alicia thought, were so young and beautiful and danced the tango so well. Sucking her flower, which was a lollipop, Alicia reached the end of the avenue. It stopped at a grand palace painted on a canvas, where the muses were removing their clothes.

That city was like a model on a colossal scale, like a grand amphitheater for dolls. To her left, another rigid boulevard collided against a barrier of columns; to the right, a small plaza vaguely opened. When Alicia made up her mind to walk to the plaza, she noticed she was being watched. Yes, a gentleman with a mustache was staring fixedly at her from the opposite sidewalk. His features were trivial and poor; alarm was making his ugly chameleon eyes bigger. Alicia tried to offer him her lollipop, which was also an ice-cream cone, but the man shook his shoulders and pointed to the end of the boulevard. "Go away, leave this place!" The man seemed angry or sad; some scabrous misfortune manifested itself on his yellow face. "How did you get here?" the unknown man asked her. "Pablo and Rosita are dead," Alicia answered, sucking on her ice cream. "Go away!" repeated the man, until his eyes horrified Alicia. "Go away immediately!" But she did not know the way out, so she remained there, next to the window where the couple was dancing, until she fell asleep.

...

Mamen's eyes were two dark mouths that led someplace distant and profound. Those eyes were observing Alicia from the other side of the desk bearing the Matisse calendar and that mass of ballpoint pens Mamen used to distract herself, spinning them between her fingers as she listened. There had been a threat of rain for more than a week, and that Tuesday the clouds exploded in a storm that soaked the sidewalks.

"Tell me everything," said a curious Mamen.

"Something new happened, Mamen, something changed."

"Your dreams?"

"Yes, Mamen, but it's really strange."

Alicia hadn't been scheduled to make another visit to the office for two weeks, so they could check the effects of the treatment on her insomnia. Which is why Mamen was so shocked to hear Alicia's voice on the telephone, anxiously demanding a session that very afternoon. Alicia's tone was undefinable on the other end of the line—an incongruous hybrid of terror and hope was deforming it. When she reached the office, she didn't even stop to take off her raincoat; instead, she collapsed in the chair and took out her pack of Ducados, patiently allowing her umbrella to flood the beige carpet.

"You're scaring me." Mamen lit a Nobel. "Want to tell me what the hell it is once and for all?"

"Everything started a week ago," she began. The rain had glued Alicia's bangs to her forehead. "Until then I'd had the typical sort of dreams—Pablo, my daughter, you know. One night, I had no dreams whatsoever. Now that did seem odd to me."

"It's not odd at all."

"It is, Mamen, it is odd. In my case, it's odd. Besides, I was in a deep sleep, as if I were sealed up in a cave. I had the feeling I'd sunk into a sleep that was so deep there was no room for images."

"And . . ." Mamen's hand picked up the cigarettes.

"And, well." Alicia was desperately looking for an ashtray. "The fact is that the next night I did have a dream. And it was the oddest dream I've ever had in my life."

Under Mamen's suspicious scrutiny, Alicia described a city of painted buildings walked by men who kept their backs to her. The layout of those streets left a kind of trace within her, as if it planted a seed in her mind. She suspected that the city contained a secret, that it possessed a meaning, that it was the symbol of something in the same abstract way in which a melody can stand for happiness or a white arrow makes you take a certain road. Once she was back on this side, sitting on the edge of her bed shaking her pack of cigarettes (that's the curious thing about dreams—we're always forced to interpret them through the filter of the faded memory they've left in our awakened mind), she tried to do a step-by-step reconstruction of the phases of her excursion: The memory contained symmetrical doses of attraction and repulsion. Those theatrical boulevards were saturated with that old childhood fascination which found an epiphany in all things and events. In a certain sense, the city in her dreams was a violent return to the age of innocence. On the other hand, that very innocence concealed a trap. All illusion is poisonous because, if it were to come true, we'd be on our way to annihilation. The night of unknown stars, bodies without features, the shadows—so anonymously beautiful—that carried out their dance, all aimed tangentially at something, at something unknown covered with thorns, a mere glimpse of which terrified Alicia and made her retreat. Perhaps what was waiting there, inside, was the atrocious nucleus of the truth, the eye without a lid, the broken mask.

"What's the city like?" Mamen stared at her with a stormy brow. "What did you say was there?"

"When I was little, I always thought there had to be cities like that on the moon, cities with silvery neighborhoods, ashen cities whipped by the sirocco. The city is like an opera, like a stage set. I don't know."

"So there's a clock." Mamen's hand was inaugurating another Nobel. "A yellow clock in the middle of an avenue."

"Yes, an avenue that ended at a palace with Greek statues. And that plaza on the left."

Surrounded by cigarette smoke, Mamen leaned back in her chair until her face was a gray, imprecise thing. The pen was no longer dancing in her hand. Her fingers were nervously tapping on the desk, between the vase filled with pencils and her car keys.

"I don't know what to tell you, Alicia." Mamen again leaned forward over the desk, and Alicia again fell into the colorless grottoes of her eyes. "I have to recognize that, yes, it's strange. I don't know, try increasing the tranquilizer dosage by another half a pill. The truth is that the whole thing is intriguing. Maybe it would be a good idea to try the hypnosis sessions again."

"No, we've already seen they were useless."

"Okay, half a pill more and call me next week if the dream recurs. But now you'll have to excuse me because I postponed three visits to see you."

"Of course, Mamen, I'm sorry."

"Don't be a dope."

Armed with her umbrella, Alicia was on her way to the office door, murmuring a good-bye.

"Alicia." Mamen spoke to her with her back turned, looking out the window at the storm that was erasing Torneo Street. "Did you see anything else?"

"No, not that I can remember. I'll call."

It went on raining.

...

The excursions through the city did at least include the relief of eclipsing Rosita and Pablo, who did not reappear, alive or dead, in any of her nights. Displaced by that new mystery, they seemed to dissolve in the memory saturated with poisons that favored them, and Alicia could ask herself from time to time if something really had happened and not only if it was true that her husband and daughter had been expelled from the world by the sadistic conjunction of a highway and a car moving at an improper speed. She would occasionally ask herself if those empty faces multiplied by the photographs on dressers and sideboards, those voices with muffled echoes that went on repeating themselves in certain corners of the apartment, had ever really existed.

It really was useless to deny it. It was stupid to hope for liberation, for a recovered life, for a past as soft and clean as sheets just laid on the bed. She had the city in her dream, but the ghosts were still lurking in the corners ready to collect their debt, to disrupt the routines Alicia wanted to preserve through repetition. It was a feeble, easy trick to give in to the belief that no rubble would ever again hinder her afternoon strolls, her peering into bookstores and linen shops, her conversations with Nuria or Esteban, the cloudy plumage of her *conibras,* her pleasing encounters with Harvey Keitel in the movies or some videoclub, the interminable labor of shelving and cataloging books every morning from eight-thirty to two in the General University Library.

At least there was the city. She'd found a respite in the descent that, after the water and the pills, would return her dawn after dawn to the preliminary avenue where the yellow clock divided into two sections and in one of whose windows the shadows she loved went on with their eternal tango. At the end was the palace with the muses, then to the left a high pavilion with columns which, when she'd observed it at closer range, she noticed were engraved with myriad mythological characters: gorgons, Erinyes, and sirens. Beyond the pavilion, the dome of an observatory rose, with the barrel of the telescope pointed toward the stars, and behind the observatory a tower with slate pinnacles. In that part of the city, the streets became narrower and shorter, and the walls played labyrinth games, creating the fiction of a dead end just to improvise, almost at the moment of making a turn, the passage that connected to an armor museum with a semicircular theater on whose proscenium actors' masks and sandals had been abandoned, with mirrored galleries that broke and warped her reflection, with cabinets stuffed with violins and clavichords or organs with their fans of tubes spread out in the light without the volume of the constellations.

Traversing interwoven arteries, she would reach pergolas and ministries, bird shops overflowing with cages, barracks where mechanical hussars paraded on cardboard chargers with flower garlands in their bridles. And that puerile joy of creating everything as she went along touching it continued, as if the roundabouts and roadways opened before her only because it was her feet that sought them out. Sometimes, backs gathered together would appear a couple of blocks ahead and scatter like pigeons when she approached. She also seemed to recognize, on one occasion, visitors like herself, people with fronts and faces who walked around the city as if it were a show and who stopped to admire the peristyles and balustrades.

One night she saw, from a distance, girls wearing hair nets pulling children's wagons up ramps and flights of stairs, and domes with exposed patios where circles of manikins were gathered. Another night, she reached a plaza, a flat, naked plaza flanked by pavilions, which the emptiness and silence rendered as vast as insomnia. At the center of that square plaza there was a statue, a beautiful bronze angel with a maimed foot. That night, Alicia had the impression of having profaned a secret, of having broken the first of the seals that protected the mystery of the dreamed city.

The stars slipped along the angel's coppery wings, sticking silvery pins into his feathers. She returned to that plaza many times and to that ubiquitous feeling of awakened sacredness, that numinous presence shared by the liturgy and by sacrilege. Then, from the depth, from the infinitely distant pavilions, that man came running, that humiliated man begging her to leave. The echo of his shoes was the only voice left in the air of the remote wooden city.

...

The door buzzer on the point of bursting into flames, pushed by an all-too-impatient finger, yanked her out of bed. With barely enough time to slip into Pablo's robe, she slid back the bolts and discovered that Marisa and Joaquín, with their usual, symmetrical smiles, were occupying the landing. They left an amorphous paste, whose source Alicia prudently refrained from inquiring into, in the kitchen. But Marisa, her neck furrowed by a new necklace from Madagascar or Angola, announced that it was a certain kind of highly efficacious vegetable meat. True, that combination of words might seem to produce a slightly absurd, even dumb, binomial, yet it really was vegetable meat, that is, the pulp of who-knew-what dried vegetable ground until it turned into something that was a distant relative to hamburger but infinitely healthier, of course, than that swill soaked in God-knows-what filth.

"Alicia, what *conibras* you have. They're so beautiful. How do you get them to last? Mine die immediately."

"The secret is to water them four times a day. Not one time less, not one more."

Usually, Alicia was amused by Marisa's vegetarian furor, which concentrated all the dietetic and medicinal goodness of nature in the versatile potential of a few greens whose names she would repeat as if reciting incantations. She was amused by Marisa's mania for herbs as long, of course, as it did not collide with her own dietary free will. Thinking about Marisa's complicated cure, Alicia watched the black torrent of Marisa's hair, held in place by three or four hairpins. She was fascinated by Marisa's hair, that anarchic, dark squid made blue by the indirect light.

After listening with very tranquil eyes to Alicia's descriptions of insomnia and nightmares, Marisa had prescribed a prolix series of remedies for Alicia and intermittently threatened her lunches with batteries of vegetables, infusions, omelettes of a dubiously green color, and equally improbable soups. All that accompanied by a bit of bucolic life, clouds, streams, little birds and not the ashen claustrophobia of the city, which can do no one any good. Marisa decided that morning that it was a stupendous Sunday, an absolutely ideal day to spend in the country.

Scratching her own mop of hair to prove she needed an urgent shampooing, Alicia objected that it had been raining too much. There would be nothing but mud and puddles. With the skill of a duelist, Marisa counterattacked with the little farm out in the hills that had a well-stocked fireplace and the little garden with which they could amuse themselves by weeding. But country life did not seem especially idyllic to Alicia, aside from the fact that she didn't have the slightest damned desire to be in mud up to her ankles, so she said no and thanked Marisa and Joaquín for the vegetable meat until the two of them, rather down in the mouth, disappeared into the elevator. A few seconds later, before she'd put the coffee in the pot, the buzzer again startled Alicia. Resigned to withstanding Marisa's final attempt, she put the receiver to her ear.

"Hello."

"Alicia, it's me, Esteban. Will you let me in?"

Esteban walked in with a newspaper under his arm, voicing the obligatory praise of the beautiful weather: This parenthesis of sun would save them from drowning to death. He placed a cardboard container soaked in oil on the kitchen table, and all Alicia had to do was unwrap it to find a succulent spiral of freshly made *churros*.

"Chew slowly. You're going to choke. Hey, how great your *conibras* look."

"Don't they? Today they're happy. It's nice and sunny."

The day before they'd strayed from the stipulated schedule for visiting Mamá Luisa—the obligatory profaning of cadavers and the archaeological exhumation of rusty sensations that sent her home wanting only a shortcut to oblivion and sleep. Alicia accepted the Saturday visit as a punishment, the tortured silence where she hung the comments of the old lady, harassed by some heavy and distant evil that took pleasure in perforating her with its stilettos, in flagellating her soul until her eyes closed, their lids loaded down with questions. What did she get from putting up with all that? If at the beginning she'd agreed to accompany her mother-in-law in her solitude to provide her a helping hand, she was now totally resolved to let her consume herself in that enraged bitterness in which she was drowning, in which she'd been thrashing around like a lizard since the day Pablo exchanged her for a softer and lighter woman. No, she hadn't gone to visit Mamá Luisa that Saturday. The new landscapes in her dreams were supplying her with rather spacious pauses where she could rest from Pablo and the girl. She did not want to waste those scarce breaks with more red-hot memories. It was enough to have to dodge them the rest of the time.

"Why didn't you come by?" Esteban cut a *churro* in half and turned off the coffeepot. "Mom asked for you."

"I don't know, Esteban." No, she wasn't going to retreat a single inch. "She's going to have to get used to seeing me less."

"Seeing you less?" He turned to face her. "What do you mean, Alicia?"

"Nothing, it's nothing, silly. Take the cups out of the dishwasher, those over there must all be dirty." Alicia's hair was decidedly ready for the best Scotch-Brite shampoo. "I've got other things on my mind. Yes, things."

"I don't understand how you can drink this coffee. It's pure chicory, vacuum packed. What things?"

"Things." Drawings of snakes began to circulate in the back of her eyes. "Listen, Esteban."

The silence became voluminous, as if it were charged with revelations. It was that thick silence that covers the gaps between major statements, between begging sessions, between insults. Esteban knew he should forget the cups and lean forward over the table, his arms crossed, perhaps smoking a cigarette.

"You don't have to look at me that way. I'm not going to reveal that I've murdered someone."

"That takes a load off my mind." Esteban opened a new pack of Fortunas. "Well . . . ?"

"It's dreams, Esteban." Alicia in turn lit a Ducados. "For a week now I've been dreaming about a city."

"Which city?"

"I don't know which city. It isn't any city in particular, it's a city like—an abstraction. It's like a city with dollhouses, painted, false houses, a stage-set city. The dream, actually, would be of no interest whatsoever if it didn't come back night after night, never missing, and always the same. Understand? The city is the same night after night. I always begin at the end of a boulevard at the center of which stands a yellow clock, and a couple dancing tangos."

"Are there people in the city?"

"No, barely any. People with their backs to me, manikins."

Esteban was disappointed that Alicia's dreams were so academic.

"Sweetheart, your dreams are museum dreams. Magritte, Delvaux, de Chirico. Surrealist trickery."

"Kiss my ass. I won't stand for any more teasing. Come along, I'll tell you more while I shower."

Decorously facing the hall, finishing off his cigarette so he could start the next one, Esteban heard the rustle of Alicia's clothing as it separated from her body, falling into little piles on the bidet or the tile floor. Then came the diagonal noise of the water falling and crashing into the tub, her naked back intervening in that curtain like a hot finger, in that delightful pecking which was probably sliding toward her backside, which would warmly lick the cones of her breasts and that final throat between her thighs. Esteban sighed. The shower stall disfigured Alicia's anatomy, finally dissolving it in a mass of pallid smudges.

"Okay then, tell me." Esteban tried to speak over the monotonous snore of the water. "Is that city so special?"

"Yes it is, Esteban. There's something inside it, which I can't explain. The city gives me a sensation, a mixture of sadness, horror, and fascination."

"Why?"

"I don't know, there's nothing objective, that sensation doesn't come from anywhere in particular. Doesn't it happen with you that your dreams are like excuses, like secondary products of a feeling that directs them?"

"Yes, that's what Coleridge said." The silhouette behind the glass was rubbing something that was about at the height of the thighs. "First comes the vertigo, then fear, and finally the precipice and the free fall materialize."

Wrapped in the robe, her face streaked by a mass of black tatters, Alicia led Esteban to the study. She and Pablo had agreed on that vague title for this labyrinthine warehouse of books, records, yellowed postcards, rolled-up posters, and diskettes chaotically piled up on both sides of the PC's monitor. The light from the paper lamp slipped over the shelves, partially caressing the golden names of Michael Crichton and Vázquez Montalbán, or detoured toward the sardonic face of Groucho Marx, with, below it, the inevitable phrase, "Madam, excuse me for not rising."

Pablo's profession fomented that heterogeneous abundance of typographic material, where, to the great confusion of the startled visitor, the Greco-Roman classics were mixed in with Barbara Cartland's latest brilliant exercises, to say nothing of juicy monographs on reincarnation, astrology, and chiromancy, all certified by authorities with last names both musical and improbable. Alicia handed Esteban a thick volume about the same size as an atlas, with a forest on the jacket and a title in English: *The European Engraving in the Eighteenth Century.* On page 138 appeared a series of bizarre geometric architectural ideas—cubes, spheres, and pyramids that had the pharaonic air of extraterrestrial monuments. Esteban checked the captions below the illustrations: Etienne-Louis Boulée, *Newton's Cenotaph* (1784); Claude Nicolas Ledoux, the house of the Water Director, the Workshop of the Woodcutters, Arc-et-Senans.

"Are these the things that appear in your dreams? They're horrible."

"No, they don't appear." Alicia's hand slid over the satiny surface of the leaves. "But it's the same sensation. What do those buildings mean to you?"

"I don't know." It was like a great cemetery of forms, like a beach covered with polyhedrons. "Uselessness."

A few pages ahead he found Piranesi's famous prisons, confused intestines lined with pedestals and complicated, lugubrious stairways. Yes indeed, drawings like that had the asphyxiating density of nightmares. Esteban went on leafing through the book until Alicia in jeans and a sweater decorated with rhomboids called him from the living room. She was holding a notebook in her hand, the same hand that held a recently lit cigarette.

"I've made a schematic drawing. Look."

The sheet contained a clumsy chessboard scribbled over with place-names. Arrows and asterisks located on that nonsense of lines, a yellow clock, an observatory, houses covered with mirrors, and a military academy. Below, to the south (because it just had to be the south), there was an empty square, and in the center a dot. Beneath it, a nervous hand had written: *Angel.*

"And what's this? An angel?"

"That's the best part." She let herself be swallowed up by the black leather sofa. "That plaza, Esteban, is surprising. Don't ask me why, but there is something there. That angel, so pretty, alone there, right in the center of that enormous plaza, well, it's enough to make you cry."

"What's the angel like?"

"An angel, with two wings and all the rest. His name's on the pedestal, but I don't remember it. He's lame."

"Lame?"

"His foot is folded back at the ankle, like this"—Alicia twisted her right boot to illustrate the dislocation.

Sitting on the arm of the sofa, Esteban took another cigarette. He had the notebook before him. On other pages, Alicia had tried to draw, with less skill than good intentions, some of those strange architectural examples about which she'd been speaking to him in her sickly bedazzlement. He didn't know to what to attribute this new obsession, didn't know if he should give her the benefit of the doubt and agree with her that all this dream urbanism was really very strange or if he should reduce all that raving to a maneuver intended, simply, to create confusion, like the curtain of smoke that would save her from facing up to the subject of her visits to Mamá Luisa and, above all, to the matter of Pablo's successor. No, of course, he was in no hurry to suggest the alternative, but perhaps with that trick of the city of dreams she was trying to apply the remedy before the wound bled, to set about washing her hands, slowly but confidently, of Pablo's world and its ramifications. On the other hand, there was one final possibility, though Esteban preferred canceling it because of its sinister aspect.

"Have you spoken to Mamen?"

"What do you mean?" Alicia's rage flared up.

"I don't mean anything, just if you've told all this to Mamen."

"Yes, Mr. Psychiatrist, I've told her. Poor little Alicia's gone nuts." Her voice was bitter.

"You told her everything?"

"I told her everything, sir: city, boulevard, tango dancers, plazas, backs, the harassing . . ." Something stopped Alicia short. "No, not everything. I forgot the man."

"What man?"

"There is a man as well." She seemed to be pushing aside the cobwebs on her memories with her hand. "A man with a mustache who harasses me. He tells me to get out of there, to run away. I'm not crazy, Esteban."

What did it matter if she was crazy, if she went on living within that warm wrapper of green eyes that was Alicia freshly emerged from the shower, what did it matter if it was the doll city or the dried-out cadavers of Pablo and Rosa, except that because, of course, accompanied by those figures in their shrouds, she was closer to Esteban, who would support her, to Esteban, who offered her his lap and began to let his fingers slide through her chestnut hair and to whisper words to her, words of consolation first, words about courage, then to finish with those other words, the axial words, the words to be spoken after synchronizing their eyes and, as it were, releasing that asphyxiating weight in the pit of his stomach.

Freedom, what a bent coin, what an empty pocket, what a freshly sharpened pencil without a stinking page to write on; of what use is that grand, embroidered word, if it's empty and broken, if it contains nothing, if it's all the same to exercise one's liberty or go to the movies, have a conversation, or watch a bad TV show at two in the morning. Freedom, Alicia was thinking, walking around in front of the shop windows, is an undesirable gift, because when it falls on top of you, sticky and gummy, coating your fingernails and eyelids, you've got nothing left but sleepwalking, indifference, inertia; you've got the paralysis of someone who dies of hunger with a hot pizza in front of him because he doesn't know which slice to eat first. Alicia's freedom was that handsome, empty pocket calendar that Pablo and Rosa had given her, the diary without a single bad comment about which she'd be obliged to write, even if it were only in the fictitious task of convincing herself she still existed.

Which is why it made no difference whether it was tea or coffee, a novel or a movie, meat or fish, Seville or Betis. That afternoon, which had already begun to slip smoothly toward a darkness dotted with streetlamps, she chose to take a walk but she could just as easily have done something else. She'd picked up that hygienic need to walk, which consisted in a more or less tolerated random wandering through the downtown neighborhoods, stopping in shops, looking into bookstores, satisfying the occasional whim of a lead soldier, postcards, or a book on Renaissance courtesans.

She also owed Pablo her habit of making an exhaustive perusal of secondhand bookstores, of walking along with her hands in her overcoat pockets, and perhaps with a cigarette butt in her lips through interminable squadrons of lined-up books, in one of whose titles was hidden, perhaps, the after-dinnertime of the next few weeks or the half hour before switching off the bedside table lamp, or that small treasure with its beaten-up binding, which was a real pleasure to place on the shelves in the hall after a bit of glue for that very nice price. So when Alicia ventured into the bookstore on Feria Street and began to run onto the reefs of the complete works of Alvarez Quintero and the inevitable reports about alien life-forms or life after death, she was simply following the itinerary she had learned with her husband and to which they would abandon themselves on Fridays or the Saturdays when the girl was devouring cookies in her grandmother's house.

That bookstore was much like a garbage dump, and not only because of the generous stock of dust on the volumes or the deplorable aspect of many Lafuente Estefanía notebooks that looked as if they'd been saved from a Dumpster, but above all because of the piles of rusty tools that covered the floor mixed in with shattered wooden frames, yellowed fascicles, and the odd portfolio of lithographs. The old man behind the counter, a venerable variant of the ragman or junkman, tried to make a neutral sign of complicity by raising his eyebrows the instant Alicia greeted him with a parallel movement of her hand. It was the same old man with whom Pablo would often get involved in infinite conversations about the virtues and negative qualities of new binding techniques or the old-time newspaper serials. It was to that bookstore that Pablo had led her by the hand on a night long past to give her the marvelous edition of Lewis Carroll with engravings, composed in a soft typeface that made her think about lavender, siestas, and summer.

"Good afternoon, miss."

Seduced by some vague curiosity, Alicia crouched down and looked through the portfolios. Her hands opened a wrinkled flood of nineteenth-century photographs, bleach advertisements from the forties, maps ripped out of French encyclopedias, posters. Boredom would definitely have had her toss all that old paper into the same corner from which she'd rescued it if it hadn't been that underneath a retouched portrait of Concha Piquer there appeared a print that set off a flare in some corner of her memory: It was an avenue, a long boulevard in eighteenth-century style, upon which antlike, long-coated pedestrians strolled. No, it wasn't the same boulevard, but it looked so much like it to such a strange, surreptitious extent that it seemed linked to that other boulevard by an undeniable family resemblance.

The inscription revealed that it was the Graven in Vienna in 1781, leaving no room for greater mysteries. It had been taken from an illustrated biography of Mozart. In any case, the picture magnetized her to such a degree that she decided to buy it. She removed it from the portfolio just clumsily enough to scatter everything all over the floor. Her annoyance was rapidly dissolved by a wave of stupefaction, of madness. She closed her eyes, opened them, without managing to repress the painful hammering of her heart. On top of the fascicles and broken frames, there was an engraving of a square plaza with an angel at its center, a fragile, androgynous creature with a twisted foot.

Three

S he waited for him sitting at the marble table, mechanically stirring an all-too-black coffee. Her appearance revealed nothing alarming, so Esteban, who hadn't stopped running since getting off the bus, stopped to catch his breath. To begin with, Alicia had called him at school, breaking a rule and doing something he could forgive only in really extreme cases—death, winning the lottery, things of that sort. During a boring session of Cicero translation, which he was slogging through with his twelve students, the secretary barged in and confusedly referred to a certain Alicia and something important.

Fearing some undefined disaster involving his mother or a hospital, Esteban awkwardly picked up the telephone. She didn't try to give him any explanations, but simply asked him to meet her in the Coimbra as soon as classes were over. While he did return to the classroom and did try to concentrate on that *quo mortuo me ad pointificem Scaevolam,* etc., he couldn't get Alicia out of his thoughts, neither her nor the ever more scabrous and sinister turns her neurosis had lately been taking. Mamen should have taken a stronger hand in managing her, because who knew what cliffs those bitter, nocturnal calamities would throw her from. Esteban slammed the portfolio overflowing with Caesar, Sallust, and Cicero down on the marble circle and sat down to pant. Alicia took him by the arm with that hand of hers—all fingers.

"You ran all the way here?"

"Yes," he gasped. "And this better be important, because if it isn't . . . Order me something, please."

Alicia asked for two glasses of anisette and unwrapped a pack of Ducados. The long ceremony of extracting a cigarette, putting it in her mouth, and lighting it made Esteban start tapping his fingertips on the table. After the first puff, he burst out with: "What's going on?"

She handed him a paper cylinder with an elastic band around it, which Esteban accepted without knowing what to do.

"What's this? Are you giving me a poster?"

"Take a look at it."

At first, when his eyes collided with the austerely geometric surface of the plaza and the three walls tattooed with windows that enclosed it, Esteban watched Alicia out of the corner of his eye, more interested in the expression on her face than in the content of the print. Then he noticed the angel and raised his eyebrows. Finally, when he discerned that the leg of that hermaphroditic thing was bent into a ninety-degree angle at the ankle and, therefore, represented quite accurately the physical defect Alicia had described the previous Sunday, he began to shuffle possibilities and discard alternatives while a smile of good-natured stupidity spread over his lips.

There was the possibility of a joke, but Alicia wouldn't have interrupted his class for something like that, or, for her sake, he hoped not. There was the possibility of giving up followed by repentance; that is, Alicia understands that the fantasy of the city and the angel is a dead end and confesses that the whole thing has been nothing more than a chimera based on the engraving, which she found God knows where. But the look on her face negated that interpretation. Finally there was chance. That's it, chance, nothing more than that, in the same way that when you remember a movie you saw a long time ago and really want to see again and you turn on the television and—Jesus!—there it is, get some popcorn and take the phone off the hook. An accident, like getting in the same cab twice or dying on your birthday, who knows?

"You're right, what a coincidence," attempted Esteban in a not particularly convincing tone. "An angel like the one in your dream."

"Coincidence my eye," Alicia cut him off. "It *is* the plaza in my dream. It's exactly that one just as you're seeing it there, except for one tiny detail."

"You don't say. Which detail?"

Alicia's pointy index finger moved to the angel's pedestal and pointed to a tiny lion curled up next to the statue's left foot.

"In my dream, it's not a lion but a bull or a cow, some animal with horns. Also, the name on the pedestal is similar to the one in the caption, but it isn't the same. Yes, and there is a Hebrew letter too, but it isn't that one."

Esteban read: *Samael.* He had an angel's name, sure; somewhere Esteban had heard that the suffix *el* meant "spirit of God" or something like that, which is why there were Michael, Gabriel, Rafael, etc. As to the letter, yes, it was Hebrew, or at least looked Hebrew, though it might be Aramaic or Canaanite or taken from who knew which Semitic alphabet—his ignorance of Near Eastern languages was absolutely complete. The print wasn't signed, but some faded notes on one margin referred to a remote French printer and cited the original source. Esteban recited the Latin title with all the rhapsodic elegance five years of classic philology and a certain intimacy with Catullus and Virgil conferred upon him: *Mysterium Topographicum, seu arcanae caliginosae eximiaeque urbis Babelis Novae descriptio.*

"So?" He put the print down on the table and lit a cigarette.

"I told you there was something in that city, Esteban." Alicia had decided on some sort of strategy that Esteban was as yet incapable of penetrating. "This means that the dream isn't *my* dream. Or at least that it isn't only mine."

"Enough of that, Alicia. Where are you going with all this?"

"I'm going wherever this thing takes me." There was no sign of weakness in her eyes. "I have no idea how I entered that city, but the fact is I'm there, and that I return to it night after night. And I'm not the only one who returns. That engraving proves that the city has been visited by more people."

Yes, a coincidence, curious, but nothing more than that. Really curious in any case, but to carry the thing to such an extreme was to distort it completely, all because of a pure coincidence. It wasn't possible to admit the existence of a city built inside there, inside the dream, the way someone would build a chalet on a mountain. And then, to accept the existence of a collective dream, as if at some point in its geography the dream was common and shared, and each person entered it by going down the hatchway of his pillow: an ecumenical and absolute dream any sleeper could visit.

"I'm going to look for the book from which this picture was taken," Alicia announced. "I don't think it will be that hard."

"Oh no?" Esteban was laughing with no damned desire to do so. "Where will you start, the British Museum or the National Library in Paris?"

"It's in the university library," she stated dryly. "I know from the author's name."

"Achille Feltrinelli," Esteban read. "You know this guy?"

"No, I'm not Umberto Eco." The anisette softly burned Alicia's throat. "I remember that last name, Feltrinelli. For two years now, we've been recataloging the library collection to computerize it, and that name caught my eye. Feltrinelli is a publisher in Milan that Pablo used to work with."

Naming the ghost placed a glass barrier between them, and for a few moments each one began drowning in private memories, in images and words to which neither wanted particularly to return, because they quickly seized on the engraving as a life raft.

"So the plaza is identical," Esteban said absurdly.

"I'll need you," answered Alicia, toying with another cigarette. "I'll need you to translate that book. I'll copy a few fragments, and you'll translate them for me."

Silence returned to the table, thickening the atmosphere in which their eyes gave themselves over to a duel without concessions, each one trying to humiliate the other and stretch the enemy out on the streaked marble, the ashtray, the pale white hands holding glasses. That ocular pulsation lasted until the lighter burned Alicia's Ducado with a yellow snap.

"This is for real, Esteban," she said, with her nose clogged with smoke. "So I have to ask you if you're with me or not."

How was he going to say no, to beat around the bush, to put his hand back in his pocket now that she needed to have it on her shoulder, a place from which, perhaps, it might escape into that chestnut mane, toward the unpolluted valley that ran between her shoulder blades. Of course he'd be with her, and not because of the angel, the city, or all that nasty paraphernalia, of course, and he would lend her his help mortgaging each act and resource in the hope of presenting her the bill when this matter was resolved or diluted in a new obsession or a new madness in who knew which remote zones of dreamland or the real world. Perhaps, if his strategy were examined coldly, it would merit censure or a silent repudiation, but the paths of passion are not always clean and have no reason to be that way. Yes, of course he was with her, at her side, the chameleon poised, ready to snare his fly.

"Of course I'm with you, silly girl," said Esteban, taking her hand.

...

She was trying to create a more or less balanced omelette by methodically shaking the frying pan when the intercom buzzer made her abandon the stove. She recognized the voice with its spacious vowels asking her to let her in, pressed the button, and looked for her cigarettes. Marisa took just enough time to come up to make the retired gentleman on the fifth floor understand that the elevator was not his private property, and, as always, after those creamy, pink kisses that left Alicia's cheeks like pieces of rubber, she ran to caress the *conibras,* dedicating to them her usual raptures and praise.

She was on her way to her herb shop two blocks closer to the center of town, and it occurred to her to come up for a moment to drop something off, after that afternoon when Alicia described the strange city she'd begun visiting in her dreams. She emptied her burlap bag on the table, and, her tangled hair pouring down her shoulders but still looking like a magician pulling a rabbit out of a hat, extracted a pair of sunglasses, a lost earring, papers (lists or recipes), two hairpins made to look like slices of dry lemon, a little bag of suspicious herbs, and a book with a black binding and a sonorous promise in its title, *How to Interpret Your Dreams*.

Alicia's hand took the volume while the hint of a smile elevated the cigarette between her lips. Marisa, meanwhile, taking advantage of having found her hairpins again, imposed order on the thick, black jungle occupying her head, pinning it at the back of her neck. She went on observing the *conibras* between the twin waters of fascination and resentment, not understanding why she, who had dedicated her entire life of sacrifice to spreading the gospel of plants and the benefits of the natural life, was not allowed to have creatures like these in her own house, with all their white plumage waving ornithologically above the pistils. They didn't even last the seventy-two hours that guaranteed the success of transplanting. The smoke of Alicia's cigarette, insolently whipping her nose, made Marisa turn to her: "Still smoking," she grumbled. "Like a truck driver. Joaquín's the same. Haven't I told you how many deaths tobacco causes every year?"

"Why did you bring me this?" laughed Alicia, holding up the book.

"I think that's clear enough," Marisa said, leafing through it energetically. "It's a book that helps to interpret dreams.

Don't laugh, dummy, dreams are very serious things. Our dreams speak to us about our real selves, about the condition of our vital energy in symbolic language. Look at the expression on that little face. Twenty times now I've asked you to come to see Ramón, my acupuncture guy. He'd explain to you that the body is like a battery, that vital energy runs through it, the *chi*."

"Well, my battery must be ready for the recycling pile."

"After talking to you yesterday"—Marisa's fingers were frenetically exploring the pages—"I remembered I had this book at home, and I looked up what it might mean to dream about a city. And look, just look what I found: *To wander in an unknown city generally means indecision, lack of resolve, problems with bringing a given project to completion. Immaturity. Frustrated aspirations in the immediate future. Do not put large-scale plans into action for a while.* It goes on like that for a whole paragraph."

"The author of your book is a real psychologist," said Alicia, annoyed, crushing out her cigarette in an ashtray. "Come into the kitchen, come on now. I'm going to slice some tomatoes to go along with my omelette. Have you eaten?"

Marisa's goodwill would have been something to be thankful for if it hadn't been for her shortsighted obedience to the wild theories of the natural life and her esoteric knowledge, both culled from the lessons of supermarket best-sellers to which she ascribed the sacred veracity of a guru. The problem was that for Marisa the solution to any problem always resided in the power of a mysterious herb that grew only in a remote swamp in eastern Pakistan or in an educational excursion through the fifth dimension of the astral plane or some other, equally risky zone in spiritual geography. Which meant that her advice, despite all the altruistic intent with which she delivered it, was usually as useless as an expression of consolation in the wrong language.

Insofar as Alicia could remember, Marisa's fury for friendship with plants and excursions to other worlds went back at least to adolescence, when the two of them would get together in one or the other's room to listen to Radio Futura and recite catalogs of possible boyfriends. She'd always been interested in extraterrestrial visits, evidence of Atlantis, the secret room that would open with death—all the sort of exotic unknowns that the kiosks helped to resolve for the modest investment of two or three hundred pesetas. Not that she was naive; she was equally distant to fanaticism and mysticism—Alicia knew she was safe from the tentacles of all those sects and gnostic societies that supplied wisdom in exchange for the number of your bank account. Marisa believed in other worlds with her own personal conviction, freely chosen, because you've always got to believe in something and both Christ and communism seemed too old-fashioned to her.

We've all got to believe in something, Marisa had declared to Alicia on some occasion when a concern or a glass of red wine had unleashed her sincerity, you've always got to cling to something, especially if all our broken hopes will not allow us to have faith in the future. Perhaps her esoteric credos became insincere dogmatism when the doctor told her that her womb, sabotaged by a strange sickness tests had imperfectly noted, would never hold the child she wanted. Ever since then that impossible presence, the never-to-be-born child, accompanied her solitude and her herbal investigations and made her feel, despite Joaquín's perennial attention, a bit more abandoned.

She'd wasted many tears and spoken many blasphemies in the pursuit of that unattainable child. Once, in a cloud of marijuana or cognac, she'd even asserted that it wouldn't matter if she had to sell her soul to the devil to obtain that prize. But she, Alicia thought, had her vegetables, her inhabitants of the great beyond, her incredible universe full of echoes and surprises: Only a nail can remove another nail, only a stronger obsession can extinguish the one that torments us. After searching like a mole through the inside of her bag, Marisa had put before Alicia, in the kitchen, a kind of visiting card with a half moon and two or three stars painted on it: The card fell onto the platter and sank into the juice from the tomatoes. *Asia Ferrer. Learn your future. Specialist in cartomancy, chiromancy, oneiromancy, and other methods of telling the future.*

"She's a specialist," Marisa assured her, dipping a slice of tomato into a bowl of salt. "Pass by her place and tell her I sent you. What have you got to lose?"

"Maybe later." The underside of the omelette was a brown and black relief map. "But I do thank you for it, Marisa. Though, in any case—and please don't take any offense—I don't know what use it would be."

"Look, if you don't like those dreams, she could get them to stop bothering you."

"Sure, right away." Irony inscribed a right angle on Alicia's mouth. "She changes the cassette, and voilà, a different dream."

"It's simpler than you think," Marisa retorted with a sudden severity in her voice. "There are people who can dream whatever they like, people who have trained their psychic energy with the intensity necessary to govern their subconscious. Meditation exercises, concentration, yoga. There are even masters who can make you dream what they want. Like some people who can infect you with joy or sorrow without your knowing why."

"Okay, I promise I'll go, but not for a while. What would you like with the omelette?"

"Omelette?" Marisa seemed to return suddenly from another place. "No my dear, look at what time it is. The herb shop will be closed by the time I get there. I'll leave the book with you."

"Fine."

The juice from the tomatoes left a dark rubric on the card.

...

It could all turn out to be stupid or just another chapter in her neurosis, this one marked by extravagance and that outsized obligation to find answers to gag other voices and images threatening to emerge from down below. All of it might be nothing more than a distraction maneuver—movies or embroidering or a distant subject of conversation that makes a concern or a dilemma less bloody. If she sat down on the sofa in silence, staring sleepwalker-fashion at *le douanier* Rousseau's flautist, which Pablo had placed between the baffles and the majolica vases, if she closed her eyes while she misted the *conibras* taking care not to flood the pots, if for a moment she were able to unblock her thinking to allow a place for the dry harshness of sincerity, she would find that neither the city nor the crippled angel were worth so much work, that they really did not deserve this fury of inquisitiveness which so insistently ordered her to resolve the enigmas surrounding them. It was all, of course, a way to plaster over her memories, to pacify those memories with their sharpened jaws, those memories filled with rage and curses for those Alicia vainly thought she had already paid enough. The dross of the past, the rubbish of Rosa and Pablo transformed into a kaleidoscope of phrases, gestures, kisses, and promises intruded into every empty square, invaded every unused parcel of her time and space, with the result that the city was necessary, with the result that the angel, that the book in Latin whose title Esteban had recited in his theatrical voice at the table in the Coimbra were sadly but absolutely necessary.

However, Thursday morning, after creating a space between the cataloging of new acquisitions and the redistribution of the psychology section, after she'd typed in all entry information on the library's search screen—authors, subjects, publishers, and titles—and after she reviewed three times over the columns of green letters that winked on the monitor with the hope of correcting some conceivable carelessness, the book appeared nowhere: Fell, John Barraclough; Fellini, Federico; Felten, Yuri Matvéivich; Feltham, Owen; Feltin, Maurice. Nevertheless, she was sure she'd had that name before her eyes—Feltrinelli—that she'd copied a catalogue card with worn corners into the same computer that was now presenting her with a labyrinth of unknown names.

For a few moments, she left her partner Juanjo in charge of the cataloging and descended to the second floor, where she deciphered the cards in the Old Collection. Feltrinelli was missing as well from that stream of yellowed cards typed out with ancient typewriters. For a moment, puffing a cigarette opposite the portrait of the gloomy professor who watched over the vestibule on that floor, she came up with the objection that perhaps a memory short circuit could have caused her to locate there something that took place elsewhere. But no, she could not have noted that book in any other computer, she could not have had in her hands the stamp of any other library—eight years of work don't go by in vain. The guard on that floor was a bald and freckled thing who sat at his desk boring himself to tears laboring over an eternal crossword puzzle.

Alicia opened fire with perfunctory comments on the rain.

"You've got to let me in for a moment."

"Why, sweetheart?"

"There's a mistaken reference in the computer. We can't get into the eighteenth-century catalogue."

"The director hasn't said a word about it."

"It would only be for a minute."

With the man's smiling acquiescence, she penetrated that cathedral of books whose bindings had been wrinkled by the irreverent weight of the centuries. Fabulous editions of Galen and Pliny, bursting with engravings of rough descendants of medieval bestiaries, made her pause in the stacks, fascinated by the monsters and the herbs—amphisbaenas, hellebore, mandrake, and mistletoe. There was no Feltrinelli in the eighteenth-century section or in the seventeenth. In the sixteenth, she resigned herself to contemplating the beautiful drawings in *De historia stirpium* by Leonhard Fuchs. She made her way down to the fourteenth century, where the incunabula began and a harsh sign prohibited portfolios and ballpoint pens.

At first, Alicia thought she'd have to recognize that once again her memory had played a bad trick on her or that it had wanted to amuse itself at her expense by having her wander through a thicket of Latin titles. Suddenly it occurred to her that someone could have very patiently set out to erase any traces. She smiled at her movie-inspired fancy, but the possibility of being in competition with someone did not seem so crazy to her. After all, the mystery would be that much more exotic if she were to accept the existence of a hand, of a secret, ubiquitous player who arranged the pieces on the chessboard as he pleased and went along challenging her movement by movement, leading her to the end of the game, where all secrets would be revealed. The labyrinth of the city and the angel became, therefore, a kind of bait, an invitation to go deeper into the grotto to see just how far her curiosity or daring would lead her.

As if illuminated by her hypothesis, she ran to the farthest stacks in the collection. Kept there, in a special, alarmed room where the humidity was maintained at a constant level, were the university's bibliographic jewels: a Gutenberg Bible, a mutilated *Celestina,* Nebrija's *Grammar.* And down below, tossed aside, there was a more recent or more modest binding, without all those gold flourishes and vegetable curlicues typical of the more ancient volumes. The sticker with the catalogue number had been ripped off the spine, and the title was illegible. All Alicia had to do was open the cover with a smile to reveal that she already knew the long paragraph on the first page: *Mysterium Topographicum, seu arcanae caliginosae eximiaeque urbis Babelis Novae descriptio, a ministribus Domini nostri exaedificata ad maiorem Sui gloriam.*

Someone had tried to obliterate any trace of that book, to suppress its existence along with the trail it left behind in card catalogues and book catalogues, someone wanted to convince her that Achille Feltrinelli had never written a work in which there appeared an engraving with a maimed angel. But her heart skipped a beat when she noted that between the end-papers of that volume not only awaited her the plaza surrounded by pavilions but that there were views, also impossible to confuse with any others, of the observatory, the hemicycle theater, the palace with naked muses, the interior neighborhood where the streets turned into somber, strict galleries and where it was barely possible to make out the constellations. While there were differences—the clock on the avenue was not the same, and the store with the manikins looked like an arms shop—the book was, without any doubt, a kind of tourist guide to the city in her dreams, a manual for new visitors with a complete map included in its central pages. A circular nucleus produced spirals of buildings spreading toward the periphery, stopping in four square plazas connected by passages. In each one of those plazas, as Alicia confirmed by consulting the illustrations, there was an angel, a maimed angel with a small animal at his feet. Most certainly, then, there did exist a game, a hidden game to which, without knowing why, someone had invited her, placing her in front of the board and the cards. She had to show all that to Esteban; she had to copy some fragment she would hope to be meaningful so he could translate it. Yes, she needed paper and pencil, and she had to breathe for a while, sitting down somewhere, and perhaps a cup of coffee, and, most definitely, a cigarette.

...

The giant's eyes swept over the pages of the notebook while Esteban, bored, turned to the door to observe the plaque eaten away by ruse: SANTIAGO BERRUEL. WATCH REPAIRS. Only then did he remember that before this visit he'd noticed that repellent stench of burnt sulphur that seemed to emanate from the back room and that blocked his nasal passages. Above, the sun could not decide to come out and remained camouflaged in the white mountain chains of storm clouds. For sure it would rain again.

"No, it's not ready yet," said the giant with his index finger stabbing a notation in his book. "Your watch is a Lancashire, correct? It isn't ready."

"I brought it in a week ago," retorted Esteban.

"Yes sir, I know"—the notebook returned to the shelf from which it had sprouted—"but more urgent jobs came in. Besides, I told you that it was difficult to repair the Lancashire."

"Okay." Esteban's chin dove down into the neck of his parka. "When should I come back?"

The giant was still undecided. The mummified hand scratched his face, where a scar outlined on the diagonal recalled some act of past carelessness.

"Come back in a week," he finally decided. "We'll see what can be done."

The antiques shop on the corner had a new guest. Esteban stopped to contemplate the dilapidated bust of Hadrian that amused itself contemplating the passersby from the window. It was a block of something vague, between marble and plaster, deposited on top of a Doric pedestal. The years had chipped away his cheeks. For Esteban, all old things had an air of acrid melancholy, that smell of a closed-up room or a beach on a rainy day: too much literature.

When, having used up all the possibilities of coffee and three or four stores, he went over to Alicia's house to see what had come of the tale of the city and the angel, he had to resign himself to the landing and pushing her buzzer many times to confirm that there was no one there to hear it. Alicia had slipped away once again, what the hell could she be doing at that hour but feeding those zany lucubrations about angels and dreams in some bookstore or shop window? After all, they'd made a date to translate the damn book. He knocked. Maybe she was showering and didn't hear the buzzer. Half a dozen knocks later, he decided to turn around and take the stairs again. The change of plans transformed his afternoon into a depopulated, ashen wasteland where there was nothing to amuse him. Thinking he'd simply resign himself to the inevitable Agatha Christie novel that awaited him on his night table next to the postcard of Agrippa's Pantheon, he shook his pack of Fortunas to get the last cigarette and saw Nuria come out of her apartment with two swollen bags of garbage in each hand. He relegated the cigarette to the pocket of his parka and grabbed the two bags, which stank of sawdust and ammonia.

"Thanks," said Nuria, elevating that mouses's nose of hers, which reminded Esteban of some cartoon character. "Help me, we'll throw them out downstairs, and I'll make you coffee."

"It's a deal."

The Dumpster had barely enough room for one more object, but the bags found a tight resting place mixed in with stacks of cartons and two or three sticky magazines. Nuria and Esteban went back upstairs talking about music—they could choose between the Velvet Underground or some Bach delight. The same stench of ammonia mixed with rancid wood was floating in the living room, where a devastating battle seemed to have taken place. Coffee cups and teaspoons languished next to carpentry tools; the odd sandwich forgotten after two bites was stained by soot next to the stove. A random pattern of cigarette butts carpeted the floor, which was half covered by sheets of newspaper. In between, a few steps from the balcony where the blinking neon sign from the ice-cream store across the street was beginning to pulse, a resigned figure was receiving a coat of something yellow, between honey and sulphur: a one-eyed Virgin.

"Don't get upset." Nuria smiled and made her way on tiptoe through the living room so she could run to the stereo. "You caught me right in the middle of a gassing. The Virgin is giving me a lot of work."

"I imagine so."

Trying not to squash a container wrapped in aluminum foil and filled with a reddish unguent, Esteban made his way to the Virgin, whose face, violated at the level of her eye by a violent, black gash, filled him with a suffocating vertigo. During the first strains of Bach's *Wachet auf,* Nuria asked about Alicia, and he answered without paying attention to what he was saying, entranced by that black abyss in the figure's head.

"Now I'll give you paper and pen, and you'll leave a note for her if you like. I'll go get the coffee."

"Let's have it."

Later, whenever he thought about that moment (because he'd repeat it), he'd tell himself that the spiral attraction the broken statue transmitted had been nothing more than a prelude, the prologue or first warning of the other thing, the really important thing, which he would find when he stepped a bit to the left to observe the Virgin's mantle from behind and discovered the brownish chip in the shape of an elephant that marked her back. At first, he noted nothing unusual because he was still trapped by that black hole, by that hungry maw that trepanned the statue's forehead, but as soon as he blinked to focus on the back corner, there, next to the pile of magazines, his vertigo took on the dimensions of an enormous yellow and black funnel, and he thought he was going to faint.

A slap numbed his cheek. He blinked twice, walked over and touched. In the corner, on a sheet of plaster-stained newspapers, flanked by the magazines and a J&B bottle with a half-burned candle stuck into it, there was a bronze angel with a maimed foot. Esteban caressed the surface of its wings and passed his fingers over its hair, covered with undulations. Yes, it was absolutely identical to the one in the engraving except, of course, for its size and for that tiny human figure that took the place of the lion next to its left foot. The statue couldn't be more than half a meter high and had a vaguely baroque air. It reminded him of the angel blowing the trumpet in the facade of the university. Nuria was coming back down the hall when Esteban confirmed that a mass of signs covered the pedestal. There was a name, *Azael,* a Hebrew letter, two Latin words, *Dente draco,* symbols and letters in Greek that he'd need time to translate. Nuria held out a blue cup to him and it warmed his hand.

"Like it?" she said. "It just came in last night."

"It's superb," Esteban stuttered, still unable to believe it.

"Eighteenth century," said Nuria, using her teaspoon to make it ring like a bell. "I have to clean it and take off a bit of rust on the hair, but aside from that it's in pretty good shape."

"Who brought it to you?"

It seemed Nuria didn't like the question.

"What business is it of yours?" She licked the teaspoon until it shone like a mirror. "Know what that thing they call a 'professional secret' is? I can't go around telling everyone who my clients are."

"Okay."

Two ideas collided noisily in his head. The bronze figure on the newspaper next to that junk heap of wood and equipment placed him at a crossroad he was in no mood to face but which obliged him to decide once and for all between following Alicia's fantasy like some cow, and covering her mouth with his hand to make her leave this detour and return to the highway of reality. Although he was convinced that the figure there in the neighbor's living room stopped Alicia's tales dead in their tracks, a little voice was calling out from the depth of his conscience to defend her, to vindicate her. Every time he understood—the evidence was blatant—that Alicia was fooling him and everyone to escape from the assaults of memory, he collided with a sticky spiderweb of objections.

"When did you get it?"

"Last night, I just told you."

"Not earlier?"

"What?" said Nuria.

"You're sure it wasn't before last night?"

A smile tried to camouflage itself behind the lip of her cup.

"What's wrong with you, Esteban? My memory still works fine."

To give in to Alicia's imagination would suppose admitting that those angels had crossed some sort of threshold, the border separating reality from dream, that confused and turbid universe below as well as our routine composed of poor certainties. To pass from one side to another just like that, like passing from the living room to the kitchen and remaining quite calm: What was that tunnel connecting two irreconcilable orders, two antagonistic areas of geography and architecture? Over the course of an enormous half hour, Nuria talked about the apartment, about remodeling, and about God knows how many twists and turns in the mortgage. Esteban didn't hear a word. About the time the *Gloria sei dir gesungen* rang out in the Bach, he thanked Nuria for everything and picked up the paper and pen. Without knowing what exactly to say to Alicia, he hastily scrawled out: *I must see you. It's urgent.* Then, a bit disquieted, he left, dragging his feet; Nuria lost sight of him only when he disappeared down the stairs.

...

Until she walked up to the shoe-store window to take a better look at the boots that had drawn her over from the opposite corner, Alicia could not be sure that her life was at the point of crossing a certain line, that she already had one foot on the other side, which marked the future, and that the future was populated by a growing horde of creatures and faces that were not exactly pleasant. Her heart began to stutter when she recognized, reflected in the glass she was looking into, those ashen and impoverished features cut through by a mustache, features she associated with a remote plaza lined with pavilions.

For an abysmal instant, Alicia closed her eyes with the burning desire to be mistaken, and her nails almost pierced her palms she was squeezing so hard. But what her mournful eyes found when she again stared into the window was the same procession of bluish individuals, the same girl holding the same child by the hand, the same old man trying to adjust the same dubious cap over his temple. And, with an anxious detonation in her ribs, Alicia saw the same man with the mustache, beaten down and needy, tediously contemplating something that had to be in front of her, in that landscape of beige tones spattered with shoes.

She took three deep breaths before turning around and making her way as best she could through the crowd looking into the shop window. When she was alone, standing next to a traffic signal, she thanked the gusts of cold air blowing up from the avenue, trying to keep her from placing a tremulous cigarette between her lips. She hadn't stopped to keep an eye out, not even the corner of an eye, for the shadow that then stationed itself to her left, loaded with a shopping bag, that brushed against her elbow just when she'd finally rescued her lighter from the depths of her purse. To turn around and feel that suffocating collision right in her lungs, and to free her lips again from the cigarette's filter, mechanically, as if taking it away from someone else's face, was a rush of sensations that her memory, later, would subordinate to a single image: that of an unknown man with a mustache who was standing next to her, fixing two black eyes on her, eyes from which arose the same odor of disbelief or irony, with another cigarette indolently fixed in his mouth, using his thumb to pretend to light an invisible lighter: "Can you give me a light, please?" The lighter shook and got lost among her fingers before reaching the man's face. The flame, orangeish and thick, turned if only for a second into a sardonic mask from Greek comedy. The man immediately thanked her and said good-bye with the same subterranean squint that terrorized her in her dreams.

The shadow of the unknown man went on moving around in clandestine fashion through her memory until, almost running, Alicia reached the door of Mamen's office. She entered the elevator that frightened Rosita so much and pushed the button for the fourth floor. The mirror showed her a cornered, stupefied woman, panting in anguish from the depth of eyes that broadcast dark thoughts. Then she too began to fear the whole thing, she too began to fear she'd dropped the reins and found herself, without having noticed it, on the other side, expelled from the civic sanity that enables ordinary people to see what everyone sees and to share the normal meaning of words. Suppose she really was going insane. When Mamen, who'd stayed behind in her office all that afternoon to review case histories, saw Alicia's face so convulsed, she ordered her to sit down immediately in one of the armchairs in the waiting room.

"Well now, what's wrong?"

"I have to tell you more things, Mamen." Alicia could barely breathe.

"Okay. In a minute, but I'm going to make you some herb tea. What a look you have on your face."

In the office, with a Ducados in one hand and the other warmed by the hot cup, Alicia seemed to calm down. Night had fallen; outside, Torneo Street had turned into an erupting anthill of advertisements and stoplights. The desk lamp poured its glow over Mamen's hands; her cigarette contaminated the surrounding darkness with spirals of smoke.

"The other day I forgot to tell you something. Well, the fact is that now I've got a lot of things to tell you."

"Are you still involved with the city?" The voice emerged impersonally from the hands. "I thought you'd be over that by now."

"No, Mamen, listen. I've discovered that the city is not just a dream. Not just my dream at least."

The hands remained silent. An excessively golden bracelet glittered on her wrist.

"Let's see if I can explain myself. Look, in that city there is a plaza with an angel in it and a man with a mustache. The other day, in a bookstore on Feria Street, I found an etching with the angel, and the man with the mustache just asked me for a light out on the street."

"A man with a mustache." The hands seemed to meditate.

"Yes, a poor man." Alicia snuffed out her cigarette and dug around in the pockets of her duffle coat for the pack. "He's the typical character you think of when you think of a poor man. Imagine: He's balding, narrow shoulders, a functionary, he's henpecked, things like that."

"Okay. What about the angel?"

"The angel is maimed. Actually there are four angels."

"Four."

"There are four angels, one in each corner of the city. It's all in a book I found in the library that describes everything. Incredible, Mamen. That author, an Italian of some century or other, was there. Down there, in the city of my dream."

Alicia suddenly fell silent, as if for a moment she'd been given the opportunity to duplicate herself and listen to herself from the other chair, that empty chair on which Mamen had piled a dozen portfolios. It was then she understood the alarming paths to disaster to which her outburst was leading her.

"Mamen," she moaned, "am I crazy?"

The hands abandoned the hole of light, and Mamen's shadow walked around the desk and sat down next to Alicia. She must have been staring intensely at her, but her eyes had dissolved in the thick darkness that hid the office.

"Alicia." That way of pronouncing her name, between accusation and reproach, did not herald a promising diagnosis. "Alicia, listen to me: Forget that city once and for fucking all."

"Is it up to me?"

"Yes, to a great extent it is up to you." Mamen was sitting down on the desk, and the lamp was flashing splinters of light off her costume jewelry. "Let's see if you understand me. The city is nothing but an excuse. The city, the angel, all those fantasies you think so intriguing or so interesting are just projections or detours from your principal obsession, the obsession that is really eating you up, the one we both know very well."

"Pablo and Rosa," Alicia sighed.

"Yes, Pablo and Rosa." Mamen looked like the indulgent teacher who discovers her student copying during an exam. "It's a widely documented psychological defense mechanism, and very often it keeps us from going crazy, but other times it can be fatal. And you're leading yourself astray with this. Are you listening to me?"

"Yes."

"I'll tell you what we're going to do."

The hands went back within the light and shuffled through some papers until they picked up a prescription blank. The right, with the help of a pen, inscribed signs on the paper, while the left, now being strangled by the excessively golden bracelet, held it in place.

"I'm prescribing you some new pills. They're stronger, but I think that the way things are going, you'll need them."

"More pills," grunted Alicia from the side of the chair.

"Yes, more pills." The look in Mamen's eyes left no doubt about the need for the new prescription: It was a categorical command. "I know all this annoys the hell out of you, but you'll see. There's the name: Peramerol. Don't confuse it with anything else. I'll underline it."

Thanking her with no excess of enthusiasm, Alicia was getting ready to snatch up the paper in order to bury it in her bag, but Mamen's hand stopped her. The pen hadn't finished writing.

"Take these tranquilizers, one after each meal. And at night, half a pill more. You're going to call me the day after tomorrow to tell me how you feel. Then we'll see."

"The day after tomorrow is Saturday."

"So what?" Mamen's tone was more relaxed. "You think health takes off on weekends too? Wait, I'll walk out with you. I've got nothing more to do here. Want to get a beer?"

It was soothing to let herself collapse into Mamen's arms, to turn a blind eye to her horror in order to pass it to those hands that would obliterate it and not leave a trace, giving back to her a smile or comforting words of consolation, which she would accept, closing her eyes. Alicia relied on Mamen as if she were a panacea, as if the mere fact of following her prescriptions would lead magically to the cessation of her malady. Yes it was true, Pablo and Rosita had to continue their patient invasion of her mind, making their way through obstacles until they were scratching that last stronghold of sanity whose fall would mean surrender, the end, the compass broken and the iceberg against the hull, cessation. The city was nothing more than another camouflaged avatar of that cruel conquest, of that infection multiplied on various fronts that would wipe out, unless she stopped it, the vegetation of her nerves.

Repeating to herself, as was only proper, her resolution to mend her ways, she and Mamen went down in the elevator and emerged into a vast night cleansed by the light rain. The humid air that flooded her lungs convinced her for an instant that an alternative was still possible, that the letter could be begun again by tossing the sheet full of corrections into the waste basket and taking a new sheet. But when she looked in the other direction, she realized that it wasn't all so easy, that she could not rid herself of her incubi with a mere flick of the wrist and the decision to go back to ordinary life. The man with the mustache was waiting two doorways to the right, huddled in his raincoat gloomily finishing off a cigarette. All of Alicia's projects disintegrated in an instant, and once again that urgent itch to find answers ran through her body, that amorphous combination of curiosity, pleasure, and fear that attracted her to the city of wooden avenues where she saw the clumsy-looking man with the mustache who was now tossing away the butt and drilling a hole through it with his eyes.

"There he is," whispered Alicia, taking hold of Mamen's arm. "That's the man from the dream."

"Where?"

With the face of a beast on the hunt, Mamen scrutinized the doorway where the inoffensive figure was waiting. He intermittently checked his wristwatch, as if awaiting the arrival of someone who was hopelessly late, perhaps the person who would receive the plastic shopping bag he had wrapped around his wrist. Then the man allowed himself to be seen perfectly in the glow of a streetlamp, and, raising the collar of his raincoat, he began walking up the street until he disappeared at a corner where there was a branch office of a bank. Mamen's gaze remained suspended in the air, frozen in the contemplation of the bank, engrossed in something that only she was able to witness. Alicia shook her and again repeated: "That was the man in my dream."

Mamen's head turned mechanically.

"Didn't I tell you to forget all that. Do you want to go crazy? Come on, let's have a beer and to hell with this stuff."

Right at hand, there was a bar, and they were playing Julio Iglesias.

...

To visit, successively, the four plazas, each of which was oriented toward one of the four cardinal directions as promised by Feltrinelli's plan, with the help of which one could learn to calculate the most beautiful or the shortest of itineraries (for those in a hurry), all you had to do was walk around the city along those four streets that marked its limits. The city ended at a vast fictitious wall adorned with painted mansards or cute Venetian bay windows. It was impossible to reach anything beyond that barrier. Although waking up carefully erased the names on the pedestals, there were four angels, four identical sentinels in what seemed four precise repetitions of the same plaza, the same laconic space walled in by the pavilions. The only detail that distinguished each one was the small animal crouching next to the angel's left foot, the healthy one, and these were a bull, a lion, a little man, and an eagle.

Alicia explored other zones of the city, searching for some sign that might help to clear up or at least to make less dense one or another of all those questions, which so anguishingly demanded an exit. But at her feet there opened only more narrow lanes, fantasy grottoes, pantheons, academies, and botanical gardens. The same unreal calm went on floating over the city like a magic spell, a silence never profaned by any echo. Within it, Alicia made the soles of her shiny patent-leather shoes snap. Again the idea flamed up within her that the city had to be the remains of an empire, of some ruined civilization some cataclysm had annihilated at the peak of its splendor.

And yet one night she heard footsteps: not the regular, pacific footsteps of a passerby but the furious gallop of dozens of feet, a horde of feet that made their way along the streets, carrying through a quest. Hidden inside a doorway, Alicia confirmed that the footsteps ceased, that they were replaced by a long pause in which only whispers reached her. Then the thunder of the shoes once again shook the air, and the pack of dogs checked the neighborhoods, whipped by rage for having found nothing. Alicia suddenly understood that they were looking for her, that she was an intruder, that they wanted to exterminate her. She'd made her way into that place without explicit permission; she'd strolled through that foreign territory as if it were her own city, as if her mere presence gave her the right to enjoy that urban scene. Yes, if they found her, they'd expel her, punish her, perhaps even do something worse. The roar of that gang of shoes contained a hint of cruelty, a blurry fierceness that appeared in their terrible way of hammering the silence.

It was then the black scorpion of fear stung her stomach, and she understood that by playing that game she was risking her life, that the decadent beauty of that architecture concealed an atrocious secret which was winding more and more into a tangle that could trap her like a spiderweb until it would be too late to change her mind and hope for salvation. The patrol of shoes wanted her, wanted her to pay for her curiosity, wanted to punish the inquisitiveness that had brought to light something that was not supposed to circulate in the ordinary world outside. Perhaps it was for that reason the man with the mustache had repeated to her that she must flee, that she was in danger, perhaps for that reason she again saw him come to her, perhaps for that reason he was hiding in a ballet school and, sweating, grabbed her by the shoulders and again begged her to leave, repeated that she had to escape, that she leave with her eyes closed and not take a single step back.

Four

The air gently caressed her forehead and cheeks, and Alicia, closing her eyes, liked to imagine that a pair of blue lovebirds was flying across her face, planning the mask of her face and dissolving it, the same way the gaze of those enormous birds that fly over the bottoms of valleys and the mountains reduces the earth to a gray-brown cartography. Then she opened her eyes again and followed Esteban, indecisively strolling to the far end of the avenue of poplars, walking in circles, stopping to light cigarettes or examine statues, training her eyes on the cloud of chestnut-colored butterflies fluttering in the treetops. The sunlight, sullied by the clouds, gave the avenue the artificial quiet of a winter garden.

"He's got a mustache," Alicia repeated.

"What kind of mustache?" inquired Esteban.

"A mustache, Esteban. I can see it perfectly. The same kind I saw on him the other afternoon when I went to Mamen's office."

"You went to see Mamen?"

"Yes, the afternoon I saw him, the day you left me the note. By the way, what was it you wanted to tell me?"

On those vaguely rainy days, María Luisa Park had the Parisian air of a cemetery for poets or the rusted remains of ancient glories. The vegetation and the rats shared the grandiloquent architecture of the 1929 exposition, moss was eating away the busts of eminent men of the Hispanic world placed in the crossroads, plastic bags and papers had taken the place of the fish and the geese in the stinking waters of the ponds. They liked strolling along the useless avenues flanked by palm trees and willows because there it seemed possible to isolate oneself from the vulgar routine of the city and domestic obligations.

"Nothing important," answered Esteban. "Nothing at all. Wasn't I supposed to translate something for you?"

After reflecting for a few minutes, Esteban decided, for the moment, to say nothing about Nuria's angel. Yes, the existence of the angel would corroborate Alicia's most alarming hypotheses, but to inform her of its existence meant yielding to her all-too-disorderly way of seeing things. Naturally, everything should have an explanation, and the pieces in the puzzle would compose a reasonable figure once they were properly arranged. Esteban assumed responsibility for finding the right combination, but on his own terms. This meant not giving Alicia information that would lead her only to improper conclusions.

"Yes, here it is." Alicia held out three sheets of paper covered with hasty handwriting. "I took it all from the book, which, as I told you, was in the library. Someone tried to hide it."

"Hide it?" Esteban examined the pages.

"Hide it or destroy it. I found it on a stack where it didn't belong, between two incunabula. The last person to enter the Ancient Holdings did not fill out the appropriate identification card. They simply put in the title and catalogue number for the book they were looking for. And that, naturally, could not be Feltrinelli. All this is beginning to look sinister to me, Esteban."

Alicia noted that the sun was beginning to peek over the clouds in a cowardly way and that, at times, it made the sad carpet of fallen leaves golden. Almost at the same time, a gust of wind scattered them along the entire avenue of poplars.

"My dreams have warned me," she recited, like a sleep-walker. "That man appears in my dream and has told me to run away again and again. I'm chased. There are people who chase me down there, people who know I'm trying to unmask them."

"Chase you?" Esteban looked at her. "Who's chasing you."

"I don't know. I don't see them. This thing's going to kill me. Maybe Mamen's right, and I should forget all of it. But how, how?"

Esteban's hand traveled to her cheek and touched it with two fingers, tracing a vague caress. Alicia understood that Esteban's eyes were filled with something, that a deep, warm tide was screaming within him to flow from his pores and at times took control of his gestures and words. She thanked him for the sign of his hand, but lowered her eyes and restricted herself to searching hastily for a cigarette. She was afraid, afraid as well of what was shimmering in his pupils, afraid too of the future in all its forms and subdivisions. The black scorpion of her dream had injected her with a muffled horror of everything, of her decisions and the unforeseeable effects they could un-leash. Rosa and Pablo had delegated their power to the city; the chase was still the same even if the setting had changed.

"This thing is insane," snorted Esteban, reading the pages.

"What does it say?"

According to the poor, academic Latin of the text, the city had been built with the help of scores of disciples over a period of many years in order to praise the glory of the Gatekeeper of Hell, the Great Enemy, the Prince of This World, the One Crowned with Stars, and it was destined to shelter his ministers and apostles in the millenary war they were waging against the miserable Jesus Christ, his lackey the pope, and all the repugnant scum of Holy Mother Church. The faithful would patiently await the coming of the Promised One, who would return twisting that which was straight and overturning thrones and basilicas.

He would be assisted in carrying out his plan by words pregnant with worlds (*verba orbium gravida*), a name of devastating dimension (*dirutae magnitudinis nomen*), Four Fundamental Letters, Four Roots, Four Beasts, Four Commanders, and an Allpowerful Woman. Strictly on his own merits, the author of this insanity would have earned his own plaza in the appropriate asylum. Finally, on a separate sheet, Alicia's chaotic script had recorded what seemed to be a dedication and a handful of verses. Unless Esteban's Latin was incorrect (which would have been sad at this stage in his life), the book was dedicated to *Egnatio Alpiarcaense, golden creator, rival of the angels, conspicuous competitor with nature in the forge of beauties and marvels.* As to the verses—they didn't exactly cut a swath through that jungle of bad metaphors and bizarre ideas.

Connected to the final sheet by a paper clip, a parallel to the poem, there was also an engraving. Esteban looked it over for a few seconds, enjoying with a touch of intrigue its enigmatic aroma of secrets from the past, of archaic, buried revelations. Above a landscape of ruins and fog, a lizard, a squalid relative of the monsters in stories, was biting its own tail, illustrating the ring in an ancestral myth. It was the Ouroboros, the serpent that devours itself, ancient symbol of time, which ends up swallowed by its own drain. Esteban scrutinized the verses with the tip of his finger.

> *Dira fames Polypos docuit sua rodere crura,*
> *Humananaque homines se nutriisse dape.*
> *Dente Draco caudam dum mordet et ingerit alvo,*
> *Magna parte sui sit cibus ipse sibi.*

"Approximate translation," he announced with a not really sincere touch of tedium, "and forgive my hesitations. *Terrible hunger taught the Polypos to gnaw their legs and taught men to nourish themselves from human things. The dragon bites his tail with his teeth and throws it into his stomach so that a great part of himself will be his own food.*"

"And just what does that mean?" Alicia's hands were jumping every which way.

"It's a description of the engraving, dummy: the dragon bites his tail, feeds on himself. Like time. It regenerates by consuming what's already gone behind."

Like memory, thought Alicia. The future chewed the tail of memory, digested and nullified it, turning it into blood, flesh, skin, and nerves. Life, by definition, was the opposite of the past. Lucky dragon, she said to herself with a mix of confusion, repugnance, and tenderness. Lucky him who could calm his hunger chewing his appendages, those miserable, sterile peripheries that could only hold her back. *Dente Draco caudam dum mordet.*

"The poem and the engraving came together?" asked Esteban.

"Yes," said Alicia, just as her thoughts evaporated. "Yes, yes. At the end, as if they were set apart, after two blank pages. It would be possible to think they'd been included later, with no relation to the rest of the book, but it's not so. It's as much a part of the binding as the first page. I photocopied the engraving so you could get a look at it. What can it mean?"

"That I don't know." Esteban was still looking at the dragon, which was concentrating all his attention on ingesting himself. "What seems clear is that it has little to do with the rest of the book, even if it was bound in with it. I don't know. Perhaps it's a riddle."

"A riddle."

"Yes." Esteban's eyes did not want to reveal too much interest. "Maybe the dragon, the tail, the Polypos—whatever they are—all mean something. It could be a message."

"A message about what?"

Esteban was nervous, and Alicia could not help but notice that his wrist was trembling as the flame from his lighter made its way to the cigarette. There, in the distance, the silhouette of a man wearing a raincoat was waiting in the shadow of the willows.

...

After a short telephone conversation in which the theme of persecution was discussed and all the bodies in the case accounted for, Mamen, in no uncertain terms, prescribed a rest for Alicia and said she would take care of the necessary paper work for securing her leave from work. Her job was to rest, get lots of sleep, and most importantly amusement, perhaps a little trip. Mamen's voice was drowning in a tide of static and buzzing, as if she were speaking next to a bonfire or a jetty; yes, she had no choice but to call her from her cell phone, she'd been in Barcelona at a congress about pathologies of something or other, and would remain there at least for a week. Toñi would take charge of the sick leave if she brought the forms to the office.

Alicia hung up the phone and curled up on the sofa, hypnotized by a TV miniseries. As she consumed a cigarette facing the bald cranium of Antonio Resines, she reasoned that the break would really be the right thing for her, that perhaps a sudden interruption of that daily grind into which her ghosts had inserted themselves would be the right way to exorcise them. That's it: She'd dedicate herself to reading, music, taking care of her *conibras,* taking walks if she felt like it; she would go to Malaga to see her sister.

Just after noon, Nuria turned up wearing a T-shirt spattered with plaster and the usual Cruzcampos. Scraggly clumps of blond hair hung down her face. She opened two bottles, put on some Leonard Cohen, and gladly accepted the pickled mussels Alicia had poured onto a plate. Alicia felt a confused happiness because she had Nuria in her house. Her presence was like a guarantee, like a talisman or a promise that assured her that life could still be a carefree and hedonistic act one should take advantage of; no, she should not miss the train. So she clinked her bottle with Nuria's in a toast to create a vague rendition of a xylophone arpeggio, and they drank.

"I'm making progress on this job," said Nuria with something like a touch of boredom. "I've set aside the Virgin a bit, and now we're concentrating on a San Fernando who's missing his sword for slaughtering the infidels. My poor little Fernando's sword is nothing but crumbs. What time can bring about. Really, your *conibras* are a poem. You can see them in the afternoon from the balcony, what plumes."

"The secret is in knowing how to water them."

"Things like that make you happy. That's why you look so cheerful," Nuria smiled. "How are you feeling?"

"Well, let's see," answered Alicia. "How do I seem to you?"

"You look great. Besides, I'm sure taking a break from work is going to be wonderful for you."

First we take Manhattan, threatened Leonard.

"Right, I did ask for a medical leave," Alicia drank. "To rest and all that, but I do feel much better. How did you know about the leave?"

"I don't know. Maybe you told me yourself, or maybe it was Lourdes."

Dear Leonard was passing from Manhattan to Berlin and was saying no one knew much about a monkey and a plywood violin, but it was enough to arouse the anger of the person in the apartment above, who now began to punish the ceiling with the usual pounding. The music couldn't possibly be reaching him, because Alicia and Nuria could barely hear it from the kitchen. Besides there was no danger of waking anyone up at two-fifteen in the afternoon, so it was possible to attribute those annoying warnings from the tip of the broomstick, those Flamenco-dancing heel exercises, or whatever the hell you call it, only to her neighbor's simple urge to mortify someone, either that or it was a sensorial defect that made any sound louder than ten decibels unbearable to him. Nuria suggested they respond by turning the sound up to the maximum, and even though Alicia was tempted for an instant to blast him out with some strident sound from Wagner or Dizzy Gillespie, her long-suffering civic virtues ordered her not to counterattack. She resigned herself to cutting off the music the moment Nuria left, still fuming with a homicidal rage.

In the withered light of an afternoon devoid of color, Alicia became bored, successively, with television, with the ambiguities of the French novel she'd started the previous week, and with the hall guarded by Indonesian masks. She took a bath, cleaned some squid, looked over the arts and leisure supplement from last Sunday's newspaper, and went downstairs to buy cigarettes with a freshly opened pack in her bag.

When she got back, Mrs. Acevedo was waiting for her in the kitchen putting a shine on half a dozen plates and a pair of platters that for the past four days had rendered the dishwasher unusable. The old lady was carrying out her chore as if it were the most natural thing in the world that Alicia would find her there, rubbing away at the glass with a scouring brush. On top of the table stood indefinite objects wrapped in aluminum foil.

"What are you doing, Lourdes?" Alicia muttered stoically. "You were waiting for me to go out so you could slip in, right?"

"Because that's just the way you are, my dear." Mrs. Acevedo fixed the turquoise syrup of her eyes on her. "If I'd asked you if you needed anything, you wouldn't have let me help. And just look at the state this kitchen's in. I told Blas to look over the pipes for the washbasin, the thing you told me about."

"Thanks, Lourdes, but you really didn't have to bother." The foil masked frozen chickpeas, little empanadas, and an arsenal of croquets of respectable caliber. "What's all this?"

"*This* is something for you to eat, child. And there's nothing more to say about it."

"But Lourdes"—all this concern was unbearable for Alicia—"listen Lourdes. You know I'm very, very grateful for all this, but really I can take care of myself perfectly well."

"Now, now." Mrs. Acevedo swatted aside Alicia's words with the back of her hand. "You're in no condition to do anything, I can see that. You need rest. You need tranquillity, and that's why you're taking the medical leave of absence. Just keep quiet and eat this stuff. Look, I've brought you a wonderful juice."

Her hand, tortured by wrinkles, emerged from the sink and pointed to a cylindrical jar on the counter. Inside, a violent stench of unripe oranges had accumulated.

"How do you know I'm taking a medical leave?" Alicia blurted out.

"Yesterday your girlfriend with her hair dyed red." Lourdes waved her hand over her head, as if wanting to color the thicket of cotton covering her temples.

"Mamen."

"No, not Mamen. She told me her name was Marisa. She rang the buzzer two or three times and waited. And since I saw her a couple of times with you, I said hello."

"Marisa? With red hair?"

"Yes, Marisa. We talked for a while. She told me about your leave, that she'd come to drop off some herbs for an infusion or something like that. Said she'd come back."

"And that was yesterday, Lourdes?"

"Well, I think so." The old lady looked dubiously up in the air.

"Why didn't you tell me before?

"Child, I have no idea." For an instant her blue eyes seemed to catch fire. "I don't always remember to tell you about everyone who comes. The other afternoon your brother-in-law was here. A nice boy, and how much he resembles Pablo, poor thing."

Don Blas was in the bathroom, busy with a complicated archaeological dig that required him to crawl around on all fours under the sink to reinforce and shine the intestine of pipes that led rustily to the toilet. *Pablo, poor thing.* After everything, the ghost came back to break the truce in the dumbest but also the most inevitable way, as if in any case the natural path of events or words would lead to those memories, as if that ominous taboo were the obligatory terminus for any conversation or act begun with the naive intention of disinfecting memory or clipping its wings; a hypothetical new life was passing through the formalities of that past, through the painful customs gate where everything she wanted to abolish would be reclaimed. But she would have to take a chance, run, jump, if necessary, get over the wire, until, on the other side, she could breathe easily and believe that at least she'd no longer have to look back over her shoulder. She had to try.

"All finished," Don Blas said and stood up, brushing off his sweater. "Nothing big, just that stupid connection. It's loose, my dear, call in a plumber once in a while."

"But since I have you . . ." Alicia smiled.

"Right." The old man quickly returned her smile. "I really wish I could earn a living as a plumber. It might get us out of the squeeze we're always in. Because as far as my pension goes . . ."

He slowly picked up the toolbox he'd left on the toilet seat and made his way out huffing and puffing—but not without taking along an S. S. Van Dine novel with a catchy title: *The Kennel Murder Case.* A short time later, when she was alone and had smeared her face with moisturizer, Alicia discovered a dirt-colored case in the soap dish on the bathroom sink. It contained glasses with heavy, dense lenses that made objects enormous and dissolved them in swirls of color. When she put them on to see the effect, Alicia experienced nothing more than a plunge into shadowy forms and a yellow spume she could never locate. About fifteen minutes later, Don Blas came back for them. He was always leaving them somewhere. Without knowing why, Alicia was sorry to give them up. Sometimes she wanted reality to be something else, even if it was reduced to that swampy, turbid limbo that came into being through the lenses.

. . .

He attempted two hardly credible coughs to advertise his presence, and after only a couple of minutes Mr. Berruel popped through the little door that perforated the shop on the right and slid toward the counter with the sinister elegance of a vampire. His mortuary hands again investigated the appointment book, until his eye recognized a note, and he put the book back on the shelf.

"You've come for the Lancashire, right?" he said in a voice close to a snore. "Well, I don't have it."

"You don't have it? But you told me."

"I don't recall what I told you, young man." His vigilant hands took up their place on both sides of the counter. "Look, your Lancashire is giving me headaches. The platen is defective, eaten away, and the bridge has fallen, because the watch is all platinum. I have to take it completely apart and readjust the axes."

After muttering an amorphous intention of protest or resignation, Esteban went back into the rain, where the hasty silhouettes of a few umbrellas were circulating. The heavy downpour smashing down from the awning to the sidewalk did not allow him to stop at the antiques shop to see if there were any new acquisitions, so he limited himself to scrutinizing, from the cafeteria across the street, the vaguely Oriental carpet in the window and the poor Hadrian, frozen in his marble majesty.

Even though he decided to wait until the rain let up a bit before going to Alicia's house, two anisettes convinced him that the rain was going to keep on coming down, so he finally accepted the fact that his parka would get soaked, and skirted terraces and hills. No voice answered the intercom. Esteban was afraid she wasn't home, despite the horribly stormy afternoon. He went up the stairs two at a time, and, his chest burning, pushed the buzzer until he got bored. Inside, locks unlocked, the door slowly opened to reveal the flattened, mixed-up, distant face of a post-siesta Alicia.

"Do you think this is the proper time to be sleeping?" Esteban ran to the laundry room to wring out his parka. "It's already seven o'clock, my sweet."

"I don't know." Alicia's brain was sinking in a translucent ocean without tides. "It must be the tranquilizers. I've been terribly sleepy all day. I can't stand up for more than ten minutes at a time."

"So much the better. That way, you'll rest. We'll have coffee. What's that?"

When he opened the plastic cylinder, Esteban received the blow from a smell of bitter oranges.

"Lourdes brought it," answered Alicia, getting out a Ducados.

"Your fairy godmother."

"Yes, and you can't imagine how much of one she is. I don't know how she does it, but she finds out about my life before I do."

"Sophisticated radar system." Esteban was walking in circles around the kitchen, checking the place mats. Some had designs uncomfortable to the naked eye. "Remember who Argus was? A giant in Greek mythology with a million eyes."

"Disgusting philologist." Alicia put the cigarette in her mouth and crossed her arms. "But it's funny what happened to me with her this morning. She told me Marisa'd been here to bring me some herbs. The herbs she uses, you know."

"So?"

"Well, Lourdes tells me her hair was red. Either she's dyed it or she's put on a wig, because the Marisa you and I know has pitch-black hair."

"Hmmm. Maybe she confused her with Mamen."

"No." The white smoke from the cigarette erased Alicia's nose. "It seems the redhead told Lourdes her name was Marisa. Anyway, it couldn't be Mamen because Mamen called me a while ago from Barcelona to tell me she was spending a week away from home. Besides, why the hell would Mamen say her name was Marisa?"

"Who knows?" The lost personalities puzzle was beginning to bore Esteban. "Probably Marisa was on her way home from somewhere and was wearing a disguise that included a red wig, who knows? Or it could be it was neither Marisa nor Mamen, but the Third Woman. Or perhaps the old lady was simply trying trick you just to see what kind of expression you'd have on your face. Mysteries of identity, my dear."

Carrying their cups, they went to the living room, where Esteban praised a Charlie Parker "live" recording that he immediately inserted in the CD player. Gently rocked by a tropical rhythm, Parker, accompanied by Miles Davis, inaugurated a night in Tunisia. Staring at the *conibras* from a distance, noting how carefully settled they were in their pots, Esteban could visualize through the music souks, mosques, deserts tamed by the neutral pallor of the moon. To the surprise of Alicia, who was emerging from her sleepiness sip by sip, the neighbor upstairs did not take a stand against the cautious meandering of the saxophone through Maghreb landscapes and let Parker wind his way even to "Lover Man," where he then seemed to feel obliged to inform them of his presence by means of the usual detonations.

"What's that?" asked Esteban staring toward the sky.

"New neighbors." Alicia gulped down her coffee, feeling restored. "They feel the compulsive need to demonstrate that they too hear the music."

"It's that these days they make the damn floors out of paper."

Esteban's hand amused itself by playing with the loose hairs slipping off her ears. His fingers tripped softly on her cheek, attempting a caress made awkward by timidity, by the uncertainty of fingertips that didn't dare show all the warmth of their feelings. The presence of someone else's skin at that point on her face freed Alicia's stomach from some dark weight, but at the same time it brought back to her another skin, another hand that so many times had taken the same path, the hand of an unburied cadaver that watched from the hinges and the electrical outlets, prepared to veto her freedom of choice. Carefully, so as not to offend Esteban, she turned her face aside, shaken suddenly by a bitter repugnance. He noticed it and pliantly sent his hand in search of a Fortuna, without moving it from the edge of the cup inside of which was nothing but a brown circle. He felt obliged to improvise some kind of conversation.

"Know where I was this morning?"

"Where?"

"In your library. Your pal, the one with the glasses, must not have been very informed about your medical leave, because he was waiting for you to do some cataloging or other. But anyway, you can't imagine the things I've discovered."

"Come on! Surprise me." Alicia snuffed out her cigarette in the ashtray.

"Your friend Feltrinelli," said Esteban after inhaling, "had a pretty turbulent life. Let's say he wasn't exactly an angel."

"You don't say."

A gelatinous laziness stretched Alicia out on the sofa, rendering her perfectly indifferent to Esteban's revelations. She didn't understand why suddenly Feltrinelli, the city, and the angel seemed a used-up chapter, a canceled phase of her own self, like the book put back on the shelf or the film for which the lights in the theater constitute an epilogue. Perhaps she'd become bored with all that dumb crossword puzzle stuff, which could have been fine for brightening up a dull Sunday but which could not be prolonged so that more important obligations be overlooked. For now, all she wanted was to turn off, fall asleep, go on sleeping; a spongy mist blocked her thoughts and softly forced her to stumble in her dream.

"And since I was there," Esteban went on, "I amused myself looking at other books."

The dream, Alicia repeated to herself. Then she was intrigued to notice that the city, from there below, had begun to dilute itself that very night, to become imprecise and turbid like a reflection in a pool broken up by the impact of a stone. For the first time, she noticed, that night, that the city and its plan seemed singularly vague, misty, coming to resemble the chipped images of the memory that tries to reconstruct the most distant past. The city was beginning to lose solidity, allowing itself to be dragged toward the inert and watertight darkness of the background, toward a landscape free of cadavers, avenues, shoes on parade, and individuals with mustaches. She didn't know if she should be happy.

"I found out a few things," Esteban said, caressing an ashtray. "Feltrinelli's book appears in the bibliographic index of the *Revue du dixhuitième siècle,* which mentions at least two editions, neither dated, but both probably between 1740 and 1745. The place where they were printed is also uncertain: perhaps Florence and Rome. Then I consulted Koestler's *Biobibliographia latina,* where I found the book noted there as well, in volume twenty-four, along with a tiny biographic note on this Feltrinelli guy."

"Who was he?" Alicia could just make Esteban out through a screen of hair.

"He was born in Cremona, where the violins come from"—he pulled a sheet of paper out of his trouser pocket— "in 1698; he died in Venice, by hanging, in 1759. Feltrinelli wasn't his real name; it was Andrea Messauro."

"He was hung? Was he a criminal?"

"Worse than that. He was condemned for sacrilege, sodomy, perjury, and devil worship. According to Koestler's short note, he entered the church in his hometown and rose to the dignity of apostolic ambassador in, successively, Rome and Paris. The first accusations against him date from his French period. Rumors circulated that he kidnapped little boys to rape them and cut their throats. He liked to move around. The list of the places he visited comes right out of the travel agency display window: Venice, Milan, Salzburg, Vienna, Stuttgart, Prague, Metz, and Madrid. Around 1753 he disembarked in Lisbon, where he met the person to whom this book is dedicated: Inácio da Alpiarça, a goldsmith and sculptor who at the time was working for King José I on a titanic commission. He was charged with creating a colossal statue of each of the patriarchs of Israel, which would decorate the basilica of the convent of Mafra. He never made more than two. Not so strange since, as it seems, each statue was supposed to be more than ten meters high. And there were almost a dozen patriarchs."

"Sure, but what about Feltrinelli."

"Yeah, Feltrinelli." Esteban seemed to chase ideas as if they were butterflies. "He also went to Sicily, where he renounced the priesthood and changed his name to Feltrinelli. It was also there, it seems, where he wrote his only work, the *Mysterium Topographicum*. In Naples, he visited the house of Giordano Bruno, who at the time was the heretic and Antichrist par excellence. On the way north, he was arrested on the Austrian border and turned over to the Venetian Inquisition. They executed him after a suspiciously short trial. The authorities decapitated the cadaver and burned it on a pyre of green branches. The last fact Koestler supplies is that Feltrinelli was a member of the society of the *Coniurati*—the Conspirators.

Demolished on the black leather sofa, Alicia observed Esteban from within a soft, interior muddle that made his words seem superfluous. She didn't know if she wanted to go on listening, but she was sure she didn't intend to move a single muscle.

"The next trail was the *Coniurati*," Esteban went on, increasingly exhilarated by his bibliographic exploration. "I consulted Hope Robbins's *Encyclopedia of Witchcraft* and found an entry more than two columns long under that word. Apparently this was a satanic society of intellectuals originally founded in the Rome of the Borgias that counted among its members distinguished political and artistic personalities connected with the papal court, perhaps including Alexander VI himself. It's possible that Lucrezia Borgia's death in Ferrara in 1519 was somehow related to the sect, which was furiously persecuted throughout Italy beginning in that year. Scores of philosophers, poets, musicians, and architects were arrested, tortured, and executed in Florence, Venice, Modena, Milan, and Pesaro. The indictment accuses the defendants of celebrating, on certain stipulated days of the year, illicit meetings in which they acted out a sacrilegious version of the Mass using inverted crosses and black hosts. Control over the group was held by a woman, the papess, supposedly the concubine of Satan himself. And I'll bet you can't guess where they confessed to the tribunal that they held their meetings. Guess."

"Tell me. Where?"

"I don't know if I should tell you: 'A city named New Babel, with four square plazas oriented in four different directions.'"

Alicia understood nothing.

"The *Coniurati* were silenced in Italy, but the cult of the devil in some way transplanted itself in France. According to some, the person responsible was a certain Paolo Exili, a poisoner and fugitive from justice locked up in the Bastille in 1665, honored by the Marchioness de Brinvilliers, a courtesan of necromantic tendencies, with intimate friendship."

"What a huge cast," grumbled Alicia, exhausted.

"Listen, listen," Esteban went on, checking his notes. "Somehow or other, the *Coniurati* enjoyed a true golden age in the court of the Sun King, Louis XIV, where in certain circles they were known as *Les Montespannients* because they clustered around one of the king's beautiful lovers, Françoise Athenaide de Rochechouart de Tonay-Carente, Marchioness de Montespan."

"With a name like that . . ."

"The marchioness most certainly had the role of papess in Paris, although another of Louis XIV's girlfriends could have boasted that honor: Marie Olimpie de Mansini, niece of Cardinal Mazarin and wife of the Count of Soissons."

"Esteban . . ."

"With them joined a cell made up of witches and fortune-tellers who specialized in the preparation of filtres—Filastre, Chanfrain, and, especially, Voisin, lover of the Paris executioner, who supplied them with fat, bones, and the hands of hanged men for the service of the Black Mass. The liturgy was celebrated by the priest Guibourg, an expert poisoner who lived with a prostitute by whom he had several children, some of whom were sacrificed in the cult of Satan."

"Esteban, Esteban . . ."

"The Black Masses were held in sacred places in order to consummate their sacrilegious function more perfectly— in the chapel of the castle of Villebourin, which belonged to the Marchioness de Montespan, or in the oratory of her abandoned house in Saint-Denis, where Guibourg officiated in a spermatic mass, with the semen of a hanged man, for a certain Mademoiselle de Oeilletes, who was seeking the death of Madame de Fontanges, one of the king's favorites."

"Enough, Esteban." Alicia's voice was brusque, and her body had finally flung itself forward toward the table. "Great, a splendid feat of research, but enough is enough."

Esteban couldn't decide if his sterile display of erudition had been dictated by an obscure desire to mortify Alicia by showing her the insane routes her obsession with the city and the angels was leading her along, or if he'd accumulated all those facts with the intention of solving the puzzle. He felt he should have the confidence to tell Alicia something, but his uneasiness tied his tongue.

"Look, Esteban"—she was picking up another cigarette— "I don't know if all this is worthwhile. I've talked it all over with Mamen."

"So much the better. Maybe now you'll finally come to your senses."

Esteban's hand again flew toward Alicia's face, ready to inscribe another terrible caress on her skin. She didn't know if she could stand it. Alicia could respond to Esteban's love only by taking an instinctive step back. Fortunately, before the hand managed to touch her, the door buzzer stopped it in midair. Alicia jumped, as if activated by a spring, and stood up.

"Were you expecting someone?" asked Esteban.

"No, and much less with the kind of night this is." A storm whipped by lightning flashes was moaning outside the balcony. "It must be some advertising campaign."

The buzzer sounded three times before Alicia brusquely picked up the receiver. On the other end, a wrinkled, obscure voice tried vainly to string together a few coherent words. Alicia twice asked the voice to identify itself, but the words went on fighting one another, slipping in a kind of swamp that wouldn't allow them to combine, to say what they were trying to say. Finally, when she was about to hang up and write off the matter off as a joke in bad taste, Alicia seemed to understand what the voice was unsuccessfully trying to tell her.

"Esteban," said Alicia, frightened by the tone of her own words, "it's someone asking for help."

"Don't be ridiculous. What are you saying?"

They went downstairs slowly, imitating, with the proper theatricality, the caution of detectives in movies, rejecting the elevator without knowing why. The staircase was totally dark. As they went down, the light in the lobby got brighter, more voracious. Alicia, wrapped tightly in her sky-blue robe, clasped Esteban's elbow (but she shouldn't hold on too tightly), imagined that the growing nearness of the glow, of the yellow light that floated over the lobby from a paint-encrusted globe, also signaled the proximity of the voice, that voice like broken rock summoned up from inside old fear—she was sure she'd heard that voice before.

"Stay still," said Esteban.

From the bottom step, it was possible to see the entire lobby—the sofa covered in synthetic leather with its cigarette burns, the bored plastic fern that observed the elevator; at the far end, next to the chessboard of metal mailboxes, a black figure was leaning against the front door. The glass, misted over by the rain, made seeing his features impossible. Walking closer, Alicia and Esteban only partially made out an opaque shape that wasn't moving. Esteban tried to move forward, but Alicia held him back with her hand; something ordered her to be the one to turn the knob, to push the door slowly on its hinges, so that suddenly a glove made of frost could seize the back of her neck. A man fell on top of her. Wracked by screaming hysteria, she violently pushed him off, letting him crash silently to the floor and sprinkle the tiles with an unmistakable red liquid. Esteban turned the man on his side, revealing the two holes that pierced his clavicle, the tranquil red spring dying his shirt collar.

"My God," stammered Alicia.

"Who is it?" asked Esteban.

"That's the man, Esteban. That's the man."

The mustache eliminated any doubt. A reluctant, thankless mustache, grudgingly staining the lip holding it up. Even though Esteban insisted he not try to speak, a mound of words still seemed to want to slide from between the dying man's teeth. His hand pointed to something on his side that Esteban tried to find by hastily feeling around and daubing his fingers in that garish liquid. From his soaked raincoat emerged a bronze object Esteban carefully accepted before allowing the stranger to sink definitively into a seamless sleep. It was an angel with a twisted foot, an elegant, cold angel absolutely identical to the one Alicia had described. Horrified, she was now observing the trophy, which had occupied the center of the plaza in the engraving, which had adorned the corner of Nuria's living room except, to be sure, for the eagle, which on the left side of the pedestal was preparing to take off.

Five

With ill-concealed suspicion, the police accepted the mistake theory. They did not seem completely disposed to believe that the murdered man was looking for someone else and that an error—the wrong floor, the wrong street—had caused him to end up dying in the arms of an unknown woman. But the inspector, a solid man trapped in a much too tight suit, preferred to let the matter pass for the moment as he accepted one of Esteban's Fortunas. The police limited themselves to removing the body, taking some photographs, and announcing vaguely that they would be back.

As soon as they had disappeared through the door, the Acevedos invaded the apartment, causing poor Alicia to collapse. By then, she was incapable of controlling her feelings and swung back and forth between silence and weeping. After sending her to bed, Esteban took charge of thanking the neighbors and saying good night to them with all the haste decorum would permit, not without first nodding his approval of Lourdes's detailed instructions, her usual dietary advice.

"The most important thing of all is for her to drink the juice. That juice is incredibly good."

"Don't you worry, ma'am. I'll tell her. Good night, bye."

"The juice, you won't forget now, will you son?"

"Bye, ma'am."

He also had to hold off Nuria's incursion—this time her Cruzcampos were not accepted: Alicia's asleep, thanks anyway; along with that of a strange couple muzzled in robes Esteban promised to call in case they needed anything. He watered the *conibras,* then smoked a calmer cigarette in the kitchen as he fried up some croquettes, which he placed, along with some salad and a little glass of the juice, on a platter he carried into Alicia's room. He found her sitting on the bed with the bronze angel between her knees, studiously running the tips of her fingers over the signs on the base. She seemed more serene, although a chaos of horror and perplexity still muddied the depths of her eyes.

"Think we did the right thing?" she asked. "Shouldn't we have turned the angel over to the police?"

"Of course we did the right thing." Esteban placed the tray on the quilt. "Eat a little something, go on."

"I don't feel like eating anything. Now do you believe me? See how it was all for real?"

He took the angel and traced his finger over the smooth path that led from its temple to its knee. It was an exact duplicate of the one he'd discovered with the same stupefaction in Nuria's house a few days earlier. Even the symbols that covered the pedestal seemed the same. The name was there, the Hebrew letter, the strange sign made up of parallel, symmetrical mortised lines, the two Latin words, and the stream of Greek terms he had no difficulty in translating:

I salute you, guardians of the Axis, sacred and terrible captains, who, under the power of a unique order, give movement to the zodiac axis in the continuous movement of the heavens . . .

⚏.AZAZEL. ⚎.HUMANAQUE.HOMINES. TESIDRV.AETAESME.IN.INSAENE.EVMPTE . . .

"The eagle," noted Alicia pensively. "This angel stands in the plaza on the left in Feltrinelli's plan, the west plaza."

"Just eat this," retorted Esteban pointing to the tray. "There are two Latin words, but the rest, well, I don't know in what language it's written."

"I'm not hungry. But, okay, I will drink the juice."

This must certainly be a message in code, a kind of cryptogram that this Feltrinelli, a heretic condemned more than two hundred years ago, was trying to send to them by means of a beautiful bronze figure that could also be present in the center of a plaza accessible only in dreams. But if there were four angels with four sets of signs, the message could be reconstructed only by reuniting its four parts, bringing the different inscriptions together, no matter how indecipherable the results might be.

"Why did that man come looking for me?" Alicia repeated to herself aloud. "Tell me, why did he have to bring me this angel?"

"Who knows?" Esteban handed her the juice. "There are many questions: Who was that guy? What is this angel? Why did he have to give it to you, yes. And, most important of all: Why was he killed? Drink."

She emptied the glass and stretched out on the quilt.

"Listen," said Esteban, "no one should know about the angel. No one, understand? This is going to be our little secret until we find out what's going on. Now you'll have to forgive me, but I should have been with Mama since ten, and look what time it is."

Alicia's hand caught his arm; the palm softly rubbed the path that led to his shoulder; it drew him to her. Suddenly she was overwhelmed by the need to have Esteban at her side so that something wouldn't die. She knew she'd pay for what she was going to do, but despite that Alicia opened her lips, ascended to Esteban's face with the delicacy of a reptile, and kissed him deeply, darkly, holding her breath to pour it into the other breath, emptying herself. Then Esteban held her against his throat, caressed her, untangled the four unruly hairs that fell on her cheeks. He kissed her again, returning something that was similar to the bite of a squirrel. He got up, put out the light before leaving the room. When the bolt in the lock slid home, Alicia's night was an uninhabited territory: sparse, filthy grass; garbage; bones.

...

To emerge from the dream, she had to swim several strokes inside the black pool until she reached the surface, which more or less coincided with a precarious wakefulness and where she could finally breathe with all of her lungs. She wavered indecisively for a few seconds on the edge of her dream, making an exhausting effort to hold up her eyelashes. It was hard work, something like taking off a backpack loaded with rubble, but she understood that she had to wake up: A sound in the form of a serpent, which was becoming clearer and clearer and more biting, was trying to warn her that someone was ringing the doorbell.

She awkwardly dragged herself down the hall, bearing the weight of her body, which was more solid and compact now, and crossed the living room without recognizing herself in the brusque, robotlike movements of her legs. The eyebrows of Joaquín and Marisa, who were waiting outside the door, bent like aqueducts when they saw Alicia's face reduced to a tangled rag.

"Are you okay, Alicia?" asked Marisa, whose eyes were occupying half her forehead.

"No." An uncertain growl burst out of Alicia's lips. "Come in, come in, you can't just stand there like that."

Even though the curtain hid half the sky, a flock of elephant-colored storm clouds was floating over the balcony, threatening them with an imminent storm. The proximity of those discharges, when the air became as heavy as granite, usually upset Alicia's character, so Marisa concluded that the disarray of her face was the result of a mere meteorological inconvenience. With a sense of emergency, Joaquín ran to the kitchen and set about slamming closet doors as he asked where the coffee was kept. No sooner was he informed than he urgently rinsed out the pot and loaded it with a flood of black powder sufficient to raise King Tut's blood pressure. That toasted aluminum instrument began to whistle and emit foam just when Joaquín placed his pack of Cohibas in front of Alicia. She accepted a cigarette in the same reticent way a child accepts some change from an older person in exchange for his silence or obedience. Marisa, back in the living room with the watering can in her hands, dedicated the same reproving frown to the smoke that settled like cotton on the lamp and to the howl of the coffeepot, which seemed about to start chugging its way out of the station.

"That's right," Marisa bellowed, "just go on poisoning yourselves, you two, while I water the *conibras*. Destroy your hearts. This is your sixth today."

"The fourth," Joaquín disagreed, making sure the coffee was proceeding properly.

"What a liar you are. And after your solemn promise not to smoke more than half a pack a day. It's only for your own good, you animal. And besides, you're drawing that child into your ill-fated vice."

"Poor little thing." Joaquín and Alicia exchanged a stoic look. Her features seemed more normal.

"What's wrong with you?" asked Marisa as she extracted some jars from a plastic bag. "You had a face on you when you opened the door, that, well . . ."

A bad night, that was all. Of course, she left the corpse, the angels, the plot, and all the loose ends behind in her bag of secrets. These weren't subjects to be revealed with a grin. She'd had difficulty sleeping the past two or three nights, waking up at sunrise with her mouth cracked like dry mud, and when she did manage to get to sleep it seemed she was swimming underwater in an aquarium filled with hands and faces. Finally, an authoritarian sleep had taken control of her, flattened her, left her exhausted and defenseless on the pillow, and forced her to sleep mercilessly until, when it was time to wake up, she didn't know at which point in the rotating cycle of nights and days she'd opened her eyes again. It seemed that Marisa was just waiting for the negative health report to show, with a gesture of triumph, her containers. A grunt of resignation fled Joaquín's mouth as he poured the coffee into two cups.

"Look, what I've brought here is so perfect for you that I couldn't have planned it that way." Marisa's wooden bracelets rattled. "The other day, after seeing you, I remembered about your sleeping problems when I was in the herbalist's shop, and I bought you something that should suit you to a tee. Take the container. You boil some water and toss in this infusion of vervain and a touch of rosemary. And these little seeds I'm giving you."

"What are they?" Alicia accepted the jar full of black birdshot.

"Ex-Lax," suggested Joaquín, instantly scalding himself with the coffee.

"Idiot." Marisa's eyes were fleetingly those of a tiger. "It's called Palm of the Prince, and it's very good for relaxing tensions and nerves. Much healthier and more natural than all that garbage Mamen prescribes. No doubt about it. Because you are taking that stuff, right?"

"Yes," answered Alicia like an obedient student, "aside from a little juice my neighbor brings me."

"I talked with Mamen yesterday." Marisa seemed to have corrected her intonation. "She's in Barcelona, right?" She was the one who told me you were on medical leave, that I should look in on you, see how you were doing. We've got to take care of our little girl, we don't want her getting any worse. Wait, finish your coffee and then talk. What do want to ask me?"

"Were you here the day before yesterday?" Alicia blurted out, her tongue turned to charcoal.

"Day before yesterday? No."

"And you weren't wearing a red wig or anything like that, right?"

"Of course not." Marisa's eyes, now wide open, were trying to find the joke. "No, carnival is in February, isn't it? And you can see my hair is still black. A few gray hairs, but that's it."

"My neighbor, the old lady, must have confused you with someone else. She's not all there. She says that the day before yesterday there was a woman named Marisa here who had red hair."

"For God's sake. Getting old is horrible," Joaquín intoned in a complaining voice, saddened as well by his unrelenting baldness. "Who knows if the woman really wasn't blond."

"Now that you mention it, she doesn't really see all that well." Alicia smiled an ugly smile. "But the part about the red hair is weird."

"That would be your neighbor who makes the juice?" Marisa's eyes were reflecting. "I don't know her. But I have spoken with her husband from time to time about antiques. Don Blas or something, isn't that his name?"

The mysterious redhead opened the way, after two more Cohibas made their debut, for Marisa's respiratory retreat to the kitchen and for the ineffable Asia Ferrer, specialist in reading cards, dream analysis, etc., whose place of business Alicia had inexplicably not as yet visited. Trying as graciously as possible to get around her obligation to make the visit, Alicia promised she'd go. She then drank the rest of her coffee and, from behind the cigarette smoke, pointed out the inconveniences of time, work, her insecurity. Marisa wanted to hear nothing of that. Her fortune-teller, who also aroused Joaquín's irreverent comments, deserved more credit than a good number of those so-called experts who hid behind the nameplate on their door in order to perpetuate the nonsense of their diagnoses.

Marisa then repeated that dreams are a kind of energy storehouse which can provide fuel to many of the functions of the soul, and that any obstacles in their way, any interferences with them required explanations that would shed light on the spiritual disorders that could be tormenting her. People with proper training could break into that storehouse and distribute its energy as they pleased, so the visit to Asia Ferrer could only bring her benefits. And, having didactically repeated all that, Marisa withdrew to the bathroom.

"She's going through a bad period," Joaquín said to Alicia when the two of them were alone. "It's all that stuff about the damned kid. She too stays awake night after night crying or thinking. She too has a jar of that shit of the Prince stuff. I don't think it will help her much, just so long as it calms her down a little."

Marisa's way of reacting to the harassment of her anguish was this counterattack, this rabid consecration to the religion of herbs and horoscopes, as if that museum of roots, leaves with nerves, and conjunctions between stars reduced to mythological animals could remove her from the density and banality of a much more pedestrian and annoying world, from this world of daily bureaucracies where every disillusion was as insidious as a fly in one's soup. Alicia envied Marisa's ability to take flight the instant things became too uncomfortable on this earth. Then Marisa came back and forbade any more cigarettes, and Alicia once again began to feel that overloading of her thoughts, that weight of lead and mist dragging her down toward the opaque pool that she had to fight by standing up and suggesting another round of coffee, despite the fact that Marisa's mouth was hanging open in wonder as she predicted Alicia would end up exploded and with a heart like a rotten apple, so much coffee, so much coffee just wasn't possible.

...

Inspector Gálvez opened two envelopes, and an avalanche of papers and photographs spilled onto the desk, concealing the paper clips and ballpoint pens. A too-tight shirt was strangling his torso, so his movements were like those of a robot. As he went over a pair of documents marked with seals, he offered, in a neutral way, his pack of Winstons, which Esteban and Alicia declined with hand gestures. On the right, a secretary angrily machine-gunned at his typewriter.

"This individual's name"—the inspector showed them the photograph of the dead man with the mustache—"was Pedro Luis Benlliure Gutiérrez, age forty-eight, a resident of Barcelona. Married with three children, who still can't believe what happened. His wife has declared he came to Seville simply to carry out a business deal. Do you two think his visit could have had some other, hidden, motive?"

"Maybe he had a girlfriend," Esteban ventured.

"Maybe," answered the inspector from behind a rigid smile. "Though he'd come a little far to look her up, don't you think? But suppose he was here to see you two and for some unknown reason ended up dying on the doorstep of the young lady here?"

"Thanks for the young lady part," Alicia retorted, "but I'm married. Well, I used to be married."

With his huge, butcherlike hands busy shuffling papers, Inspector Gálvez scrutinized Alicia's gloomy face hiding behind her sunglasses. What with the quantity of rain falling, it wasn't, of course, a day for sunglasses. The drumming on the cement roof tiles of the police station mixed with the clicking of the typewriter, which the secretary kept pounding on the table to the right.

"Mr. Benlliure was registered at the Inglaterra Hotel," the inspector went on, "where he had a single, which he'd occupied since last Tuesday. Which is to say, he'd been in Seville almost a week. The desk manager has testified that he made numerous telephone calls from his room, and that he also received several. A woman usually called him."

"See what I mean?" Esteban snorted. "The girlfriend, couldn't be any clearer."

"Shut up," Inspector Gálvez harshly ordered. "That woman could easily have been you, ma'am. Right now, you're the only person to whom we can link Benlliure in Seville. What was he doing at your door? You stated that he buzzed your apartment from the street."

"I explained it to you yesterday." Alicia turned to her Ducados. "He got the address wrong."

The inspector had a way of staring that he supposed intimidated the people he was questioning, or suggested that the steely intelligence hidden by his eyes would end up unmasking them. That gaze poured over Alicia without her feeling even slightly nervous.

"I've told you that Benlliure told his wife he was coming to Seville to wind up a business deal," the inspector said, consulting his reports, "something he'd been working on for about a month that was related to an important piece of merchandise. Do you two have anything to do with the world of secondhand furniture?"

"What do you think?" retorted Esteban.

"Benlliure was a secondhand furniture dealer?" added Alicia, sliding her glasses down her nose just enough so her green, hemispheric gaze would fall on Inspector Gálvez.

"Yes, secondhand furniture dealer, hardware dealer, antiques dealer, a little bit of everything. He dealt in old things: from used jackets to dressers from the last century with broken feet. Everything of the highest quality, his wife insists. Does this mean anything to you?"

Alicia and Esteban said no at the same time.

"The luggage Benlliure stored at the hotel was ordinary"— the Winston was burning between the inspector's yellowed fingers. "Shirts, ties, a couple of detective novels, pills for his ulcer. Everything very normal, except for the box. A box just under half a meter long, about like this," he said, raising his hand almost to the height of the lamp. "Benlliure must have brought something valuable packed in that box because it was reinforced with rubber and cloth. Naturally I suppose you two have no idea what that box could have held."

"You suppose correctly," Alicia answered hoarsely.

"And of course you know nothing about this tattoo." The inspector's gross hand held out to them a photograph of a forearm—just beyond the wrist there was a small wound whose shape looked something like two *T*'s divided on a symmetrical axis. From Alicia's mouth came a sigh that seemed to flow from very remote zones of either her breathing or her fatigue. Esteban hermetically observed the photo for a few minutes; then he returned it to the inspector.

"It's a fresh wound. The medical examiner says it had to be produced during the hour just before the murder. Take a good look, he did it himself, trying to draw the tattoo. Strange, don't you think?"

"Very strange," Esteban admitted, his eyes having strayed to a pencil.

Inspector Gálvez's fat hands joined together on the desk, composing something that disgustingly recalled a severed head. He shrugged his shoulders, making a sign with his head that he was giving up.

"Look, we have no positive links between you two and the murder of this man. For one thing, the Walther PPK used to kill him hasn't turned up. For another, several witnesses said they saw him collapsed against the front door as if he were drunk, all of which seems to indicate that he was already wounded when he got there."

"Therefore?" asked Esteban.

"You two take me for a fool. I know you didn't kill this guy, but I also know for a fact that you know things you're not telling me. That's your business. You're making your bed, and you're going to lie in it. We'll be in touch."

They crossed Gavidia plaza in the brief interval between two cloudbursts. The rain began falling again just when they pushed open the cafeteria door. While they waited for their coffee and anisette, Alicia took off her sunglasses to reveal a flat, inert face as opaque as that of a puppet. Esteban felt he was in the presence of a poor replica of the person he knew.

"What's wrong? The look on your face would scare anyone."

"I don't know," she answered, with a hesitance that wasn't typical of her. "I don't know, Esteban. I'm so tired, so really, really tired. It's hard for me think clearly. Every time I stop, I feel as if I'm going to fall asleep."

"A coffee will fix you up, just wait."

They also ordered croissants. Concerned, Esteban could see that Alicia was able to follow his conversation only with difficulty, and that from time to time her head nodded in spirals that threatened to crash it into the table unless a hand was quickly placed on her shoulder to steady her. She accepted his advice to moisten her temples and the back of her neck. Refreshed now, with her features softer and her voice less guttural, she asked, "It was the same sign, wasn't it?"

"The one on his forearm?" Esteban dunked his croissant in the coffee. "Yes, of course, the same sign. The same one on the pedestal."

Alicia's hand hastily snatched a Ducados. She seemed to have unblocked her mind, to have become once again the vigilant, wary creature she always was. Outside, the rain lashed the few passersby, who fled in search of doorways.

"Last night I looked in the encyclopedia," said Esteban. "I haven't found out what the sign might mean, but the Hebrew letter isn't difficult to identify. Its name is *tet,* and it's pronounced *t,* which doesn't reveal a great deal."

"Have you found out anything about the text?"

"The one behind the two words in Latin?" He crumpled up his Fortuna pack. "I don't have the slightest idea. I've never seen anything like it in my life. It reminds me of one of those nonsense things in Tolkien or Lovecraft: *rlyeh Ctulhu klō Yog-Sothot,* etc. I've always wondered how the hell that's pronounced."

"Charming interpretation."

"Glad you like it. As for the Greek, it wasn't very hard. I wore myself out translating things just like it during five years of graduate work. Vulgar Hellenistic *koiné* adulterated with Latin and Hebrew interpolations, fourth century at the earliest. It's a standard incantation used in the later Roman Empire to invoke minor deities and demons."

"So this stuff is leading us to hell." The smoke of Alicia's cigarette swirled around, creating faces.

"You have no idea how deep in hell. Azazel, according to the encyclopedia, was one of the rebel angels under the command of Lucifer who challenged the government of Jehovah before the world was created. According to the apocryphal *Book of Enoch,* Azazel was the prince of the *egregon,* the guardians, captains of the insurgent angels who, two hundred in number, descended on Mount Herman to have sexual congress with the Daughters of Men. From their union were born the monstrous giants who would be exterminated by the archangels Raphael and Michael. From their bones would spring more demons."

For a moment, absolute fatigue again darkened Alicia's will, drawing from her a sigh and placing her at the point of a long axis of tunnels, of an infinite vegetation of catacombs and galleries that lead to a uniform, black barrier. Mamen had insisted very severely that she separate herself from the city in all its forms, that she make an effort to overcome the gravity attempting to trap her on that side, that the slow return to a healthy, normal life depended upon her giving up all those obsessions. And although she wanted with all her heart to abandon that ambush of charades and symbols, she found she was too involved in the enigma, in that extravagant crossword puzzle spattered with blood. Fleeing the wooden city populated with backs had become as futile as definitively burying, once and for all, the bodies of Pablo and Rosa. That certainty anguished her, encompassed her neck in a collar of black links. She did not understand why she had to fight to find the key, to have the solution in her hands, if memory was going to pursue her all the way to that far end of the road, if memory was going to go on spurring her toward the exit without allowing her to catch her breath. Again, she was sleepy, very sleepy.

"Are you okay?" Esteban's hand was a cool remedy on her cheek. "You feel sleepy again?"

"Yes," she answered with a sagging voice. "I don't know what's wrong with me, but for the past two days I haven't been able to stay on my feet. The more I sleep the more I want to sleep. And the little time I spend awake I'm like this, like a dead person."

He slowly took another cigarette. Anyone could see that his way of staring at the table, from time to time averting his eyes in a cowardly way toward the window where the complex ceremony of the rain was still being celebrated, meant Esteban had something to say, something important beyond coffee and croissants but something that for some reason became uncomfortably stuck in his throat. He waited to enjoy the first drag of the cigarette to tap his fingers nervously on the edge of the saucer and to inaugurate his confession with a tranquillity he was not feeling.

"Alicia, I've been beating around the bush here," he muttered.

"Around what bush?"

"The angel and this entire story." He seemed sincerely upset. "I have to tell you honestly that at the beginning I didn't believe you very much, because since the accident and all the rest, and Mamen, well, you know."

"Okay," Alicia said firmly, with a gesture that obviated his preambles.

"Well." Esteban's throat was attempting to swallow stones, lots of stones. "Listen carefully, as carefully as you can. I know I shouldn't ask you this, but I'm going to, and may my guardian angel forgive me. Do you see that there are too many coincidences in all this?"

"In all what?"

"In the story of the angel. Have you ever thought that it might possibly be a trap?" Esteban seemed to be working his way around the outskirts of a word without being able to invoke it. "A kind of conspiracy?"

"No," Alicia lied. "A conspiracy? Against me? Why?"

"I don't know." Esteban lowered his eyes and focused them on the cigarette he was holding in his hand—the ash was patiently conquering the defenseless paper cylinder. "It horrifies me to say this: Your neurosis has spread to me. Okay, I've been busy connecting certain possibilities, and I see a few things it doesn't seem you've proposed to yourself. Of course the most important of those possibilities is one you don't know about, so . . . Anyway, it's all my fault. Alicia, promise me you won't get mad."

Of course she promised, but as Esteban spoke it became clear to Alicia that she could never keep the promise. Amid the voices, Alicia wondered aloud, after some not especially polite adjectives, why she went on wasting time with an investigative partner like Esteban when any freak on the damn street could offer her more guarantees of sincerity and, therefore, facilitate a more cooperative and fruitful investigation.

Until the blood that was blocking the arteries in her temples cooled and only until then, she went on banging her lighter on the cafeteria table and attracting the disapproving glances of the waiter—miss, if you can't control yourself—she was incapable of seeing even slightly clearly the meaning of what Esteban had just revealed to her: the angel in Nuria's house.

"Bastard," she barked again. "What do you mean you didn't have time?"

"I'm sorry," Esteban repeated for the thousandth time, cowering against the fierce onslaught of insults. "But listen, what's that angel doing there?"

"In Nuria's house?" Alicia went on looking obliquely, not knowing why the conversation was still taking place. "It's logical, or did you forget that Nuria is a restorer, you bastard?"

"Who owns the statue? She wouldn't tell me. She's got it there, behind the stove, sort of hidden."

"So what are you getting at? You look like a chick choking on his feed, poor little thing."

He was almost thankful for the blessing of that rage falling over him, over his shoulders shamefully bent over the remains of the coffee and the butts, because it had something of a ritual of exemption, of paying, of expiation through punishment. Each whiplash sinking into the skin of his pride compensated for those prayers—never sufficiently purged—about Pablo's future, about the love of Alicia, who now hated him noisily with all her saliva and bile, as if to reestablish a previous and wounded balance.

"I mean," Esteban went on in a voice he feared came from his throat, "well . . . This entire story is crazy enough that in principle no hypothesis must be discarded. When did you begin feeling sleepy? I mean when did this sudden need to sleep begin?"

"I don't know." The sudden change of subject caught Alicia off guard. "I don't know, two or three days ago."

"When did you start drinking that juice Lourdes left for you?"

A green flash illuminated her eyes.

"Okay. At about the same time," she admitted. "That means Lourdes is part of the conspiracy, right?"

"You told me that your recent dreams of the city have been blurrier. When did that start?"

"Three or four days ago," answered Alicia, consternated.

"Well." Esteban didn't dare to smile. "What a coincidence, don't you think?"

"It could be because of the pills Mamen gave me," she hastily retorted. "She increased the dosage."

"Yes, of course. Just keep tying these threads together. Those neighbors of yours, the ones who are such a pain beating on their floor, the ones upstairs. When did they move in?"

"I don't know." Alicia felt like the astonished spectator watching a magic show. "Three weeks ago or something like that."

"Wasn't it about then you began dreaming about the city?"

Now Alicia's brow turned itself into a right angle that sank toward the center of her forehead.

"Okay," she growled. "Where are you going with these things?"

"Count them up." Esteban put his left hand forward and went over each finger. "Some people you don't know who are highly incensed at any noise you make but who don't get annoyed if you speak too loudly. Are they listening? Who knows? A helpful old lady gives you something to drink so that a city you're dreaming about will disappear—just as you're learning things about it. A neighbor hides an angel that closely resembles the figure in your dreams. Both of them suddenly know you're on medical leave without anyone's having told them. Do they have radar? A man you don't know but who's in your dream turns up dead at your building, a building that, oddly enough, is the place where all those bizarre characters also appear. What does that suggest to you?"

"That you're a jerk." Alicia was digging through her change purse. "Besides, I'm sleepy and want to go."

"Look"—Esteban's fingers slid toward her wrist—"let's go home, and you go to bed for a while, then we'll see how you feel. I'll take the angel out of the closet and bring it to an antiques dealer I know to see if he can at least give us some idea about who the sculptor was or the date when it was made."

"An antiques dealer?"

"The one opposite the watch repair shop I use. Sometimes I stop to look in the window. Marisa knows him; he's an old friend of hers from someplace or other. He might be able to orient us a bit. Maybe it's nothing more than junk or a joke, which it could be."

"A joke that got someone shot to death," a funereal Alicia couldn't help but comment.

...

The rain had opted for a slight parenthesis. Taking advantage of the break, people dashed outside in order to race through the puddles or decipher their watches in the veiled light seeping through the thunderclouds. A vast tide of pitch coming from the east infected the sky.

Before crossing the threshold, Esteban noticed that the poor, chipped Hadrian in the window had been replaced by a horrible young miss with a ribboned bonnet who twisted her porcelain neck with a studied gesture of disdain or indifference toward the ancient armillary sphere that rested below her. Despite the tinkle of the little bell that trembled over the door, no one came to receive him, and Esteban was able lose himself delightfully among tapestries with unicorns, tea services illustrated with hunting scenes, platters and pitchers, amputated armor, tiny, diffusely Oriental boxes that contained brass butterflies. His eyes, fascinated, were wandering inside a light blue cameo that represented an erotic scene when a false cough informed him the owner's assistant was there, and observing him from behind the counter was an individual wrapped in an impeccable blue suit with a handkerchief protruding from his pocket.

"Good afternoon," recited the man. "May I help you?"

The assistant beatifically withstood Esteban's gaze, placing his palms flat on the ebony counter, itself supported by two spiral columns. Esteban placed the package on a chair covered in red tapestry and slowly loosened the strings. The assistant began to drill holes through him with eyes in which stupor mixed with impatience in a not especially promising way.

"I wanted to consult you about an object," Esteban explained, tangling his fingers in the knots he'd made. "I've come to you because we have a common friend, Marisa Gordillo."

"Marisa Gordillo." The man sounded out the name with an eloquent smile but without relaxing his rigidity. "Of course. How is she?"

"Fine, as far as I know." Esteban regarded that part of the matter closed. "Look. It's a family heirloom."

With a mechanical gesture, the man leaned over the counter. His senses seemed to be on alert, as if he expected to catch a spy hidden in the old wood and metal that filled the shop. The blanket revealed an elegant bronze head whose face was turned to the left into an improbable wind romantically tousling its thick hair. The assistant did not descend from his attitude of polite suspicion until he saw the wings appearing along with the small eagle on the pedestal that brandished a fierce, gray beak, with the suppressed glitter of ancient coins.

Some comment or other must have choked him up in the vicinity of his Adam's apple, something most certainly linked to his manner of staring—somewhere between horror and shock—at the figure. In any case, he decided to hold it all in his lungs in order not to reveal too much interest. So when Esteban pushed the angel toward his belly, marked by a powerful belt with a golden buckle, the man limited himself to examining the mantle and the hair with a kind of clinical detachment, like a surgeon who has to struggle with a routine appendicitis.

"Where did you get this?" he asked, turning the angel over on its back.

"It's a family heirloom," Esteban repeated with an expression of feigned ignorance.

"You must have a well-to-do family." An amorphous, lying smile traced itself on his lips. "No matter. If you haven't become excessively fond of it, I could make you an interesting offer."

"No, I'm not interested in selling it."

"Think it over."

Esteban's head swung from side to side ratifying the negative while his hand, almost instinctively, tried to grab the pedestal by its edges. He did not like the way in which the figure was moving away from him across the counter where it would end up enfolded in the belly of the assistant, who was squeezing the statue with a disturbing ferocity. The offer burst from the same lips three, four times, growing larger and larger without Esteban's head ceasing to move back and forth. Finally, the man sighed and pushed the angel back to the center of the counter, to that neutral space where it seemed his greed could not snare it. It was then Esteban realized that the last sum quoted had made him dizzy: "Is it really worth that much?" he asked blinking.

The assistant simply pointed to a place on the figure's back, where the shoulder blades divided and the wings began like the leaves on a date palm. A letter was engraved there, a kind of inverted N that Esteban studied with the tips of his fingers. Then he looked into the assistant's face as if that man had just spoken to him in a strange language

·14·

"This is the monogram of Inácio da Alpiarça," the antiques dealer explained, as if staring down at him from the top of a tower. "Do you know who he is?"

"Vaguely."

"You don't know." His smile squeezed his eyes until they were reduced to two tiny peepholes. "If you did, you'd have no doubts about the value of the piece. Inácio da Alpiarça was an eighteenth-century Portuguese sculptor who can be compared, without modesty, to the great Italian masters of the

Renaissance and the baroque. Just look at this technique." His hand traced the angel's arms in a prolonged ecstasy. "The bronze seems to breath; it's alive. Look at the finish. The skin is as soft as a baby's ass."

"It is," replied an indifferent Esteban.

"Officially, this piece is listed as lost." The man's eyes suddenly took on a threatening ferocity. "Of the four in the group, only two were registered in catalogues. The four angels, I mean."

"It's a family heirloom," Esteban stubbornly insisted. "What do you know about the artist?"

The assistant straightened out the handkerchief in his jacket pocket so that it was a small triangle; he was proud of his elegance.

"Da Alpiarça's life is interesting, worthy of a nineteenth-century adventure novel. What do you know about him?"

"That he had friends in Italy," Esteban replied mechanically.

"He studied there," said the man. "I've had the chance to sell a few da Alpiarça pieces on a couple of occasions. Common tableware, nothing, of course, like this."

"Well then, it seems I've come to the right man."

"Yes." The man's voice was perfectly devoid of enthusiasm. "As a young man, he spent five or six years in Rome, studying with different masters, working sporadically for the pope. He was famous as a carouser, drinker, and whore chaser. In the forties or fifties, he returned to Portugal and joined the famous sculpture school at Mafra, which was directed by an Italian, Alessandro Giusti. In no time, he became a master. He became famous and rich. He was named official sculptor to King Jose I and received commissions from nobles all over Europe. He spent as much money as he could, buying four palaces within and outside of Lisbon. He even financed a private zoo where he wanted to keep a rhinoceros. He was obsessed by the rhinoceros. Da Alpiarça's drawing books are filled with rhinoceroses, monstrous animals more related to extraterrestrial fauna than with the pacific pachyderm that appears in documentaries. He was promised a rhinoceros. It was brought from Asia. Shipping it was costly, and maintaining the creature required astronomical sums. To finance the shipping, da Alpiarça accepted a commission from the king that was worthy of a titan. He was to decorate the basilica at Mafra with gigantic statues of the twelve patriarchs of Israel. He consumed what little he had left of his youth in the project, but he did have his rhinoceros. He spoiled it like a child, cleaned it himself, brought it perfumes and silks from its remote Orient. He saw it in his dreams."

"Did he finish the Mafra statues?" asked Esteban with ill-concealed haste.

"No," said the antiques dealer. "One night, da Alpiarça had a dream. He saw a bronze rhinoceros in the center of a plaza, and he saw that the rhinoceros melted away until there was nothing left on the ground but a gray, thick mass. The next day, his rhinoceros, the one brought from Asia expressly for him, fell ill. He called in charlatans, veterinarians, surgeons, but none could overcome the fever that was destroying the animal in his stable, eaten away by his own excrement and vomit. Da Alpiarça was desperate. He sought cures in churches, paid for Masses officiated by bishops, made a pilgrimage to Santiago de Compostela, but the rhinoceros did not get better."

"A strange obsession," Esteban absurdly observed, as if to prove he was still listening.

"Yes." The man's voice had become elusive and dark. "Since he lost confidence in God, he asked help from the competition. He made contact with an occult sect that celebrated devil worship and Black Masses in Lisbon and destroyed the two patriarchs he'd just poured. From the bronze of one of them, he made the four angels."

"For what purpose?" Esteban was staring out of the corner of his eye at the figure waiting on the counter. It too seemed to listen in silence.

"It isn't very clear," the man said and made a gesture of exoneration. "They were certainly linked to some sort of ritual, but I can't tell you what it was. See the signs on the base? They must have some meaning."

The two pairs of eyes patiently made their way around the circumference of the pedestal, crossing the Hebrew letter and the strange sign made up of lines, and foundering on the long, incomprehensible versicle that preceded the Greek: *Hvmanaqve homines tesidrv aetaesme in insaene evmpte . . .* Then their eyes met. In the antiques dealer's gaze, Esteban recognized the fact that he still had the energy to fight for that misplaced relic which the tide of coincidence had carried to his own shop. He couldn't let an opportunity of these proportions slip away.

"Are you sure?" asked the man with orthopedic friendliness, again pointing to the angel. "I really wish you'd reconsider your decision, even if it's only for the sake of the friendships we have in common."

"What happened to the rhinoceros?" answered Esteban.

"It never got better. It died. The famous Lisbon earthquake trapped da Alpiarça during a sinister celebration the details of which were never recorded, a ritual that seems to have had at its center a woman who acted as high priestess. The building where the acolytes gathered was demolished by the earthquake, but da Alpiarça managed to escape along with one other man, an Italian."

"Achille Feltrinelli," noted Esteban.

"Correct." The antiques dealer's eyes expanded to the very edges of his cheeks. "I see you know who he is: a bandit who would be burned in Venice a few years after. When he got home, da Alpiarça was horrified to discover that the earthquake had knocked down the stable and that his rhinoceros had died, buried under the rubble. Some versions say he committed suicide immediately afterward. Others say he died in the conflagration that devastated the city for three days in a row. No one knew of the existence of the angels until about midway in the nineteenth century when a French collector reunited them. Their history since then is blurry. They've changed hands constantly and been lost on several occasions. The last time they were together was in Berlin during 1945. The capture of the city by the Allies again scattered them. It's known that one was destroyed. Hold on a second."

The man stepped into the back room with his index finger frozen in a kind of warning signal. By going around a collection of rusty apostles, Esteban reached the rear area of the show window. He could see the armillary sphere, the carpet stamped with a vague elephant in combat, and the back of the neck of the young miss with the ribbons, which in the light reflected from the street gained in charm. Outside, animated by an afternoon of brownish tones that looked like a brief armistice between rainstorms, people boiled on the sidewalks, walked in circles around the kiosks, disappeared behind the bakery windows filled to overflowing with cakes.

Esteban wanted to smoke, but he understood that it wasn't the best course of action for the health of those old and venerable things. He heard the man return to the counter. An enormous folio volume monopolized his arms. His hands fluttered through the pages of the book until they stopped at a certain point. Esteban's eyes poured over some tightly printed text in three columns dotted here and there by black-and-white photographs that had the cloudiness of charcoal. In one of them there was an angel with a twisted foot. He read the cascade of words at the foot of the illustration:

Inácio da Alpiarça (1709–1754): Angel (1753?). Bronze and birch with silver inlay, 47 x 3 x 28 (wingspan) x 19 (pedestal diameter) cm. Monogram: IA. Destroyed.Last of a series of four angels that, according to legend, the artist created the year prior to his death for the Italian Achille Feltrinelli, who resided in Lisbon for six months. This is a conventional baroque angel of the Spanish school, wearing a tunic and sandals, with a bull at his feet and his right ankle twisted. This last element has suggested the angel's connection with Satanic cults. (Lucifer was rendered lame when he fell from paradise to hell.) The name on the pedestal, *Mahazael,* which seems to designate this particular angel, supports the hypothesis that the four figures were made to take part in some kind of ceremony connected to Satanism: Mahazael was one of the first rebel angels cast out of paradise by Saint Michael. The group was broken up in 1945. Azazel disappeared, and Mahazael was destroyed in a bombing raid. The third,

Azael, appears in the catalogue of the Margalef Collection in Barcelona, and the first, Samael, is in the collection of the Adimanta Foundation in Lisbon. The text on the pedestal is a combination of Hebrew, Greek, and Latin characters. The Greek part has been identified as an incantation for summoning the spirits of fire; the Latin section is corrupted with words in another language, which Du Pressis suggests may derive from Aramaic or Coptic. The catalogue of the Falkenhayn Collection (Berlin, 1936) establishes the complete text of Mahazael as follows: ק .Mahazael. ‡ .MAGNA.PARTE.BISSCSV. VEISEI.PIIEISEIOETI.PANTA.DI.AUTOU. EGENETO.KAI.CWRIS . . .

Esteban had recovered a notebook and a pencil stub from some remote grotto in his parka and was now writing down the content of the text in a calligraphy that would have baffled even the most talented handwriting expert. Opposite him, the assistant again coughed, causing his flabby cheeks to shake, and again looked at the angel on the counter with the eyes of a diabetic in a sweet shop. His pink, elegant hand amused itself by caressing the wings.

"Margalef Collection, in Barcelona," Esteban read.

"It no longer exists," said the man, as if all too happy to disillusion him. "Old Margalef died and his heirs divided the spoils. A shame. They didn't make as much of a profit as they thought they would."

"So where is their angel?"

"Sold, most certainly." The antiques dealer seemed to be chasing numbers in his memory. "I don't know to whom or for how much. You'd have to consult the annual auction reports."

An image like a comet plowed through Esteban's brain: He saw that other angel, another paralyzed, cold animal with a little man about knee-high, stuck in a corner on a pile of old newspapers next to an unclean stove. Nuria could have picked up the figure in any antiques market, and its price might not have been prohibitive. It was possible that the urgent need of Margalef's heirs to fatten their bank accounts had made them lower the price. Esteban's eyelids softly descended over his brown eyes. His accusatory imaginings evaporated all too soon, because the most plausible, ordinary explanation, one stripped of all strangeness, was right before his eyes, reduced to a single word. Restoration. A simple job, nothing more. The person who bought the statue, Mr. X, gives it to Nuria so she, emulating what the Spanish Royal Academy was supposed to do with words, can clean it, polish it, and give it splendor and then it can be set on the sideboard in the living room. A simple coincidence. Just one more. Of course these coincidences, because they recurred, ended up losing credibility, losing power.

"The Adimanta Foundation," recited Esteban. "Lisbon."

"Sebastião Adimanta." The antiques dealer's voice seemed to swerve toward a dead end. "A paralyzed, eccentric old man taken care of by a Swedish girl. Before an accident imprisoned him in a wheelchair, he would say he was a medium and things like that. A fraud. He set up a foundation for the study of paranormal phenomena that also has a small museum of curiosities. It's a museum that specializes in the devil."

"Maybe you have the address?"

The dealer's eyes were like those of a calf being led to the slaughter.

"I can give you the address, in exchange for which you'll promise to take my card. Promise me you'll keep it, that you'll think about my offer for the angel, and that you'll call me. How's that?"

"Give me your card." Esteban tried to smile, but his mouth froze in the attempt.

Outside, he found that a solid, sapphire-colored sky was outlining the dome of the El Salvador church, a kind of tarantula made of brick and tiles that scuttled over the roofs of Plaza del Pan. With the angel conveniently concealed in the neighborhood of his ribs, he made his way along Puente y Pellón amusing himself by looking into shop windows: manikin couples seducing each other with abbreviated caresses, lamps, alarming toys, prints with color geometries. He had no idea where he was going but was amused by the fact that his wandering stroll was the appropriate correlative to the traffic of his own thoughts, which kept on walking without seeking any definite direction.

He had no idea what he was after. Why had he let Alicia put him out to sea on this raft with no rudder so that the conflicting currents of his enthusiasms made him pitch from one side to the other, made him seasick, wishing he could walk on solid ground. But of course he knew the answer. He knew it perfectly well; he knew what prey was waiting for him at the end of the hunt, the goal that would make the madness and the mud less annoying. It might also make less annoying his finding himself every afternoon stuck at a crossroads he wasn't sure it was worthwhile to leave. That angel, still packaged at his side, was, curiously, beginning to weigh more than it should. But the angel was the key to getting the Alicia he wanted, the Alicia in whose ear he would be able to whisper, without fear of sliding his fingers along the skin of her shoulders or cheek during an avalanche of warm words, words to be spoken in half-light and that taste like bitter chocolate in the back of your throat.

It wasn't until he found himself standing in front of the School of the Arts, the package at his feet for a moment so he could light a cigarette, that he began to feel there was something dangerous in continuing to connect his thoughts in that way, to allow them to run along happily speaking all the words that prudence recommended not be said. With a growing disquiet, as he again placed the angel next to his ribs and walked more quickly, he perceived with all clarity that his skull had a hole in it and that some disrespectful eye was intruding into the interior, disturbing the content, spying on him.

He took a long drag and forced himself to stop, to breathe, to reflect. He wanted to clear away that absurd suspicion simply by convincing himself of how outlandish it was, but he found, to his horror, that the eye was already inside and knew everything, that it was running through the grottoes of his brain copying all the information he thought was exclusively his, his certainties, his fears, his shame. Making a desperate effort not to shout, Esteban tried to follow the wake of the eye, to retrace its path, to find out where it came from. He understood that someone behind him was watching him from perhaps five or ten meters way, that whoever it was had camouflaged himself among the flock of passersby on Laraña Street.

His heart was bursting in his chest, rendering the fear solid and painful. He began running, holding the package furiously tight under his arm, not wanting to think. He couldn't allow himself to be caught. He knew that the eye had been left disconcerted for an instant because of his sudden departure, but by now he could detect the person like a wasp at his back ready to continue the plunder. He turned up Cuna, slamming into couples, stumbling on a curb that was just about to send him smashing into the sidewalk. He spun onto El Salvador, trampling three hippies drinking beer, and stopped again. His pulse was exploding in his wrists while it seemed an elastic vertigo had pitched the plaza around him into a funnel.

To continue the chase in a straight line seemed to him more or less synonymous with letting himself be caught, so he twisted his way left and went around the church from behind, entering Plaza del Pan. Instinctively, he had the idea of taking refuge in a little shop he knew. "Good afternoon," roared Esteban, placing his package on the counter, dazed by the stench of sulphur.

"Good afternoon," repeated the giant, as if coming to his senses after a blow to the head. "What's the matter? You look as though you're being chased by the devil."

Esteban didn't manage to answer.

Six

When Esteban reached Alicia's apartment on Reyes Católicos, he found the door open, the bolt dangling, and a porcelain harlequin reduced to confetti on the vestibule carpet. The devastation continued in the living room, whose charming elegance poor Alicia was incredulously trying to clean up. It was a dump of pillows without stuffing, drawers thrown into corners, and pottery smashed against the carpet. Esteban made his way through the wreckage, picking up decapitated figurines and worrying about reconstructing ashtrays. The mop of chestnut hair that carelessly concealed her face gave Alicia the orphaned aspect of a victim.

"Isn't this incredible?" The words clogged up like marbles in her throat. "Some son of a bitch paid me a visit and had some fun."

Esteban crouched down. Under the slashed foam rubber of a cushion, he'd recognized a piece of that ceramic Colosseum he'd picked up as a souvenir for Pablo during his last trip to Rome. In a flash, he saw the window of that gift shop on Via Veneto, a place somewhere between a junk shop and a butcher shop. He saw infinite Colosseums and Trevi fountains in different sizes, all pornographically arranged in display cases. A vulgar Colosseum, the gift he would have chosen for someone he didn't know, like giving someone an Eiffel Tower or the Giralda here in Seville, a promise you keep in the moment when you're in a hurry and don't give a damn.

"How did this happen?" Esteban stuttered, throwing the piece of his souvenir back onto the floor.

"I got here half an hour ago," Alicia answered, "and I found the place this way. I was coming back from buying milk and renting a movie. I was very tired, but I couldn't go to sleep."

"What was stolen?"

"Stolen? Nothing." She crumpled up the Ducados pack and furiously tossed it to the back of the living room. "Nothing I've been able to discover until now. The little money I usually keep in the house is there, Mom's necklaces and broaches were moved around, but nothing's missing."

Broken vases, emptied shelves, drawers hysterically emptied onto the floor or the armchairs revealed something more laborious and obscure than a simple robbery attempt. There was the suggestion of speed in the attack, of anger, of minute attention to detail. Whoever was responsible for that cataclysm had not been attracted to Alicia's apartment for a handful of jewels or some succulent appliance. The invisible hand had chosen her door and no other, had searched, with artistic dedication, every corner of every piece of furniture, emptying each tiny portion of space that could have served as the hiding place for the object they were looking for. An object, by the way, Esteban suspected he was holding under his arm, untidily wrapped in an old piece of cloth.

"Nothing." Alicia was trying unsuccessfully to smile. "I'll have to declare the living room a disaster area. Oh God, the little figurines we brought from Mexico."

"They broke the bolt," said Esteban from the vestibule.

He was amusing himself by making the mangled bar of aluminum swing flaccidly back and forth. A pair of thin incisions were a souvenir of the very respectable kick the door had taken.

"They kicked the lock," observed Esteban wisely.

"Yes, that's what I thought at first," said Alicia walking toward him with a Mayan head between her fingers, "but look. The bolt is broken, very graphically by the way. But there isn't a single scratch around the keyhole."

"You're right."

Esteban's index finger confirmed the idea, suspiciously feeling its way around the edge of the lock: not a sign of a scratch, not even the tiniest sign of a splinter out of place. The kick had smashed the door and dislocated the bolt, but the lock itself hadn't been touched. The intruder had thrashed an open door.

"Whoever it was used a key," stated Alicia, observing Esteban from the end of the hallways of her eyes.

"How many people have the key?" he asked.

"Mamen has one." The fingers of Alicia's right hand made ready to give a helpful arithmetic demonstration. "Marisa, who every so often comes in to water the *conibras.* My sister, just in case some day she comes from Málaga and has to get in. The doorman. Lourdes."

"Lourdes," repeated Esteban in a diabolical voice.

"Yes, Lourdes," said Alicia, annoyed at having to repeat that name, at having to stain it in that pool of oil. "I know, I know, your favorite explanation. This supports your conspiracy theory. But I'm afraid the motive is less romantic. José, the doorman, told me that someone broke into the locker by the entrance and stole a bunch of keys. He must have tried mine among all the keys he grabbed."

"A thief who doesn't steal," he insisted.

"Enough, Esteban." Alicia's eyes tried to be dismissive. "Forget that. Oh my, the *conibras* too."

The pots had been smashed below the stucco shelf, and a bubble of black dirt darkened the floor tiles. The poor *conibras* had the torpedoed look of a sinking yacht. Armed with a dustpan and broom, Alicia tried to plant them in a pair of wicker baskets, which until then had been used to hide handkerchiefs. She set about carrying the plants with the pediatric delicacy a puppy would require. She set them in the baskets, sweetly caressing their plumes as if to alleviate their alarm or disgust. When she'd replanted all of them, Alicia stepped back a few paces, tripped over the leg of a dresser, and stooped with the intention of observing them from afar. The distance showed them to be in good health and unconcerned. After all was said and done, perhaps the disaster wouldn't affect them very much.

"Did you go to the antiques shop?" she asked without getting up, the weight of her body making her knees ache.

"I did. And when I left, something happened to me I didn't like."

"Wait. Let's bring the *conibras* into the kitchen and water them. Meanwhile tell me."

The *conibras* thanked her for the dose of water and chlorine by proudly raising their plumage. Holding them far enough away so his sweater would not get soaked, Esteban spoke in a confused voice about four angels, about a message, about some Portuguese guy who dreamed about rhinoceroses, about an earthquake, and about the devil. Through the window over the sink, it was possible to see the traffic jam on Marqués de Paradas, and there, on the far sidewalk, a man and a woman were chatting under a streetlight. Without knowing why, Alicia's thoughts crossed the street and remained hanging in the light coming through that filthy glass as if expecting an event that just wouldn't take place. Esteban's voice repeated: "The message in code is the key."

"The message," said Alicia.

"We have to find out in which language, aside from Latin and Greek, the text is written. But before anything else, we have to bring together the four parts of the message."

"Right."

"Nuria."

"What?" Alicia suddenly came back to herself.

"One of the missing angels is in Nuria's house."

Life, thought a disquieted Alicia, was rapidly cracking into two semicircles separated by an unbridgeable chasm; the ghost she'd awakened by trying to capture the meaning of her dream and resolving the flagrant coincidence of the etching was floating over her head. Like an ectoplasm, it was taking over the wills of other people. The dream and all its macabre paraphernalia of suspicions and threats was beginning to contaminate that geography of her life in which she'd wanted to search for air after the catastrophe. The routine pastime begun a couple of weeks back was beginning to acquire the disturbing dimensions of a nightmare, which was also troubling those around her. No, the devil, madness, the redundant, crippled angels: none of that had anything to do with Mrs. Acevedo's care, with the beers and smoked oysters and laughs opposite the poster of Jimi Hendrix wearing an eloquent hussar's coat. They were two halves of her existence she did not want to combine.

"Forget all that, Esteban," she snorted, lighting a cigarette.

Esteban recognized that, yes, okay, perhaps her neurosis had indeed ended up affecting him through an irremediable contagion, affecting him more than it affected her. But he couldn't forget, shouldn't forget. Since the deaths of Pablo and Rosa, she'd tried to dive into that tank, the tank of forgetting, to submerge herself in its waters, abandoning the insolent light of the surface, the long ritual of daily asphyxiation. She'd tried to forget her name, her past. Each night became a sterile exercise in renunciation, a desperate effort to scrape and scrape at the plaque of memory in order to see if it could be scraped clean and engraved with new images.

But there was only one thing missing, and she had to know it: forgetting. Every act, every episode suffered, was weighing on her shoulders with the unbearable tonnage of promises and guilt. Taking shape behind her was the growing globe of a world overflowing with names, telephone numbers, verses, faces, hopes, terrors that occupied shelf after shelf in an inevitable museum. And every word left a groove, a scar that her fingers could trace, remembering the moment when they were said, everything they swore, everything they were forced to carry through. And the words and gestures could be brandished like accusations, and then they turned into tarantulas or knives, weapons that had to be rendered useless before they were handed over to the enemy or lost in the exchange.

"I suppose you'd also prefer to forget last night," said Esteban with a failed, cinematic pathos.

"Yes." Alicia fled the kitchen in horror, searching for some surviving ashtray. "Yes, it would be better to forget it."

"Run away, that's right, run away." Esteban's voice was tinged with the bitterness of a child deprived of his toys. "Flee your responsibilities, just turn off, get under your quilt and repeat to yourself: I want to forget, I want to forget. And you can do it all with such joy."

The cigarette was beginning to heat Alicia's fingernails, but that small threat between her fingers lacked any relevance. To hide her head as her venerable teachers had told her ostriches did; leave the party when you hear your name spoken; drop out of the game when you're sure that you've been dealt a hand consisting of a modest two pairs. Certainly, the task of living was something too wide and sonorous for the awkward way she had of walking around the house, certainly life demanded an intelligence or a resolve from which predestination or genetics had precluded her. Faced with the two paths in which a dilemma split, she'd always preferred the third, the exit. It was better not to speak in order not to deserve an answer; it was preferable to erase words and pretend they had no impact on others, that they were inoffensive silhouettes. But now Esteban was demanding she pay the debts of her promises, that she not try to go back to erase the ship's wake and change course. The previous night she'd turned to him, slid her hand over his shoulder, sought his breathing in order to feel less bereft. And she had to understand that everything, even asking for help, had a price.

"I'm all confused, Esteban," she stuttered, as her fingers created furrows in her chestnut hair. "I know what happened last night, I know I made a fool of myself, but you have to understand I'm having a hard time. And on top of that all of this. And Pablo, and Rosa . . ."

Both of them knew the absolute, invincible quality those two names had. Just saying them had the effect of cutting off all discussion. They marked a border that neither of them would dare to cross. With a strange, hungover feeling, Esteban coughed and stuck his hands in the pockets of his parka. The hallway smelled of boiled cauliflower.

...

All the Valium brought was a sleep like a spiderweb, a defective sleep with jagged edges. When she woke up, Alicia had the ashen impression of having spent the night in a puddle. The dream again evaded her pillow after she'd spent an entire week drowned in pitch, after waking up so many mornings with her mind clouded over by the effluvia from a swamp that never completely disappeared when she opened her eyes, that cried out to return and wrap up every instant of her waking life, her torturous waking life. It was true that for the time being she'd given up the pills and Lourdes's juice, but her insomnia had to be the result of some more elemental, more direct cause: the attack on her apartment, her doubts.

Sitting on the bed, she noted how the rising sun dirtied the openings in the blind, and she again felt the return of that fractured feeling that caused her, the day before, to reproach Esteban. Despite everything, it seemed that the spur of reticence had hit its target, so now she could no longer face certain names with ease. Two days back, she would not have been suspicious about the sudden appearance of Nuria so soon after Esteban had left and her all too nonchalant way of taking in the scene of the crime, as if finding the furniture upside down and the dishes smashed all over the floor were an everyday event. A venomous voice whispered in Alicia's ear that Nuria was behaving artificially.

"What can you do?" asked a detached Nuria. "A couple of days of work, and it'll be fine."

"Right, it'll be fine."

She never before would have been suspicious of Nuria's invitation to have lunch—the way things are here, it would be better if you came over to my place—but now everything seemed to her like different sequences in a masked maneuver, movements in a strategy whose objective was a slippery, occult destiny. She'd gone to bed with that struggle in her head, with the sting of distrust; the dawn brought her the same indecision, and when she caught sight of herself in the mirror, tired and broken, she didn't know if she would go down to Nuria's to eat because of the bonds of friendship or to tighten the knot of the enigma.

Coffee with too little sugar, a shower, Leonard Cohen's "Tower of Song": none of those things led her to the exit she desired, the exit that should lead her off the highway of those shopworn thoughts. Suddenly she was struck by the certainty that she should play her cards more attentively, because despite the laughs and the pats on the back the game would not allow her to take refuge in the softness of friendship.

When she got out of the shower, she looked at herself in the mirror. She saw that she was trying to maintain a balance between faith in a bravery she'd yet to put to the test and the definitive escape, annihilation, perhaps Australia or an extra tranquilizer. She wondered, with another coffee in front of her and with Leonard singing the whole record over again (*they sentenced me to twenty years of boredom*) accompanied by the upstairs neighbor banging on the floor, what would happen if that balance came to an end, if one of the sides managed to establish hegemony.

Either she would trust Nuria and the Acevedos as she had until now or abandon them to suspicion. She should admit the possibility that they might not be what they said they were, what for an offensive number of years they'd pretended to be, perhaps in order to use her, to extract from her a service that as yet had not taken definitive form.

That Roman Polanski–style idea twisted her mouth into a grimace, either of laughter or horror—she didn't know which. And imagination, as disloyal as always, wasted no time initiating its siege. What devilish jungle of coincidences forced her to begin dreaming of a city where there was an angel like the one Nuria was holding? Why was it that the book containing the plan of the city was no where else but in the library where she worked? Why was everyone in the neighborhood fully informed by some source unknown to her whether or not she was going to work? Why was it that by merely not drinking the bitter juice Lourdes was bringing her every night she was able to shake off that unctuous drowsiness she had been feeling for a week? Why had this person who'd come into her apartment in order to steal nothing kicked open an unlocked door? The more she wanted to bury those armed questions, the more they poked through the sand of her conscience, leading her to empty the coffeemaker, wash it out, and search for the coffee can without seeing the labels on the others. In the living room, Cohen was whispering his songs to a pair of sofas that couldn't manage to stand up.

...

The precooked cheese cannelloni Nuria unwrapped with badly disguised repugnance did not, of course, constitute an offering worthy of exquisite chefs, but her labors in the dear old chapel left time for nothing else. Fortunately, Alicia's bottle of Rioja wine served as a counterpoint to the vulgar, microwaved dish that was intended to placate their appetites. The Virgin was almost ready, after two nights of orthopedically regrowing the first knuckle in her fingers, but now a San Fernando with a shameful nick on the edge of his sword was impatiently awaiting his refurbishing so he could again become the veteran conqueror he was six hundred years ago.

Alicia had seen him when she entered the apartment, there in the center of the living room, next to the other image dotted with patches, with his left arm raised in what seemed a kind of invitation to the dance that his partner, the Virgin, was demurely trying not to accept. Around the wooden figures, Alicia's nervous eyes discovered nothing more than the usual tools, amputated wood, the device that reminded her of a flamethrower filthily abandoned opposite the stove. Nuria was talking about the San Fernando, showing her a plan of the chapel that Alicia's eyes looked over rapidly as they tried to flee toward the corner, there, under the display cabinet, toward the corner camouflaged by cans of turpentine and linseed oil.

She had to put up with the same boring speech at the kitchen table, over two agreeable glasses of wine and two less agreeable servings of pasta, nodding her head affirmatively each time one of Nuria's silences called for the gesture. But her thoughts were moving in the opposite direction to Nuria's words, far from San Fernando, the Sevillian baroque, and the seventeenth-century eucharistic altarpiece, far from Tom Waits, who was howling from the loudspeaker of the boom box. She was concentrating on that presence waiting for her in the living room, voicelessly calling her from a corner of that

room so she could finally use what she'd hidden in her trouser pocket, still uncertain about Nuria's friendship or her
vileness. Nuria, Nuria sweetheart. The sentence she had to
pronounce stuck in her mouth like an underdone steak.
"Nuria, I have to pee."

"Okay," commented Nuria, annoyed at seeing her lecture on Sevillian religious imagery in the seventeenth century
interrupted. "At the end of the hall, you know where."

As she walked down the hall not quite on tiptoe, Alicia noticed that a pair of eyes was nailed to her throat: Jimi
Hendrix was nebulously observing her from the window of
his poster, stuffed into his humiliating orange dress coat. She
closed the bathroom door in such a way that the sound of
the bolt could be heard everywhere in the apartment. Then
she nervously ran to the living room. She didn't know if her
pantomime of muffled footsteps and lies shamelessly plagia-
rized from some spy movie deserved seriousness, but an explosion of convulsive laughter was almost on the point of
betraying her maneuvers. Instantly, however, she thought
about the body of that bald, flaccid man, Benlliure, collapsed
on top of her with all its smell of wet raincoat, and her mouth
stiffened.

She'd taken the precaution of strategically leaving the
kitchen door ajar before making her way to the hall, so that
to see her activities in the living room from the doorway would
require a complicated contortion. She carefully made her way
between the trash can where the bits of wood were tossed and
the tools; she went around the two figures who could not
make up their minds to dance. San Fernando was staring into
a corner of the ceiling with the astonished expression of someone surprised by a revelation or a heart attack.

In the corner Esteban described, she found a battery of rubber and plastic pails and chemical products for softening or removing encrustations. She turned her head precisely ninety degrees to confirm that the sound that had suddenly poured into her ears did not belong to the kitchen entrance, from which Tom Waits's monotonous litany continued to flow; her blood was pounding in her temples. She began moving aside the pails of caustic soda and bleach; she pushed aside the wall of acrylic paint, varnish, and, much to her surprise, a bottle of shoe polish. Only after a few, eternal seconds could she find the corner and the sparkling, black figure waiting at the rear.

It looked younger, cleaner, and stronger than Benlliure's. The effect of the solvent was obvious on the forearms and the edges of the wings, which shone with a soft, bluish enamel. Alicia contemplated him with a vengeful fixity, as if by staring she could pay herself back for an old offense committed against her. His eyes were not empty; they were not like those of the other statues, where a smooth but cutting screen erased the presence of the iris and the pupil. Alicia could perceive that the angel, Azael, was returning the ferocity of her own gaze, that his eyes were two mirrors where her rage and horror were replicated. But beyond the eyes, the charm of evil and pride ceased. The angel's perfect anatomy grew to a height just short of half a meter, and from his chest to his legs he was covered by a doublet and a tunic that fluttered to the rhythm of a petrified wind. He was beautiful, serious, and inflexible.

Luckily the clatter of plates that reverberated from the kitchen reminded her that her action was secret, that it should be secret. Why was Nuria hiding the angel behind that wall of cans and pails? Why had her conversation become like the suburbs of certain themes, which she cleverly seemed to avoid by always choosing secondary roads that never flowed into the thing that Alicia really wanted to discuss: What was an angel like the one in her dreams doing hidden in the studio she called a living room?

An annoying film of perspiration covered her hands as she went through the pockets of her trousers, a sweat that soaked the piece of tissue and mixed with the charcoal to produce a sticky, black paste. She didn't want to stop to think. She wanted her actions to unfold behind that severe voice that had always corrected her decisions. With the movements of a sleepwalker, she placed the paper over the inscription and pressed down while the charcoal softly rubbed over the surface. The paper crackled like a pile of leaves being trampled. Then a vaporous, black cloud formed around the pedestal. The letters, reversed now, started appearing in that magical way in which secret messages appear when someone breathes onto a mirror. She had no idea how long it took, but when she peeled back the paper, she felt she was the laborious author of the message which she was now holding in her fingers.

𐤔 .AZAEL. ⛌ .DENTE.DRACO. TGIVGERED.ROAGD.MGEGD.MVTEE . . .

She returned the paper, now rolled into a ball, to the bottom of her pocket, where she cruelly crushed it together with the piece of charcoal. But she did not stand up. Hunkered down, she went on observing the beautiful bronze adolescent, captivated by his magnetic elegance. There was an undefinable pleasure in watching him hold that pose forever. Again she contemplated the eyes, where the same incendiary gaze was projecting itself toward some place behind her. She stared at the thighs emerging unpolluted from the tunic, the right foot broken in a right angle at the height of the ankle, near the place where a tiny human figure was embracing the shin.

She moved closer to observe that image she hadn't noticed in her first examination of the angel: The little man, dressed in a kind of cloak and cape, had his arms wrapped around Azael's leg. His face, as small and difficult as the wrinkles in a walnut, was inexpressive. Alicia recalled that the other angels, in the same place, were escorted by a bull and an eagle. Now there was a man. It seemed clearer and clearer to her that what she had before her were the scattered words of a message she should patiently continue putting back together, juxtaposing, inserting each new one in the place of the previous inscription, linking it with the following one in order to produce a sequence she could then throw herself into translating; prior to the interpretation of the enigma came the assembling of its signs. She was repeating the need for that basic program when she noted that the angel's eyes were becoming darker, that a cloudy shadow was obscuring the corner of the studio where the figure was hidden. When she turned her head, Alicia found that Nuria was standing in front of the pails of abrasives and varnish, and that her face had taken on the rigid expression of a manikin.

"That's not where the bathroom is," she said in an empty voice.

A ball of harsh canvas blocked Alicia's breathing, blinding her words. Her heart was pounding while she cleaned off her knees and made way so Nuria could reconstruct the wall of cans and pails.

"It's such a pretty figure," said Alicia, unable to keep herself from stammering and betraying her anguish. "What a shame you have it hidden there. It would shine so much more if you took it out of there."

Nuria had never looked at her that way; her eyes seemed to be infected with the same tranquil fury that just moments before she'd discovered in the angel's eyes. Alicia fearfully thought it must be her own nerves that made such an absurd connection. Nuria's gaze was that of the poker player who tries to guess what cards his adversary sitting on the other side of the table is holding, the gaze of the detective in novels who is about to begin pulling apart the plot behind the murders that have dotted the story. There was a strange flow in those eyes, a tide of bitter feelings quickly circulating from eye to eye and then calming with the same suddenness with which it had appeared.

Stupid, more than stupid, a huge jerk, Alicia rigorously insulted herself, hoping perhaps that those adjectives would take away her disorientation and shame. Of course, you'd have to be very stupid not to check the kitchen door just a little more carefully, very stupid to forget that everything could fall apart in exactly that place, very stupid to forget the threat while she amused herself with her usual silliness looking at the features—like those of a shelled walnut—of the little figure hugging the angel's tibia. A good thing the charcoal and the paper were safely put away in her pocket next to the keys, which were digging, just a little, into the place where her thigh began. She tried to excuse herself with some formula which would sound more casual than her previous babble, but Nuria cut her off by waving her hand in the gesture of removing the dust from the top of some piece of furniture.

"Don't worry, my dear," she said, deploying a smile that ineffectively attempted to reestablish confidence. "I don't want people to see it because it's a very special commission. The person who's having me restore it doesn't want it to be seen."

Alicia thought Nuria was opening a closet.

"Who is it?" Alicia asked, with an artificial ease.

"I don't think it matters really." The smile fell off Nuria's mouth again, and that dark tide returned to her eyes. "Excuse me for talking that way, but it's a very special commission, as I said. And I wish you wouldn't mention it to anyone."

"No, no."

"Let's go." The smile once again traced a semicircle from cheek to cheek. "I've got fruit compote for dessert. Wait until you see how good it is."

The compote was very delicious, but Alicia couldn't concentrate on those sudden, sweet charges the spoonfuls of gelatin left on the back of her tongue. She mechanically repeated the act of introducing that stainless-steel utensil into her mouth again and again, without ceasing to observe Nuria at the other end of the table, also busy emptying her bowl with rigid, precise spoonfuls. For a moment Alicia felt absurd, felt she was following a silly choreography, as if she were trying to communicate with a deaf mute by inventing her own sign language. The clatter of the teaspoons against the glass helped them by filling in any inopportune silence that might require words.

Tom Waits had finished singing, and no one bothered to find out what was on the other side of the tape. Alicia almost jumped out of her seat when the doorbell rang, and Nuria found the perfect excuse to abandon her unfinished compote and got up, shot Alicia a fleeting, diagonal glance, and left the kitchen closing the door behind her. Alicia had to finish her wine before she went back to linking her conclusions, still with no kind of fear or suspicion until she realized that Nuria had closed the door when she had left the kitchen.

The compote had gotten all over her thumb; she was tenaciously licking the trace of gelatin that tasted of molasses and apple as she went over to the door and found out that the knob wouldn't turn in her hand. That is, it wouldn't turn even if she were to scrape off the skin on the palms of her hands trying to turn that obstinate piece of yellow aluminum. The thought came to her to find a relationship between her unexpectedly being locked in and her being discovered minutes ago with the angel, spoiling a secret that Nuria definitely wanted to keep in the shadows.

Again she tried to open the door. It wouldn't budge. Her hearing, growing more sensitive by the second, told her that there was not a hint of Nuria on the other side of the door, even though the vestibule was no more than two steps away. She plastered her ear to the door to confirm that suspicion: nothing. As her hands went on skinning themselves against the knob, Esteban's words fell in an avalanche over her consciousness, blinding the limited capacity for analysis she still retained at that degree of hysteria. She understood that all of Esteban's points followed a single trajectory. The neighbors upstairs, who protested about music but not about voices; Lourdes, who found out about her sick leave the same day she took it and who lied; Benlliure, who died on her very doorstep, with the angel in his hands, trying to find someone living there; another angel like his, just a short distance from that door—which would not open—hidden because it was preferable that its existence not be known.

She felt like Mia Farrow in *Rosemary's Baby*, backed into a corner, incapable of accepting the web of machinations that her intelligence, liberated by panic, would not stop tracing, filament by filament. For the first time, it occurred to her to establish a diffuse link between the fact that she dreamed about a city with four angels and the fact that there might be people in her own building spying on her, persecuting her, a diffuse link connecting her solicitous neighbors and the sect of the *Coniurati* Esteban had spoken about, the one that gathered around a papess, Satan's concubine.

By this time, resorting to punches and kicks did not seem insane to Alicia. She discharged the electricity of her nerves against the door, which accepted each blow without changing, without yielding. She put her fingers against her temples to try to force her thought processes to work more quickly, more clearly. It was obvious that Nuria had locked her in so she wouldn't snoop at her angel again, so she'd pay the price of her curiosity and understand the fatal consequences that could result from her lack of respect for the secrets of others. At the same time, Nuria's absence could only mean she'd gone out, that she'd left the apartment, perhaps to get reinforcements.

With the taste of compote still on her tongue, she ran to survey the kitchen window. It overlooked a courtyard dotted with archipelagos of moisture because the sun shone on it only ten minutes every day. First looking down to the bottom and then up to the piece of sky that was just possible to make out above the upper floors, her eyes tripped over clothes-lines, some as naked as broken harps with green strings, others abandoning to the breeze a flutter of sheets and pajamas. She'd always wondered if those synthetic ropes that held up coats and quilts would be able to hold up a not overly heavy person, a person like her. She dragged the table over to the wall and got on top of it using the bench as a step.

The kitchen now seemed narrower and less important: The future would depend on the upstairs clothesline. She'd have to stretch out her right arm with all due care, not look down, forget the four floors below that were waiting for her with their mouths open, act with the nonchalance and aplomb of a trapeze artist who's learned her lesson. Her heart and her index finger were almost touching the ropes above when the kitchen door opened with a kind of muted clap of thunder. Nuria found Alicia standing on tiptoe on top of the table trying to reach the flowerpots of the next-door neighbor.

"Alicia." For an instant Nuria could say nothing more than that name. "What are you doing?"

Alicia didn't move. She suddenly felt like a ballerina finishing an extraordinarily marvelous or ridiculous ballet step.

"I couldn't open the door," she said turning around.

"Right." Nuria lit a cigarette to digest the situation from a more philosophic point of view. "Sometimes the knob sticks. But you weren't going to go home through the window, were you?"

"No, of course not." Alicia's ears were approaching the temperature at which metals melt. "Actually, I was leaving, but by way of the door. Who was it?"

"Come down from there now."

They walked to the vestibule, Alicia with the impression she'd been found naked in a public park, Nuria with her eyes focused on the burning tip of her cigarette, not saying anything. Their eyes never met.

"It took me longer than it should have because I had to go to the apartment upstairs," Nuria reported with a suddenly glacial voice. "It was Lourdes. Someone's looking for you. For you or for Esteban. It's the police, I think."

Alicia's tongue still tasted of compote.

Seven

S itting on a stair, Inspector Gálvez had just finished his cigarette, taking good care not to let a speck of ash dirty the tiles on the landing. Seconds earlier, a lady with nostrils like those of an ox wielding a mop had greeted him harshly and stared reprovingly at the cigarette he held in his fingers, to the point that Gálvez became ashamed and tried to either hide or get rid of the cigarette. But he found no receptacle where he could make it disappear. So when Alicia appeared and muttered something, Gálvez stupidly raised the Winston up to his chest, under which his left hand acted as well it could the part of resigned ashtray.

Maintaining that dressmaker's dummy pose, he entered the vestibule, sighed, and waited for Alicia to put her keys on the side table and extract her own cigarettes from her trouser pocket. It was hard to walk through the living room. It seemed to him that some kind of hurricane had flipped over the furniture onto the rugs, smashed the china, and scattered the books. With each step, an uncomfortable crunch would call attention to the fact that a shoe was landing on a not especially convenient place. Gálvez was left cornered at one extreme of the massacre, unable to move either foot, with the Winston transformed into a gray and flaccid thing on his chest and his left hand stupidly turned into a seashell below, with that asphyxiating shirt of his squeezing his torso. Alicia was walking back and forth among the pieces of glass and majolica, until finally the inspector could restrain himself no longer and asked, "Do you have an ashtray?"

"Use the floor," said Alicia calmly. "A bit of ash won't even be noticed."

The inspector's finger obediently followed instructions, and the little mound of ash darkened what looked like the head of a fox terrier.

"Well, well." Gálvez tried to smile, but did so very badly. "Have a fight with your boyfriend?"

"Oh, this is nothing," Alicia responded with the same cramped smile. "The study is in worse shape. There was no fight, I just like to keep the place this way."

The inspector made no comment. He was a timid man. For a moment, Alicia was sorry for that enormous visitor trapped in his shirt. His disrespectful receding hairline and the raincoat unwilling to have anything to do with his shoulders made him look like a shipwrecked man seeking rescue. She led him to the center of the living room, next to the table whose magazines had also been scattered around, and had him sit down on a Moroccan hassock which, miraculously, was still upright. Then she vanished behind the kitchen door. From his seat, with his knees almost at the same height as his ribs, Gálvez contemplated the jungle of broken pieces that ravaged the floor and amused himself trying to guess which piece went with which. He guessed right with a pair of dogs, an ashtray, perhaps a jar of pencils. But suddenly, he felt, with a hint of urgency, he was wasting too much time. He had to begin the conversation somewhere.

"Your neighbor, the little old lady, told me you were downstairs," he shouted.

"Yes, Lourdes," Alicia answered from the kitchen. "I was eating with a friend. Want a beer?"

"No." Gálvez thought for a second. "A whiskey would be better, if you have any."

"No. I've only got Coke."

"A glass of water then."

The inspector was handed a glass holding a rather turbid liquid in which a few wood shavings were drowning. This obliged him to practice a courteous smile. Setting aside her can of soda, Alicia set upright a little wrought-iron tea table she'd bought in Tangier during some distant Maghreb summer and sat down on top of it, with one leg crossed over the other. She rejected the inspector's Winston and lit a Ducados. To Gálvez it seemed that even her way of smoking was angry, as if she were exhaling insults or punches.

"Well, then"—Gálvez moistened his upper lip with his tongue—"I wanted to talk with you and your brother-in-law. But he doesn't seem to be here."

"You might think I'm lying when I say this, but he really isn't."

"Okay." The inspector again tried that penetrating stare that put the fear of God into the criminals in his station. "I don't know if this has anything to do with the death of Benlliure, but I do know that yesterday afternoon your brother-in-law was in an antiques shop on Puente y Pellón."

"You don't say." The can was revolving in Alicia's hands. "Did you have him followed."

"Our job is to know everything." Gálvez suddenly felt proud of his aphorism. "Is it true or not?"

"Is what true?"

"That your brother-in-law was there yesterday."

"Ask him." Alicia drank.

"Everything at its proper time." His gaze became more intense, more skull-piercing, more useless than ever. "To tell you the truth, I don't know why you answer my questions with such suspicion. In principle, you've got nothing to fear."

"Thanks."

"Which is why I'd appreciate your help." Inspector Gálvez drank from his glass of water, and the gesture was absurd. "You may deny it if you like, but I know your brother-in-law was in that shop yesterday, between six and eight P.M. The girl working in the pastry shop opposite recognized him because he'd stopped to look in the window on many other afternoons."

"Is that a crime?"

"Let me finish. I'm not looking for him because I intend to accuse him of anything. I want to talk to him because his testimony may be useful. Someone killed the owner of that shop yesterday afternoon, shortly after your brother-in-law's visit."

The inspector had emitted the last sentence in the same tone he might have used to make some prediction about the next day's weather or his verdict about some soccer match. the intonation was routine, distracted. Even so, Alicia felt that her heart had hit a pothole, that a soft impact, like being hit with a bath towel, had altered her breathing and her pulse for a second. She had no idea why she'd become so nervous;

she didn't know that man; there was no direct, tangible relationship between his death and the city or the dream. But she mysteriously perceived that some subterranean path linked those two dead bodies, that of the individual she didn't know, whose face she could not draw, and the other that fell on top of her with water and blood pouring off his raincoat, the man with the face that appeared in her dreams transformed into a stained, pitiful mask. In some obscure way, the new murder made Benlliure's death more authentic or definitive.

"How did it happen?" she asked very slowly.

"Someone smashed his skull by bashing it three times," said Inspector Gálvez, trying to make himself more comfortable on the ottoman. "The wound had to be produced by something heavy, hard, made of metal most probably. The body was found behind the counter, under an avalanche of figurines and fragments of antique weapons. He dragged a shelf down as he fell, while he was being beaten. The motive for the crime is still not clear. It doesn't seem as though anything's been stolen. However, an enormous book was found next to the body, the size of an atlas: *Antiques Yearbook 1979*. The murderer ripped out a page."

Alicia's contracted throat tried to swallow saliva. She found her saliva bitter and harsh.

"Don't worry about your brother-in-law," said Gálvez.

"Esteban," Alicia retorted without looking up. "His name is Esteban."

"Don't worry about Esteban." The inspector attempted a kind of compassionate smile. "The medical examiner determined that the man died at around nine-thirty or ten P.M. The girl from the pastry shop has testified that she saw Esteban leave the shop just as it was getting dark, and later other people went in. The shop closes regularly at nine, so no doubt this was a previously arranged meeting. The murderer and the victim knew each other. Don't worry about Esteban. Besides, he isn't nearsighted, is he?"

"Nearsighted?"

Gálvez's hand submerged in the right-side pocket of his shipwrecked man's coat and presented a small plastic bag containing something long and dark. It took Alicia only a few blinks to understand what it was, but when her eyes figured it out, horror and thirst again left her exhausted on the little tea table. She rested her hand on her thigh.

"Glasses for a nearsighted person," snorted Gálvez. "One lens was broken, as if it had been stepped on, perhaps during the escape. High magnification, so the guy must not be able to see much. Stigmatism too, worn-out eyes, probably an older person. But Alicia, you seem to recognize this frame. Are you okay?"

Yes, of course she remembered the frame. On the soap dish by the sink, just a few days back, after the plumbing work and the S. S. Van Dine novel. It was useless to deny it; her pallor and her suffocation betrayed her. She meekly said yes and dropped her soda can onto the floor, but please don't ask anymore questions.

...

The coffee machine was at the end of a long hall partially blocked by plastic flowerpots. To exorcise the disturbing impression that its length was infinite, that it would never end, the hall had to be traversed as quickly as possible. During the day, the furious percussion of the typewriters and the slamming doors punished the corridor, so that it was virtually impossible to reach the exit with one's hearing fully intact. Now that night blinded the windows, and the offices became even more enormous, the silence enhanced the hall's seeming endlessness, suggesting to the visitor that to enter into its space was to allow oneself to fall into a defective and elastic temporal orbit, like that of a spiderweb.

Alicia and Esteban did not share that fear, but as they made their way toward the far end beyond the final ferns, both felt that their footsteps were useless, that they'd need a thousand nights like this to reach an eternally postponed objective. As she put coins in the machine—the cappuccino was the only choice that was moderately digestible—Alicia compared her present perception of things with the distorted sounds a tape recorder emits when the speed is changed: Voices become threatening shrieks, contaminated with an odious resemblance to animals or ghosts, and lose that nearness that makes us seek them out to take refuge in their lulling sound. The world was no longer the beautiful Rousseau that had always decorated her living room, above the book case, next to the majolica vases. Now it had become sinister, like a Kirchner or one of the most deformed of Francis Bacons. Stirring her coffee, Alicia took her place in one of the rows of chairs in the waiting room; Esteban accompanied her, with his fourth consecutive Fortuna between his lips. On the wall opposite them, almost camouflaged by the artificial palm, half a dozen faces were spattered on a poster. The words below the pictures advised the viewer that the mysterious multiplicity of the faces was only apparent: *This man is very dangerous.*

"I had no choice but to identify him, Esteban," said Alicia after a sip of coffee, answering a question no one had put to her. "He didn't give me a chance to deny it, not even to think about whether I wanted to deny it. He saw how pale I'd become, and that was that."

"Well there's nothing to be done now." Esteban was fascinated by the crowd that was the man on the poster. "Besides, you had no reason to hide it. I don't want to become annoying, but you know what I think of all this."

"But Blas, Blas." Alicia bit her lower lip. "I can't believe it, Esteban."

He leaned forward and planted his elbows on his knees. The smoke from the cigarette was making his eyes water.

"No matter who it was, they knocked off the antiques dealer because of what he knew about the angel. There was nothing missing from the shop, the motive for the crime does not seem to be theft. Except that, and think about this, they tore a page out of an antiques catalog, the same page he showed me, the one with all the details about the piece. I don't know if it was Blas who killed him, but whoever it was wanted to erase connections. Remember they also tried to hide the book."

"But Blas."

"Blas or whoever it was," said Esteban with a slightly obstinate tone. "But you tell me what his glasses were doing there on the floor next to the body."

"Now he's going to tell us," Alicia answered as if defending herself from a reproach. "All I'm saying is that it's hard for me to believe it, Esteban."

"Yes, it's hard for you to believe it. But I have the impression that whoever it is is closing a circle, Alicia. There is a fence getting tighter and tighter, and you and I are inside."

A voice called out their names from the hall. The interrogation was going to begin. They made their way slowly to the door from which Gálvez was summoning them and entered a cubical office where a number of men were breathing. The light from a table lamp vertically interrupted the suffocating darkness of the room. Esteban, cornered next to a desk, was afraid the walls might collapse like a tower of cards and trap them under the entire deck.

Behind the violent rip of light, it was possible to make out the face of Blas Acevedo, patiently at his post on a chair. For an instant, he dedicated a glance like that of a hungry jaguar to Alicia, but she could not see that threat. Her eyes were still incapable of focusing easily in the swamp of black presences that swallowed her as soon as she crossed the threshold. It actually took her a couple of minutes to guess there was someone else sitting next to the wall, someone whose flannel trousers she slowly began to make out, a shirt whose sleeves were rolled up to the elbow, a corpulent typewriter. After emptying his lungs with a sigh, Gálvez closed the door and scurried into a corner. Now Alicia could see only the swath of light colliding with a plastic ashtray, which housed cigarette butts on top of the table, and the head of Blas Acevedo, a bit farther back, broken by an enigmatic, unpleasant smile.

"All right now, Mr. Acevedo," the gritty voice of Inspector Gálvez spoke from behind Alicia's back, "I want you to repeat in the presence of these two people the answers you just gave me. Take as long as you like, maybe you'll remember details that escaped you when you told me what happened. First, is it true you visited the antiques shop belonging to Rafael Almeida, the victim, after ten last night?"

"Yes," answered Don Blas without hesitating. "It's true."

"The shop was already closed," the earthy voice continued.

"Yes." Blas Acevedo's smile made an affirmative grimace. "It closes at nine."

"So you and Mr. Almeida had made a date beforehand."

"Not exactly." The smile lost its balance.

"Not exactly," repeated the impatient voice occupying the space behind Alicia. "But you and Mr. Almeida knew each other."

The smile, deformed into a kind of fleshy crevice, allowed an exhalation to flee; Blas Acevedo's eyes, more and more feline, tried to blaze a trail through the darkness of the office, through the shadows, to look for Alicia's and pounce on them. Alicia lowered her eyelids whenever that furtive hunting was repeated. Her pulse or her nerves were convulsively agitating her eyebrows. She understood quite clearly that this was virtually like stabbing Blas in the back, good Don Blas, to pay him back with a low blow for all those years when he'd acted as her surrogate father, years of plumbing repairs, candies for Rosa and his sweetness always alert when she needed a hand.

She was hammering the best of her past to bits, the showcase with the china of her life. But she couldn't avoid it, as she'd said to Esteban. She had seen the frames of Blas's glasses in the inspector's hands, and her face had been transparent, more transparent than that dubious glass of water the inspector, surrounded by broken things, had drunk on her ottoman. Until then, her low-cost happiness had depended on her neighbors, but after Rosa and Pablo, it became the untouchable requirement for her to go on playing with the enigmas of her dream, the city, the book, the angel: a crossword puzzle that was entertaining at times, that would not contaminate what was truly important, essential, the safe little square of her existence. Now not everything was so clear; she couldn't stop to reflect much on it, but she seemed inclined to skip over those guarantees in favor of the risky exploration of the truth, if that thing actually existed. She was sorry, Blas, really, but he too would have to understand her. Esteban tried to take a cigarette out of the pack. The man at the typewriter stopped him with a whisper.

"I did know Mr. Almeida," admitted Don Blas with some slight embarrassment, but with the same visionary pride as a martyr facing a gang of lions. "We'd known each other for quite some time, ever since a friend of my neighbor, Alicia, introduced us. We were involved in business deals together, buying and selling watches, still lifes, so we saw each other with a certain frequency. I would regularly come by his shop after he closed. Last night, at about nine-thirty, I received a telephone call. A woman's voice told me I should visit Almeida immediately, we were going to finish off the deal we'd been working on."

"What deal was that?" interrupted Gálvez brusquely.

"I was surprised a woman called me," Blas Acevedo went on without reacting to the interruption. "I know that Almeida had a secretary who set up his appointments and kept his agenda in order, but he'd always contacted me himself. So I left the house, and it took me about twenty minutes to get to Puente y Pellón. I do have a lot of health problems—age never lets up on you—but my legs still work fine. The metal gate had been pulled down over the upper part of the front window. There was very little light inside, just a little lamp with a green glass shade near the counter. Everything suggested the shop was closed."

"Did you call out for someone to let you in?" asked the voice.

"Didn't have to," answered Blas with immense, crushing naturalness. "Whenever he expected me, Almeida would leave the door open. I walked in, just as I'd done many times before. It was dark, you could barely make out the things in the vitrines. The light from the green lamp gave everything a strange, ghostly air."

The dry dirt voice made a comment in which he praised Don Blas's capacity to create atmosphere for his descriptions. He'd just offered the ideal setting, in literary terms, for an atrocious crime, like the one they were all involved in. Blas Acevedo's mouth again twisted to compose that martyred smile, in zigzag, which Alicia didn't recognize in him. He confessed he'd spent his life reading detective novels, and that their atmospheric protocols had finally rubbed off on him.

"But," the old man went on as if piecing together a story he knew by heart, right down to the exact synchronization of glances and gestures, "I quickly realized that something was wrong. My nearsightedness would allow me to see only that there was a pile of mixed-up things on top of the counter. I took my glasses out of their case and carefully examined what it was: pieces from some shelf that had been smashed, a shotgun whose butt was covered with blood."

"You touched it," ordered the earthy voice. "Your fingerprints are on the shotgun."

"Yes," said Blas with a powerful brown stare. "I picked it up to bring it close to my eyes to verify that it really was blood. That's when I got nervous. I followed the path of objects that had been knocked down and went around the counter. Almeida was there, on the floor, in a small pool of blood. His head was twisted to the right in a very strange way, as if he were a clothes dummy."

"What did you do next?"

"I became very nervous." Don Blas's nostrils expanded. "My hands started to shake, my grip isn't as strong as it used to be. My glasses fell out of my hand, and I didn't realize it. I fled, yes I did. I was scared out of my wits and thought, overcome with fear, that no one had to know I'd been there."

In a slow interval of silence, Blas Acevedo scrutinized the darkness of the room with animal fixity, as if trying to drill through the black veil behind which the voices that answered his were hiding. Scratching her fingers, Alicia again told herself that the white head, covered with grooves, sliced off its trunk by the violent cone of light from the lamp, was far from being the amiable old man who on so many occasions had served her as a handkerchief or crutch, who had made afternoons less bitter. She felt that something was moving behind her in the office, that there was something like the sliding of furniture, when the dry-mud voice of Inspector Gálvez again rang out nearer the light and the sliced-off head, threateningly close.

"There is one question you haven't answered. What deal were you involved in with Rafael Almeida?"

The sinuous, wary smile again emerged from Don Blas's lips.

"Do I have to tell it to you again?"

"Repeat it."

The brown eyes turned to sweep bitterly through the parcel of darkness that was supposed to hide Esteban and Alicia.

"Well, my old-age pension doesn't go far," Don Blas began, nodding. "Not very far at all, especially if you have your vices. When I was young, I became fond of playing cards, nothing serious at first. It was when I retired, when I had to spend the whole day without knowing what to think about, that led me to this addiction. You know there are games where people gamble away their bank account, their furniture, their house."

"I can't believe it," whinnied Alicia.

"Believe it, my child," he said in an odious parody of his previous sweetness. "I lost money. Lots of money. My wife had valuable antiques, jewelry especially. Little by little, I emptied her writing desk, substituting the jewels with fakes ten times cheaper that I had made up whenever some small winning let me recover. Rafael Almeida was my usual buyer. I assure you he took a big cut for himself. My wife had necklaces that had once belonged to important families in the aristocracy of Seville."

"Lourdes knows nothing." Alicia breathed with difficulty.

"Of course not, child," answered Blas Acevedo to the curtain of darkness that had spoken to him. "She would die if I confessed to her. And I hope you won't be so cruel as to stab her in the back."

A cold serpent squirmed on Alicia's back. She understood that Blas was reproaching her, virtually throwing a glass of water in her face, her betrayal, her thanklessness. She bitterly wished she could light a cigarette.

"What deal did you have this time with Almeida?" asked Gálvez.

"The silver cutlery," said Don Blas, bowing his head and sketching a scribble in the air with his hand as a sign of farewell. "He was going to pay me well. But now you'll have to excuse me. I don't feel like saying anything else."

Inspector Gálvez led Esteban and Alicia out of the room. They both felt as if they'd been deafened by a roar that had broken their eardrums. The fluorescent light in the corridor hit them, and they had to drop their eyes to the floor while they hastily looked for cigarettes in their coat pockets. Gálvez's hand held out the lighter, then, in a worried way, rubbed the bald area that timidly stopped at the frontier of his ears. They walked slowly toward the coffee machine; none of the three daring to break the silence. Esteban noted, out of the corner of his eye, that a disorderly and fragile rain was again beginning to sprinkle the windows.

"All right," the inspector finally snorted before they'd reached the plastic ferns. "At first sight, this looks like a very simple case. Your neighbor, Blas, gives the cutlery to Almeida, but Almeida hasn't given him all he owes. Blas turns up at the time he knows Almeida will be alone and kills him to settle the bill. Then he's afraid because of what he's done and runs away, leaving his glasses behind. Almeida's secretary, whom we've also interrogated, says she did not call Don Blas that night, because she had the day off. And there were no calls from the shop to his number. It all seems to fit into the typical pattern of a murder for money, but I just don't believe it."

"Why?" asked Esteban, taking out his change. He only had enough for an espresso.

The inspector exhaled so energetically that his lip trembled in the current of air. He put a coin in the machine, holding his Winston in the corner of his mouth.

"You're better off with a cappuccino," he suggested. "No one can stomach the other stuff. You ask me why, and your little comedy goes on. Very well, you two can go on thinking I'm an asshole, but we all have our pride. I'll ask you a question: Why do you think I wanted you to witness the questioning. I don't know if Blas Acevedo killed the antiques dealer or not, but what's clear is that the motive here is something other than a simple matter of money. We still don't know why the page was torn out of the antiques year book or who the woman was who called Blas to involve him in the crime."

"Unless he's lying," Esteban said and stirred the mud-colored liquid the machine had spit out.

"Unless he's lying, of course." For the first time, Gálvez's eyes reached a temperature sufficiently unpleasant to disturb Alicia. "But I intuit, I don't know, that he's telling the truth. And I've also got the feeling that this death is related to the one that took place a few days ago, the death of that Catalan junk dealer, Benlliure. He died on the Acevedos' doorstep, which is, oddly enough, also yours, Alicia."

So it was not only she who suspected, not only Esteban who was capable of connecting the pieces. The figure was taking shape strangely, sketching itself out on the paper blow by blow, with dirty sweat and blood; the image was mysteriously appearing on the plate while it was being shifted back and forth in the revealing tank. One figure was closing, a polygon whose sides were coming together, allowing its principle edges to come to the surface. But the shape was not yet recognizable. With a rather brusque admonition to enjoy the coffee, Inspector Gálvez said good-bye and promised they'd all see each other again. With regard to Don Blas: It was possible the judge would recommend bail. By the time they reached the street it had stopped raining, but the sky was stained by a mob of swollen, red clouds. They walked away.

"What coincidences, yes indeed." Esteban blinked. "It turns out that Don Blas knew the guy forever, and we had no idea. And he says so just when he can't find any other way to justify his presence in the shop."

"Well, it was supposed to be a secret."

"Could it be true that one of your girlfriends introduced them? Marisa was a friend of Almeida."

"I didn't know that either."

They stepped into puddles silently. The neon sign from a hamburger shop was inverted in the small pool of water, more diminutive and hesitant.

"Blas's alibi is too innocent," murmured Esteban when they'd reached a closed café. "Too reasonable to believe it. I'd almost bet he left his glasses there on purpose. Do you remember 'The Purloined Letter?'"

"The what?" answered Alicia in a daze.

"We've got to go back to the classics, my child: Edgar Allan Poe. That story about the hidden letter, which at the end turns out to be on the mantel or on a table, I don't remember which."

"Yes, sure. What about it?"

"Think back. The story begins with a digression about two boys playing a game where one has to guess how many stones the other is holding in his hand. One of the boys begins by hiding two stones. When they play the game a second time, he doesn't know how many stones to hide. He calculates what his opponent might be thinking. No doubt the opponent will think he's going to hide only one because he's just hidden two and wouldn't be so stupid as to repeat the same play. But a calculation elevated to the second power is also possible. Since the opponent will believe he's going to hide one, he will hide two as he did the first time, even if it seems the stupidest thing. It's thinking in the mirror. That's what Blas did."

"Think so?" Alicia looked at him with the eyes of a virgin ascending to glory.

"Of course," Esteban said, then stopped. A street person was snoring under a cardboard box nearby. "What's the most skillful way to manage being thought innocent of a crime? By planting an eloquent number of clues against yourself. Alicia, Blas killed that guy. And he killed him because of everything he knew about da Alpiarça and the angel."

She snorted. "Esteban."

"Yes, yes." He was putting another cigarette between his lips. "The dream led you to learn about a sect's obscure secret, Alicia, a sect that occupies the block where you live. The upstairs neighbors, who want to hear you. Nuria, who hides the figure. Lourdes, who gives you juice to make you sleep. Someone with a key who dismantles your apartment. Benlliure, I don't know how, but by means of your dream, knows about you and comes to give you the angel. Benlliure chased you, wanted to communicate something to you. Someone kills him, but he manages to hand his angel over to us. Little by little, we gather together the inscriptions, closely followed. They, whoever they may be, are right behind us, they know every move we make. They've been leaving us clues, but always warning us that we're picking them up with their consent and only because they expressly desire it. The book deliberately put on the wrong shelf in the library that ultimately turns up, Benlliure who dies but who can still hand over the piece, the antiques dealer murdered only after revealing the inscription on the fourth angel and telling where to find the first . . . They want us to solve the puzzle."

"Why?"

"That I don't know, but they're pushing us forward little by little. And what else is there for us to do? We'll have to resolve this enigma just to see what we find. We're inside the figure, Alicia, and we can't escape."

It was true. She had to admit it once and for all. She was hemmed in, trapped in the closed domino game of her dream, and escape was impossible. To bring about an opening she would have to submit herself in a disciplined way to the rules of the game, let herself be carried away by the enemy's tide to find out on which beach the landing was set to take place. Taking military strides, Esteban was crossing Plaza del Duque with a cigarette between his teeth. He stopped at the statue of Velázquez, washed by the rain.

"Maybe it would be better if you left your apartment for a while," he said. "You could move in with Mom and me."

"I don't think it's a good idea, Esteban." Alicia was annoyed at having to go over that matter again. "I'd rather stay in my own place. We'll see what happens."

"Is it because of Mom or because of me?"

"Cut it out, Esteban."

Sooner or later, she'd have to face that alternative, she'd have to turn the corner and decide which path to take, because Esteban had savagely grasped the hand her irresponsibility had held out to him on a night when it was more important to allow herself to be lulled to sleep than to think about the infinite lines into which life multiplies itself. Something at about the same place as her diaphragm, something that lived together with her viscera, something that was as intimate a part of her as the marrow in her bones and certain fears she could not renounce, wanted to banish that substitute once and for all, to forget the idea of replacing Pablo with a younger, more-in-love puppy version of him; but her intelligence, the room within her with more light and better equipment, had insisted on holding out her hand, on allowing him to go on hoping. They said good-bye under two lightning flashes that were the prelude to a new storm: Velázquez's face became covered with wax or porcelain. From a distance, almost at the corner of La Campana, Esteban seemed to Alicia a poor, troubled little turtle.

Eight

It was then she really felt she was at the edge of the abyss, that her fingers were trembling on the handrail, and that her stomach was beginning to anticipate the vertigo of the fall, the long, black esophagus that would take her to some place in the depths, her hair burning over the nape of her neck and her ears, and her arms striking out blindly in the air. Then, suddenly, at the bottom, where the chimney ended, once again, there was the same boulevard, with photographic precision, the same sidewalks, the same identical walls like sentinels flanking her first terrorized steps, her hesitations, the final decision to turn aside to touch the walls or examine details—arabesques, stucco-work clearer than before, more solid, more real, and thicker than ever, so distant from that defective, cloud-in-a-puddle glimpse she'd had until then, as if the avenue and the pediments and the streetlights and the robots had not until that moment been any more than sketches for a drawing which only now had been made, only now became definitive and exact.

Now the city was pounding at her five senses, drowning them, overwhelming them, proposing drawings over the doors, drawings that until this night had been only disorganized scrawls, scattering in the air shreds of the green scent of wet trees that her sense of smell had always, inexplicably, resigned itself not to notice. The edges of the buildings were as sharp and violent as knives; wrinkles and expressions covered the faces of statues which before had been indifferent and anonymous. Each star staining the night's lid was recognizable and distinct, so that it would be impossible to lose it among the tide of constellations and luminaries, the shadows the streetlights projected were not reduced to that crude, black paste they'd thrown until that moment at the feet of objects. Instead they possessed subtle, gaseous gradations of grays, chiaroscuros. The patent leather of her shoes was more metallic than ever, she was more wide awake in her dream than ever, to the point that for an instant she feared that the city had finally passed through definitively by mocking the controls and leaping the barrier. She feared that, without knowing it, she was strolling on the wrong side of the border.

She could feel her thoughts with total clarity, perceive how the premises were finding one another and joining together with the same affinity as side roads flowing into the main street. If wakefulness and sleep can be told apart only by slight shades of sharpness, the city deserved, with all propriety, entry into that world outside, the world above, the world of toothbrushes and coffee in the pot just before knotting one's tie. She walked slowly, rejoicing over the sound of each footfall, attentive to the multiplied echo the soles of her shoes raised at the corners; she stopped opposite windows and saw how the shadows smoked, read, asked one another to dance; she explored intersections whose existence she'd never noticed before and that led her, after an intricate investigation, to the same spot where she'd begun.

She visited the palace of the Muses, the observatory, the academies, and the ministries. Biting her lip, her fear not allowing her to manage her feet with all the speed she desired, she approached, little by little, the enormous plaza, more enormous, more deserted, more lunar than ever. The pavilions seemed to her a cemetery of infinite facades that obsessively repeated the same progression of windows or niches until it erased them in the distance. She heard the reptile hiss of the wind, felt it play its blades over her face.

At the center, the angel awaited her like the prince presiding over a reception of legatees. She saw him grow gigantic as she approached, become heavier, become a frozen, black bird. When she was before him, she tried to look into his eyes, but they were occupied in something else. They were traveling over the city, flying over the towers and roofs, sinking into the night like emissaries of an impenetrable will. She wasn't afraid. She spoke his name, *Mahazael,* pronounced each one of the syllables, which she recognized easily, inscribed into the pedestal. Then the vertigo returned. The night became a funnel turned upside down where the stars finally slipped through. She understood that she was being called elsewhere. She again perceived the rubbing on her skin, that breath of a sleeping animal, and the chimney picked her up again and she fell on the opposite side: above, toward the bog of sheets, the taste of bitter saliva and dirty ashtray, where, disconcerted, she saw in red numbers that it was barely fifteen minutes before five.

...

She couldn't get there in time because she hadn't finished brushing her teeth, and the ringing of the telephone caught her with the plastic bristles tangled in her gums. She ran down the hall as fast as she could, trampling more fragments of ashtray and shards of glass. She'd just managed to knock the telephone off the back of the sofa, where she'd set it up. When she put the receiver to her ear, there was only the intermittent beep of a dial tone in her ear. She suspected nothing until the phone rang again. This time the telephone was at hand because she'd decided to improvise a jigsaw puzzle with the pieces of an Oriental vase and had only to stretch out her arm to know that her picking up and the other side's hanging up were almost simultaneous—a kind of crackling of brown paper and then again that intermittent siren in her ear. The third call took place while she was in the kitchen. She walked slowly to the living room, taking her time, giving that anonymous hand the opportunity to abort the attempt before the wires again connected their two mouths. This time the unknown caller did not hang up. Over a dense curtain of silence, Alicia asked twice who was calling. Her words disappeared in that void; the connection was broken again after a few seconds.

Returning to the kitchen to finish watering the *conibras,* Alicia shrugged her shoulders. The three consecutive calls could simply be a mistake, a pay phone that swallows the coins before the connection is made, something like that. But the more suspicious part of herself, that double who had gradually been awakening while her doubts about her neighbors took flight, suggested, doubtlessly aided by examples from movies, that someone could also be calling her to see if she was at home, alone in her apartment, a fact that would allow or prohibit who knew what kind of subsequent operation.

She shook her head. She refused to go on thinking, refused to allow these arguments to go on galloping unbridled through her head. She put the pots under the tap. But Esteban had recognized the night before, the night before her new dream, purer and more transparent than ever, that there could exist a kind of conspiracy, a secret strategy among people who knew her, no matter how absurd and crazy the idea might seem to her, which it did. She shut the faucet and sat down on the kitchen table with a cigarette nervously trapped between her lips. The window opened over the interior courtyard, over the crisscrossed clotheslines; from one window below hers came the sound of water pouring into Nuria's sink. She was running water into some receptacle. She remembered the scene she'd made the previous day in Nuria's kitchen, practicing ballet on the table, and she was attacked by an annoying combination of tenderness and shame. She did not know whether Nuria deserved her terror and suspicion or not, but she did not reject the reasons that urged her to make her way to the window and climb up the clothesline.

Reason repeated that there was nothing to be afraid of, that a plot like the one Esteban had woven, obeying the most liberal suggestions of his fantasy and fed by all that shock literature he loved to consume, would eventually collapse under its own weight. Too bad reason was so nearsighted, so deaf, so incapable of assembling the figures despite having all the pieces on the table, impeded by its own protocols, by its dumb, scientific, and moral obligations. While she was still smoking her cigarette standing at the window, something other than reason pressured her to leave the apartment immediately without entangling herself any longer in pros and cons. She accepted that warning the way one accepts a promise or a diagnosis, feeling that things will take place as someone has dictated and cannot take place any other way.

Into her bag she tossed her cigarettes, her sunglasses, her French novel, and her wallet—never checking to see if she was short on cash. While she was pushing the elevator button, stubbornly red—the retired gentleman on the fifth floor loved to spend the day on the terrace waving to people—she asked herself what her real motive was for running away. What was provoking her to abandon her flat this way, as if she wanted nothing to do with an annoying date she'd prefer to avoid? And as she tripped her way down the stairs, she answered herself saying she was trying to avoid a hand, free herself from the threads of a threat, pull her foot out of an invisible trap that, without knowing why, she sensed was closer and closer to her shoes. She was entering the mezzanine when the elevator opened with a kind of flutter, and Nuria appeared standing inside it, opposite the mirror, stuffed into her leather pea jacket, like a doll inside its box that the little girl hasn't dared to unwrap. Running into Alicia seemed to slow her down, calm the urgency with which she'd pushed the elevator door. As she walked over to say hello, Alicia noticed that something had broken in the space between their eyes, something had dynamited the bridge that connected them.

"Hi," said Alicia with the spontaneity of an actor on a TV soap opera. "Where are you off to?"

"Cigarettes," Nuria grumbled without completely looking at her, advancing on the three stairs that separated them from the door. "I don't have a single cigarette, which means it's impossible to work."

"I'll give you one of mine, if you like."

"Black tobacco? Never, for God's sake." A wormish smile illuminated Nuria's features for a second. "Thanks all the same."

Nuria's last sentence sounded so courteous and polite that Alicia was tempted to slap her face. The day, above the sidewalk at the entrance, was wide and cold; there were no clouds to interfere with the sky. The porter's booth was empty. A magazine open to a soccer player dressed in white was patiently waiting for José to finish his errands. Held back by words that didn't want to be spoken, somehow Alicia and Nuria could not manage to part. For an instant, something seemed about to jump from the trampoline of Nuria's lips, but that intention rapidly dissipated. What her lips did whisper was: "Bye now, stay well."

She had no intention to become a spy; her brain as yet hadn't found the cure that could neutralize the disquiet left by the hang-up calls. With a kind of automatism, her feet led her to the bar on the other side of the street; just as mechanically, she ordered coffee and anisette and sat down at a table that gave her a panoramic view of the entrance to her building through the glass and the backward ads for fish and chips. She'd never situated herself that way, facing her own doorway, taking unfair advantage of the anonymity of the voyeur or hidden camera which allowed her to peek into the spontaneity of people and events free of all premeditation, free of the varnish of simulation or suspicion that taints all encounters, all words.

She saw a man enter carrying portfolios whom she nebulously identified as her upstairs neighbor; she saw that José went out and came back loaded down with hammers; she saw two Jehovah's Witnesses cross the threshold strangled by their ties; she saw Lourdes leave, and something pinched her heart. Down what miserable ramp had Esteban's suspicion made her slide, in what latrine was she tossing her peace of mind, the comforting words, the warmth of hands with which she could caress the future? She wondered if everything she'd heard Don Blas say the previous afternoon could possibly be real or if he'd lied, or if she'd dreamed it. The Blas of her past and that unknown, cornered man in the police station were as dissimilar as a face and the memory that reconstructs it.

Barely a chestnut-colored circumference remained in her coffee cup when she realized, without intending to, that Nuria was taking much too long to buy a simple pack of cigarettes. After all, there was a tobacco shop just one block up. Reason and instinct were sharing her brain equally, each contradicting the conclusions of the other, like the waves that continually wipe out the words we write in the sand.

A sudden attack of prudence made her wonder why she hadn't called Esteban or Marisa or Mamá Luisa to see if one of them had tried to contact her by telephone instead of that ghost supposedly threatening her. She asked herself if it made sense to talk about a conspiracy, if she should, as a preventive measure, abandon the apartment, if the decidedly unnerving facts in Blas's supposed crime could be part of a conspiracy, and what about Nuria's hiding the angel, her dream, Lourdes's juice, and the apartment trashed and turned upside down? But if that's the way it was, why didn't these people act, why didn't they pass to action and bite, what did they expect from her, what signal were they waiting for? She wouldn't have hesitated to pay the price for discovering in one fell swoop that all her neighbors belonged to a secret plot if that would resolve the uncertainty in which she debated these issues.

With her second sip of anisette, she once again focused on the entryway. A new figure was demanding her attention:

A woman dressed entirely in black was pushing her buzzer. Alicia narrowed her eyes so the distance wouldn't trick her; it was her number, no doubt about it, and the woman's black gloves pushed it every five seconds, spurred by an urgency that was difficult to conceal. Alicia did not recognize the woman. A long, black, tubular overcoat covered her down to her black knees. Sunglasses erased her face sheltered under a cap of black cloth. She moved like a shadow, like an insect, like the invisible man in the movie, covered by her disguise.

Suddenly, like being slapped, Alicia realized that this woman was the one who'd made the three calls. Her heart grew braver, and the anisette and the cigarette ceased to be important. Her green eyes traveled along the street, fixed themselves like pins onto the black woman who would look back and forth and push the button calculating her movements with the suspicious care of a fugitive. A woman dressed in black, a concealed, clandestine woman. Yes, that's it, there was a woman involved in this entire matter, a latent and continuous presence that never came to the surface. Hitchcock in a Hitchcock movie, passing through without seeing himself, all the while being the person who governs the intrigue. A woman telephoned Benlliure; a woman told Don Blas to come to the antiques shop, a woman; a woman wearing a red wig passed for Marisa at her house. The members of the conspiracy gathered around a woman, the papess, Satan's concubine. A woman seemed to be the nucleus of the enigma, the heart of the mystery, perhaps the same woman in black Alicia continued to observe without breathing and who now, after furtively sweeping the two flanks of the entryway with her eyes, ascended the three steps and went into the mezzanine with the same forced ease of a badly trained animal.

The decision burst out of Alicia's tormented will before her cigarette had finished burning on the saucer. She paid without looking at the coins and walked out onto the street to receive the lash of a metallic, cold wind. As she crossed the sidewalk, she tripped over a student carrying a portfolio who spit out an insult. She did not stop outside the entryway even though José was coming back from somewhere carrying screwdrivers and raised his hand in a kind of admonitory greeting. She had to find out if that woman, the woman in black, had gone up to her apartment. The elevator was available, but she rejected it—because seeing herself imprisoned inside that oblong box would make her feel that she was putting off, floor by floor, the essential meeting. She dashed up the stairs two at a time, with her pulse dripping in her temple, with her mind as empty as an unused cassette: a rapid eternity of silence.

The future and its plans concluded in the imminent collision with the unknown woman. Her imagination could not manage to go beyond that; she had no idea what would take place beyond the beacon guarded by that mysterious black silhouette. Her lungs were wheezing in her chest like a broken accordion when she stopped to survey her landing: The door to her apartment was correctly shut, neither Lourdes nor her other neighbor was visible, and over the stairway there reigned a crushing appearance of normalcy. She went up the last stairs with her nerves completely on edge, expecting to run into the black figure at any turn, perhaps expecting her to detach herself from the solid black shadows the ceiling lamp projected over the wall and the tiles.

She stopped outside her door, listened closely, held her breath. The absence of signs only alarmed her more. The woman could have gone to an upper floor, she could have given up, she could be on the terrace, she could be visiting a friend who was not Alicia, whose number she might have mistakenly pushed downstairs. Even so, a kind of irresistible sense of fatality forced her to take her keys out of her purse, insert them into the door lock, and slowly turn the knob, her eyes never leaving the blue and yellow carpet. The same unknown force took control of her head and made it reconnoiter the barely half-closed kitchen and the vestibule where the first constellations of broken porcelain began.

She took a step. A piece of glass crackled under her foot with the voice of a frog suffering from a cold. The sunlight stamped itself on the balcony window, clearly outlining the sofa's profile, an upside-down armchair, the speakers, and the shape of a feminine presence, unmistakable in the curvature of the hips, a presence that was holding something heavy in its right hand.

Alicia dizzily thought it was she, that she'd entered her apartment, that she had to speak to her, that she seemed to guess what the thing was she held in her hand. The silhouette, warned by the sound of the door and the crushed glass, had turned cautiously toward the vestibule, allowing a ray of light to reveal the fact that her fingers were squeezed around a black metal object. Alicia's heart needed no further details. It made her flee with her brain short-circuited from surprise and horror. It occurred to her that continuing to go upstairs could provide her with a chance for salvation. She ran up ferociously, abusing her legs, paying no attention to pain or anguish. That escape maliciously imitated the plot of her cruelest childhood nightmares: being chased up a labyrinth of stairs that never ended, chased by a rhythm of footsteps that never turned into a body, but which constituted a warning about an unbearable presence that was trying to annihilate her. As in that terrifying scenario of years gone by, Alicia began to hear that rhythm below her, one or two landings below her, high heels that were pounding stairs in pursuit of her. A quick glance into the stairwell confirmed that the black phantom was following her, that she'd accepted her role in Alicia's game, in the choreography of hunter and prey. She felt that fear was deflating her thoughts, but that her knees were strong.

The metal door that led to the terrace was open; the lock had been eaten away by rust years earlier. Enraged, Alicia pushed it and found herself surrounded by antennas and towers on top of an asymmetrical chessboard of red tiles soaked by the recent rain. She ran, perhaps with the secret intention of flying when there were no more tiles to run on. She slipped. Her hip and her ribs received a kind of gray impact, her breathing receded. Out of the corner of her eye, she saw that the black shadow was about to leap onto her. She tried to drag herself away and couldn't. Then she shut her eyes and saw Rosita with pigtails in the vestibule, the image she'd always retained photographically in her memory so she could take refuge in it before abandoning this world.

...

She felt a bare hand clutching her by the arm. She felt herself get up, felt that her muscles were drowning, incapable of putting up any more resistance. She felt that the hand, before pain came back to her leg and side, was trying to caress her forehead. The voice that reached her ears made her wish, like a breeze, to have a cradle where she could fall asleep, clean sheets, a sweet lavender perfume with which to impregnate the drawers where she kept clothing.

"Alicia, have you gone insane? What were you going to do, jump down to the street?"

Marisa's black mane had poured tumultuously over the lapels of her black overcoat, and her horrified black eyes were contemplating Alicia's face. For her part, Alicia didn't know if she should die of relief or shame. She let herself be helped up and limped her way to one of the poles holding up a clothesline. The sheets of her neighbors were fluttering in the air to the rhythm of a tide. Marisa offered her a cigarette, which she took without putting up any resistance; she accepted the metal lighter, which the treacherous light of the balcony had made her think was a pistol; she laughed, releasing in the fragile giggle all the anguish that had suffocated her; she puffed, more thankful than ever for the taste of smoke. Only then did she become aware how bizarre it was that Marisa, of all people, had offered her the cigarette.

"Forgive me, Alicia, forgive me, I beg you." Marisa swallowed the smoke with not a hint of prudishness. "I called, but I couldn't speak with you. I rang your buzzer, but you didn't answer. I let myself in using the key you gave me so I could wait until you came, because I have to talk to you, have to talk to you."

Marisa, her voice shattered, was on the verge tears. No, she wouldn't cry, but she had cried before, a very short while ago. Alicia was sorry to think it, but she did have the sense that Marisa was taking too much advantage of the fact that she had the key; how could Alicia be sure that Marisa wasn't there a few days before turning drawers upside down. But there were so many questions to answer; adding yet another to the list seemed useless to her. Marisa, her fingers trembling around the cigarette, seemed willing to offer answers on the spot.

"I know you must be asking yourself a ton of questions, Alicia"—Marisa wouldn't look her in the eye. "What could justify my turning up this way in your apartment dressed this way?"

"I have no idea," replied Alicia, showing no mercy.

"And I'm even smoking." Marisa inhaled. "I'm sorry, I know I've pestered you a thousand times with sermons about how bad tobacco is, but I think I need it. Yes, I really need it because of nerves and things. I stole a pack from Joaquín and ran out of the house before he could follow me. He's been very suspicious for two or three days, constantly keeping his eye on me. I think he knows what's happening. I called you from home, but he was right there, so I couldn't talk. I put on all this black shit, the hat and the glasses, so no one would recognize me. I had to see you, but I didn't want him to know about it. No one should know about it. Poor Joaquín."

"Marisa"—Alicia adopted an imperative tone, appropriate for important conversations—"what's wrong with you?"

"This morning I found out listening to the radio." Marisa's voice again weakened, became liquid. "Someone murdered Rafael Almeida."

"Yes, that's true. What about it?"

Silence and some strategic wailing eloquently expressed why Marisa was devastated by Rafael Almeida's death. It also explained Joaquín's suspicion, her futile dedication to astrology or special diets: the search for the absolutely necessary child through paths matrimony had closed to her. Alicia knew, because Esteban or perhaps Marisa herself had made some offhand reference to it, that she and Almeida knew each other, that she'd bought things from him, that from time to time there appeared on the walls of her apartment antiques whose value was outrageous, objects that were perhaps worth more than she had in the bank.

Alicia wasn't annoyed by the silence, the lie through omission committed by not confiding the whole truth to a friend, this piece of Marisa's life that had just emerged from the waters after a strict silence. But Alicia now found she was starting to get used to her stupid little girl's deafness to the secrets of others, secrets other people had decided she couldn't digest because of her emotional immaturity. Now, nothing from the past importuned her; the present was much more urgent and bothersome, transformed into a thick violet pain in her thigh and ribs.

"How long had this been going on, Marisa?"

"Two years," hiccuped Marisa, puffing at the cigarette. "Don't ask me if he was better than Joaquín, he certainly wasn't. Or he was, I don't know. The fact is I decided not to discard either of them, and now destiny has done the job for me."

"How did it begin?"

"With the porcelain vase I have in the living room. Remember? I bought it from him. You know I've always been mad about old porcelain. He found things for me, and I could see how detail conscious he was. I don't know, Joaquín is good and obedient, but sometimes I feel that as far as he's concerned I don't deserve any more attention than a piece of furniture. Rafael took me out to dinner, there were even secret trips, well, you can probably imagine."

"I can imagine," Alicia concluded modestly.

"I had to tell you about it, Alicia, I just had to confide in you. I heard the news, and it screwed up something here, in my chest. I was asphyxiated, I was going to die, and Joaquín was staring at me, wondering if the coffee had done something to me. Hearing the news was like being stabbed. Can you forgive me for having hidden it from you all this time?"

"I'll get over it."

"Thanks." Marisa squeezed Alicia's hand, not as warm as she'd hoped. "I know I should have told you everything before, you of all people. But the two of us decided to keep it secret, not only because of Joaquín. We barely allowed ourselves to be seen on the street, barely in the yoga classes, those dinners I told you about, the movies. Everything turned out much better when everything was kept in its place."

"Could you do it?" asked Alicia without much conviction. "I mean, put each one in his pigeonhole and not allow him to get out."

"Yes, I know what you mean." A touch of distrust brightened Marisa's eyes. "To you dividing a life this way seems artificial and even horrible—forks on one side of the drawer so they don't get mixed up with the spoons, everything in its proper place so it won't disrupt the healthy flow of existence. I know that for you I'm nothing more than a bit of that, health and order, nasty balance, no cholesterol, no excesses, no promiscuity, everything hygienic and boringly perfect."

"You're the one who's saying it," answered Alicia without contradicting her.

"Okay, you're right. I cried, but I won't cry anymore. I didn't know if I had to cry. I don't know what the protocol of feelings orders in such a case. I don't know if I cried for him, for myself, or for Joaquín. It goes without saying of course, but I hope you'll understand that this conversation has to remain strictly between you and me."

"Of course."

Alicia found no response to give. She supposed that all of the handy words of consolation were too hackneyed, that they were like stained handkerchiefs, and that perhaps silence would seem more friendly. She essayed a light but forced caress of Marisa's black hair and smiled. But she still had something to ask.

"Was it really Don Blas?" Marisa's voice woke up with a snort. "The morning newspaper gave his first initial and his last name. Did he do it?"

"I don't know," said Alicia. "He was questioned."

"Life's ironies. I talked to him about Rafael and sent him to the shop. One of the two tiny times I ever spoke with him. He asked me advice about a piece he wanted to have appraised or something. I sent him to the shop, and he kills Rafael. It's as if I'd killed him a little myself, isn't it? An intermediary."

"Forget about it."

Alicia's arm over her shoulder was warmer and more sincere. They walked back to the stairs. They'd need Palm of the Prince more than ever that midday.

...

There were many reasons why the obligatory visit to the little apartment on Francos Street was unappealing, and not only the fact of having to stand guard like a statue for an hour or two, while the coffee got cold or the TV soap opera finished, over the old woman's crumpled body, encrusted on the sofa with her anguished, lizardlike breathing. If it came to that, Alicia could even overlook her repugnancies, but the apartment harassed her with a circus of atrocities so difficult to put up with that they fatally transformed the Saturday visit into a calvary forced on her by compassion or by a masochistic variation of habit she'd agreed to respect. She recalled having repeated it to herself that Saturday while she calmly walked up the four flights that served as a prologue to the vestibule, the horrible vestibule from which she received the greeting—like a whiplash—of Pablo's face slapped by some summer smile on the sideboard. She walked up the steps one by one with her hand on the rail—the metal was cold, her thigh hurt with an elastic pain—and again asked herself about the inertia that ordered her to go on obeying the date of the visits, to go on taking her place on the same sofa with the poppy or sunflower or who-knows-what pattern, discreetly averting her eyes so she wouldn't face the other photo, the one she'd hide in the twinkling of an eye among the panoramic views of Paris or the muscular young men wearing togas, because that other photo, much more than the one that received her from the vestibule with its vexing smile, did indeed constitute a violence, an express declaration of war against her battered, half-ruined tranquillity.

This old woman, whose life was filled with absence, this old woman Alicia had learned to detest, knew perfectly well that Alicia had swept her apartment clean of all photos of Rosa and stuffed them into a bulging garbage bag that would help her to bog down less in the swamps of memory. Alicia could not stand the watchfulness of that face, of those eyes locked behind the glass and inside the frame as if lost under the surface of a lake Alicia could only touch with the tips of her fingers. Nevertheless, Mamá Luisa kept it on the shelf, perpetually in front of the encyclopedia and the copper watch paralyzed at five-fifteen, perhaps to suggest with all the concealed cruelty with which she usually did it that the child or her mirage went on observing her from somewhere, reproaching her for trying to forget.

For this reason, whenever Alicia entered with her two kisses and the half dozen cookies for diabetics, she would strategically choose the armchair with its back to the books, even if the television set required a complicated twisting of neck and shoulders, and amid the storm of themes and commentaries the old woman brought up, she would concentrate on contemplating the balcony and the flowerpots. Mamá Luisa was fascinated by *conibras,* knew that Alicia's grew healthy and svelte, and lamented, somewhat theatrically, that even though she'd tried to cultivate them on several occasions they barely lasted two weeks. Alicia would repeat—although she was never sure the old woman listened to her—that tenderness was essential.

"Mamá, you have to water them and caress them, so they understand that you love them. They're very sensitive about things like that. If they realize you're doing it without wanting to, they refuse to live. They starve themselves to death."

Certainly, Alicia thought, the *conibras* must intuit that life demands a certain minimum level of quality below which it made no sense to go on being stuck in the flowerpot, abandoned to the fatuity of the future. She hadn't, but, at the same time, she never accepted the hand that wanted to protect and caress her. And that hand belonged to Esteban, who, at ten minutes before seven, turned up half an hour late wearing his still soaking wet parka from the previous night and with a kind of hidden thought in the back rooms of his eyes. He walked over to kiss Mamá Luisa and received from Alicia the pressure of her fingers on the nape of his neck, an ambiguous gesture that could be interpreted with the same degree of surprise as a caress or as a sign of disapproval.

"Excuse my lateness, girls," Esteban said, fixing his shirt collar after tossing the parka into the sink. "I came straight from the watchmaker. It seems the bastard will need at least two years to fix Dad's watch."

"The thing about that watch," Alicia laughed, "is that it's ready for the junkyard, and here you are expecting miracles."

"Very good sources have told me that this watchmaker has salvaged other lost causes." Esteban carefully omitted any references to his sources. "His name is Berruel. His little shop is in the Plaza del Pan and it always stinks of sulphur. Near the antiques shop you and I know. Like a coffee?"

Alicia's stomach had barely had time enough to digest the first coffee, but the convincing twist in Esteban's eyebrows told her that a trip to the kitchen was obligatory. She crossed the vestibule without looking right or left with two cups in her hand; Esteban was waiting for her next to the counter pensively puffing on a Fortuna. His shirt collar wasn't quite straight, even if he'd tried, just moments before, to negotiate a more or less balanced relationship between his sweater and his neck. Alicia straightened things out with a mother's attentive hands, in the same way Esteban had seen her adjust Rosa's uniform before the child went to school, the same way someone arranges the costume on a manikin or a doll rather than the way one would dress a person, a thing that breathes, spits, and gets dirty. This sudden attempt at closeness, having Alicia right under his nose correcting his collar, brought on a cramp in the base of his esophagus. Of course, any prox-imity could be taken advantage of to take a big bite, but he suspected a secret strategy would materialize if he were to leave himself open to enemy fire.

"Did you get soaked last night?" she asked suddenly, slapping him mercilessly with her eyes.

"Just a little," he answered, stepping back. "Well, my parka got wet, you probably saw that, but nothing serious. I got home, put Mom to bed, went to bed myself, but couldn't sleep."

"You couldn't sleep." That information seemed to arouse in Alicia's mind the need to say something. "But I did sleep, Esteban, and I was down there again."

"In the city?" Esteban stepped forward and was again so close that he could smell the coffee on her breath.

"Yes," she said distractedly. "It was clearer and sharper than ever. I saw everything perfectly, just as I'm seeing you now, as if I were awake. After all that insomnia, now this."

"The juice," said Esteban, smoking with passion. "Did you discover anything new?"

"No, it was the usual stuff, but more detailed, that's for sure. How do you think the dreams come to me?"

"Flying?"

"Yes." She dropped the cups into the sink and turned on the water with a karate chop. "Last night you said there was a possible relationship between the fact that my neigh-bors were part of this supposed conspiracy and the fact that I started dreaming about this damn city. Do you think I inter-rupted a private party or something like that, that I jumped over the fence without anyone's allowing me to go in?"

"Something like that."

"What I've been thinking might seem stupid to you," said Alicia, leaving the handles of the cups irreproachably clean, "but if this has something to do with getting to the bottom of dreams, maybe I should consult an expert."

"A psychoanalyst?" Esteban spoke through his cigarette. "I thought Mamen had already warned you about the evils of Dr. Freud."

"You didn't understand me." The cups were scurrying around in her hands. "I'm talking about a fortune-teller. A few days ago, Marisa left me a card: chiromancy, cartomancy, oneiromancy, fancymancy, and shmancymancy. It's near the Alameda, we can take a walk."

"Yes, but you'll have to go alone," said Esteban from the door, next to the calendar with a photo of the Alhambra. "Come here, I have to show you something."

Mamá Luisa was floating in the images on the TV screen (a man and a woman followed mutual slaps with an enormous, voracious kiss), so she couldn't see how Esteban and Alicia ran from the vestibule to the hall, where the two parallel series of hunting-trophy cases began, with those gray bird cadavers. Alicia never knew if they were partridges or pigeons. She didn't follow Esteban to his room at the end of the corridor, from which he returned after a brief tumult of things stirred up with a wrinkled piece of paper in his fingers. He extended it to Alicia. The diagonal light from the living room barely allowed her to decipher a confused skein of names and arrows.

"I'm going to Lisbon tomorrow, first thing," Esteban informed her, lowering his voice below that of the leading man on the television show, who swore he'd never return. "I'm going to visit Sebastião Adimanta."

"To Lisbon," Alicia repeated in the same tone she'd use if she'd just discovered the true identities of the three wise men.

"Look at the paper." He pointed to something within that ocean of wrinkles and folds. "We have the inscriptions on three of the angels, but we're missing one. The missing inscription is in Lisbon, and I'm not going to ask them to fax it to me."

Her long-suffering eyes, by pushing the darkness toward the corridor, discovered they already knew three of the lines they'd scrawled down from the folio.

ע .AZAZEL. ╫ HUMANAQUE.HOMINES. TESIDRV.AETAESME. IN.INSAENE.EUMPTE

ש .AZAEL. ⊶ .DENTE. DRACO. TGIVGERED. ROAGD. MGEGD. MVTEE . . .

ק .MAHAZAEL. ╬ .MAGNA.PARTE. BISSCSV.VEISEI.PHEISEIOETI.ISSIE . . .

"We're missing an essential fragment of the message," said Esteban as he touched his chin. "But there is a relationship we never noticed until now, look how stupid we are, a relationship that doesn't clear things up much but which could provide some clues. Look at the elements in each inscription. A Hebrew letter, the name of an angel, a little sign we don't recognize, two words in Latin, five in that language that sounds like clucking, the Greek exorcism."

"Right, that's what we have." The sea of wrinkles trembled in Alicia's hand.

"The two words in Latin." He stared at her as if he were digging under her eyelashes. "Don't they sound familiar?

Don't you know them from somewhere? *Humanaque homines, dente draco, magna parte.* That's the beginning of the three final verses of the poem you discovered in the book, the one with the dragon biting his tale. Remember?"

With a spark between her eyebrows, Alicia remembered the engraving: an elusive, circular monster, dragging itself through the dust of a post-disaster landscape stained with ruins and crevices. Esteban had salvaged those verses in his hand and with them their enigmatic translation: *Dira fames Polypos docuit sua rodere crura,/ Humanaque homines se nutriisse dape. /Dente Draco caudam dum mordet et ingerit alvo,/ Magna parte sui sit cibus ipse sibi.*

"*Terrible hunger taught the Polypos to gnaw their legs,*" she read, savoring each word as if it were a spice, "*and taught men to nourish themselves from human things. The dragon bites his tail with his teeth and throws it into his stomach so that a great part of himself will be his own food.* So there exists a relationship between these verses and the inscriptions on the angels."

"Yes, an inscription that also contains an exorcism." Esteban went through his pockets in search of cigarettes: shit, the kitchen. "Inácio da Alpiarça and Achille Feltrinelli were friends in Lisbon. In Italy, Feltrinelli was the leader of the famous sect of the *Coniurati,* and da Alpiarça prayed to the devil to save his rhinoceros. Both were connected to a sect that worshiped Satan through a mysterious woman, the papess. The *Mysterium Topographicum* is the detailed description of a city—we don't know if it ever existed, but the *Coniurati* were sure they'd meet there. In that city, there are four plazas with four angels that da Alpiarça sculpted with four inscriptions. And it turns out that the content of the inscriptions leads, at least in part, to a poem that closes Feltrinelli's book."

"Each point leads to the others," Alicia admitted, drawing a fleeting geometric form in the air. "As it would in a circle."

"The circle of the dragon," Esteban answered with flashing eyes. *Dente draco caudam dum mordet et ingerit alvo.* Why does the inscription on the pedestals point toward those verses? There's more. What does that poem mean? *To teach men to feed on human things.* Cannibalism?"

"Silly." She smiled, and the oppressive tension in the air relaxed its cords. "So you're going to Lisbon and leaving me alone."

"It will be for only three or four days." Esteban's fingers needed a cigarette. "I want to see Adimanta, see the angel, chat with him. Apparently, he's a specialist in occultism, and maybe he knows something about Feltrinelli or da Alpiarça. As to the trip—Lisbon is cheap, and I can always skim some of the money I've got saved up to buy an apartment. I suppose you can look after Mama."

It was the moment to say something, to stick in the wedge that would bring about the opening that would serve as an air vent. Beginning that morning, Alicia knew that the future was decided, that she had to ignore that remote repugnance that defined Esteban as an extension of Pablo, as a reduced recovery, a remnant of that eternally dead man who'd caressed her. Yes, most certainly, Esteban was nothing more than a prolongation of the epilogue, a continuation of the same thing with the same dissatisfactions, but also the same, necessary guarantees. And even if her heart rebelled, went on

rebelling against that solution of going about the house, con-
forming with a provisional abolition of her hunger, the alternative had to be discarded because it was inaccessible: solitude,
memory, darkness, cessation.

She should throw herself into Esteban's arms despite all
that reticence typical of a little girl not trained to eat properly, the kind who say, I don't like chickpeas and much prefer chocolate. It was no betrayal. He wanted her, wanted to
cradle her, and warmly touch the place where her hair began,
like his prototype, like that distant Esteban of yesteryear. She
had to give herself, quickly. But when her mouth began to
open, and her whipped will pushed her toward the opposite
body, an intangible barrier, a wall that was like denying that
two and two made five, stopped her muscles and put words
in her mouth.

"When you get back, I want to have a talk with you,"
she said, turning red with shame.

He looked at her with a smile; or it was the light that
came from the living room, partially blocked and defective,
which painted that expression on her lips. He caressed her
with the same fingers he'd used to caress a plush doll and
kissed her chastely on the cheek. Then he went back to the
kitchen, because for a long time his exhausted lungs had been
begging for another cigarette.

Nine

omething inside him was thankful for this rediscovery
of that dusty odor of felt and cheap deodorizers, which
served as protection against other, more unconfessable
smells, that fragrance of the past that combined termite-
chewed wood, worn-out sheets, the fried grease they used
to cook peas in the narrow kitchen upstairs, and a junk room
with a stove and a few broken tiles. Following the map his
memory supplied him, Esteban stubbornly insisted on asking for the same room—fourteen—that faced the center of
the plaza where the valiant João I had wielded his majorette's
baton.

The lady in charge, who was also the same as before,
offered no resistance to his whim, and even though rooms
twenty-three or thirty had spacious bathtubs that made the
sarcophagus-like rigidity of the shower stall unnecessary, she
handed the key over to Esteban as if she were surrendering a
besieged city. It was the same woman, enormous and swar-
thy, with the same swollen wrists, the same one, with the
perpetual lentil-shaped mole above her unshaven lip. Esteban
walked up to the second floor in order to prove to himself
that the stairway was still humpbacked, tilted to the right,

deformed by the footfall of an improbable colossus. He walked along the corridor where that entire coalition of smells became more precise, intensified, until he reached the door.

His memories seemed to cease when he introduced the key into the lock while holding his suitcase—barely enough clothing for three or four nights, the obligatory book that would remain relegated to the corner of the night table to support cigarettes, a wallet, the odd postcard. But when he opened the door he realized something was opening as well over his eyebrows, and the images ran wild, like a pack of dogs. Usually, memory forced him to respect those kinds of symmetries, even if they no longer held any meaning, even if they'd become the mechanical liturgy of a nonbeliever.

He was taking a morbid pleasure in comparing his past happiness with his current madness, in placing each one on the scale to find out their specific weight. Walking over to the window to draw back the curtains, he recalled the huge Christmas tree that in the Lisbon of the past—about five years back—had supplanted the statue of João I, of which now he could glimpse only the most unworthy haunches of his horse. Eva hadn't come to mind for years, probably because that pavilion of memory did not merit being revisited, but from the moment he stepped off the train, at around seven in the morning, with an awkward sunrise that could not decide if it should break over the gigantic supports of April 25 Bridge, he realized this brief visit would bear the stigma of that old love, of those twenty-five comfortable and tedious months in common that she dared to end one lucid afternoon.

If not, Esteban smiled that morning, he would still be dragging around the same good-natured routine of movies caught by chance at a videoclub, Bitter Kas, and hygienic

Christmas vacations every January. He was thankful to Eva for being so brave as to cut the ties that were tying them together even though both had less and less desire to be weighed down that way. And even though for a few months, at sunset, he would suddenly feel he was missing something, he soon had to recognize that the company he needed was someone else, someone more akin to the impossible person his brother had already snatched away from him.

Esteban tried to reconnect that bifurcation in his memories by shaking his head, forcing himself to deal with the chore of unpacking his bag and reviewing his plan of action. His lungs hurt a bit because of all the cigarettes he'd smoked, but he wasn't excessively tired. He'd traveled by train all night, lulled by the rhythm of his evocations, feeling vague glimmers of hope whenever he steered his thoughts in the direction of a certain face. The dawn, an ashen marine scene by Turner with gray silhouettes and fog, came on as the taxi carried him along Avenida Ribeira das Naus to the Hotel dos Franqueiros. A worn-out, filthy Lisbon was waking up outside the taxi's windows. Perhaps something like a courtesy toward his body might have suggested he dedicate the rest of the morning—it was eight o'clock—to resting and sleeping, but he wanted to resolve the enigmas that had brought him to this city, the city of the past, as soon as possible. Because Lisbon was a city that always seemed to take place in the past, or perhaps he'd read that somewhere.

The walls of the cafeteria where he wolfed down a Neapolitan and a coffee that tasted of resin were tattooed with infantile illustrations of Belem tower and the Marquis of Pombal, taken from an anonymous portrait that reappeared in all the tourist guides. While he labored to put the exact amount of money for his breakfast on the counter, he asked, in a Portuguese adulterated with Latin and Italian, to borrow a telephone book. He wanted to confirm the Almeida information. The counterman, a veteran at deciphering the babbling of tourists, handed him an enormous volume, pieces of whose cover had been bitten off, and which was attached to the bar by a comic piece of clothesline.

Esteban had no trouble finding the correct address at the same time that he extracted the next-to-last cigarette from his pack of Fortunas. The Adimanta Foundation had two telephone numbers and the tiniest of letters indicated it was on Largo das Portas do Sol, number four. "Alfama," answered the counterman when Esteban asked him where that street was, as if those three syllables explained everything, as if it were unnecessary to add anything. Covered by a dense layer of fog, he crossed Praça da Figueira until he came to Rosio. Above, a bit to the left, the Castle of Saint George seemed truncated by a brusque stump of earth and squeezed-together houses. He could walk to his destination and in the process clear his lungs on Lisbon's cruel hills, but the gravitation of certain memories, which since the previous night had been forcing him to circle around places, names, and ceremonies, made him take the number 28 tram, packed with Americans wearing sneakers.

He and Eva had agreed that Lisbon revealed itself only if seen through he window of a trolley, through that peephole of polished glass that can change the color of the air. Only seated on that groaning plank of wood and rust was it possible to discover naked Lisbon, the moving theater of a city that flows along peacefully through the windows following a secret clockwork principle that orders the alternating scenes: leaden streets inhabited by functionaries, short, white churches, disorderly, broken houses seemingly abandoned on piles of rubble. The tram left the Sé, with all its warlike crudity, off to one side, and Esteban noticed that just as the tram went uphill scratching at its rails as though complaining, his soul embarked on a parallel ascent, leaving the past below in order to make its way toward the more succulent offerings of the future.

Alicia would be waiting for him when he got back from that fleeting excursion, ready, finally, to reveal all her feelings, not to allow stupid objections to block the exercise of a possible happiness without interferences. The future was that clear path toward which events were kindly inviting him to stroll. And with a confident smile, his lips approved those guarantees that made him raise his imagination higher and higher, like the tram which now, having just raced through a demanding curve, was stopping to vomit out blond retirees loaded down with cameras.

A tile hanging on a chipped facade advised him that this was also his stop: Largo das Portas do Sol. The blond tourists, with red flesh and transparent ears, were running in a herd toward the Miradouro de Santa Luzia, where the ill-mannered fog of the morning barely revealed a confused mass of cotton and amputated buildings. Esteban stopped in front of the statue of São Vicente and observed the scythe-shaped semicircle the city effected at that point, pouring a cascade of roofs and terraces over the estuary of the Tagus. The sea and the port had been annihilated by that enormous wave of white foam. Even so, he amused himself counting the spires on the bell towers that stood out like bishops' miters among the masses of tightly squeezed houses.

Alfama was a fragile accordion of land that descended toward the coast. Leaning on the railing, he smoked an entire cigarette thinking that the fog made Lisbon more extreme, more liminal, more end-of-the-earth, cornered at the far end of the world, balanced over that corner of the peninsula where a new, unknown, and strange world began. The city seemed to dissolve obediently into nothingness, the last witness of a continent coming to an end. Then, crossing the street, he saw that a fleshy woman dressed in black was hanging out towels and that a bald man in his undershirt was leaning out a window to exhibit obscenely a jailbird's tattoos. The music that came to his ears when he finally stopped opposite number four must have been coming from that man's window. Esteban would have wanted a fado just to complete the composition of the place properly, but this was a disrespectful tropical melody.

The door, wood and glass, was ajar. Inside, it was possible to see a dark, nineteenth-century vestibule, tiles attempting a deficient chessboard. A stamped poster on the glass solemnly announced that the Adimanta Foundation would inaugurate its weekly lecture program on the sixteenth, on the exciting subject *Life After Death: Testimonies by Voyagers,* which would continue over a handful of sessions with subjects that were no less stimulating: *The Truth about Lost Civilizations, Secrets of Reincarnation, Tao and Mandala.* At the bottom, a simple line above a kind of Egyptian eye, which must have been the foundation's logo, noted that admission was free.

The intense stench of bleach in the vestibule barely dispelled the weight of the humidity, the nearness of salt and sewers. The floor-tile chessboard snaked to an interior patio bathed in a disturbing grayish light, and a shoulder-wide stairway twisted toward upper floors. Esteban paused opposite the mahogany desk to one side of the entrance. On it, someone had left behind a puzzle magazine, a calendar, a pencil, and a copper bell. The flow of time in that badly ventilated reception area seemed defective. The concierge, or the diminutive, dark person who fulfilled that role, took an intolerable amount of time to appear. He did not understand Spanish and did not understand the hodgepodge language Esteban had invented. At each word, he shook his head in simian fashion with a kind of passion, as if trying to free himself from an accusation, a persecution. Esteban pronounced Sebastião Adimanta's name, drawing each vowel with his lips, until the gorilla's face made a sign of approbation. The man scrambled up the stairs and came right back down. His hairy hand ordered Esteban to ascend to the next floor.

A gray light received him as he reached the head of the stairs. Five windows opened over the quartz glitter of the patio, which was on one side of a corridor broken into right angles and dotted from time to time with old wooden benches and small lithographs, imitations of drawings by Blake. Esteban walked down the hall. He stopped each time he came to a door, where windows informed him, successively, that groups of people sitting at desks were listening to men who covered blackboards with signs or were playing, in a circle, mysterious card games.

Some of the classrooms were empty and dark, impregnated with that smell of bleach he'd also noticed in the vestibule. The corridor was interminable. Each right angle promised to open onto the end, onto stairs or an exit, but the ashen light repeated itself perpetually, along with the benches and lithographs—like an abandoned museum. At long last, after a final turn, Esteban saw that the hall terminated at a half-open door. He walked more quickly, the pounding of his heels on the tiles seemed monotonous, like rain. He stopped before entering, stared courteously from the threshold without wanting to insert himself into the room. Above a window with a chestnut frame, he could make out the statue of São Vicente in front of which he'd stepped out of the tram as well as the confused cascade of roof tiles that made up Alfama flowing toward the Tagus.

The room, luminous and square, had that air of a prize office, of a casino for the retired, an air many Lisbon interiors had. The furniture belonged to a venerable style of the past that could not conceal its feebleness and its fatigue. A solid office table covered with papers and packages, chairs with striped backrests, a distant, gray metal file cabinet that supported an old, useless fan like a flower set in wire.

On the walls, in the isolated spaces not occupied by masses of books, floated portraits of sepia men, among whom Esteban thought he recognized Emanuel Swedenborg. The only person in the room did not seem to have noticed his arrival. Next to the bookcases, consulting the index of some book, stood a woman on top of two endless legs. The blue tube skirt ended at her knees, leaving in the open air two fine tibias as hard as white masts. Her hair, combed back, fell in ringlets over her blouse. Her eyes, which Esteban could just make out behind her glasses, were blue and solid. Esteban coughed, and the woman directed him a musical question in a Portuguese he did not understand. He tried to excuse himself in his recently invented Esperanto, and then the woman thought she recognized his accent.

"You're Spanish," she said with a hard, Castilian accent and perfect consonants.

"I am."

"Come in, please. Sit down." The woman placed her book on the stacks and observed Esteban's looks with a fleeting interest. "I've been told you want to see Mr. Adimanta."

"That's right."

"I'm Edla Ostmann, the vice director of the foundation." Esteban grasped a hand with fingers like needles. "I'd be happy to help you if you'd be kind enough to tell me what your visit is about."

The woman's language was melodic; there was an orchestral charm in her style of ordering words. Sitting on the old chair, Esteban felt comforted, satisfied, as if he were being caressed.

"My name is Esteban Labastida. I'm a journalist. I work for the cultural weekly *Sphere*. We're preparing an issue totally dedicated to the devil, and I've been told that your institution has a library and a small museum dedicated to that subject."

His lie had turned out as completely convincing as a spontaneous confession by an unknown person—someone who, in principle, has no interest in altering the truth. As he walked along the corridor, Esteban had elaborated his story step by step, paying minute attention to the details of the fraud so it would sound as irrefutable as a passport in proper form. Even so, the woman looked at him in such a way that it made him sit back in the chair, squeezing his cornered vertebrae against the back support. The woman's eyes were translucent and clean and seemed to filter Esteban's lie to the point of making him feel that his introduction had been stupid. Then her blue eyes descended to the table, where her hands picked up a little box marked with golden volutes. She offered him some small, black cigars that gave off a mild aroma of wood. Esteban declined.

"So you're a journalist," said Ms. Ostmann, placing the cigar in her mouth, and Esteban immediately knew she was fully aware he was lying. "What exactly are you looking for?"

"Well"—for a moment his words stuck on his tongue, as if it were impossible to reconstruct the detailed explanation he'd planned earlier. "I've gathered some information about satanic cults, sects, sacrifices, things of that sort. All the studies I've consulted mention the society of the *Coniurati,* led by Achille Feltrinelli, as one of the most important groups in the history of satanism. It seems your foundation possesses objects that belonged to members of that society."

Edla Ostmann's eyes looked like twin telescopes placed symmetrically on either side of a mouth that was expelling complicated spirals of smoke. All obscurity, all mist, all veils dissolved in the bifocal power of those two blue lenses. Slowly, without wanting to recognize it, realizing in the same way we realize the sole of our shoe has stepped on chewing gum, Esteban became aware that he was entering a complex ritual dance in which his obediently carrying out the role assigned to him was absolutely necessary if he was to achieve the objective he was pursuing, the one for which he'd suffered a long night of insomnia on a train with cigarette burns, ambushed by memories. Ms. Ostmann recognized the lie, the turquoise fire of her eyes had incinerated his charade, but even so the ballet went on, each one carrying out his movements with all the naturalness expected of a well-trained ballerina. Esteban sensed he was being allowed to approach the center of the web, to advance to the nucleus of the star made of white threads, until such time as the sting would make his escape impossible. He had no choice but to move forward step by step, risk his integrity in order to saturate himself in the unknown.

"I don't want you to have a mistaken idea of our institution," said Edla Ostmann, as if reciting a sentence written for her in a libretto. "We're not a sect, and we don't foster the sentiments of sects, especially of satanic cults. Mr. Adimanta founded this society with the disinterested participation of a group of subscribers for the purpose of scientifically studying paranormal phenomena, a field in which we can boast of having become a pioneering organization. Our specialists not only catalogue, classify, and describe all kinds of experiences related to spiritism, extrasensory perception, telekinesis, and mind reading but also are able, in the laboratories we've built expressly for that purpose, to implement the abilities of those subjects who have shown rudimentary aptitudes for the supernatural use of their psychic energy. Aside from being a research center, we've also and especially become a parapsychological school."

"What about your museum?" replied Esteban, cutting his way through that jumbled mass of publicity jargon.

"If you're going to write about us in your magazine, I suggest you begin by making that point quite clear. We're dedicated to research and not to cults."

"I'll make that very, very clear."

To celebrate his recent transformation into a journalist, Esteban had bought, in the train station, an improbable red notebook and a ballpoint pen that refused to write, engraving grooves in the lined paper before grudgingly emitting a precarious thread of ink. Esteban violently traced four or five abbreviations, trying his best to make it seem clear he was obeying Ms. Ostmann's conditions. Then he put the notebook on the table, next to a letter opener in the shape of an owl, and asked permission to smoke. The woman, leaning back on her cracked-leather chair, crossed her unending legs to breath in the smoke of her cigar, with which her right hand drew gray, ephemeral letters in the air. The match she held out to him burned Esteban's Fortuna while her blue gaze bathed him in a kind of lubricious curiosity, the kind that makes imagination strip the clothes off unknown passersby in the street. Instead of tempting him, that gaze brought nothing to Esteban but a splash of alarm.

"Would you be so kind as to follow me." The woman stood up and again observed him from the height of her legs. "I'd like you to see a few things."

They went out into the corridor, to the benches with their rancid varnish, to those careless imitations of Blake. Taking his first steps, Esteban tried to orient himself by comparing the path they'd just begun with the one he'd followed to reach the office, but two right angles and a brusque detour that collided with a closed window sabotaged his intentions. All he could do was second the footsteps of Ms. Ostmann through the corridors, the metallic impact of her high heels against the tiled floor. She went on speaking to him as she walked, but her voice, distorted by the sound of her heels and her height, was hard to decipher.

"I'd like you to observe some of the laboratories where our specialists work. No, we won't interrupt them. There are windows on our classrooms that will allow us to watch without getting in the way. I hope you'll take good notes on everything for your article."

"I certainly will."

The window they stopped in front of revealed a dark room occupied by a vague number of individuals seated at desks. The porous, vague light was barely sufficient to pick things out, but Esteban glimpsed some thin cables like tendrils connecting the desks to the temples of the men, who were dotted with electrodes. At the rear of the classroom, next to the blackboard, a person wrapped in a white bathrobe was pointing to objects on a screen. The slide projector cast a star on the rectangle, then on a mountain, then on a pencil sharpener, then on the moon.

"This exercise is based on Thorndike's experiments with stimuli," said Ms. Ostmann, briefly sucking on her cigar. "Our students are gifted with incipient extrasensory capacities, which this kind of work will help to develop. It's a standard exercise in telepathy. The professor thinks of an object, and the students must read it in his mind. If the perception is sufficient, an electrode stimulates the subject's hypothalamus; if he's mistaken, he receives a small discharge. Everything at a very elementary level, as you can see, and scientific. Take note of it."

Esteban scribbled in his notebook to satisfy Ms. Ostmann. There were no ashtrays; he had no idea where to toss his cigarette. The hall was as clean and threatening as a hospital corridor.

"Who can enter your school?" he inquired, suddenly inspired by the itch of journalistic curiosity. "I would imagine you have a rigorous selection process."

"You imagine correctly," she answered, once again marching down the corridor. "The candidates are given an entrance examination and a series of tests. We try to thin out the applicants, to filter out thrill seekers and the merely curious, both of which abound. The Adimanta Foundation has a reputation, Mr. Labastida, and it must maintain it. We have to be very sure of the raw material shaped in our classes."

"And do many people take the tests?"

"More than you'd think." Edla Ostmann suddenly acquired a bureaucratic harshness. "And even more would take them if not for our having imposed a requirement that has served as a constant theme for the majority of our detractors. To take the test, the candidate must deposit in a specified bank account the sum of two hundred American dollars, to cover the costs of the examination above all. Our enemies call us swindlers. But write in your magazine that they shouldn't expect us to turn into sisters of charity."

"I will."

Before they reached the end of another corridor as complicated and tortuous as plumbing, they passed another window on the other side of which a game of cards was being played. The individual in the white bathrobe would place the deck on a little cloth-covered table about three meters from the first row of desks. Then he would show, with his palm open and that radiant pomposity typical of television magicians, the first card: a four of diamonds. He was speaking to the group hunched over their desks, but the words faded before they got to the window. As Ms. Ostmann explained, it was an exercise in telekinesis. The students were supposed to try to place the bottom card in the deck on top without moving from their seats. Esteban nodded, and they moved on. At all times, his mind refrained from admitting or repudiating the outlandish teachings of the Adimanta Foundation. After all, they did not seem so bizarre in this incongruous universe of ours where only the ordinary seemed surprising.

They reached a metal door covered with notices. It was clear that years ago it had been painted green. It was the door to a freight elevator that had to go to the lower floor. Edla Ostmann pushed a button; a sharp shriek like the one the tram made when it went up Lisbon's hills came slowly through the wall. The interior of that rusty, sad cage could barely accommodate Ms. Ostmann. During their brief ride, Esteban amused himself by looking at the knees covered by stockings. He found them pretty and substantial. His eyes, accustomed to the quartz light that saturated the entire upper floor with whiteness, could barely make out the room that received them when the elevator door opened. He took three steps, following Ostmann, and felt that his soles were treading something elegant and hard, marble perhaps. Slowly, the long library began to take shape around him, the two walls, a mosaic of book spines and stitching that stretched toward the patio. The unmistakable smell of old paper, leather, that mixed-blood smell of wood and stagnant water came to meet him. It was not easy to make out the titles. There were some in Hebrew and Greek, but most were in Latin. Wearing a smile over his teeth that was somewhere between amusement and irony, he read: Richard Bovet, *Pandaemonium,* Bartholomäus Anhorn, *Magiologia,* Peter Binsfeld, *Tractatus de Confessionibus Meleficorum et Sagrarum,* Balthasar Bekker, *De Betoverde Weereld.* Edla Ostmann's voice almost startled him— distant and vibrant, it revealed the true length of the room.

"Take a look at a few of them if you like. They might be useful for your article. Mr. Adimanta has given you permission to consult them."

It was only then he noticed that the woman was speaking to him from the other end of the room, opposite the window that faced the patio, and that a small, static shadow was resting next to her leg. Esteban walked forward in a time that seemed excessively dilated to him. He stopped opposite the window. Mr. Adimanta was an old, curled-up body, inert, trapped in a gray suit and tie, imprisoned in a wheelchair. Some cruel sickness had destroyed his joints and sabotaged his limbs, rendering him a series of white-haired, useless bags. He was a cadaver with an intense blue gaze. Esteban was astonished to find a fire that powerful in those two diaphanous eyes, which, curiously, possessed the same glitter of sharp intelligence as those of Ms. Ostmann. With a touch of alarm, he noted that, in the mere lapse of a second, an indefinable flash circulated from the old man's eyes to those of the woman. Esteban suspected that some mysterious circuit allowed that exchange of impressions.

"Sebastião Adimanta," said Edla Ostmann, pointing to the shape tucked up in the wheelchair. "An unfortunate accident exiled him to that poor body which inactivity destroys a bit more each day. His body is a broken machine, but his mind shines more brightly than that of all sound bodies. At the beginning, after his accident, Mr. Adimanta cursed the Creator and tried to find consolation in suicide. But with the passage of time, he could only thank God for having singled him out for this honor. He'd been liberated from matter, he was a pure spirit who could dedicate himself freely to thought, to taking flight. As you can see, his eyes are the only part of his anatomy that still tolerate some movement. Communication between his mind and the world is impossible through merely physical means."

The old man's eyes approved those words with a tired blinking. Esteban thought of Dumas, of the Count of Monte

Cristo, of old Noirtier de Villefort, also reduced to two imprisoned and loquacious eyes. It occurred to him that his incurable vice was literature, and that his life was the vague territory that remained beyond the plot. Sebastião Adimanta, joined to his chair, achieved in the patio's interior light the majesty of a seated statue. Rocklike and serene, he seemed to emulate the eternal giants of Abu Simbel. His blue eyes thought something; immediately, Ms. Ostmann communicated: "Mr. Adimanta has been informed of the reason for your visit. Usually, he does not receive journalists because they are inevitably people with narrow objectives, but you intrigue him because you've come asking questions about the *Coniurati*. What, specifically, are you looking for?"

"I think I explained myself," answered Esteban, fully aware that one by one his words were leading him to the center of the spiderweb. "I read about the *Coniurati* in an encyclopedia. I think they founded a city, where there were statues of angels."

As it turned, the wheel on Mr. Adimanta's chair emitted a disagreeable screech, like a rat being stepped on. Ms. Ostmann pushed his useless body forward until Esteban had him at his feet. The old man's eyes, more alive and electric than ever, gestured toward the long row of books to the right. Warned by that gesture, Esteban glanced vaguely at the volumes. The woman indicated a stack and an exact place. He removed from the wall an aristocratic, dark book, which covered his forearm. The cover bore no title, only the confused swamp of cracks and blemishes embossed on it by humidity and time. On the first, perfectly preserved, page, he read the title he already knew:

MYSTERIUM TOPOGRAPHICUM
ACHILLE. FELTRINELLI.
Seu arcanae caliginosae eximiaeque urbis Babelis
Novae
Descriptio, a ministribus Domini nostri
Exaedificata ad maiorem sui
Gloriam

"There you have it, the *Mysterium Topographicum*," said the woman or the old man. "A unique work, extremely rare, sought after with equal fervor by the fanatics of Satanism or seekers after curiosities. It's a perfectly preserved first edition."

"There's no proof it was the first," retorted Esteban, carefully turning the pages. "There's neither a date nor a place of publication."

"True enough, Mr. Labastida." Adimanta's eyes smiled coldly. "Of course you aren't a journalist like all the others. You're easily recognized at a distance, there is in you another will, one that's more interesting, if you'll allow me the observation, more impassioned. You must be able to read Latin well. Do me the honor of reciting the first line of the work."

Esteban obeyed with the uncomfortable sensation that he was sinking deeper and deeper in a bog, first his ankles then his hips, that the suffocating mud was beginning to surround his waist: *Moses affirmat (Genesi cap.XI, v.4) ut homines aedificaverunt turrem altam quam caelo ad Deum ad duellum provocandam. Nos aedificamus urbem totam ab gloria sua obsistindam.* Edla Ostmann's voice proffered the translation with a special emphasis on the *p*'s and *l*'s: "*Moses affirmed that men built a tower as high as the sky to challenge God. We are*

building an entire city to combat His glory. An entire city dedicated to rebellion, to apostasy, to deserting God. The return
of Babel, the sacrilegious city. A city of dreams, made of dreams,
an architecture of dreams. Observe the engravings, they're
impeccable. A compatriot of this house, Inácio da Alpiarça,
created them one by one in tortured nights of insomnia. The
engravings have been copied in many other books dedicated
to irreverent publicity, books of engravings including Piranesi,
Doré, also the exquisite pages of Robert Fludd. Which is
why it isn't unlikely that some of these drawings seem familiar to you."

All of them were in fact familiar to him. All of them
aroused in his soul, as he made his way through the pages with
a growing anguish, the vertigo of some buried feeling that
spoke to him of an earlier, prenatal, impossible life related
obscurely to that lunar and terrifying city. Each illustration
brought him that ancient horror that has neither name nor
reason for being, that atavistic fear of disinterring a shredded
memory that birth erased, barely allowing the disquiet of some
ruins. It had occurred to him at one time or another, with
Magritte's paintings and certain musical compositions, discovering with a bitter pellicle on his tongue that in some way or
another he knew that situation, that image, that combination
of scales, but that his identity and his Cartesian certainties,
his mirror and his DNA, had managed to push them aside,
making them alien and threatening.

"It's one of the twelve copies that survived the fire," Edla
Ostmann when on. "Only twelve in all the world, and one
of them is here in the foundation's library, the most complete
library on Satanism, witchcraft, and demonology in the world.
In the Vatican library there are five copies, in that of the

Kremlin two. Another is in the University of Uppsala, another in Seville, one more in the Library of Congress in Washington. Except for the one in the Okono Collection in Tokyo, they all belong to public institutions. Which means that they all require fussy permits and licenses to be read, to be studied. Here it's completely at your disposal."

Esteban's eyes had fallen onto the last page, isolated from the rest of the text by two or three inexplicable blank pages. He once again met the circular monster who headed those four enigmatic verses, the dragon with the stupefied gaze over a nuclear-holocaust landscape. He recalled his fleeting conversation with Alicia, the Ouroboros, the eternal beginning. It was unnecessary for him to read the lines that followed below to recover the mysterious music of the conundrum: *Terrible hunger taught the Polypos to gnaw their legs* . . . Sebastião Adimanta's blue eyes had anxiously exalted the book's frontispiece and, collapsed because of some sort of excitement or fury, were contemplating the engraving of the dragon.

"You too are intrigued by that engraving, as is only natural," said Ms. Ostmann. "Relegated to the end of the book, with no apparent relationship to the rest. But it was printed with the work, beginning with the first edition. As a point of information, I must note that it isn't original. It's one of the emblems in the *Scrutinium Chymicum* by Michael Maier, accompanied by his epigram. The *Scrutinium* was an alchemical text composed in the seventeenth century, clearly inspired by the Rosicrucians."

"What's the engraving doing here?" asked Esteban.

"That's a hard question to answer," said Ostmann while Adimanta's eyes flashed. "Most probably it's a warning, most probably there's a key. The Ouroboros, the serpent that bites its tail, is a symbol of alchemical work, of all projects. Most certainly it's also a symbol of the project of restoration—the One Crowned with Stars returns to Earth. That, of course, is just a hypothesis."

"But this text is repeated on the angels."

Adimanta's eyes spun cyclically, like a kaleidoscope made of glass and frost. For a moment, with terror or vertigo, Esteban understood that those eyes were the two diminutive spy holes that connected the universe with a mind that was an abyss, an inaccessible dung heap of wisdom that lived perpetually dedicated to its onanism, its contemplation, to mitigating time by getting lost in the voluptuous complexity of its own labyrinths. Edla Ostmann muttered something in Portuguese that Esteban did not understand until they went out onto the patio and the white light bathed his eyelids: *O museu.*

Months later, comparing magazine articles and some insulting books, Esteban would learn that Sebastião Caumedo, the man who'd been Adimanta before becoming a manikin stuffed with sand on a wheelchair, was born in Santarém in 1932. None of his traits as a young man prefigured his later dedication to the exploration of esoteric realities. At the age of twenty-four, he had few books, a transitory girlfriend, a career as a naval engineer truncated by tedium, and he had the entire Lisbon police force at his heels because he had killed a man. The motives behind the fight are unknown, but it seemed to be proven that it was Caumedo, a young, thin man with Nordic eyes, who, in a bar, had savagely attacked a killer from the port area with a knife, to the point that he'd exposed the man's liver.

The manhunt sent him to Angola, where he changed his name to Sebastião Açorda and made a meager living writing articles for a local newspaper. Either seeking his fortune or trying to clean his record of the crime, he joined the colonial militia. One afternoon, his division departed for the north to put down an uprising that threatened the frontier with the Belgian Congo. Near Macocola, his group was ambushed and had to fight its way out. According to the testimony of the officer who commanded him, Sebastião Açorda fought bravely, using up all his ammunition and defending his life with his machete. Before dawn, an enemy bullet smashed his skull. Açorda fell on a stream of cadavers and was thought fatally wounded. He was brought to the Luanda hospital, where he began to show the strange symptoms of his lesion. There were no physical consequences, but his brain fogged over with incongruous ideas whose source he did not know. Over time, he came to understand that he'd become vastly more receptive to the thoughts of others, that the sensations and intentions of others filtered into his head, and that these could be read by simply holding up to the light the marks they'd left in his mind.

Sebastião Adimanta, the fortune-teller, was born in 1964 on a colorful circus poster where he shared his stardom with a contortionist and a dragonfly trainer. He toured Angola for five or six years presenting his fortune-telling act in bars and theaters, accompanied by a fierce mulatta named Letizia Olaias whom he'd married after living with her for a few months. Slowly he was becoming famous as a mysterious man gifted by nature with a miraculous aptitude for digging out secrets that eluded the intelligence of a normal person. Finally, he himself reached the conclusion that he should use his illness, if it could be called that, to dive into the most hidden of the mind's secrets, concealed from ordinary mortals.

He returned to Portugal alone, continued with his show, and won a precarious popularity. In 1978 he was run down by a truck on a Lisbon avenue. It didn't kill him, but it did reduce him to an inert manikin who couldn't move his own wheelchair. Assisted by friends, he tried to kill himself with poisons, but no one wanted to assume the penal responsibilities, so he was left alone. He'd accumulated a modest fortune before the accident by, it's said, making predictions about lotteries and soccer pools, so he was able to open a foundation in his own name dedicated to the study of esoteric subjects. Twenty years later, the source of his finances was not very clear. Aside from monthly payments from students, the society survived thanks to an obscure system of donations paid by its members around the world. Many remained anonymous.

Except for very specific cases, it was chance that principally governed the chaotic combination of curiosities and rarities that occupied the Adimanta Foundation Museum. The hall, rectangular and disproportionate, repeated the layout of the library. To look at the engravings and paintings that covered the walls, it was necessary to detour around two or three strategically placed and intermittent tripods that served as pedestals for wood or ceramic images. At the same time the echo turned his footsteps into muted, threatening blows, Esteban felt that honorific fear of being the only visitor in a museum. Sometimes, beginning during his childhood, he thought that at night museums, when closed to the public, were the setting for secret meetings among the characters in the pictures, who would take advantage of the silence to flee their frames, wander the galleries, dip into the still lifes, or take part in some battle filled with lances. All the works in the Adimanta Museum had a common denominator. All, directly or remotely, were connected to ancient horrors and superstitions, those nightmares that tasted of thirst and insomnia as the sun rose, those presences intuited in stories that occupied nights around a fire, that truculent fauna from the abyss which had frightened mankind from its origins in the cave and that now peered into the indirect lighting occupying prints or pedestals.

The tragic image of a prince reduced to a monster was repeated in all the pictures: a distant figure in Persian terracotta with the head of a dog and the wings of a crane; flocks of misshapen, insane creatures harassing Saint Anthony in several parallel engravings; the reptile that bit the dust under the sword of Saint Michael or some other officer of the angels in canvases veiled by time with brown, dense haze. But the devil was not the only protagonist in the museum even if he certainly did indirectly summarize the intention of the works. There were also examples of the devil's apostles on earth, ancient ironwork and torture tools that had served to dissuade his acolytes, awls and scissors used to unmask witches. Finally, at the end of the rectangular corridor, next to an illustration from Milton's *Paradise Lost,* Esteban found what he was looking for: the last angel, the fourth member of the family, identical to the others. It allowed itself to be bathed by the light from the spotlights, like any other object in the collection, like an ordinary statue, forgotten in the stormy past of death and sacrilege of which he was the protagonist. The animal that stood guard next to the angel's left tibia was a lion. The pedestal offered the lines of signs Esteban was expecting, and he diligently copied into his notebook:

〕.SAMAEL. ❙❙ DIRA.FAMES.VSVTSVE. EDRDD.ESADVDC . . .

"Years ago," said Ms. Ostmann in a ventriloquist's voice, "there lived in Paris a Hungarian magus who presented a rather heterodox version of Genesis. Stanislas de Guaita, which was his name, asserted that when God pronounced the famous formula *fiat lux,* He wasn't lighting the lamps of the world or separating the light from the darkness, as generations of biblical scholars have wanted it. That 'Let there be light' was the creation of the firstborn of the creatures, the one who was in himself the torch of the world: Lucifer, the Bearer of Light, the most beautiful being the universe has ever known. He was prince of the most powerful rank of angels, the seraphim, according to Suárez. Certain legends say that the Morning Star was encrusted in his forehead; others that he was adorned with a diadem with a gem of the most powerful shine. But you know that angel was seditious."

The wheelchair advanced along the hall. That unbearable screech of a beaten animal grated on Esteban's ears.

"The book of Isaiah tells that Lucifer wanted to scale Heaven, install his throne over the stars of God, and sit on the Mountain of the Testament. Saint Thomas attributes his rebellion to pride, which instigated him to emulate his creator, while Duns Scotus charges him with an enigmatic sin he calls 'spiritual lust.' For Tertulian, Saint Gregory of Nisa, and Saint

Cyprian, the Prince of Creatures envied man, created in the likeness of the Most High, and that moved him to revolt. Suárez proposes that he refused to adore God made flesh because he, a pure spirit, would not kneel before an animal made of passions and blood like man. In the sixteenth century, Ambrose Catarino, archbishop of Ponza, presented an interesting thesis:—that Lucifer became indignant because he wanted the Word to become flesh in his person. The angels revolted, a colossal battle ensued in Heaven. Johann Wier, in his *Pseudomonarchia daemonum,* calculates that the rebel army consisted of 6,666 legions of 6,666 soldiers each. You know how it ended: *Videbam Satanam sicut fulgur de Coelo cadentem.*"

Adimanta's eyes remained closed for a few seconds, as if he were trying to capture a cloud of fading memories. Esteban breathed without making a sound, fearful of violating those dramatic silences by just turning the page in his notebook or changing position.

"Lucifer was exiled to the depth of the world, chained in a stinking pool where he dedicated himself to weaving his revenge. His name became Satan, Beelzebub, Astaroth, Leviathan. The gem that crowned his diadem dropped from his forehead and fell under the power of the Saint Michael the Archangel. It would later be fashioned into the Holy Grail, which would catch the blood of Christ. Lucifer transformed into a monstrous creature, which drew from Dante a beautiful commentary in *Inferno: S'ei fu sì bel com'egli ora brutto* . . . Then began the secret work of plotting, of conspiracy, of espionage. Distributed around the world, his agents dedicated themselves to preparing the return. The priests of Satan multiplied, authentic artisans of evil. Here I hope you'll allow me a brief parenthesis. Do you know the work of Arthur Machen?"

The question disarmed Esteban, who suddenly wanted to light a cigarette. His movements, the slow maneuver of abandoning his notebook in the pocket of his parka to gain a little time or a proper answer, were engraved on the blue eyes of the old man with a miniaturist's precision. Esteban coughed: "A man who wrote horror novels," he timidly noted.

"Yes." Edla Ostmann's hand rested on the backrest of the wheelchair. "He's usually called a precursor of Lovecraft, though I'm afraid his interests are slightly different. In a fragment of his novella *The White People,* which Pauwels and Bergier also quote, Machen explains that true evil, Evil with a capital *E,* has little or nothing to do with those tiny things we consider evil in domestic life. The authentically evil person, like the authentic saint, are much stranger and more uncommon creatures than the hydra or the unicorn. True evil is related to the spirit, not matter, with theology and not technology. The wretched drunk who kicks his wife to death is as distant from evil as the charity of the old lady who gives alms to the homeless. A person can be a terrorist and still be good-natured. Anyone can be a conscientious citizen, a perfect father, a well-known philanthropist, and practice the most chemically pure kind of evil. It was not in vain that Shakespeare warned us that the Lord of Darkness is a perfect gentleman."

"In that case, what is the essence of evil?" Esteban interrupted.

"Allow me to leave that question unanswered." Ms. Ostmann smiled. "It's as if you were asking me to describe the state of grace or the nothingness that preceded creation. Try to accept this brief formula: Evil is negation. Of everything you can imagine, evil is the other, the opposite. Many of those who innocently stroll the streets under the innocuous mask of shopkeepers, lottery vendors, prostitutes, or impresarios can be members of that sinister society of black swans. They adore Satan, the dark side, the contrary side. For centuries, they've been secretly preparing the arrival of an order of things that should be the exact antithesis of what we know. What I'm trying to tell you is that evil is a metaphysical not a moral concept."

"For centuries?" Esteban's lips passionately desired a cigarette.

"Yes, for centuries. Men are usually dissatisfied with what they have, so they demand that the poor creature with horns prepare a program of opposition"—the old man blinked. "Satanism has a long and elaborate history. Gilles de Laval, marshal of Rais, slaughtered children in the fourteenth century in order to preside over Black Masses. The Marquis of Villena, translator of Dante and Virgil, set himself on fire in order to gain knowledge of hell, and with that knowledge he would come back to life with a new body and new intelligence. Catherine de Médicis, queen of France, wore on her stomach the skin of a murdered child with ciphers and letters that would invoke Satan. Diverse treatises testify to the existence of demonic societies beginning in the sixteenth century: the *Questio Lamiarum* by Samuel de Casini, the *Tractatus de Strigiis* by Bernard de Cóme, the *De Striginagarum Daemonumque Mirandis* by Silvestre Mazolini, and also the books written by Barthélemy de Spina, Jacques van Hoogstraeten, or Pedro de Ciruelo. In 1667 Milton is showing open admiration for the devil, and he presents him in his *Paradise Lost* as a kind of exiled king who deserves our admiration. Schiller's *Masnadieri* tries to convince us that it's far better to burn in hell in the company of daring and contentious spirits than to share glory "with all the vulgar imbeciles." At the end of the eighteenth century, Leopardi composes a hymn to Satan in which he will be followed by Giosué Carducci and Michelet, who attribute human progress to the hand of demonic rebelliousness. Many more names could be added to the list: Byron, Vigny, Erhard, Bierce. Today there exists in the United States an Official Church of Satan, whose bible, composed by a certain Anton LaVey, proposes a systematic work of disobedience and rebellion."

"What about the *Coniurati*?" asked Esteban.

The old man's eyelids veiled his intense blue gaze, announcing that the answer to that question would have to wait. Edla Ostmann draped a red and black blanket over his tangled legs and slowly turned the wheelchair around, facing it toward the patio. For an instant, Esteban thought Adimanta himself was also a part of his museum, that he was another piece in this contradictory collection that paid homage to a dethroned prince. His insubstantial body belonged more to that order of minute and repellant objects than to the domestic order that began on the other side of the door to his museum. The chair moved off with its screeching voice until it stopped opposite the whiteness of the window. There Ms. Ostmann turned around and asked Esteban, "How long will you be in Lisbon?"

"Two or three days," he answered.

"We'll meet again tomorrow, Mr. Labastida."

At long last, he could get out his pack of cigarettes.

...

The suitcase and the two canvas bags had found all the space they needed in the trunk, but that outlandish lamp adorned with relief carvings of birds which Mamen had fallen in love with on Paseo de Gracia required two or three attempts to settle into the car. Finally it took up the backseats with the window on the right side open so the birds could timidly peek their little heads out. Alicia did not speak much on the trip back from the airport. She drove with both hands on the wheel, mechanically, though it was impossible to say whether it was from concentration or distraction. Mamen interpreted it to mean that the half hour delay of her plane had exploded Alicia's fragile patience. But what was really happening was that despite driving around the Capuchin circle, braking properly at every light—the lamp with the birds on it was bending while Mamen looked on in horror—her mind had escaped its natural receptacle and, on its own, had undertaken a five-hundred-kilometer journey.

Esteban had telephoned her the night before and brought her up to date on his new discoveries. He dictated the message of the fourth angel, which was a bit like saying nothing, then described meeting Sebastião Adimanta and his secretary with such passion and precision that, after seeing them with photographic clarity in her imagination, Alicia felt the impulse to run off to Lisbon at that precise moment instead of having to resign herself to biting her lips. Their entire conversation of the previous night had been reduced to his giving an account of the business with the angel and a port city Alicia knew only indirectly from postcards. In point of fact, she would have wanted some words of commitment, some audacious words, the kind that would have made her hang up the phone with a slight tremor in her fingers. The dialogue avoided the truly capital confessions, the only ones that could excuse a conference at one-thirty in the morning and only suggested them without diving into their oblique waters. No, Alicia repeated to herself in pendular fashion, she would have wanted and would not have wanted to hear those words dedicated to her ears. She'd want to hear them because they would have fortified her decision to begin creating a space for feelings about Esteban where it seemed there was none; she wouldn't want to hear them because the words would have been the last station on the border, the beacon to indicate the point of no return. But, for the moment, she would have to shoo away all those contradictions as annoying as flies, which were causing her not to pay attention to poor Mamen, resigned behind her sunglasses to burying herself in the swift parks that passed by the windshield. Alicia tried to find the most careful of tones when she asked, "Well, tell me. How was Barcelona."

Mamen stared at her, shocked to discover that Alicia had a voice in her throat.

"My dear, now that you've descended to planet Earth," she said looking for a cigarette in her bag. "I told you before, an unbelievably boring congress on pathologies and socioaffective disorders. Exchanging impressions with colleagues, listening to papers, attending roundtables especially designed to combat insomnia, a couple of dinners, a flirtation here and there. No big deal. Barcelona on the other hand is divine. Open spaces leave me cold, everything's enormous, a lot of sky. And around here, how are things? Esteban?"

"Esteban's in Lisbon," answered Alicia, instantly growing alarmed at giving out such information.

"In Lisbon." Mamen repeated the name with a cigarette in her mouth. "What a pretty city Lisbon is, I like it enormously too. Have you ever been there?"

"No, never."

"It's charming, it's got a kind of decadent air. And what's Esteban doing there? Is he on vacation?"

"Not exactly."

She knew that if she confessed the reasons for Esteban's trip she'd be unleashing the whirlwind, admitting that she'd taken to an insane level an obsession she should have thrust aside the instant Mamen had told her to forget it along with the handy prescription for tranquilizers. With an unsuccessfully confident voice, Alicia reported that the snowball of the angel and the book had gone on rolling down the hill, and that many more mysteries and a pair of corpses had also joined the avalanche. Yes, Mamen could become serious, bawl her out, she could tell her she was worse than a little girl, but the plot had thickened behind her back, the cloth was growing thread by thread and had finally ended by wrapping her up, trapping poor Esteban as well, who had given in to her because he was in love. Mamen snorted just as Alicia expected she would and smoked two cigarettes without making a single comment until they were opposite the Torre del Oro and there were only a few meters left before the car passed through the portal to her street. Double-parked and with the hazard lights on, they unloaded the luggage. It wasn't until they were upstairs, having passed the sidewalk, the vestibule, and the elevator, that Mamen skewered her: "Alicia, you're completely irresponsible."

Yes, yes, she recognized all that. Absolutely, she should have obeyed Mamen's decree and obliterated her obsession while it still hadn't grown large enough to constitute a threat. But now all those laments were beside the point. By some strange process of osmosis, reality, everyday external and domestic reality, had become saturated with the strange conditions of her dream, with the zodiac of mysteries and enigmas that surrounded it. Without her having moved a muscle to connect them, the inside and outside realms had entered into a sort of pact, proceeding symmetrically, each one following the other, each grafting itself onto the affairs of the other. She might be going insane, but there did exist a real and objective enigma to resolve. Why was that man with the mustache looking for her, why did Nuria have an angel like the one in the city, why did the plan in the book coincide with the urban landscape of her dream, why was Don Blas a suspect in the murder of the antiques dealer, that's right, the antiques dealer who was a friend of Marisa.

"Rafael Almeida," said Mamen, her forehead waxen.

"That's the man. Did you know him?"

A slight hesitation revealed that she did know him. Mamen had a moment of weakness, but she quickly recovered her aplomb and began talking about making coffee or, perhaps better yet, an herb tea. The apartment had the thick smell of a closed-up space; it seemed to emanate from the furniture and statically arranged objects in the salmon-colored living room. Alicia scurried to put the lamp with the birds in a corner, in front of a Matisse print that had the vague air of a blue, underwater sunflower. Her attention was caught by an antique sculpture of Saint Elizabeth that stood below it on a short-legged table next to the sofa. She bent down, picked it up, and studied it. Conclusions took shape with increasing rapidity in her limping brain, and she felt as if the pieces in an enormous puzzle were beginning to come together.

"I bought that very piece from Almeida," said Mamen, who had suddenly appeared behind Alicia smoking a cigarette. "Don't jump to any conclusions. I just knew him."

"I'm not jumping to any conclusions," retorted Alicia, putting the piece back on the table, understanding perfectly what conclusions Mamen meant.

"I met him through Marisa and bought a couple of things from him, that's all. Yes, I knew what was going on between him and Marisa. It doesn't surprise me; he was attractive, attentive, and poor Joaquín is as good as he is dull. And you say your neighbor's been accused of killing him."

"He didn't kill him. He's just a suspect. He too knew Almeida and was there when he died. I'll tell you all about it."

But it would have to be another time. The clock that was looking at them from on top of the television set was progressively lowering the right side of its mustache and warning them that six-thirty was approaching. Alicia had an appointment.

...

Inspector Gálvez awaited her indolently sprawled out on a bench opposite the Isla de la Cartuja and the symmetrical architecture of the Universal Exposition. The sunset was duplicated in the river and stained the waters with a current of blood broken from time to time by kayak races. As Alicia made her way to the avenue as quickly as she could,

always using the half-moon of the Barqueta bridge as a land-
mark to reach their meeting place, she noted from a distance
that the inspector looked like a sleepy or defeated figure smoking an insignificant cigarette, which he allowed to burn ef-
fortlessly between his fingers. Alicia's voice seemed to awaken
him, to return him to the place where his body had dragged
him. He stood up and, after shaking his trousers, greeted her
with his habitual film-style courtesy and suggested they take
a walk. No sooner had they set out than a jogging couple
passed them by; the girl's blond ponytail looked like a hand
waving good-bye. Alicia couldn't tell if it was a mirage re-
sulting from fatigue that was interfering with her way of rea-
soning and expressing herself, but it seemed to her that the
behavior of the inspector was even more measured and
stealthy than it had been on other occasions, as if each one
of his gestures and words demanded a preparation or a tech-
nical inspection before being put into effect. For that reason, his way of extracting his pack of Winstons from the
pocket of his homeless-person's raincoat and placing a cigarette between his lips seemed insufferably theatrical to her.
That manner bad actors have of ostentatiously showing that
they're carrying out a transcendently crucial act in the devel-
opment of the action just so the audience will realize it. Alicia
breathed in and out energetically. From the river came a pleasant breeze that made the rushes along the shore tremble and
caused the retirees scattered on the benches to smile. She rejected the inspector's Winston; she preferred a Ducado.

"Again I thank you for giving me a little of your time,"
Gálvez ceremoniously reiterated. "I know all this must seem
quite annoying to you, but just put yourself in my place. I'm
paid to write reports. To tell you the truth, deep down I'm

thankful I've been given a case like this one. You waste your professional life fighting with junkies, swindlers, and thugs of the worst moral sort. This is the first intellectual plot I've ever had: antiques, statues, Satanism. An embarrassment of riches."

"Satanism?" Alicia repeated, troubled by a sudden attack of deafness.

"Oh of course, I forgot that your role forces you to deny everything"—Gálvez made a Humphrey Bogart–style gesture to little effect—"or pretend you know nothing about anything. I told you and your brother-in-law that Acevedo's motive seemed too incredible. A retired guy isn't going to risk smashing open someone's head to enjoy the ten stinking years of life left to him using ill-gotten cash. The key was in that annual report, that enormous book tossed next to the body with a page torn out. I contacted other antiques dealers, and after a lot of looking around I found a copy that was intact. On the missing page, they talk about an angel, to be precise, a group of four angels, bronze statues made by a Portuguese artist who worshiped the devil. Really something out of a movie."

"If you say so."

The night was beginning to gangrene the sky, the joggers and the mothers pushing strollers diminished to make way for another population: dubious-looking women, young people with whiskey bottles camouflaged in wrinkled, white paper bags. Above, to the left, on Torneo Street, the light from the streetlamps and cars combined to create an intense, yellow anthill. Gálvez paused and took a deep drag. Each one of his gestures seemed rehearsed.

"I called Barcelona," he went on. "I spoke with Benlliure's widow. She recalled having seen in her husband's shop a statue similar to the one I described over the phone, of the same dimensions as the box found in his hotel room after his death. The yearbook said that one of the angels—there were four, as I said—was lost after the war. Excuse me for not stopping to tell you the whole story, but I'd feel like a fool. You can just deny it all if you like."

"Well . . ." coughed an uncomfortable Alicia.

"One angel was lost after the war, another was destroyed. I don't know where Benlliure got it, but it seems clear that he possessed the lost angel. It seems each angel has an inscription on its pedestal, each one part of an ancient satanic invocation. That was the reason they were created for some lunatics in the eighteenth century. The yearbook stated that another of the statues is in Lisbon, where I understand your brother-in-law is now visiting, and that the last one belonged to Joan Margalef, an old Catalan collector. I tried to contact him, but he's dead."

"You don't say so." Alicia wanted to be indifferent.

"I spoke with his son, a cold, rather stupid person. If the old man ever came back to life, he'd discover that his heirs liquidated the entire collection. The angel was sold. He didn't recall to whom, it was months earlier, after so many transactions I couldn't ask him for names. I had to repeat that I was a cop, that this was a criminal investigation. Finally, he blurted out that the buyer had been a young woman from Seville."

"A young woman," muttered Alicia, crushing out her cigarette butt on her heel.

"That's right. Any ideas?"

It was better she have no ideas. Her cranium was a beehive filled with furious insects angrily colliding with one another inside her darkened mind. The clues were pointing more and more to the place her initial suspicions had roped off. Her fear of the first days was swelling like an enormous, repugnant abscess that would have to end up bursting. But she did not want to be there when it did. Despite the fact that Esteban's initial suspicions should have vaccinated her sufficiently, it still seemed atrocious to admit something that a certain feeling lodged in some cellar of her heart refused with a decisive passion, trying to find absolutions or alternatives. Something like that occurred to her, of course, it would occur to anyone, and she preferred to run away and close her eyes and sleep a comfortable parenthesis of two thousand years. While she confusedly looked for another cigarette in her overcoat pocket, Alicia noticed that the inspector's eyes were maliciously scrutinizing her. She immediately intuited which train of ideas it was that led to that gaze.

"Wait a minute," she stuttered. "You think I . . ."

"I don't think anything," Gálvez interrupted her, looking aside. "But I am asking you please not to leave Seville for the next few days even if you feel the irresistible urge to travel, as your brother-in-law did. A question of Satanism. Did you notice the tattoo Benlliure had on his forearm when he was found? You must remember that."

"The tattoo."

"Two upside-down *T*s." Gálvez's hand made a brief drawing in the air. "That figure is repeated in the inscription the annual report attributes to the destroyed angel, Mahazael. Actually, if you've noticed, each one of the angels has a small mark on its pedestal aside from the Hebrew letter and the words. I've read some books. The subject is interesting."

"What did you find out?" asked Alicia, her patience at the edge of a cliff—Gálvez's digressions exasperated her.

"They're called *stigmata diaboli*," he answered, showing off his knowledge. "Marks of the devil. The demonologists explain that it was a small scar or tattoo Satan used to mark his acolytes so that they could recognize one another or stand up to torture if they were captured. Some experts point out that the mark is usually placed on hidden parts of the body, zones usually covered by clothing, or also in the armpits, on the back, on the interior of the eyelids, or in the anus. In women, it's placed on a breast or on the part of the sex hidden by hair."

For a moment, Alicia was afraid Gálvez was threatening to inspect her in search of the damn tattoo. She was nervous, night had definitively fallen, and a disturbing wind covered her face with a curtain of hair. She glanced at her watch without seeing the face, announced that it was late, shook hands with the enormous, tight raincoat, and fled, resisting her desire to run. The inspector stayed behind smoking next to the river. The small, blue ball of the moon was by now reflected in the waters.

Ten

R ua do Chão da Feira: The last time Esteban climbed that sadistic hill, he'd had to stop halfway up to wait for Eva, who arrived dragging herself along and puffing like an asthmatic child, and help her lean against the castle wall while he went through his knapsack looking for the bottle of water that could alleviate her shortness of breath. A Japanese man with bony knees walked over and asked in a friendly way if he could be of any service, but it wasn't necessary. Eva couldn't stand hills like those; she wasn't made for carrying baggage on trips. Vacation was supposed to be time off from work in the most literal sense of the expression, a rest, so any added effort was excessive.

The name of the street was the same, Rua do Chão da Feira. The road made of irregular cobblestones continued rising and skirting the wall of the Castelo de São Jorge, recently restored with unsightly patches of plaster and cement. But the style of the ascent that Esteban remembered seemed to have been modified imperceptibly, perhaps the effect of the light. Nothing of the soft limestone-colored Lisbon light in December remained in the uncertain mauve mist that surrounded him. He concluded, speeding up until his thighs hurt, that memory

constructs the past instead of returning it, that memory is imagination troubled by timidity that doesn't dare let its inventions
freely take wing. The Lisbon of that Christmas five years ago
was a buried, nonexistent city, a maze of streets and meetings
essentially different from the city in which he'd now disembarked in search of the end of a thread that could lead him to
the future that was his. The present had nothing to do with
his memory, that tender and boring excursion of then with the
hasty search he was carrying out now. And he found out, shortly
before reaching the Porta de São Jorge, where Edla Ostmann
had agreed to meet him, that in the same way that the Lisbon
of the past had disintegrated and become irrecoverable, the one
he was walking through in that precise instant would also have
to disappear, to continue the fate of being confined to the useless reliquary we call nostalgia.

Ms. Ostmann's navy blue overcoat was supported by two
elevated and squalid legs that were implanted in the gravel
with the solidity of a tripod. They said hello. Esteban made a
comment about the weather, and they set out. Escorted by a
flock of Nordic tourists, they passed the arch of the Porta de
São Jorge and turned toward the castle's watchtower. Half a
dozen rusted cannon were aimed at the estuary. The day had
awakened as cloudy as the one before, so an enormous white
stain made it impossible to see the ocean beyond the last line
where the stevedores were bustling about, where the cargo
ships and cranes stopped in order to turn into tiny, airy toys.
The Praça do Comercio seemed to constitute the final limit
of a disorderly model that scattered in a fan shape under the
unreal weight of the fog.

Esteban counted the churches, white towers topped with
slate tiaras; he peered into the plazas; in the distance, above

the Santa Justa Elevator, he could just make out the petrified skeleton of the Church do Carmo, a fossil multiplied in ashlars and buttresses. At Esteban's side, Edla Ostmann contemplated the panorama for a brief instant, while she smoked another of her small, perfumed cigars. Then, with a kind of courteous brusqueness, she blurted out that they were not there for the sake of tourism and led him along the edge of the fortification, to the collapsed remains of an arch. Behind, there opened a charming, circular little plaza the Nordic retirees were taking advantage of to catch their breath and take photos.

In the center of the plaza, on an austere marble pedestal, a bronze Saint Michael armed with a sword and spear forced a demon to bite his sandal. The excellence of the angel seemed familiar to Esteban or perhaps it was the style in which the violence of the attack had disordered the angel's hair and clothing. The foreshortening of that supernatural, feminine, and undulating body imitated that of another, parallel body that he knew. They went closer. The retirees were exchanging giggles in an enigmatic language infested with aspirated *J*'s. The demon was a sinewy, potent animal who did not seem subdued by the archangel's foot. A mouth bristling with fangs bellowed a cry of rebellion that the bronze had not included. His weapons, smashed by the enemy, were strewn about him scattered and battered—an Oriental dagger, a spear, a round shield with a rhinoceros depicted on it, a monstrous creature, protected by utterly fantastic armor.

"Inácio da Alpiarça," murmured Esteban, extracting a cigarette from the pack.

"Exactly," said Edla Ostmann, who was puffing the black stick of her little cigar. "One stormy night, a lightning bolt destroyed the ancient statue of Saint George that adorned this little plaza. King José I commissioned da Alpiarça to substitute it with another in the same spirit. The artist took the liberty of supplanting the saint in order to depict his master, Lucifer. Just look, good and evil are fighting furiously in the image, neither giving any quarter. Da Alpiarça's rhinoceros was dedicated to the devil."

"How did the *Coniurati* get to Lisbon," asked Esteban, accepting a light from Ms. Ostmann.

"Let's walk," she answered.

Again his will dissolved in the watery element of her eyes, illuminated by a glow that seemed to negate all attempts to dissent, to respond with some act of disobedience. That penetrating and controlling gaze in some way perforated his forehead to get further inside, beyond, below, in the place where that commerce between thought and sensation took place, a place Esteban considered exclusively his own. As they descended through the intricate streets of the Alfama, he was shocked to notice that he'd already had that same impression, that an indefinable presence was breaking open his brain and tearing it apart, appropriating hidden information. It had been afternoon when he had walked out of Almeida's shop with the angel under his arm, and an instinctive form of panic had made him run. An eye had penetrated his mind.

There was no horror in Ostmann's tranquil inspection, but Esteban perceived with a chill that for her he was as transparent as those pale eyes of hers, in which it was possible to contemplate a minuscule, blue glacier. He tried to forget his unrest by changing the direction of his reflections. They were passing by the Sé, the fortified cathedral of Lisbon that had disgusted Eva so much. She could not stand the idea that a cathedral could rise without the required Gothic pinnacles and flying buttresses. At that point in their walk, Edla Ostmann opened her pack and took out another cigar, which she caressed with two pointy white fingers.

"To know the origin of the *Coniurati* sect," she said in an impersonal voice, "certainly the most relevant and sophisticated of all those offered to us by the history of Satanism, we have to go all the way back to Alexandria, in the second or third century of our era. You know that in that period the Roman Empire witnessed a genuine explosion of mystical religions, of magic societies, of wizards, necromancers, priests for backward, strange cults. It was in that culture medium that the revelations of Basilides, the gnostics, Nicholas of Antioch, and Valentinus took form. Amid that promiscuous intercourse of theological and mystical material, the circulation of psalms, litanies, charms, and liturgies derived from the most diverse sources was not uncommon, all of them directed to the most exotic divinities with myriad intentions. In those centuries, the empire adored Jupiter, Isis, Mithras, Jehovah, and Persephone with the same eclectic furor, in Latin, Greek, Egyptian, and Hebrew.

"A certain Greek manuscript with Hebraic interpolations, written down in that period, was transported by a Byzantine savant to the Florence of Ficino and other students of Plato in the middle of the fifteenth century, immediately after the fall of Constantinople. The savant drowned soon after in a shipwreck, and the library that contained the manuscript burned. Even so, Pico della Mirandola or Ermolao Barbaro had held it in their hands, and, like them, so did an anonymous copyist who saved it from the flames. At the beginning of the sixteenth century, the only known copy of that text is in the Vatican library. There it was consulted by Rodrigo Borgia, a descendant of Valencian immigrants, the man who would occupy the pontifical throne under the name Alexander VI."

"What manuscript was that?" Esteban joined in. "I mean, what was its content?"

"It contained an invocation," answered Edla Ostmann, while her violet fingernails encircled the unlit cigar. "It was a reproach to the ancient demon Asmodeus, who mortified Job and Tobias, or to Apollyon, angel of the abyss, called Abaddon the Exterminator in Hebrew. The titles given to that obscure deity are innumerable: Belial, Beelzebub, Lucifer . . . The text of the invocation tries to oblige Satan to appear before the officiant who would then formulate a series of petitions which the demon would later carry out once the pact was signed. It's the Faust myth in its several variations, just as the legends describe it. Strictly speaking, the *Coniurati* sect was born when Pope Alexander, to put a little life into the orgies and banquets he held in the Vatican, suggested inviting the devil. Among the coreligionists figured his two children, Lucretia and Caesar, as well as other political and artistic personalities of the period. You probably know as well—it's been the stuff of countless movies—that the Apocalypse announces the arrival of a mysterious Antichrist, whose presence will inaugurate the Empire of the Last Days, itself a prelude to the kingdom of Lucifer. That Antichrist was to be engendered from the seed of Satan himself. The *Coniurati* postulated that the devil, summoned by the invocation, would couple with a human woman and make her pregnant with the Antichrist. This woman would become the supreme priestess of the cult and would bear the pompous title of papess. Lucrezia Borgia, a woman of supernatural beauty, was the papess. In his first manifestation, always following the chronicles, Satan appeared as an enigmatic combination of ram and prince. He assigned tasks to his faithful and marked them with the famous *stigmata diaboli,* or marks of the devil.

"They crossed the Baixa on foot going north. At Rua da Assunção, a tram went on ahead of them and continued up the street, packed with faces that convulsively moved their mouths and eyes. The fog had begun to lift, and the sky, above their heads and the compact blocks of apartment buildings, seemed bluer and higher.

"The demon divided the group into four churches," Ostmann blinked, "each governed by an archbishop, who in turn was under the orders of the papess. Why four? Four usually suggests totality—four cardinal points, four elements, four seasons, four temperaments. The river that flowed from the garden of Eden had four branches; in his vision, Ezekiel saw four cherubim; God visits four punishments on His people in Jeremiah—sword, dogs, birds, and beasts. Each one of the diabolical churches was under the auspices of one of Lucifer's princes, those who accompanied him in his insurrection against the Most High: Samael, Azazel, Azael, and Mahazael."

"The angels." Esteban abstractedly footnoted her staring at the tips of his boots.

The Santa Justa elevator was an elegant steel cage that connected the Baixa with the Bairro Alto. An individual decked out in a uniform with frogging took the coins Ms. Ostmann handed him and pointed to a place on the red seating that ran around the elevator's wall. Two or three Japanese tourists exchanged impressions in voices that seemed cartoonish. The individual with the uniform consulted his wristwatch and pushed a button. No sooner had the sliding door closed than the surrounding buildings began to descend outside the windows like the scenery at an opera. Slowly, Alfama hill emerged before Esteban's eyes, a parcel of earth marked with ocher and gray patches on top of which arose the extenuated pile of Castelo de São Jorge. There, to the right, the sea had freed itself of the annoying morning mist and shone enormous and deserted like a lunar circus. The exit put them on the Praça do Carmo, next to the skeletal remains of the church Esteban had picked out from the castle. They went along a long, carpeted corridor, and once again the sunlight gilded their heads.

"In 1501," Edla Ostmann said, picking up the thread of her speech with a slight cough, "Lucrezia Borgia gave birth to an unknown 'Roman child,' whose father the black legend alleges was her own father, Pope Alexander. A more audacious hypothesis identifies the child as the devil's heir, engendered during one of the Black Masses celebrated so assiduously at the time in the Apostolic See. Be that as it may, in 1502, Lucrezia married Alfonso d'Este in order to move to Ferrara and begin a new life free of those machinations. The child's throat was slit while it slept, and its remains were fed to its uncle Caesar's hunting dogs. But despite the decent life she led in her new city and her intention to reform, which turned her for a time into the most devout of creatures, Lucrezia again flirted with magic. She became pregnant with a child that caused her to bleed to death from a miscarriage in 1519. Lucrezia's death, prelude to the murder of her brother and the fall of Alexander, unleashed a furious persecution that wiped the *Coniurati* off the face of Italy. Pius III, the new pope, ordered the Borgia library burned and destroyed the liturgical objects. If it hadn't been for a servant of Alexander VI, probably one of his bastards, who lost his tongue, one eye, and one hand under torture, the fateful manuscript with the charm would have been lost. This man, who knew no Greek, carefully copied the signs and fled with them to Venice."

They'd crossed the diagonal of Praça do Carmo and were going up Rua da Trinidade, sunk in a sudden silence. Edla Ostmann's legs were tall white scissors that strode a street dotted with shops, where the windows exhibited the venal elegance of manikins they had no time to contemplate. They stopped opposite a building on whose facade were some faded angels and cornucopias. She made a sign. The bored man waiting in the vestibule behind a solid mahogany desk received three coins and handed her two tickets. They made their way into an interior room. The roof was an intersection of rotund black beams that Ms. Ostmann's head almost touched. Through a window it was possible to see a garden. The house was old. Its whitewashed walls, its floor in chessboard pattern with red tiles, and that smell of age and coolness all spoke of earlier centuries.

At the entrance, there was a rectangular hall that had the look of a dining room. Esteban found a puppet in a display case. It wore a dress coat, braiding, and a wig, like a little wooden Casanova. The badly carved features of the face expressed resignation or sleepiness; the lace at the end of the sleeves had been food for moths a long time before.

"This is one of the oldest houses in Lisbon," Ms. Ostmann informed Esteban, her voice strangely cracked by the echo. "It was one of the few to survive the earthquake of fifty-five, although one wing did collapse, and the stable in the rear of the patio was also destroyed. Today it's the marionette museum of Lisbon. It's called the House of the Labyrinth because of the beautiful hedge labyrinth that covers the garden. Look at the lower part of the walls Mr. Labastida."

Swerving his gaze away from the marionette in the vitrine, Esteban noticed a small, brown drawing that was repeated insanely at the base of the walls: rhinoceroses. The house had belonged to da Alpiarça; it was the house where he had kept his rhinoceros. That discovery transformed it in Esteban's mind into something magnetic and monstrous at the same time. It was possible to imagine the animal stretched out on its silk bed, presiding over a corps of servants, receiving visits from eminent men with its horn on high. He had the impression that the rhinoceros had to be the symbol of something, as the eagle or dove were, but its meaning was hard to discern.

"Andrea Messauro," said Ostmann, "later known as Achille Feltrinelli, was a young prelate who served as a secretary in Venice to the Castrovalvas, one of the most influential families in the Most Serene Republic. It is to him we owe the honor of having rescued the document, the copy made by the servant, from a bundle of commercial papers it had been mixed in with in the Venetian commodity market. When he realized what the manuscript promised, he decided to revive the ancient glory of the *Coniurati*. The duke's guard foiled his attempt. Messauro wandered through Switzerland, Germany, France, and Spain trying to propagate the gospel of the devil and colliding with the hostility of the authorities.

"It was in Lisbon, around 1753, where the Italian fugitive found protection in the person of the bizarre sculptor of King José I, Dom Inácio da Alpiarça, obsessed at the time with the sickness of a rhinoceros which he loved more than his own life and which he cared for like his own child in a

stable in his garden. The two of them gathered a small cell of
nobles and courtiers, stolid and bored individuals in need of
novelties, and they founded a new generation of *Coniurati*.
Their papess was an aristocratic adventuress born in England,
a woman of fiery beauty, blessed with a head of violently red
hair, Lady Hester Stanhope. Before joining the sect, she was
already controversial and aroused all sorts of passions. She
would stroll naked through the gardens of her palace accompanied by a black slave who would caress her when she ordered it. She practiced fencing and used opium. Da Alpiarça
made the four angels for her, each one with a fourth part of
the invocation, which each of the four archbishops of the four
churches was to protect."

"But the angels did not have only the invocation,"
Esteban appositely observed.

"No, Mr. Labastida, you know that very well." Edla
Ostmann's gaze became vertiginous and threatening, and
Esteban became disoriented. "Each angel carries, inscribed on
his pedestal, a fragment of the invocation text, faithfully reproduced from the manuscript Feltrinelli exhumed in Venice.
There are also four Hebrew letters that, put together, give us
nun-tet-shin-lamed, LSTN, Satan. That's the name of the
Enemy in the Old Testament. Aside from an homage, it's also
a clue. The inscriptions on the four angels have to be combined to decipher their message."

"Yes," said Esteban. "Also, we have the beginning of the
verses that appear at the end of Feltrinelli's *Mysterium* as well
as some lines in an unknown language. What does all that
mean?"

Edla Ostmann took a deep breath. They were leaving
behind, on both sides, crowds of marionettes, diminutive and

attentive spectators who watched them fixedly from the silence of their painted eyes. Small dragons with paper tongues,
princesses and knights left to moths and rust hung from the
walls like small criminals abandoned on their gallows, forgotten by the hangman. Esteban suspected they were not alone,
that all those strung-up spectators were also interested in the
atrocious and impassioning events for which the house where
they now lived had been a theater. At the door of a new room
that held a maimed harlequin, she answered, "The Venetian
manuscript did not contain only the invocation. It also gave
detailed instructions about where and how the invocation was
to be recited. Since the pedestals make no reference to that,
we have to suppose those verses and the text in the unknown
language contain the key. I don't know what the relationship
is between one and the other; I don't know what language
that is. The books of famous demonologists are filled with
fantastic languages in which those savants attempted to communicate with demons. Just look into Trithemius or John
Dee. At the same time, the rest of the symbology is not difficult to decipher. You probably noticed that next to the left
foot of each angel there is a miniature animal, a lion, an eagle,
a man, and a bull. The Book of Ezekiel, chapter one, verses
five through thirteen, contains the description of four human-
oid, winged monsters, with four faces each—the central
human face, lion to the right, ox to the left, and, above all of
them, the eagle. The monsters reappear in the Apocalypse,
but they're a man, a lion, an ox, and an eagle with wings covered with eyes. The exegetes do not agree about the meaning
of those creatures, but the interpretations swing back and forth
between the unrepresentable presence of God and the meta-
morphic force of the devil. On the bronze angels they stand

as counterparts to the four Evangelists, who, as you probably know, took an anagram from each one of those animals. As to the limping—being an invalid in all primitive cultures is a sign of perversion. The Book of Kings describes how Baal's priests limp when they celebrate his ritual dance, and Genesis says Jacob broke his leg fighting with the Lord's angel. Satan was left crippled after falling from Heaven to Earth."

The room they'd just entered was small and square. No marionettes scaled its walls, which were covered with those blue tiles typical of Lisbon that are usually adorned with grotesques and vegetable filigree and are placed above doors in sweetshops. A city poured itself out in a circle over all the tiles, a blue, pale city that seemed as unreal as a puppet theater. The blue buildings were stacked on top of one another, forming terraces, long strings of facades juxtaposed with that fantastic air of opera sets. The peristyles of the palaces yielded to the pediments of academies; circuses divided into rows hid timid blue pergolas which barely peered over the balustrades of the military schools. And in the center of each of the four walls, a circular plaza housed a small figure, a tiny, almost indecipherable body on which, despite everything, the wings were recognizable, as were the tranquil animals waiting next to a broken foot.

That amphitheater surrounding Esteban, that blue, enigmatic stage set, was the same one reproduced in the book he'd tried to translate piecemeal, the same one Alicia had wandered through, fleeing the suffocating density of her nightmares: New Babel painted on the walls, yanked out of dreams and libraries and placed in the center of a house inhabited by puppets. For the first time, Esteban contemplated it just as it was, with his own eyes and not through Alicia's hesitating descriptions. Enraptured, he made his way across each wall, stopping opposite each picture. In that moment he was struck, as if in an explosion, by the real reason for his visit to Lisbon. He'd traveled there to know the interior city, the impossible city. Seville and Lisbon were replicas, disguises, ridiculous excuses for the archetypal city, the perfect city Alicia had explored and that now revealed itself to Esteban in all the fascination of its physicality.

New Babel was as real or realer than the cities where he'd spent his life, cities where he'd fallen in love, cities he'd strolled through, cities that marked chapters in his transitory life, a life without emphasis, like water. He recalled that story in *The Thousand and One Nights* (literature and more literature) where a man who sleeps in a patio under a palm tree dreams about a treasure hidden in a house in another, faraway city. He travels to the other city, finds the house, and is expelled by the person living there. When the traveler describes his dream, the man laughs at him and tells him not to pay any attention to dreams. He dreams every night about a patio with a palm tree under which there is a buried treasure. The treasure was in the traveler's own house, but he had to go on a pilgrimage to find out. Esteban had traveled five hundred kilometers to dig up Alicia's visions.

"New Babel," said Edla Ostmann with a gesture of introduction that seemed to include the entire house. "In fact, this is the room where the *Coniurati* held their meetings in Lisbon. The first stone of the city had been laid during the rule of the Borgias. The stiffening of repression in Italy had left as the only escape for the cult members a secret meeting in latitudes diametrically opposite those where the sun shines one day after another. Spurred on by the speculations of Fludd and Bruno, who said they could use their minds to construct imaginary geographies to reinforce memory, the new *Coniurati* expanded, using the collective potential of their imaginations, the New Babylon you see here. They worked on it every night, enlarging it, each one contributing his particular passion: statues, balustrades, palaces, arms.

On the night of November 1, 1755, a special meeting was held in the palace of Marquise Stanhope. The *Coniurati* witnessed the papess giving birth, supposedly made pregnant by the devil himself. The earthquake pulverized the child and the mother and crushed all those at the meeting except two. Inácio da Alpiarça, wounded, ran all the way here only to discover that his rhinoceros was dead."

Ms. Ostmann's fine finger pointed to the window. Under a faded sun, the vast labyrinth in the garden took shape, a vegetable calligraphy that drew scrawls and coils impossible to follow all the way to a distant, low building with patched walls. They went down some stairs and once again entered the open air. The sky was an enormous turquoise tent over their heads. Ostmann wanted to show Esteban the stable that had been home to the rhinoceros, so they entered the labyrinth. He followed closely behind her, not wanting to stray from the crunching sound her heels made when they ground into the gravel. They followed an infinite corridor of rhododendrons. Esteban could not calculate how much time passed before he got lost. At one bend, he turned to the right and found that Edla Ostmann's back, supported by her two tall, rapid legs, had disappeared. He tried to retrace his steps to the entrance, but discovered that the corridor had a slight curve to it that he hadn't noticed before. He emerged in a roundabout with a fountain. He smoked a cigarette patiently, thought about shouting Ostmann's name, but felt ashamed.

He was visited, one by one, by thoughts: She'd soon come back for him, or perhaps no one could rescue him at that indefinite point, in an infinite succession of paths and flower beds. He would go on. It didn't matter which route he took, the solution did not have to respond to a logical layout—strictly topographical—of the garden's architecture. The wind had begun to whistle through the galleries, striking Esteban's face, squeezing his eyebrows. He continued impenitently for four consecutive cigarettes; he visited three roundabouts, or the same roundabout three times. Again, he reasoned that reason could not provide the key to decipher the labyrinth, that it was incapable of rising beyond the narrow corridor he was exploring. Reason became perverted in mirrors, lost its senses as well, and would founder as soon as the road ahead became more ambiguous, as he could no longer have the facts of the enigma right at hand. Closing his eyes, he had to rely on the sort of impulse that on so many other occasions before had advised him, had ordered a gesture or a word or had impeded them without supplying any explanation, simply because it seemed appropriate to the symmetry, to the secret mathematics of things. If he wanted to get out, if he wanted to find the stable, the truth, the treasure, his reason should allow itself to be guided by that instinct, by the blind hand that knows without waking up where the alarm clock and the lamp are located on the night table. He was stepping on the last cigarette butt when a hand grasped his shoulder: Edla Ostmann had appeared behind him as if she'd sprung from a hedge.

...

They'd left Mamen's study at around five, after an interminable argument about the properness of the visit, until Alicia gave a sigh that could be heard all over the apartment and decided to leave alone with her hands in her coat pockets. Mamen hastily caught up with her on the second landing, begged her pardon without excessive emphasis, the truth is that the damned visit still seemed a nonsense as big as a house, if you go on obeying that nut Marisa in a minute you're going to find yourself expurgating inquisition-style the menus of all the restaurants, but, well, if that would calm her down, fine. Alicia already knew all that and was asking her for the fourth or fifth time not to spit on her; they turned onto Torneo going toward the Alameda, while she repeated that this was nothing more than a try, that she had no reason to accept wholeheartedly like a fool whatever the fortune-teller had to tell her for the modest price of two or three thousand pesetas, she just wanted one more opinion. Mamen had to agree with her in that, after all, the matter of the adulterated dreams, as public as a park, wasn't exactly a very common matter, one that she'd confide to an astonished man who occupied an office: for strange ills, strange cures. Perhaps Asia Ferrer, no matter how bizarre and crazy, possessed the key to an intrigue as outlandish as hers.

Shaking her head negatively, Mamen accompanied Alicia in silence along Calatrava Street. Of course she wasn't going to approve Alicia's ten thousandth folly—all they needed was a fortune-teller—but she wasn't going to let Alicia go alone so she could interpret in her own way whatever that ninny was going to spring on her. Much less would she leave her in the hands of Marisa, who could end up furnishing her fantasy from top to bottom with some clever explanation based on the ambiguity of the fifth dimension. Alicia's problem was clear, if anyone wanted to see it. An obsessive neurosis that was ravaging her mind at full speed, gaining a mile every time she decided to feed the bonfire with yet another visit to who knows whom or by speaking via telephone with that irresponsible Esteban. Yes, yes she understood that he wanted to sleep with her, but there were better methods to obtain that goal.

Four hippies were beating a drum on a bench in the Alameda, sharing beers and marijuana. Alicia and Mamen crossed the parking lots to Peris Mencheta Street, where the bars were beginning to open. On both sides, they passed sick facades, the odd, dark person smoking something invisible. The number supplied by Marisa's card corresponded to a two-story house with flowerpots on the balcony and a glazed Virgin stuck in the entryway. To one side languished a veterinary clinic whose neon sign was broken. Mamen repeated that there was still time to turn around and avoid a headache, but Alicia was already going up the stairs.

The wall had been whitewashed once upon a time, but humidity and cracks had diligently scratched the white surface in order to outline huge, colorless archipelagos. When they reached the top of the stairs, a woman of indefinite age greeted them from behind a door. Makeup disfigured her face from which stood out her violently curved nose. A bazaar of rings clotted on her hands, twisted by arthritis. The best part, according to Mamen, was, aside from the more or less requisite tunic, the improbable mane of violet-colored hair that fell down her back. Courteously invited in by the woman, they entered the apartment. It was then that the stench of cat urine reeking in the corners attacked them. They made their way past a living room with a television set and then the kitchen. Asia Ferrer's study was at the end of a short hallway and decorated with prints of the signs of the zodiac.

"We were sent to you by Marisa Gordillo," explained Alicia, as if she were begging pardon.

"Oh, Marisa," answered the woman, her mouth shaped to utter a curse. "In that case, I'll give you a discount. But the discount is usually valid only if I read the cards, but since it's you, I'll do it for a palm reading."

The study was a realization of Mamen's most pessimistic predictions. A rigorous purple curtain covered the four walls; a round table received the indirect light from a spherical lamp in the center of the room, next to a sideboard carved with signs taken from some book found in a supermarket. The cat responsible for sprinkling the house with his priceless fluids was lazily napping in a chair. It was a monstrous gray and white animal, as fat as a sack. Asia Ferrer lit some little bars of incense and asked them to be seated. Laughter was on the verge of supplanting annoyance on Mamen's lips. The white, lateral light, sharpened the shadows of the fortune-teller's face, almost turning it into a sinister mask from Greek tragedy. She extended her ring-laden fingers over the tablecloth before saying, "Asia Ferrer, at your service. Ask me whatever you desire."

The good woman arched her eyebrows more and more as Alicia repeated that she did not want to consult the cards, did not want her palm read, didn't even want a reading of coffee grounds. She was there because of a dream. A strange dream it wasn't worthwhile describing in too much detail.

What Alicia wanted to know was if there existed the possibility that dreams could be shared, that is, if several people could intervene together in the dream scenario, as if they'd agreed to meet in a bar or in someone's house. She wanted to know if dreams were such common places, accessible like any museum, like any bordello. As Alicia was running over the list of her questions opposite the concentrated rictus of Asia Ferrer, Mamen allowed herself to be hypnotized by the cat: The animal observed her with yellow fixity from the depth of its eyes.

"Look," said Asia Ferrer in the same voice someone would use to explain quantum physics to a five-year-old, "what's happening to you is perfectly normal. Well, I wouldn't say ordinary, although there have been many cases, but perfectly natural. Of course to understand it you have to take into account a series of previous points."

Mamen's eyelids stoically clapped shut. Now the inevitable lesson about the secret composition of things was coming, that whole combination of ineffable truths that gave the lie to the incredible naivete of the empirical sciences. Asia Ferrer was speaking with the solemnity of someone addressing a thousand faithful listeners.

"Miss, our being is divided into seven planes—seven forms of existence, seven superimposed categories. On the lowest level we have the Physical Plane or *Sthula,* which corresponds to matter, which for human beings is the corporeal body—hair, bones, skin, etc. Then comes the Astral Plane, *Kama,* about which I'll speak in a moment, and then the mental plane or *Manas.* This last plane coincides with personal consciousness, that is, the ego each of us has, our identification marks, the thing we recognize as our own when we are in control of our faculties. As to *Kama,* the Astral Plane, it includes all that potential for psychic acts which the individual does not use; it coincides with what psychologists, irreverent and obtuse people, disdainfully call the subconscious."

"Certainly," replied Alicia, looking out of the corner of her eye at Mamen, who was on the point of exploding with laughter.

"The astral body is a body composed of a very subtle substance that adheres to matter but which separates from it in certain states: daydreaming, being half asleep, under the influence of drugs, and, especially, during sleep. Once freed, the astral body can visit space and pick up objects. Of course, what this body visits is not the material world, the world we're used to moving through, but a parallel world that has no reason to coincide with the other, the astral world."

"So there are two worlds," Alicia said, trying to clarify matters.

"There are many worlds, miss"—Asia Ferrer's answer was intended to be lapidary—"but all of them are in this world. Imagine two hotel rooms, one above the other, containing the same furniture arranged in the same way. The material body has access only to the lower room. The astral body, if it's trained, can visit both. Astral vision is what we call clairvoyance, what we call telekinesis is astral touch."

It was moving to see how clear everything was for this good woman. For a moment, Mamen's rage and laughter yielded and gave way to a sincere envy. Now she understood what advantages Marisa derived from revelations like these. Everything in its place, every object with its label, the same system applied to the bathroom that applied to the seven planes of being, entropy domesticated and the universe as clean of mysteries as the garden in the backyard. Who needed truth if it was nothing but a mutilated, partial solution that did not help anyone understand the total geometry of things?

"Astral geography and material geography do not necessarily coincide," added Asia Ferrer snatching up her cat, in whom she detected the temptation to water a curtain. "The astral replica of an object is not found, nor is it obligatory that it be found, in the same place as its material model. On the Astral Plane, things, buildings, landscapes, can move and combine, creating that contradictory and enigmatic universe we see in dreams. What you've walked through is an astral city, a city that is out there, somewhere, just as Rome or Paris are in their locations."

"But, the thing is"—the explanation was intuitively convincing Alicia—"to go to Rome, I take a jet."

"Moving through the astral zone is simpler." The fortune-teller's hand was swimming in the cat's ash-colored fur. "The merest desire to be elsewhere is all you need."

"I've never wanted to be there."

"Perhaps your case is more complicated." The cat jumped and returned to the floor. "There are exceptional persons, gifted with a very vigorous astral body, persons who from their childhood have evinced aptitudes for telepathy and telekinesis. One of those persons, one very close to you, to the point of being able to kidnap your astral body, may have brought you there without your having noticed."

"Madam," interrupted an excited Mamen, "I'm afraid your cat is going to ruin the curtains."

...

Walking down Feria Street, Mamen could still remember the expression of panic that had distorted the face of poor Asia Ferrer, doctor of the seven planes of being, and how quickly she had slapped the cat, who screeched with fury before colliding with the sideboard carved with beautiful pentacles. It was obvious that the poor lady, despite Marisa's vehement publicity, had very few clients, thanks, in particular, to the generosity of her pet, who liked to regale her visitors with samples of his most unequivocal fluids. Alicia hadn't spoken since they left the fortune-teller's rooms, and she paced the sidewalk with her hands rigidly stuck in her pockets, contemplating the ground with eyes busy seeing other things. Her cigarette slowly burned down between her lips. The enigmas that were crossing her path were becoming more and more transparent. She'd found an entryway that could lead her to the other side of the fence. Of course it had come from sources that would have made Inspector Gálvez laugh and force him to denigrate the motives with a sweep of his beefsteak-sized hands. Mamen was repeating, and she was right, that a person would have to be naive—speaking euphemistically—to believe that creature with violet hair and all her wisdom learned from the monthly magazine. But an analysis as outlandish as the one that was clogging her intelligence demanded an equally bizarre explanation.

They'd taken a detour along Feria because Mamen wanted to pass by Toñi's apartment for a moment to have some documents from the congress typed up before Thursday. They crossed Resolana to the zone of the Torre de los Perdigones, where Mamen pressed a buzzer four times without any appreciable results. On the way back to Torneo, they stopped at a crosswalk with a small group of ladies with perms carrying shopping bags. No omen clouded Alicia's mind until the first bus passed by and she saw herself reflected in the fleet-ing, crystal-lightning flash of a window. She detected a vague shadow behind her, an overcoat, and sunglasses. She turned her head in profile, piqued by a suspicion, and the corner of her eye confirmed her first impression. Behind her, facing the zebra stripes of the crosswalk, had stopped a woman wrapped in a very roomy black overcoat. She blinked without being able to keep a capricious fear from starting to erode her spine. She turned supplicating eyes toward Mamen, who was dis-tracted in the contemplation of an advertisement for sewing machines on the building opposite them.

Alicia could not make her sensation of danger concrete, give it a tangible reason, but she did intuit that a drastic con-clusion was approaching with the speed of a locomotive, and that the woman behind them, that shadow as imprecise as an image in a puddle, had a role in the performance. She brought together all the threads too late to react gracefully. Another bus was tearing up the avenue just a few meters distant from her, and a fist sank into Alicia's kidneys, making her weak in the knees. She staggered, fell forward, and had the tiniest fraction of a second to roll over before the bus would have smashed into her with a moan and a musical curse from the driver.

Her heart was about to explode into a thousand pieces, but she had no time to hold back her violence. Mamen was running at her side with her brows graphically planted in the middle of her forehead when she felt the same hand that had tried to shove her into the street seizing hold of her arm. She kicked, blinded by panic, tried to break free, felt that her heel was smashing down on something that retreated and that the pressure on her arm was relaxing at the same time. Then she ran across the street, which by then was reduced to a narrow, lightless tunnel, knocking down a lady horrified at the lack of respect shown by today's youth.

Alicia couldn't see her, but Mamen was running behind, seriously hampered by her high heels, which threatened to stamp her into the pavement if they carried out a maneuver at a higher than normal speed. She shouted Alicia's name, convinced that the poor woman was completely insane. Alicia's breathing was burning her lungs, but her leg muscles did not want to stop, couldn't stop. The brief opportunity of that leap had been able to remove her from that total annihilation that the bus window had revealed to her in a flash.

Mamen never stopped shouting, and her voice was beginning to crack. She did not understand the purpose of this stupid race until, stopping to remove her shoes and go on barefoot, she noticed that a gigantic, black body, a kind of bird with its wings spread, was trying to jump on her. There was a brief scuffle, Mamen felt her fingers getting scratched, and immediately she began running with renewed vigor and no hesitation. She saw that Alicia had stopped almost opposite the Barqueta Bridge, that she was getting onto a bus that was about to pull out. Mamen dodged the last attack by the black shadow, scrambling up the three metal steps barefoot. The bus's door closed with a kind of snort; the two women peered anxiously through the window. A black overcoat retreated toward the avenue, keeping a careful eye on the fading bus. Mamen felt her mouth was infected with a bitter, dense taste. She realized it was fear.

"Alicia, for heaven's sake," she snorted, "are you going to tell me what this is all about?"

"Just what you saw."

They were close, so close that the next movement would have burned her hand.

. . .

Night was settling onto Praça de Rossio and the Athenian facade of the National Theater when he was strolling back to the hotel. Sunset had brought the fog back with it, and fine gauze was moistening Esteban's face, keeping him from lighting a cigarette no matter how hard he tried to take shelter in some entryway and use his lighter. Taking long steps, he again thought about the confused conversation he'd had with Edla Ostmann or with the remote intelligence that spoke through her lips. His brain turned into a whirling bazaar where rhinoceroses, puppets with dress coats, and fragile blue cities filled with columns spun around. His getting lost in the labyrinth at da Alpiarça's house seemed to him the perfect metaphor for his current situation, perhaps even a sign sent by chance or destiny so he'd know the next move he should make. Because reality is a kind of secret code that constantly sends messages that might orient us if only we learned the right language, the lost language of things. To exit the labyrinth, it was first necessary to reach the center, the angular hill from which it was possible to see the complete plan of the corridors and galleries. To resolve the enigma of Alicia's dream it was necessary to resolve the mystery of the pedestals, the wax seal that would allow them to get to the page of answers. That provisional detour became absolutely necessary.

The pastry shop Esteban entered was occupied by four locals with wrinkled faces, hidden under checked caps. He sat at a side table, next to a large window dominated by the monument to Dom Pedro IV in front of which pairs of black men wearing leather jackets were walking. A girl with sad eyes brought the *bica* he'd ordered to his table along with a glass of rather cloudy water, which he pushed aside. At night, Lisbon again turned into the impossible model of the past, a stage set of another time that could subsist only in the dry geography of memories. Through the fog and the trams, he again glimpsed Eva's face, again felt nostalgia for that substitute happiness, which an all-too-corrosive clear-sightedness had ruined years ago. Slowly, that mask began turning into another, one much closer, the mask with green eyes that awaited him when he returned from the trip and certainly at the exit to the labyrinth, when all unknowns would be revealed.

His hand trembled when he felt through the pocket of his parka and pulled out the notebook where he'd jotted down his journalistic notes about the Adimanta Foundation. He tore out two pages and put them on the table in front of him, next to the coffee that was beginning to get cold and the rejected glass of water. On one, he copied the inscriptions of the four angels in the same order that chance had presented them; on the other, he wrote out the four verses from Feltrinelli's book.

DIRA.FAMES.VSVTSVC.EDRDD.ESADVDC . . .
HUMANAQAVE.HOMINES.TESIDRV.
   AETAESME.IN.INSAENE.EVMPTE . . .
DENTE.DRACO.TGIVGERED.ROAGD.
   MGEGD.MVTEE . . .
MAGNA.PARTE.BISSCSV.VEISEI.PIIESEIOETI.
   ISSIE . . .

Dira fames Polypos docuit sua rodere crura,
Humanaque homines se nutriise dape.
Dente Draco caudam dum mordet et ingerit alvo,
Magna parte sui si cibus ipse sibi.

He felt these eight lines hid, like a shell, the essence of the puzzle. Why did each one of the inscriptions refer to each one of the verses? What was the interpretation to be made of that vague alchemical poem so that the key would make it possible to open the lock? Whatever the content of the secret message was, it had to give information about a place. Ostmann had assured him it hid the exact point where the incantation had to be spoken to bring about its effect. There remained, of course, the possibility that the words on the pedestals were from some ancient, unknown, or simply invented language. That would obviate any chance to move forward.

In the cellar of Esteban's Cartesian mind was the certainty that the puzzle could be taken apart if he were to use, diligently, the scalpel of his intelligence, the analytic intelligence that made Monsieur Dupin reconstruct crimes that had taken place kilometers away from the house where he'd chatted with a friend. That same intelligence should be able to answer questions posed centuries away from the coffee shop where he was evoking a face with green eyes, sweet and wounding like the memory of an unrealized project. The dragon that bit its tail possessed the secret, the dragon that ended in his beginning like the perverse labyrinth which had confused him. He tried several possibilities, changing the position of letters, discerning Latin words through the dense gibberish of the inscriptions. He crossed out, rewrote, finished the coffee. Tedium and a headache suggested he step out for some air.

The fog was hanging from the streetlights, fabricating sacks of cotton. Esteban bought a bottle of cheap whiskey in a bar and went back to the hotel with his hands dead in the pockets of his parka. His fingers were playing with the notebook pages on which he'd scratched out his attempts at translation. The lady with the wart half asleep at the desk received him with a shock. She handed him the key to his room, number fourteen, and went back to immersing herself in the exhibition of gymnastics taking place silently on her television screen. The hotel room seemed more pleasant, more secluded, more solitary than ever. Out of some stupid inertia he pressed the button on the remote control and found himself face to face with the same squalid girls who were waving ribbons and hoops on the screen at the desk.

The whiskey was lacerating. It scratched his throat with the taste of rotten wood. When he fell into bed, next to the night table, he was attacked by the bizarre idea of telephoning Alicia. He imagined her on her pillow, sleeping naked under sheets that ran softly over the meadows of her hips. He emptied the pockets of his parka, left his cigarettes on the coverlet, the two pages of writing, one on top of the other, on top of the shade of the lamp he'd turned on. Before collapsing into the bed again and with another swallow of that poisonous whiskey, he prayed. He prayed to Edgar Allan Poe that his spirit bring him the intuition necessary to find the solution, just as he'd illuminated Auguste Dupin and William Legrand. Then he fell asleep or thought he was sleeping.

He opened his eyes later, but how much later he had no idea. He felt strangely refreshed, as if he'd just emerged from a pool where he'd spent the entire night swimming under water. Now there were no more girls on the television screen,

only a courteous gentleman wearing a sports jacket who was
pointing to an isobar map. Then, looking up and lazily exploring the ceiling, he discovered the yellow stain. The light
from the lamp smashed against the white rectangle over his
head and wrote gigantic letters, letters spattered with cross-
ings out and corrections that imitated his own handwriting
on an enormous scale. The two sheets, one on top of the other,
were superimposed on the ceiling, mixing together and creating four confused lines that gave Esteban the revelation with
the force of a punch in the jaw. His heart gave a leap. Esteban
instantly grabbed the pages and put them on the bed. Yes,
that was it, of course that was it, you had to be stupid not to
see it before. With one hand on his chest, he forced himself
to calm down while he lit a cigarette and again punished his
stomach with another whiskey. He tore another sheet out of
the notebook and jotted down two lines:

DIRA FAMES POLYPOS DOCVIT SVA
RODERE CRVRA ABCD EFGHI KLMNOPQ
RSTVXY Z

The easiest way to encode message was to change the
order of its letters only. Each one would correspond to another within a previously specified code. A code, what else
could the poem from Feltrinelli's book be? Four codes for the
four lines on the pedestals, a different code for each inscription. All he had to do was compare each verse with the Latin
alphabet to find out which letter he'd have to write to substitute for which other. In the sequence *Dira fames,* which corresponded to the first angel, the *D* would take the place of
the *A,* the *I* the *B,* the *R* the *C,* and so on. With his blood

bursting the veins in his skull, Esteban wrote out the results. It didn't clear up very much.

VSNTSVC.EDRDD.ESADVDC
VOVYOVR.FRDAA.FODRVAR

He tried it with second and third lines, but he smashed against the same nonsense. Carried away with rage, he chain-smoked two cigarettes while he paced hysterically in circles around the room. He tortured his stomach with large gulps of whiskey, as if that defenseless organ were to blame for his failure. He wanted to call Alicia and confess that all was lost, that his incompetence as a translator had ended up defeating them; he wanted to tell her that he loved her.

It must have been very late when he again collapsed onto the bed, worn out and drunk. His memory showed him, as if in a film, the Adimanta Foundation Museum, the little cigars that Edla Ostmann inhaled over the course of her tale full of demons and rhinoceroses, Alicia's ravaged apartment, the city, the dragon that bit its tail. He remembered his conversation with Alicia in the park, the Ouroboros, hermetic symbol of time that eternally vomits itself, where the beginning and the end are undifferentiated. Advancing through the thick mists with which the whiskey had clouded his mind, he reached this conclusion: The engraving of the dragon above the four verses meant that the end was the beginning. This time he did not want to allow his uncontrolled writing hand to act for him, dictating decisions that came not from his brain but from some burning substance mixed in his blood with a bit of tap water. He slowly made his way to the washbasin, looked at his eyes in the mirror. They were the eyes of a desperate man who has spent an entire night weeping, in postponing an execution, in encircling a deception. He tossed water on his temples and wrists and lit a cigarette. The window showed him that the mist over Lisbon was thicker than ever. All he could see were the white globes of the streetlights on a street erased by a disturbing, foamy coal. He again picked up the notebook, ripped out another page, again wrote out the inscription on the first angel. But now he began the substitutions with the alphabet at the other end. The end was the beginning.

DIRA FAMES POLYPOS DOCVIT SVA RODERE
CRVRA ZYX VTSRQP ONM LKIHGF EDCBA

The dragon must indicate that the code had to be figured out backwards, from the last letter to the first and not from the first to the last, as he'd tried to do it the last time. The line that materialized showed him that finally he hadn't made a mistake. The outer door of the fence was open.

VSVTSVC.EDRDD.ESADVDC
CORPORE.FILII.HOMINIS

The author of the code hadn't been demanding insofar as the correspondence of the letters was concerned. It was clear he'd tried to raise all possible barriers to frighten off the profane who might try to attack his secret. The *V* could be read as *C* in CRVRA or *N* in SVA, or even *R* in DOCVIT. The reader had to accept the letter that most conformed to the context, let himself be guided intuitively by the position of the other characters. Esteban immediately copied the second verse.

HVMANAQVE HOMINES SE NVTRIISSE DAPE
Z YXVTSRQ PO NMLKIHGFE DCBA

The second deciphered line spoke about a stone and about hell.

TESIDRV.AETAESME.IN.INSAENE.EVMPTE
LAPIDEM.CALCAQVE.IN.INFERNA.AMBULA

Ten minutes later he had the entire quatrain—the place where the invocation had to be spoken in order to force Satan to visit the officiant. That knowledge horrified him; he felt a chill, and it seemed that the fog outside was covered with eyes that silently scrutinized. He had a presentiment: He knew that his mysterious pursuers, those who'd murdered Benlliure and Almeida, the people who'd attacked Alicia's house, were trying to have him reconstruct those four verses for them, that tetrahedral combination that mentioned, without naming it, a place where the earth crossed paths with hell. Esteban read the four lines four times; he had no idea what they meant.

> *Corpore filii homini*
> *Lapidem cacaque in inferna ambula*
> *Hebreicis novem pedes tradi*
> *Latinis septme, graecis quatuor admime.*

It wasn't too late; the clock that had just appeared on the television screen said fifteen minutes to twelve. The whiskey and his fever had dilated the time of his analysis until it had become as unending as the night of a criminal who longs to die. He put on his parka, set out for the street, tripping mindlessly down the stairs. He was already at the reception desk when he realized it would be proper to telephone Alicia to transmit his discovery to her and perhaps to dedicate some other word to her, a soft word that could caress her. The lady with the wart placed the telephone before him and pressed a button. Her eyes were those of a cat drowsing on its owner's sofa, who instinctively repels the caresses of strangers. The telephone rang several times in Esteban's ear; finally, Alicia's canned voice communicated that she was not at home at that time and suggested he leave his message after the beep. Staring at the fleshy wart of the woman who had closed her eyes again, Esteban communicated to the answering machine that he'd deciphered the code on the four pedestals, that he didn't know what it meant, that he'd translated its laconic Latin for her: *In the body of the Son of Man, step on the stone and walk west, dedicate nine feet to the Hebrews, seven to the Latins, take four away from the Greeks.* Before hanging up, his throat took on a more confidential, warmer tone. Esteban pronounced a sentence composed of three words and was immediately sorry he'd done so. Then he walked out onto the street.

He took the taxi right on Praça da Figueira and whispered the address to the driver: Largo das Portas do Sol, number four. Only then, while the windows were showing him the gelatinous, black swamp the fog had made of Lisbon, did it occur to him to wonder where Alicia might be at midnight to prevent her from answering his call. He tried to calm himself, saying that perhaps she'd fallen asleep, that perhaps she'd run out of cigarettes and had to go down to the bar on the corner. He wanted to smoke, but a large sign on the dashboard expressly forbade it. His blood pressure had gone down, the furious electricity that hours before had altered his nerves yielded to a docile pool in which Esteban allowed himself to sink, sitting in the backseat of the taxi. He noticed that they were going uphill; part of a house's facade came into view on the right, stained by the yellowish light of a streetlamp. The driver stopped in the middle of a black wasteland, which seemed the center of nowhere. Esteban handed him some money and got out without waiting for change.

There was a glow at the end of the corridor, behind the glass and wood door Esteban had passed through the previous day—where the bulletin board was hung that announced the lectures of the Adimanta Foundation for the semester in progress. He knocked on the glass with his knuckles two, three times, until a shadow insinuated itself at the end of the vestibule. The elongated body of Ms. Ostmann opened the door for him. To Esteban, her legs seemed just as unending, but drier. The single streetlight shining outside next to the abyss of fog on the opposite sidewalk was reflected in tiny dimensions in her blue eye.

"Excuse me for bothering you at such an hour," stammered Esteban. "But I think I have something very important to ask you."

"It's not a problem, seriously," answered Edla Ostmann in a sibilant voice. "Come in, we were working."

He followed her down the corridor, once again ascended behind her the twelve stairs leading to the second floor. The sound of her heels was harder, more definitive than ever. The entire house was dark. To keep from getting lost, Esteban had to guide himself by that harsh rhythm. After a short stroll, they entered a large, square office paneled with fine wood. Sitting opposite the fire, the ruined body of Sebastião Adimanta was waiting. The suspicion that they were waiting for him, that they'd been waiting for him all night, disturbed Esteban. On the black wood wall paneling, the fire sketched yellow serpents, swift, pale snakes that disintegrated with the same speed with which they appeared. A miscellaneous collection of photographs filled the room. In their respective frames posed groups of ten or twelve people arranged student-fashion opposite the camera, as in class photos. Esteban observed them fleetingly and observed too the metal plaques that specified the foundation's courses in which the students had participated, beginning in 1979.

"Tell us, Mr. Labastida," said Edla Ostmann. "Have you come to finish off your article and find yourself in need of one last bit of information?"

Ms. Ostmann had turned Sebastião Adimanta's chair around, and now those steely eyes were observing him from the fireplace with a blue fire that duplicated the one writhing behind him. Esteban took his notes out of his parka and passed them to Ostmann. There was a heavy silence, like the silence before a thunderburst, broken only by the crackling of the wood in the fire. Edla Ostmann's white hand, the hand that looked like a bird or a pair of scissors, placed the paper before Adimanta's face. His eyes moved up and down; his eyelids half closed to allow a glimpse of blue challenge, the look of someone offended by a word he did not expect. That look aroused a vague malaise in Esteban. He decided to feign distraction by looking at the photos dotting the walls.

"The text of da Alpiarça's angels," Ostmann observed in a tone of calculated coldness. "Congratulations, Mr. Labastida. Although the results certainly didn't require all your effort. This old secret is useless now; it must have been revealed centuries ago."

"What do those four lines mean?" asked Esteban, surprised at his own hardness and still contemplating the photographs.

"You figure it out." Esteban couldn't see the old man's eyes, but he knew they were supporting the tranquil rage of Ostmann's response. "Now that you've shown that in addition to being a journalist you can decipher cryptograms, try to figure out this one. The Son of Man is Jesus Christ, as you know. The Body of Christ is the Church. So you'd better go to a church."

The unknown faces in the photos said nothing to him; displayed in their various frames on the wall allowed the viewer to see the world of ten or fifteen years earlier. Who might those people be, thought Esteban, decked out with beards and obsolete hairdos, camouflaged in overcoats that now had to be either matter for moths or for sale in used clothing shops, people obliged by the photographer to put on a smile they must not have felt. Of course he knew no one, which is why that face in the second row of the photo for 1982 caught his attention, making him walk over to it until he was almost touching it with his nose.

For a few seconds, his memory foundered in a tide of masks, a garbage pit of varied faces through which he searched, looking for precise signs. Suddenly he had them before his eyes. The alarm went off instantly, while his brain understood everything that the photo implied, the interminable stock of consequences that derived from the anodyne face of that woman, who answered the camera with a hybrid look of malice and irony. His heart started beating again under his ribs with a renewed anger; the explanation of the entire enigma, of all the enigmas, of the angels, the city, the dreams, Benlliure, Almeida, Feltrinelli, Lisbon, and its labyrinth all became diaphanous.

"Are you all right, Mr. Labastida?" asked Edla Ostmann in a voice sweet to the point of repugnance. "You seem to have discovered something you don't like."

Esteban did not have the time to bid farewell to those two bodies waiting for his answer before the fire: A bus was leaving for Seville before half past one and he could not miss it.

Eleven

S he returned home after midnight because a vague resi-
due of fear kept her from returning sooner. Besides,
sharing her fear with Mamen could help to mitigate it.
They drank three coffees in Mamen's designer kitchen decorated with some alarming red door knockers, and after each
had finished off her pack of cigarettes they decided they'd stay
in touch in case some other sinister apparition came along to
knock them over. Alicia did not want to sleep in the Paseo
Colón apartment. Even if it made sense to accept the offer
and even if it didn't make much sense to walk the deserted
streets of the city, now made enormous by the dawn, where
there were veiled threats in every tin can stepped on by a cat
or in the stentorian footfalls of someone returning home too
late. But she had to wait for Esteban, had to wait for Esteban's
phone call, because she sensed that five hundred kilometers
away, in Lisbon's invisible stage set, the real battle was being
fought, the tiny threads that were finally going to deliver the
prey to them were being spread out. That's right, Alicia said
to herself as she quickly walked past a closed garage door, she
needed Esteban's voice offering guarantees, certifying that the
goal was just two steps away, dedicating another word to her

that had nothing to do with this puzzle marked with corpses they were about to solve, a word that would touch her more deeply, a word like a dart that would make her hang up the phone with the sensation of having cotton under her ribs.

Which is why, when she reached home and instinctively pressed the button on the answering machine and listened to a routine greeting from her sister and Marisa's questions about her interview with Asia Ferrer, she felt that Esteban's voice, which spoke to her as if from inside a box, calmed something that was pounding inside her, resonant knocks at the door that demanded a presence. She pushed aside the remains of two or three cushions and sat down in the armchair to listen. It seemed horrible that she couldn't answer the voice that spoke for her with a formality that was false and lying, that betrayed from time to time an imperceptible sigh of tenderness. She heard the translation of the quatrain, understood that Esteban had deciphered it on his own after a turbulent night of labyrinths and whiskey, after having entrusted himself to the spirit of Edgar Allan Poe, patron saint of cryptographers and violent plots. Then, at the end, after a slight bridge of silence, the voice became watery and hot and tossed out the words Alicia wanted to hear, the words she didn't know she wanted to hear, the words she'd been demanding to hear for a long time even though her fear wouldn't allow her to assent to that certainty. She heard that Esteban loved her and felt such horror at that pornographic confession that she pressed the button and removed the tape from the machine.

The ringing of the telephone made her jump when she still had not hidden that shameful proof of love in her purse. For a second she was afraid it might be Esteban again, but it was the voice of Mamen that she heard. She wanted to make sure Alicia had reached home safely. Like an obedient child, Alicia explained that all was well and that she'd just received the call she was expecting, the call in which Esteban demonstrated that the shell of the enigma had been split in two.

After some advice about bolts and windows, Mamen said good-bye. Alicia was left alone with her silence, walking around the living room sown with crunching pieces of porcelain without knowing how to face the three incandescent words that ended had Esteban's call. Two antagonistic feelings were struggling in her interior, two thoughts going in opposite directions about the kind of future she was prepared to construct after that moment on the basis of those three words recorded on the tape. She cursed herself for her indecision, for her clumsiness. Esteban's love was the security from which she was fleeing with the obstinacy of a spoiled child, simply because she could not accept any tiny detail that could be taken as a defect of form, above all, the fact that Esteban was a reworked replica of that old dead man, Pablo, who was swimming in some swamp in her memory with the corpse of a girl with pigtails who would not close her eyes. She was disgusted at returning to those unbearable images and understood, as she lit another cigarette, that she was going back to being as she was at the beginning. She was going round and around those ominous deaths in circles and spirals, unable to free herself of them.

She sought another current of thoughts that might mitigate her anguish. She found it in the quatrain she'd received along with the terrible confession. She tried to amuse herself figuring out its meaning. She became bored after a few minutes, thought about going to sleep but was not sleepy, and confirmed that she'd run out of cigarettes. It was just twelve-thirty. The corner store left both its Coca-Cola and cigarette machines out on the sidewalk, so she put on her coat, picked up her keys, and went down the stairs unnecessarily quickly. She was aware of the fact that if she acted rapidly, her thoughts reluctantly followed her decisions and made it impossible for her to dynamite them. Sometimes her reason became that viscous pool that kept her from swimming, from reaching the other shore.

Out on the street, she confirmed that the dawn was a moist, dark space broken by the occasional green light from a taxi. Following the rhythm of her footsteps on the sidewalk, her brain began bringing her in spurts other conclusions that she hadn't before taken into account. Gálvez had told her that a young woman had acquired the Margalef angel, the same woman who popped up on the corners of the mystery that tormented her, telephoning Blas Acevedo and Benlliure, being imperfectly reflected in the window of a bus so she could hardly be recognized, a woman who perhaps had another angel in her house, hidden behind a wall of bottles and cans.

While she distractedly put coins into the cigarette machine, she looked over at the display window of a furniture store. The employees must have forgotten to turn out the lights. There was a lamp very much like the one Mamen had brought back from Barcelona, the idiot, to have carried that huge thing on the plane when she could have bought it a short distance from home. She would have to decide, act just one damn time; all her life she'd been dedicated to muddle through decisions made by others, to allow Pablo, Mamá Luisa, Lourdes, or Esteban to resolve for her the problems that vexed her. She had to act, and quickly. If suspicion ordered her to do something, she should do it before the battery of doubts stepped in and it was too late to reach any conclusion.

She smoked two cigarettes at the entrance to her street before finding the courage to take that decisive step on the marble doorway. She slowly went up the stairs to the fourth floor and stopped on the landing without wanting to turn on the light. The silence was so enormous that she could almost hear the sound her thoughts produced as one flowed into the other. She had to make certain Nuria wasn't awake, that her exploration would not be interrupted by a disagreeable surprise like the one that had canceled her inspection of the angel a few days earlier. She had to find some evidence in some drawer, cornice, or pocket, in the form of a photograph, receipt, forgotten business card, that Nuria was the woman she was looking for, the feminine specter who was nipping at her heels.

She put her ear to the door. The silence seemed just as total, perfect, and dark. Employing the same feline caution with which she'd just climbed the stairs, she went up to the fifth floor and entered her apartment. A strange superstition advised her not to touch any telephone or take off her overcoat. She went into the kitchen and smoked one last cigarette in the darkness. She tried to eliminate the pursuit of any unfounded objection by angrily shutting her eyes. The blind knocked against the window frame when she opened the window all the way. She brought the table over.

If the clothesline held up that thick quilt Mamá Luisa had given them last Christmas, it would certainly bear her weight. Besides, she was sure Nuria's kitchen window would be open because she usually left freshly varnished wood out on the terrace to dry. Thought had been prohibited in her brain, so it could not present her with the very reasonable dangers involved in trying to climb down from a plastic clothesline to a lower floor, running the risk of proving the effects of gravity from a height of four stories. She kneeled on the ledge, curiously free of fear, grabbed hold of the clothesline with both hands, and let her heels slide down the outside wall until she felt them enter a hollow space.

Now came the hard part, which her plan had not taken into account. She had to swing herself somehow to get into the window, and she had to do it quickly if she didn't want the line to burn through the palms of her hands. The law of the pendulum seemed the most opportune option. She swung twice; the line gave way and she smashed against Nuria's kitchen table. Fortunately, Nuria had left the window open, but Alicia noticed a cold puddle of varnish pestilentially soaking her coat.

For an immense instant she waited for someone to open the kitchen door, alerted by the noise. That calamity did not take place. She got off the table, knocking another can to the floor, and slowly walked toward the living room. The terrace blinds were shut, so all her eyes found was a compact black wall. She hadn't taken that problem into account. The light coming from the balcony on the other side should allow her to decipher the position of objects, which was which in the confused junk heap that usually occupied Nuria's living room. That obstacle sabotaged her decision. She wondered how she could be so stupid as to invade someone else's house at one o'clock in the morning, sneaking through a window, dousing her entire body with a fetid varnish that stuck against her whenever she moved an arm.

She wondered if she really was so certain of Nuria's guilt, and her brain, which had returned to the light, traced a rapid, robot portrait of the supposed murderess: A young woman who knew her well enough to enter her apartment whenever she liked, who could ransack her dreams, a woman Almeida would allow to enter his shop after hours, who could call Don Blas to involve him in the crime, a woman ready to sell her soul to the devil to get something that destiny or the natural order of things had denied her. She received her answer in a vertigo. She turned on the light impelled by a fear she could not silence. Her inert eyes observed the body dumped on top of the restoration materials, the long lake of blood that flowed from the cruelly contorted head against the wall. Then she felt a blow that numbed the nape of her neck and saw nothing more.

...

The first thing Esteban did when he got out of the bus was take out his pack and smoke a cigarette right there at the stop, not postponing that peremptory need any longer. He'd traveled more than six hours inside that cocktail shaker without being able to breathe a single bad mouthful of smoke, subjected to two movies about cancer and matrimonial problems. The Portugal that had penetrated his window was nothing more than a black, indecipherable patch broken from time to time by the light from some distant farmhouse: the ideal setting for his mind to pursue its usual frenetic functions, joining conclusions to premises, trying to get ahead of the future to force it through the channels necessary for his purposes.

He reached Seville at dawn. A fragmentary, filthy glow scattered itself over the roofs of the city while he drank a coffee at the station bar that tasted too strongly of chlorine. He was so close, he'd desired with such desperation during that entire, infinite dawn to find himself at this distance from his objective that now he allowed himself the masochistic pleasure of prolonging the end, slowly sipping his repugnant cup of coffee. He paid in a leisurely way, and slowly walked out of Plaza de Armas station and went down the motley stairway. It wasn't worthwhile taking a taxi. Alicia's apartment and the solution were just a few steps away—he'd walk.

The dawn looked like a difficult birth: The lights of the day could not break over the mass of clouds that darkened the horizon. The street, empty, lighted uncertainly by the odd streetlamp that served as a sentinel, seemed to him a copy of another street, that one in Lisbon, and of yet another in that impossible city spread out over the secret geography of dreams. He tried to convince himself he wasn't nervous, that the pressure of an obscure urgency on his muscles was not going to thrust him into some folly. But finally, as he was turning onto Reyes Católicos and spied the enormous fast-food restaurant that occupied the corner of Alicia's block, the questions scattered through his brain like the thousand pieces of a broken vase.

Why, when he called her the second time, just before getting on the bus, was there no answer, not even from her answering machine? Where was the tape that should have greeted him, the tape that contained the solution to the enigma? Where was she before, when the answering machine did offer him that mechanical, false replica of her voice? What would he say to her, if he ever did find her, when he'd look into her eyes recalling the three traitorous words that had infiltrated the message on the machine without his throat's having been aware of having said them?

He'd crossed the Portuguese night in about seven hours, inflamed by the absolute necessity of saving Alicia, of rescuing her from an immediate danger she could have no suspicion of, one that invisibly threatened her like a curse, like a sickness that was too deep to be detected. Now, at the door to her building, all Esteban could do was drop his overnight bag on the floor and light a cigarette, trying to keep his fear from running away with his thoughts. He pushed her buzzer three then four times. He tried to smoke the entire cigarette before taking advantage of the open door left to him by an early-rising retiree who'd left the building, and he walked up the three steps in the vestibule.

Suddenly, that sense of emergency which had suffocated him in the Lisbon station, making him smoke and bite his nails until his fingers hurt, again stirred his heart, and he ran up the first three flights two stairs at a time. Nuria's open door awaited him. He approached slowly, opened the door farther without wanting to go all the way in, as if in her vestibule there awaited him the presence he'd been fearing all night long, the presence behind the general plan of the labyrinth in which he'd been lost. Still worn out from running up the stairs, he could perceive only a vague smell in the darkness, a hybrid scent of acrylic and sugar he couldn't place. He moved forward in the darkness, kicking two metal objects. He made his way along the wall until his hand found the light switch, which he pressed. It was then he found the spectacle he had expected to find or a sadistic preview of what he'd predicted.

Nuria's studio had always been messy, but never like this. There had been a fight or a frenetic ballet that caused all the restoration tools, the cans, and the sculptures to be hurled onto the newspaper covering the floor, the same newspapers saturated by the enormous pool of blood that began at the wall, coming from the head of the broken body. Someone had beaten Nuria over the head until her skull split against the wall like a watermelon. Her neck seemed bent in two; it was the neck of a manikin tossed into a garbage can. The weapon rested on one side, under the inert hand of the dead woman who'd probably tried, uselessly, to ward off the final assault. It was the angel, the damn angel daubed with a brilliant red liquid.

Still not allowing his terror to dominate him, Esteban walked through the room looking for the trail, the clue the murderer had obviously left behind. That move had been planned for so long now that Esteban simply followed the stipulated movements, tracing the hints placed on the path he was to follow. He was supposed to go somewhere, and the name of that place had to have been left in the cemetery of utensils that covered the floor of the study. A pack of cigarettes, torn photographs, a Lou Reed tape, and then a book as thick as a dictionary with a sheet of paper folded in four right in the middle.

Blood almost stained the corner of the cover Esteban examined as he put another cigarette in his mouth: *Symbology of the Christian Temple*. On page 348, the one marked by the folded sheet of paper, there were some underlined sentences. They spoke about north and south, about orientations: "As a symbol of totality, the bishop used ash to trace an X that connected the farthest points of the nave, marking the first and last letters of the Latin, Greek, and Hebrew alphabets; this ceremony possessed a symbolism that was not only cosmic but also hermetic: Aside from containing a metaphor of Jesus Christ, beginning and end of the universe, the combined first and last letters of those alphabets make up the Hebrew word Azoth, the Philosopher's Stone, beginning and end of all processes." The folded sheet was a plan of Our Lady of Blood, the Gothic chapel Nuria was restoring. On top of the usual Latin cross plan, three lines crisscrossed, and at their farthest points they were marked with Latin, Greek, and Hebrew signs. The red line, from north to south, was flanked by the *A* and the Zeta; the green, from east to west, by the Alpha and the Omega; a third, blue line traced a diagonal from northwest to southeast and was accompanied by the Aleph and another letter in the form of a chair that Esteban did not know how to read.

The date was made. He knew where he had to appear if he wanted to close the circle, pass completely through the forbidden gate. Esteban threw the book to the floor and carefully made his way to the telephone. He noticed that someone had removed the tape from the answering machine and pounded the buttons as if in a hurry to listen to a message they didn't want to leave behind. He pushed the three numbers to call the police and waited for the ring. His fear and his anxiety were calmed by the indirect certainty that everything was over, that there was nothing left to do but carry out the final formality that would definitively seal the matter. He felt he was living the next day, the period after the epilogue to his adventure.

A sleepy, wrinkled voice asked what he wanted; no, Inspector Gálvez was not at the station, his shift didn't begin until nine. Esteban spoke an address into the telephone and demanded that the inspector come there as soon as possible. Then he hung up without listening to the protests from the voice that was demanding to know who was speaking. He quickly walked toward the stairs, with his cigarette bobbing up and down between his lips. To go up to Alicia's apartment would have been an unnecessary waste of time. It had been made sufficiently clear where she was, where she was waiting for him along with the grand drumbeat that would mark the end of the symphony.

The sky flying over Reyes Católicos was an enormous crucible in which the yellow light of dawn was pouring without completely coagulating. He took a taxi; he sank into the rear seat not wanting to think anything more until he found himself face to face with the person who would answer all questions and who would most certainly not be content with simply satisfying that interrogatory protocol. He was traveling to his doom, submissively walking into the trap he knew was set to destroy him, the trap prepared at a distance for him, to dominate and annihilate him.

He got out of the car opposite the massive door of the chapel. A small opening at the bottom corroborated that someone was waiting for him. The light hanging from the facade was still lit; an early-morning wind made it swing back and forth and dirty the wood of the portal with yellow sketches and shadows. Before going through the gate of the small garden, Esteban fleetingly realized that he needed a weapon, that he was indifferent to the need. He almost resigned himself to the disaster if that was the indispensable condition for completely resolving the mystery. He slowly pushed open the door and entered the chapel without looking up. His bones were the first to note how the humidity of the stone permeated the entire space, flying even to the high tracery of the roof. The first blow cut his cheek and allowed him to take a step back, to raise his hand to his face and stop the line of blood; the second hit him on the temple and caused his knees to weaken. An opaque night clouded his eyes and he fell.

...

When he twisted his head to the right, a noisy earthquake tortured his skull until it forced him to squeeze his eyelids shut. With painful clarity, he perceived the wound on his forehead, the rope cutting savagely into his wrists, the aroma of shampoo from Alicia's hair caressing his face. He went on moving his head from one side to the other despite that seismic pain in order to rub his cheek against hers. They'd been tied back to back with their hands bound in such a way that they could only touch each other, making movements to calm each other, which helped raise their spirits or quiet them down or perhaps to formulate promises. They'd been abandoned in the middle of a transept from which it was possible to see all the modest elegance of the chapel. A long skeleton of scaffolds and railings hid the walls, which had been stripped of carvings and paintings; cloth and plastic sheets covered the main altar like a curtain, a rhetorical stage weighed down with volutes and Solomonic columns.

Esteban's head continued its twisting search, trying to find Alicia's. Bitterly, he thought that this was one of the times when their lips had been closest to touching. The stony cold of the chapel, torn only by the diagonal of light that penetrated through a window to blind Alicia, stiffened Esteban's joints so that they moved more slowly, more laboriously. They spoke in low voices, almost camouflaging their words in each other's ear whenever they could turn to touch it. They both made sure that, despite everything, they were all right. That distant body went on busying itself toward the middle of the central nave in collecting paints and brushes, apparently paying no attention to the maneuvers of the two prisoners. The fact was that Esteban's hands, despite the negative pinching of Alicia's, had been trying for a while, deliberately flaying themselves with the rope, to undo the knots that were torturing them at the wrist. His lungs hurt him, as if they needed to be swept clean of soot, but he still wanted a cigarette.

"I found you in Adimanta's office," shouted Esteban, shocked by the enormity of his own voice, magnified by the ceiling. "There you were with a bunch of other students, nicely dressed and with your smile expressly created for the photo. A beauty. From then on, it wasn't hard for me to reconstruct everything."

"You don't say."

"Of course you know that very well." His pinky was almost free of the rope. "You depended on my being able to solve the mystery, otherwise you wouldn't have set up this theater and left us to bore ourselves to death. Thank you, madam psychologist. Thanks a lot."

"No need to thank me." Mamen was dipping a brush in a can of black acrylic and choosing a place on the floor.

"You were studying in Lisbon, yes, but not psychology or not only psychology. Two courses at the Adimanta Foundation. I suppose they at least supplied you with enough to learn how to screw up the minds of other people. It was you who put that damn city in Alicia's head, you're the one who cornered her with your shadows and your manikins until you drove her crazy. Then you prescribed some pills, and she was fine."

Esteban's back perceived how Alicia's breathing was beginning to grow agitated, whipped by the crudity of these new revelations. The beam of light that came through the window fell directly on her green eyes and barely allowed them to make out an annoying yellow limbo where there should exist a Gothic chapel, where she was learning how she'd been tricked again. Poor, deluded little Alicia, incapable of discovering the secrets of others; she would have felt compassion for herself if she weren't so furious, so desperate.

"Yes my dear philologist," Mamen said as she tried to draw a kind of circle on four marble floor tiles. "That dumb fortune-teller, Asia Ferrer, was close to the truth, but her supermarket jargon ruined everything. What bullshit about astral bodies and other crap. The dream, any dream, is the effect of a certain psychic frequency. All you have to do is force the other person to tune in to the same frequency to make them dream whatever you like. I'm not saying it's easy, but it's not a backbreaker either. Yet it does use up energy. Alicia, sweetheart, you had me in bed for two weeks after constructing the city for you along with the hardworking Mr. Benlliure, who I had to reconstruct maybe four times."

"Sorry I caused you so much trouble," sighed Alicia. Esteban's hands continued moving around like ants over her thumb.

"The years with Adimanta were profitable," Mamen went on in her semicircle. "That's right, Esteban, I was also taking a neurology course at the University of Lisbon, but nothing exceptional as you might imagine. Adimanta developed in me what from my childhood had been fighting to take control—a total transparency, an uncontrolled violence here inside my head that from time to time brought me images and thoughts whose origin I had no idea of. Apparently, it's natural; there are people born that way. But it's like having a talent to play the violin. If you don't use it, you lose it. I took advantage of those two years at the foundation. I studied, I trained, it didn't matter to me how many sleepless nights I spent if that helped me increase my strength. One afternoon I understood that if nature had given me this power, it was because I was called to play a certain role, that I had a destiny. I have no idea if you, poor contingent beings, can understand what I'm saying."

"Perfectly, Madam Messiah," retorted Esteban on the point of undoing the first knot.

"I found Feltrinelli's book in the foundation library—I found out only much later that there was another copy right here in Seville. I didn't understand Latin, but I was fascinated instantly by the engravings, those beautiful illustrations filled with palaces and statues, the angels. I looked at the last page, the one with the dragon and the poem, and it intrigued me enormously. Adimanta summarized the story of da Alpiarça and the *Coniurati* for me. In the foundation museum there was also one of the angels, Samael, the first. I don't know if you'll believe me, but in that very instant, while I was observing the bronze face of that prince of demons, I understood that my destiny was to become the papess, the bride of Satan. I had to occupy a preeminent place among mortals."

"Naturally, with all your master's degrees." By then, the fingers of Esteban's left hand were free.

"There will always be classes, my boy." The black circle was complete; beginning from the east, Mamen had begun painting another inside it, a red one. "I had to find the four angels, the four inscriptions, I had to reconstruct Feltrinelli's coded message. I began a furious search for the figures in all the antiques shops all over Europe. I walked all over London, Berlin, and Paris. I found indirect leads, oblique references, trifles. I found out that the fourth angel, Mahazael, had been destroyed during the war, but in the annals of the Frankelhayn collection I found the text on his pedestal. It was about that time I met Rafael Almeida."

"Marisa introduced you to him," Alicia interjected.

"Yes, Marisa, of course." Mamen stepped back a bit to check on the progress of her second circle. "By then she'd slept with him a couple of times. Being a psychologist allows you to be up to date on people's lives. Almeida was a skunk who liked to have certain disgusting things done to him. If you did them, he would talk a lot and even be generous."

"So you slept with him too," said Alicia, still blinded by the light.

"Not only me, little girl." The second circle was just about finished. "Almeida screwed anything that came his way. The bad thing is that poor Marisa, who sometimes seems even dumber than you, thought he was totally in love with her vegetarianism and her fourth dimensions. We'd see each other a couple of times a week at my place, in some hotel. I carefully checked every antiques catalogue that came into his shop, kept an eye on everything that came in and on the things he reserved for secret transactions—there are lots of people with money out there. One day, I discovered that because its owner had died, the Margalef collection in Barcelona was going to be sold off, and that one of the pieces to be auctioned was Azael, the third angel. I got there as fast as I could, bid so high that I'm still in financial trouble, and got it. When the auction was over, a little man with a mustache came over to me. He looked as though his wife had just beat him up. He was wearing a horrible raincoat and shoes that couldn't protect him much from the puddles."

"Benlliure," interjected Alicia. Just then, a brusque convulsion from Esteban warned her that his left hand was entirely free.

"Yes." Mamen stopped after finishing the second circle. She suddenly put the paint can down on the floor and walked toward the transept. "Esteban, darling, what are you up to?"

"Not a thing, sweetheart," answered Esteban, a solid drop of sweat running down his back. "I'm trying to get comfortable. This is not the ideal position from which to carry on a conversation, believe me."

Only then did he notice that some charming latex gloves were protecting Mamen's hands, those hands that dug around in the purse she'd left next to the wall and extracted a small, silvery toy that she placed next to his nose. Esteban recognized the look in her eyes: the ungraspable gazes he'd seen in the faces of Sebastião Adimanta and Edla Ostmann.

"Know what kind of gun this is?" she asked.

"A Walther PPK," he answered, struggling to keep his voice from shattering into a thousand pieces. "Inspector Gálvez would be insane with joy if he knew it was here."

"I can just imagine. I understand you're uncomfortable, darling, but this isn't a theater. You've got one warning on your right cheek, and now I'll just give you another on the left so it won't occur to you to do something silly. A bullet might convince you once and for all, but the butt can also be eloquent."

It was a lightning bolt. Esteban again felt that his face was on fire. It was that cutting line a diamond makes when it scratches across a mirror. He cursed just as a new cascade of blood soaked his chin. Mamen went back to her circles to write letters that couldn't be seen from the transept.

"Thanks a lot," roared Esteban. "You sure know how to treat your guests well."

"Benlliure invited me to have a drink," Mamen went on, paying Esteban no attention. "He'd seen what I paid for the angel at the auction and wanted to make me an offer. He was a junk dealer. He bought secondhand furniture and scrap iron; I have no idea how, but he came into possession of an angel with a twisted foot. Attracted by the catalogue, which included a figure like the one he owned, he attended the auction to gauge its value. I wanted to see it, and he showed it to me. It was Azazël, the second angel. The price he was asking was prohibitive, so I resigned myself to copying the inscription and told him I'd think it over. I had the complete text, the four inscriptions."

"But you couldn't decipher them," said Esteban with a half smile.

"No, darling." A swarm of characters surrounded the space between the first and second circles, and Mamen needed only two strokes of her brush to finish the last word. "I racked my brains for months, but I have to admit that cryptography is just not for me. I knew from Adimanta that the secret message had to indicate a place, I knew that place had to be inside a church. The *Coniurati,* enemies of Christ, celebrated their anti-masses in a sacred place. I consulted book after book of Christian symbology."

"And got nowhere." Esteban was smiling with open pleasure. "Then you thought of me. What an honor."

"I did think of you, my darling. Your knowledge of paleography and classical languages made you the ideal candidate. But, of course, I couldn't simply walk up to you and ask you to decipher an inscription that would turn me into the bride of Satan just like that. You know, it's a matter of decorum. Everything had to be more oblique, had to take an indirect route. The ritual demanded a human sacrifice, and that gave me the key. The plan became clear, as if it had always been there, waiting for me to put it into practice."

When she'd finished the final sign, Mamen stood up to contemplate her labors. At that moment she noticed, because of a loud slap on the transept, that a shadow was moving and running toward her. She turned in time to see Esteban coming toward her with his arms extended, jumping over floor tiles to reach her, with the untied rope swinging on his wrists. The shot reverberated in the high ceiling as if a thunderburst had bombarded the stylized Gothic architecture. Blinded, Alicia shrieked until she overpowered the noise of the shot with her voice. Esteban collapsed on the floor exhaling a growl of pain or rage. A red stream was born near his armpit.

"You bastard, you bastard," shouted Alicia, as if she were reciting an incantation. "Did you kill him?"

"No." Mamen stood next to the supine body, its legs badly jumbled on the marble. "I only shot him in the shoulder, but the poor guy's fainted from the shock. What a fool. I told him to sit still. And for the time being, I can't kill him."

"Bastard," Alicia sobbed, her mouth a swamp of saliva.

"Quiet now, little girl." For the first time, Mamen stood before Alicia, interrupting the cruel beam of light that was frying her eyes. "I have no idea why you're so horrified he's going to die when after all you're not even capable of loving him properly."

"What do you know, bitch?"

"Oh, I know, I know." From somewhere, Mamen took out a pack of Nobels and put one in her mouth. "Poor little Alicia. Indecisive Alicia. Alicia who can't resolve anything on her own. Pablo—the guy you didn't know you loved or not—died, and you still don't know if you love this poor fool bleeding to death on the floor. As long as you live, you'll be useless, my dear. That's why you're the perfect instrument for channeling my plans. Esteban madly in love with you, you with a depression and mental confusion that would allow me to ransack your dreams without making too severe an effort. It was just a matter of making you believe you were surrounded by a satanic cult, that on your very street a sect was hiding in the best style of Roman Polanski. I had reserved a perfect clockwork mechanism for the occasion, to convince the two of you. It had to seem you were discovering things for yourselves, that there existed a series of coincidences that came together in an inexplicable way. In Paris, in a little shop near the Seine, I had a nobody of an engraver make me a copy of the illustration in Feltrinelli's book in which there appears a plaza with an angel. For weeks I prepared the stage set of your dreams, then I put you into them. Remember those five stupid sessions of hypnosis, those five boring afternoons when you put yourself entirely at my disposal to take away your nightmares? Thanks to them New Babel entered your head. I took that reproduction I just told you about and left it in the second-

hand bookstore on Feria Street that I know you visited assiduously with Pablo. It was I who consulted the copy of
the *Mysterium* in the General University Library, where you
worked. It was I who destroyed the card in the catalogue, I
who abandoned the book on the wrong shelf to create the
impression I wanted to have it lost, even if it was in plain view.
I telephoned Benlliure so he'd come to Seville, with the promise of buying his angel. A couple of times, I made a date to
meet him outside my office, when I knew you'd be coming,
just so you'd see him. Finally, we met next to the doorway to
your building where I shot him three times, as you know. I
rang your buzzer, and you came down and found him dead."

"What about the tattoo?" asked Alicia. "Benlliure had
the *stigmata diaboli* on his forearm."

"The satanic sect," answered Mamen smugly. "You had
to think Benlliure was a member of the sect, that he'd traveled to Seville to give you the angel, perhaps sorry he'd belonged to that sinister gang. A gang that included Nuria and
Blas Acevedo, of course. Nuria's angel was the one I bought
from Margalef. I ordered her to restore it in the strictest se-
crecy. It was going to be a surprise birthday present for you,
I told her. I found out about Lourdes's juice by accident, and
I exchanged your pills with sleeping pills, just so it would occur
to you to connect things. I found out about Blas's dirty secrets from Almeida. It was so easy to call him and involve him
in Almeida's death that it still seems child's play to me."

"But you also disguised yourself as Marisa."

"Yes." Mamen began to drag Esteban's body to the
edge of the circles she'd drawn on the floor. On the marble,
a complex red stela took shape. "From everything you told
me, I figured that Esteban was beginning to suspect that

there was someone behind the thing, a woman to be precise. Marisa knew Blas and Almeida, so she was the ideal person. Then I got into your apartment and turned it upside down. Afterward, I went to Lourdes's house and told her I was Marisa."

"But you were in Barcelona," Alicia blurted out, immediately regretting the stupid thing she'd just said.

"No, child." Mamen's prophylactic hands again tied Esteban's wrists with the rope. "I got a hotel room and called you from there. You thought I was in Barcelona, but I was here in Seville arranging everything. The day I told you I was coming home, I took a taxi to the airport loaded down with two valises and a horrible lamp I bought right near your building. You brought me home, easy as that."

So all of it was true. How obvious her inability to live with even a minimum of resolution, to develop without fear of being smashed into a thousand pieces like a too-fragile vase in this world plagued by disrespectful hands, thoughtless people who moved you from the center of the table to the sideboard without taking care not to trip over the folds in the rug. She understood without wanting to open her eyes that her life was false, that the routine she'd established to fortify herself against those other jagged memories that lacerated her was not the charming little enclosed garden as boring as it was pleasant behind whose fence she wanted to console herself. The innocent naturalness of domestic objects was revealing itself as a curtain behind which secret atrocities took place, the innocuous appearance of the ashtrays, the bathroom mirror, the slow process of the day on the alarm clock, through its sphere of numbers masked another reality, more dense, more lethal, more perfect and wounding, with all that unbearable solidity that things have only in dreams. Behind her green eyes or in the interior of her tortured heart that wished, with every beat, to untie its cage of muscles and ribs, Alicia could no longer pretend; a bottomless horror had erased her, pouring down like tar from some hole high above, and placed a black screen between what she was or thought she was and that ferocious, labyrinthine world outside that went on celebrating its traffic, television sets, its sky spattered with stars.

"Last night, someone tried to kill me," she said through clenched teeth. "Someone tried to push me in front of a bus."

"Oh, right," answered Mamen, as if remembering something. "You'd be surprised what people are capable of doing for twenty thousand filthy pesetas. She was a woman I hired on the Alameda, recommended by someone it would be in bad taste to name, but, you know, a girl's got to have friends everywhere. The jerk just went too far. I told her to wear black and all that just for visual effect, but that shove did not enter into my plans. I was fully conscious that everything was about to end, Esteban over there with Adimanta, you waiting for your information. I was right on the edge of what I wanted. Which is why I couldn't allow you to suspect me, and the attack from that nut would put me in the clear. When you told me over the telephone that Esteban had deciphered the code, I ran to Nuria's place. I needed the keys to the church, to this church. I killed her, of course. Just two blows, she didn't suffer. Then I thought I'd go up to your apartment and remove the tape from your answering machine, but you appeared, as crazy as usual, doing acrobatics through the window. You saved me a lot of work. Now the message was crystal clear. It was not in vain that I spent hours and hours rereading boring monographs on Christian symbolism.

Nuria had a B.A. in fine arts, and she had in her collection one of the books I'd read: Strindberg's *Symbology of the Christian Temple. In the body of the Son of Man, step on the stone and walk west, dedicate nine feet to the Hebrews, seven to the Latins, take four away from the Greeks.* The body of the Son of Man is the body of Christ, the Church, any church. The stone is the altar. In all churches there is a Betel stone, the corner stone that sanctifies the space. In ancient times, the priest would trace three lines through the principal nave, each one with the first and last letters of the Latin, Greek, and Hebrew alphabets. They were three directions, three axes of coordinates. Walking toward the west, that is, toward the exit, he was supposed to take nine steps in one direction, seven in another, and come back four steps in the third. He would then obtain a point, this very spot where I've marked the two concentric circles and where I'm going to make the human sacrifice before reciting the invocation."

Without taking off her whitish gloves, Mamen dug around in her bag and grasped a menacing butcher knife Alicia had seen in Nuria's kitchen. She held it tightly in her fist and moved toward the inner circle where the fallen body of Esteban was still bleeding. She'd written an enormous scarlet hieroglyphic on the marble floor stones. Alicia's extremities trembled, electrified by fear or rage. She tried to crawl toward the rear of the nave but gave up with a snort. She wanted to gain time, but didn't know how.

"Why, Mamen? Why?" she breathed out.

"It's necessary, my dear," answered Mamen as she took Esteban by the hair. "I'll carry out the ritual, but I won't be the one who takes the rap, see? I'll get out of it. Inspector Gálvez suspects that you're the young woman who bought the angel from Margalef and knows that the bodies are all related in some way or another to you. The Satanism story was sufficient to convince him that you're a dangerous maniac, that you wouldn't hesitate if it came to slitting someone's throat. A typical psychopath, the kind you read about in cheap newspapers. Now I'll cut Esteban's throat and then, when I'm finished with everything, I put a nice bullet right through your head. Excuse my frankness, but I want to be sincere with you—late in the day, you'll probably say. The police explanation: Mad woman obsessed with the devil kills lover and commits suicide. Simple as pie."

The only thing Alicia could do with her wrists and ankles strangled by a rope she couldn't possibly break was drag herself on one side and shout. Her voice echoed through the entire nave, like a metal bird smashing drunkenly, desperately against the pillars. She screamed as if her throat was the only thing that could stop the horrible execution of the most immediate future. Mamen's left hand held up Esteban's head, exposing his throat, where some arabesques of blood were already traced out. Her right hand raised the knife; the twisted beam of light that passed through the window gave the blade an iridescent glitter. Alicia didn't stop screaming, which is why she did not note the first drumbeat that shook the walls like a huge stone. She did hear the second, the third, and saw Mamen's simultaneous fall, accompanied by a gurgle like water lost in pipes, over Esteban's body. The knife made a horrible scraping sound when it fell a few steps beyond. From the door of the chapel, his face livid, Inspector Gálvez held a mute pistol. At the cuff of his raincoat, his other hand squeezed the wrinkled plan of a church crisscrossed by three colored lines.

All afternoon, she'd been stuffing suitcases, emptying dressers without paying much attention to which things she was putting into which valise. She'd tire quickly, then sit down on either the mattress or the knocked-over armchair in the living room and smoke infinite cigarettes. Along with their smoke, they also brought her images she tried to nullify by rapidly moving the air with her hands. Marisa had already left five desperate messages on the answering machine, messages Alicia of course had no intention of answering, because the telephone was a repugnant creature she'd rapidly eliminated by pulling the connection out of the wall.

Night was almost falling on a brilliant, golden day of a kind the *conibras* hadn't experienced in weeks. It especially pained her to be apart from them, to abandon them to the irresponsibility of the future, to cut with one slice the umbilical cord that had united them to her during all that time of anguish and errors. But she had no tenderness left, her heart had become a dry, old fruit that obscurely occupied some low place in her thorax. She did not want to think, did not want images or memories that might obstruct the burned movie house of her memory.

Esteban appeared at the agreed-on time, with his left hand laboriously struggling to put a cigarette between his lips. His right hand was still suspended, along with the rest of his arm, in the white cast put on him in the hospital and which was going to force him, for at least a couple of months, to practice an absolutely necessary ambidextrousness. He had the frail and unconcerned look he always had, that of someone invited to a party who hasn't dared to knock at the closed door and has remained on the street all night getting soaked in the rain.

The luggage didn't amount to more than a pair of suitcases and a squalid traveling bag they loaded onto the elevator without any difficulty. Esteban's left hand needed no help to drag the valise he chose. They went down standing side by side with their backs to the elevator, scratching or whistling from time to time without making any attempt at pronouncing a word that could get them down from that annoying block of silence. Outside on the street, a soft sun the color of pollen was yellowing the windshields of the cars. They left the suitcases on the sidewalk. Alicia shook her hands as if trying to free herself from some substance that had dirtied them and hastily looked for cigarettes in her purse. Esteban's eyes were penetrating and hard; it was Esteban's eternal gaze, the gaze that put her on the precipice of her doubts, demanded a decision, certainly the same look he had had in his eyes when he spoke those fateful words into the telephone in Lisbon.

Alicia's first reaction was to disregard that gaze, but later she realized angrily that she had to face it. The stupid adolescent impulse to hide her head under the pillow was coming to an end. There would be no more weights at both ends of the balance; the choice was made, and she had to bury her ill-mannered childish reticence. She should speak, now, after picking up the lighter, bringing it to her cheek, and lighting the cigarette. She should begin her final testimony, the protocol that would open the way to the new order she'd sanctioned. Her mouth opened, but all she could mutter was: "Call me a cab, please."

His expression did not seem to change, his eyes did not become disillusioned, and he accepted her escape as a necessary chapter in the process that should bring them to the final confrontation, the denouement. The taxi came, they put the baggage in the trunk, and then sat down on the rear seat, their knees touching. While the avenues followed one after another in spinning fashion outside the windows, Alicia tried to work up her courage. Her body refused, her throat deserted that necessary confession which would save her life, which would make it less depopulated and harsh. Yes, it was the same thing, her perennial memory written with other names, the sentimental bureaucracy with Pablo now corrected and augmented, but there was no option because the alternative was so terrible that its pain could hardly be supposed. When they stopped outside the Plaza de Armas station, she dug nervously through her handbag, unable to find her wallet. Esteban put some money in the driver's hand and asked him to get the bags out of the trunk. The bus to Málaga would be leaving within a quarter of an hour. Alicia didn't dare have a coffee, so they left the bags at the pickup and decided to smoke one last cigarette at the departure gate.

"Send my regards to your sister," said Esteban with a repellent politeness.

She had no idea how she'd gotten there, how she'd let the knots form that would end up strangling her will in that way. She had to decide, had to speak. With a crudeness she herself resented, she told herself she did not love Esteban, that she'd never loved him, but that she needed him. She needed his parasitic love if she wanted to survive in the long insomnia the future was preparing for her. So she put her objections aside, inhaled the cigarette smoke, and exhaled: "I told you that when you came back from Lisbon we had to talk."

His eyes smiled, but it wasn't happiness that glittered in them. It was the malicious glow of someone in an interminable card game who discovers his adversary is bluffing. Esteban's left hand, the one holding the cigarette, fleetingly caressed Alicia's hair.

"There's nothing to talk about," he said very slowly. "Have a nice trip."

She was horrified to see that Esteban was kissing her chastely on the cheeks like a good brother. Unable to say another word, she got on the bus feeling that she had a lead weight stuck in her throat. As the bus began to move, she felt an infinite desolation and an infinite relief. Esteban's figure at the departure gate grew smaller in the distance. She could not cry, she could not retract anything. A tar-colored bitterness in her soul blocked out any kind of spontaneous feeling. Perhaps distance, perhaps Málaga and a sister for whom she'd never felt a very connecting affection could draw her closer, remotely, to the annihilation she sought or to that uninhabited silence no ghost could ever again bombard. She did not know. The poison did not submerge until, in the bus, she was rolling along an avenue lined with palm trees. The sun lazily infiltrated through the window, leaving a yellow electricity in her hair.

That night, after Inspector Gálvez and the interminable questions and reports, they still hadn't tried to rise up, but they again figured at a threatening distance in the end of the dream, properly included in their coffins shiny with varnish. Starting from that point, the serpent would again coil; the labyrinth would end in the same path where it had begun. Pablo and Rosa, their redundant and rotten bodies, their presence at daybreak, would be appendices as ubiquitous and inevitable as the tips of her fingernails, like the hair that had to be decimated every two weeks, like that useless wisdom tooth, like coffee. She snorted and clasped her purse, which she was holding between her knees. She thought and realized that all aspirations are impossible, because they never come to an end. The final object of desire is beyond the grasp of the runner, who will never finish his race. She realized that to free herself she would have to enter another body, explore another city, change her brand of cigarettes. Oblivion was a trophy the insane and the dead received only as a consolation prize.

...

"Here you are," said the old man, putting a shiny, cold thing like a fish into his hand.

"How much do I owe you?" sighed Esteban.

The old man's face wrinkled up, accommodating a crevice that could be distantly identified with a smile.

"Forget about it," he said. "I should have fixed it two weeks ago as you quite properly reminded me. This time, it's nothing. The next time you need a repair, then we'll see."

Esteban stored Dad's watch in the pocket of his parka— Pablo's watch, the scandalous and diminutive object that reminded him of the past like the palpitating wound on his shoulder. It was waiting inside a suffocating catacomb stuffed with clocks. Hanging from the ceiling, the crystal lamp divided the shop into green, red, and yellow zones, rendering even more improbable the exotic devices packed onto the shelves and tables or piled in unhygienic corners becoming one with spiderwebs, old newspapers, and beer cans. Scaling the walls were rows of tall coffins with damask in whose bellies pendulums swung back and forth; cubicle things marked with helixes and needles observed from the depths of vitrines; faded little tin shepherds that emerged to celebrate each quarter hour with dance steps that betrayed the not very scrupulous working of the gears. Before going out into the night and the solitude, Esteban felt the temptation to ask something. "Tell me," he said to the old man, "do you believe in the devil?"

"I don't understand what you mean." The moth-eaten hands took their place on the counter.

"The devil, Satan, things of that sort. Do you think there are people who still dedicate themselves to invoking the devil."

More bent over and suddenly more exhausted, Mr. Berruel limped through the shop and scuttled behind the counter as if behind a barrier, trying to stave off some vague threat. His eyes, cornered now, slipped nostalgically over the tools attached to the wall and deciphered the small watches in the display case. His voice began to flow from that broken mouth with a sincerity that revealed resignation.

"People just don't understand that the devil too has to retire. I think he's a functionary like any other, an employee who got stuck with the role of the villain, the bad guy in the film. But most certainly he's a tired functionary. Wherever he is, he must dedicate himself to other things, minutiae of no importance, distractions that make him forget the noises of the world. I think that no matter how much people clamor for him, the devil would not be willing to return. Wherever he is, perhaps he's even modestly happy."

"If you say so."

Esteban felt that a violent puff of sulphur was numbing his nose.